BEAUTY X BEAST

DAMSELS OF DISTRESS

DAKOTA KROUT

MOUNTAINDALE
PRESS

To my amazing and brilliant wife Danielle, the fairest of them all.

PROLOGUE

THE HIGH STONE walls of the castle loomed over Sir Gasteel Anton Leiter as he marched through the gates with his chest thrust out and shoulders pulled back, saluting each Royal Knight he walked past. Even though he had been invited here by the king himself, ignoring military protocol would have been enough reason for the Royal Knights to delay him and ruin his introduction to the peerage.

Once he had passed every living obstacle, a smirk found itself lucky enough to grace his lips. It only grew as each confident stride brought him deeper into the depths of the palace.

He found himself in good company, surrounded as he was by tapestries and portraits practically *shouting* the ancient tales of conquest and war his kingdom had gloriously waged against their ancient enemies—every inch of the castle seemed to have been created to showcase the triumphs Verdelune had managed.

"Mmm... look at *that*. A portrait for winning a duel? A tapestry for capturing a town?" His eyes gleamed as he imagined how splendid his own accolades would appear. Already, he could practically *see* his own story being drawn out, meticulously planned and painted, capturing every angle of his impeccable face and combat-chiseled body.

Gasteel shivered with delight as a light thrill shot through him. "If the rumors I've been hearing recently are true, I might have a portrait to immortalize my deeds drawn even sooner than I had expected. Who am I kidding? Of course they're true. Why else would I be here? Unless... perhaps a *statue*? A *ballad*?"

Being summoned by the king himself was no small feat, and though it had come as a surprise, Gasteel merely took it as his due. Starting in his late teen years, he'd carved out a reputation as the kingdom's most formidable hunter, able to effortlessly take down monsters and bandits alike. Even all the way back then, he'd been catching the eye of the crown. Once he'd proven even the *wildest* claims true, a clear path had been opened for him. Everyone had known he was destined for greatness on the battlefield.

From a lowly Greenhorn, Gasteel had quickly earned a position as a full Knight—a rank typically reserved only for the third son of hereditary nobles. Now, less than a decade after first stepping foot into the fields of blood and battle, his military regalia was adorned with shimmering medals of valor, with more accolades being attributed to him daily by higher-ranking officers. Every victory, every conquest, meant another medal and more recognition heaped onto him.

While that was all well and good, Gasteel could only look at the tokens clinking on his chest with each step as a single item: a ticket into the palace for an audience with the king. "Humph. Medals. Useless. After today, I'll box these up and toss them into the junk drawer where they belong."

His *earned* rank was the only reason he was allowed to openly wear his sword while in the palace, but a smaller, secondary reason was the knowledge of the Advanced Skill from his class. As it did not directly interact with his sword, the weapon was usually an afterthought amongst his peers. "Now *there's* a mistake if they've ever made one. I can cut down a bear with a single strike, and a trained knight with only three."

Still, there was something so... *enticing* about using his system-granted skills. Almost unconsciously, he ran a finger over his bare forearm, staring in delight at the newly upgraded rank of his favorite ability, ignoring the lower classes and abilities he'd been given when he was younger.

Full Class: Royal Huntsman
Basic Skill: Aim and Strike: Level 10/10.
When targeting a single point, you can [Perfectly] aim your weapon, creating a burst of gasses that will propel the projectile you are about to launch.

Advanced Skill: Compress and Spark: Level 7/10.
When activating Aim and Strike, you can compress the gasses to a single point in a [Proficient] manner and detonate it by creating a spark in the center of the volatile miasma. Until [Perfect] control of this skill has been attained, the projectile may be pushed off-course by the detonation.

Breakthrough Skill: Locked.
Reach Skill level 10 with [Basic Skill] and [Advanced Skill] to unlock!

"Yes..." His resonant voice echoed back to him in the enclosed corridor, caressing his ears and making them tingle in an extremely pleasant manner. "This is certain to be a wildly successful meeting with King Jack. There can be no doubt that I'm here for him to make me a High Knight, perhaps even a Royal Knight. No... it couldn't be... a lordship title? It's possible... yes. It *is*, isn't it? No one's earned it like I have. No one *fights* like Gasteel, slaughters other *Knights* like Gasteel!"

Just before he could break out in humming his own

praises, he arrived in front of the war room. For a long moment, he just stood in front of the immense oak doors, soaking in their grandeur and allowing himself a moment to savor the taste of impending glory. Reminding himself once more of his achievements—as he was *certain* he was here for them to be recognized and rewarded—Gasteel double-checked his appearance and took a deep breath.

Standing ramrod straight, the Knight shoved the doors out of his way and brought his hands to his sides with a flourish. As they swung open, he confidently strode forward while radiating a gravitas matched only by one other person in the room: the king himself.

Gasteel's greaves *clinked* on the stone floor as he swept into a low bow. He turned his forward march into a perfect, proper salute from a Knight to his monarch: turning the bow into taking a knee and keeping his head lowered. It was an annoying necessity, a show of respect which would be necessary to complete upon each meeting until he'd earned the higher ranks of nobility he so desperately craved. For a few *interminable* moments, he was forced to wait, and he grit his teeth to try and hide his annoyance at being intentionally kept in the subservient position.

"*Sir* Gasteel Anton Leiter." King Jack's voice cut through the air, silencing the audience of noblemen and women and also catching the bowing Knight off-guard. It was not the king's low-ranking spokesman who addressed him, but the monarch himself—a rare sign of favor. The unexpected recognition and honor caused Gasteel to flinch, but he caught himself before ruining the moment by standing without being given permission to do so. Even so, the arrogant man felt his ire cool as King Jack's drawling voice washed over the room—speaking as much to the assembled peers as to the Knight on display.

"Hunter turned war hero, renowned for ruthless efficiency

in service of the crown… and your ability to pierce through any non-magical armor with a single blow of your many mastered weapons, even *without* the requisite system skills. Your reputation precedes you."

Feeling his chest swell with pride at being acknowledged by the king himself, Gasteel felt his mind race with ways this conversation could be leveraged to further his ambitions. "*Thank* you for your kind words, your majesty-"

"Some of it good, some of it *very* bad," the king pressed on darkly, cutting off the knight and sending the still-kneeling Gasteel back into frustration—as well as a low level of concern, which the bowing helped him hide. "You have served the interest of Verdelune with impressive bravery, fortitude, and… *decided* efficiency. In the early days of our kingdom, you would have already earned yourself a position among the high peerage. But we are a more matured kingdom, with laws in place meant to *prevent*-"

"Husband." The queen's murmured words broke in, forestalling the king's next words. Chancing a glance up, Gasteel's eyes were drawn to her… more specifically the green and black system-sigil on her cheek marking her as a Witch. Unlike the stuffy nobility, Gasteel only felt greater respect for her at that moment.

This was a person willing to do what was needed to gain power. Since the day she had married the king, their territory had *doubled* in size due to their endless conquest of the neighboring kingdoms.

"Rise, Sir." The king announced after a moment of waiting, showing the room that *he* was in charge, even if his wife objected to his statements.

The tension in the room shifted in a direction Gasteel was unhappy with. As he looked around, he noted dozens of faces turned in his direction, each of them wearing expressions as if they'd been carved out of granite. After a few heartbeats spent scanning the assemblage, merely several dukes and other members of the high nobility, Gasteel felt his nervousness fall away. As a seasoned hunter, he knew that people like *this* didn't come out to hunt prey.

No, they were here for political maneuvering, and that could only mean only one thing: they were either setting him up for a grand victory… or a disastrous blow to his reputation, which would leave him forevermore unable to climb through the ranks of the kingdom.

That didn't scare him. Straightening his shoulders and smoothing all emotions from his face, Gasteel tried to think why this crowd specifically would be here—and decided it didn't matter. These nobles, with their centuries-old bloodlines and incessant scheming, were the backbone of Verdelune's economy and power structure. While that was wonderful for *them*, the Knight couldn't help but look down on them. Everything they had, they'd been *given*. But he had always believed in cultivating his own power. Power earned through raw strength had a noticeable feel to it, and it was the opposite of the aura these prissy nobles exuded.

As a self-made man in a room full of people who had inherited their titles, he was a potential asset *and* a threat.

"My council has decided that your talents are needed in a… different capacity. 'Delicate' times approach us, and as we walk forward into the future, we must determine the path the kingdom as a whole will walk upon. Your rather… *direct* approach on the battlefield, while effective, has been causing too many eyes to turn toward us."

The king's eyes narrowed, and a hint of a smirk played at the corner of his mouth. "As much as *I* appreciate what you've done for us, I will be frank with you, Sir Gasteel. It's been a decade since we've pushed our border south, and my queen has reminded me that it is high time we return to our glory days. Conquest is on the horizon. When that happens, you will be allowed to return to the front lines. Until then... we need to make them think we're not making any moves."

As much as he wanted to interrupt, doing so could cost him his head, no matter how much favor he'd garnered with his devotion to the crown. He fully understood that this was a test to see if he, a man known to leave behind no survivors, could also somehow contain enough political savvy to bow his head and follow when the need arose.

There was no way the nobles judging him could know this, but patience was Gasteel's greatest strength. Just like when he'd been acclaimed as a hunter, he fully understood how a little patience—*waiting* for the perfect time to claim what was his—could mean taking home a larger trophy.

Several long moments passed, and a tiny spark of approval appeared in King Jack's eyes.

"I am pleased to see the good things I've heard of you are true. Sir Gasteel, on my command, you are to be elevated to the rank of Baron. While this title does come with a parcel of land and a manor, it will be managed on your behalf while you complete your first year of service to the crown, as is to be expected of any new member of the nobility."

Gasteel froze at the news, not able to say a word as his brain tried to catch up with what his ears had told him. Though he knew he deserved it, a barony was still outside the realm of even his more ambitious expectations.

King Jack's words rang with authority, turning his statements into orders. "Your task will be to recruit the finest soldiers and support staff in our kingdom. You are not expected to train them, merely, hmm, *encourage* them to sign on the dotted line. So long as you fully understand the laws of our land, as is to be expected of each member of my court, you should have no issues at all. Every failure... well, I'm sure you will give a full accounting to *all* of us. For. Every. *Single*. Failure."

This time, when the king paused, Gasteel understood the

cue being given to him. This was where he was meant to graciously accept, displaying humility and devotion to the kingdom at the same time. "Your majesty, I don't deserve this honor, but I shall uphold the dignity and laws of Verdelune with an iron fist."

The simple words couldn't convey the way that his heart was pounding in his chest, the storm of emotions that was filling him at the moment. Gasteel was analyzing the situation, just as he would scan the terrain when stalking dangerous game. While this was ostensibly a promotion, it was in actuality a thinly veiled insult, a move calculated to curtail his meteoric rise in power and remove him from a position where he would be visible to the impressionable troops.

No one wanted a battlefield hero who could stage a military coup. Not unless they controlled them absolutely.

Even so, it was well-understood that the fastest way to grow combat abilities was to perfect them in the crucible of battle. He had only *three* levels to go with his skill before he'd unlock his Breakthrough ability, an achievement almost unheard of for someone only in their early thirties. Even as he railed against this reassignment internally, he had to give King Jack credit. If *he* was in the same position as the ruler, this is exactly what *he* would do to ensure his power wasn't questioned.

Even so… pulling him from the front lines, from the thrill of the hunt? It was a bitter potion to swallow. He had worked his entire life defining himself as the one called on to draw blood from powerful creatures, whether animals, monsters, or humans. Earning a noble title might be prestigious, but it was a mere bone thrown to a dog to placate it.

Gasteel was no beast to be tamed. He would not be locked in a gilded cage nor allow himself to be muzzled under the guise of recognition.

"Your majesty, truly I'm grateful for this opportunity.

However, I am a *hunter*, a *warrior*, not a... recruiter. I desire only to serve you to the utmost of my capabilities-"

"Then you will do as you are *told*." A royal guard was the one to speak, stepping forward and staring Gasteel down, a hand on the hilt of his sword as he waited for the Knight to show another *hint* of defiance.

"At ease." King Jack lazily waved the guard away, though Gasteel was wise enough to understand that the guard wasn't being countermanded. Likely, the monarch simply hadn't wanted to show his own ire and had specifically ordered the guard to verbally slap Gasteel using a secret signal. "This decision is final. This strategy is crucial to our final success, as we strengthen our forces, build alliances, and prepare an invasion under the noses of our watchful neighbors."

Fists clenching at his sides, the metal and leather of his gauntlets creaking, Gasteel sharply returned to his kneeling position, using the gesture of respect to hide the inner turmoil he was enduring. When the man made no attempt to move or argue further, King Jack offered a small concession as recognition of the newly minted baron realizing his error and showing proper deference once more.

"As you know, Gasteel Anton Leiter, having three names is traditionally a sign of being a common-born individual. With your rise to the status of baron, one of your names will be removed in order to make way for the title of baron. Typically, we would do this by merging the first part of your first name, and the second part of your second name, but as a personal token of appreciation for your years of service, I have determined that *you* may choose your first name."

King Jack paused, an eyebrow raising ever so slightly as he leaned forward and mildly inquired, "Would you go as tradition dictates and take 'Gas' from your first, and 'Ton' from your second, to become Baron Gaston Leiter, or will you maintain the name that has earned you fear and respect on the battlefield and become Baron Gasteel Leiter?"

Gasteel's mind raced for ways that this situation could be exploited to his advantage. The king's favor was a valuable commodity, but in this… his ambition and pride won out. He knew this was a test, but Gasteel had no intention of weakening his name. With a steady voice, he made his choice. "In my service to Verdelune, I wish to remain your steadfast steel, hardened by the hammer of war and the crucible of combat. With your blessing, King Jack, I would take the name Baron Gasteel Leiter."

"Then rise, and know that you are the founder of a new line of nobility, Baron Gasteel Leiter." There was no approval or angst shining through the words of the king, leaving the baron wondering if he'd passed… or failed. "Go and do your duty, in service to the crown."

The new lord genuflected one last time, then stood, turned on his heel, and marched out of the war room, the heavy oak doors closing behind him with a resounding *thud*. Just before they finished slamming shut, he could hear a collective sigh of relief escape the mouths of the Royal Guardsmen.

It was just enough to return a small smile to his face.

"Each of them would've been a worthy fight, but they needn't have feared. They outnumbered me five to one, and even *I* don't like those odds against such powerful men." His mind returned to the thought of being forced away from his soldiers, from the thrill of the hunt, the scent of blood. An unbearable pain filled his gut: emptiness and acid all in one.

In a slight daze, he accepted the tome a royal clerk handed over. A glance showed it to be a logbook of all of the rules and regulations he'd need to follow during the recruitment process. "Ugh… books and paperwork. Tasks for lesser men. Wait… perfect. I know just the sycophant for the job. One year. Just one year away, then I'll be at the forefront of an invasion. It'll be worth it, in time. It *has* to be."

"Nobility on the floor! At-ten-*tion*!" As Gasteel walked through the courtyard, all of the knights in various stages of training stopped what they were doing and shifted to salute him. At first, he was startled, but then his small smile began to quickly spread across his face. Gasteel walked taller, intentionally making his way past every High Knight in the area to ensure they needed to stop what they were doing and salute him.

"Perhaps there *are* some perks to this new title, after all."

ONE

DANIELLE MARIE TINKERSDOTTIR walked down the cobbled streets of Frontière, a small town in the furthest reaches of Verdelune. Each step was filled with confidence and poise, an undeniable natural grace shining through despite her best efforts to hide it. She wore plain clothes befitting her station as the daughter of a humble Tinkerer, a toymaker who earned just enough to allow them to live peacefully in the sleepy border town.

Only one small addition to her clothing set her apart from any of the other young women in town: a thin veil that fluttered in the wind slightly with each step, an unfortunate necessity for shielding herself against the prying eyes that far too frequently turned toward her, no matter what lengths she went to in an attempt to blend in.

"But all of that changes tomorrow." Danielle promised herself, a determined light shining in her eyes, though her coverings ensured no one could see it. "A terrible Basic Class, an absolutely *brutal* Advanced Class, but with my eighteenth birthday only a dozen hours away... all of the research and effort I've put into following in my father's footsteps means I'm *sure* to unlock a Tinkering class at the very least. No, with my attention to detail and ability to adjust them after they're completed... perhaps I'll even unlock a specialty class like Researcher!"

She ran a finger along her forearm, leaving behind a golden trail that turned into words denoting her abilities, vanishing from her skin and being replaced by the next line each time she finished reading the previous one.

Basic Class: Charming Child
Basic Skill: Alluring Assemblage: Level 10/10.
When arranging items, you [Perfectly] align them in such a way that is pleasing to onlookers. Items arranged by you will be [Perfectly] pleasing to the eye, making even unpleasant tasks desirable and wares worth more for sales or bartering.

Advanced Skill: Graceful Movement: Level 10/10.
Every motion you make is [Perfectly] controlled, enhancing your flexibility and fine motor control. As you progress through this skill, you become deft, adding a [Perfectly] captivating modifier to every motion.

Breakthrough Skill: Permanently Locked.
You failed to reach Skill level 10 with your [Basic Skill] and [Advanced Skill] before advancing your class!

Advanced Class: Blessed of Beauty
Basic Skill: Resplendent Reflected Self: Level 10/10.
Resplendent Reflected Self passively, continuously, and [Perfectly] amplifies your beauty in response to the admiration and attention you receive, based on the preferences of the people you are spending the most time around. Your looks and grace will grow more potent with each glance, with each pertinent compliment increasing the speed of adjusting to the aesthetic of the 5 people you are around the most by [10]%.

Advanced Skill: Aura of Refinement: Level 8/10.
Your presence subtly, permanently, and [Extensively] enhances the beauty

and charm of people and objects within your vicinity based on the local aesthetic, reaching up to [8] meters from your body. This effect is gradual and automatic, becoming more pronounced the longer you are around people and objects, or the more focused attention you give them with this skill.

Breakthrough Skill: Locked.
Reach Skill level 10 with [Basic Skill] and [Advanced Skill] to unlock!

Her Basic Class had been a product of the combination of her father's technological assembly and her mother's unknown capabilities, as Danielle's father had never spoken about her mother. In fact, any time she tried to get him to open up, he would turn cold and ignore her for at least the remainder of the day.

Even though her skills hadn't aligned perfectly with what he needed, from ten years of age, when she'd first unlocked her Basic Class—as all children do—she had been able to help in his workshop, everything from placing his tools and cleaning his workbench to adding finishing touches to some of his works. Truly, it had been a delightful childhood, where she had thrown herself into advancing her skills with the fervor most children had.

All of that had changed, practically overnight, when she'd unlocked her Advanced Class at the age of fourteen. That was the earliest that the second class, and the new skills that came along with it, could be imparted to a person by the system. She had unlocked her Advanced skill in a year, the fastest anyone had ever seen, all because the people of Frontière had never been able to keep their fool mouths *shut.*

Compliments poured onto her like water falling from a cliff, progressing her Advanced Skill at a record pace as well. She'd only managed to keep herself from achieving a third skill from the hated class—a Breakthrough Skill, which would further empower the effects of her current skills—by donning a veil to reduce 'pertinent compliments' and refusing to actively enhance people. Otherwise, it was likely that there would be no escape from gaining the attention of some highborn and becoming a bird in a gilded cage, forced to boost their looks while never being able to go into a public space herself.

Danielle kicked a rock, blinking as her thoughts returned to the present. Her gaze dropped to the basket she was carrying, filled with small wind-up toys which should appeal to boys and girls alike: knights in shining armor and princesses bejeweled with cut glass. Simply being in her presence meant that, even now, they were ever-so-subtly becoming more beautiful, appealing, and able to inspire desire. A smile appeared under her veil, and Danielle decided she had earned a bonus for herself.

"Know what? I'm going to mark these up today. I've been carrying them around for a *week*. Whoever gets them won't be overpaying, even when spending at a premium. I know Francois has been hiding a new booklet *On the Artistry of Architecture* in his shop, and today, I'm going to *make* him part with it! He's been holding out on me for too long already."

"Ah, *Belle*, grace me with a smile!"

At the shouted plea, the smile that she already had on her face—luckily hidden behind the thin silk—dropped away instantly. The streets of Frontière were already buzzing with activity so early in the morning, a time she'd chosen specifically in an attempt to avoid large gatherings of the tightly knit community. She had hoped the early hour would give her some cover, a chance to blend in, to be just another face in the crowd as people started their day.

Unfortunately, ever since her father had moved them into the Kingdom of Verdelune, her 'exotic' origins of roughly two dozen miles away—yet still across the border—made her an oddity in a community that had lived together for generations. Each time she walked along the streets, her presence was like a stone dropped into a puddle, creating ripples of attention that followed her no matter where she went.

"Lift your veil for my son, and you'll have a genuine marriage proposal as soon as your Full Class is unlocked!" a mother called out in a voice brimming with eagerness. Her grown son flushed a bright red... but he didn't try to hush her. Why would he? What young man *didn't* want the most beautiful girl in the entire kingdom, and what mother wouldn't be thrilled to have a daughter-in-law who could restore a youthful appearance and ensure graceful aging?

For Danielle, passive beautification was already a side business she was partaking in. When she simply sat among a group of women in the town who would trade favors with her, Danielle's power smoothed out their wrinkles, gave their skin a healthy glow, whitened teeth... the list went on.

While she couldn't *actually* return people to good health, she could make it *appear* that way. Frankly, it was the only reason the ladies of the town tolerated her presence. Even as they sent cool glares her way, they wanted to look in the mirror and see a reflection of beauty.

As per usual, Danielle responded with a polite, yet firm refusal to the shouted proposal. In an effort to hide the discomfort of the constant shouts, she kept her eyes forward, her steps brisk and purposeful. She'd set a goal for herself, and when she determined her next step, she wouldn't be tempted off of her path by anyone or anything.

"I'll show them, someday. I'll be recognized for my ability and contributions to people's lives... not just my system-granted appearance." Danielle held her head high, speaking quietly to herself. She would happily tell anyone who would listen about her dreams, but in a town like this, they would only smirk knowingly and shake their heads at her. "I *will* be a standout person, respected for what I can do, who I am. Not... not for the classes the system practically *cursed* me with."

As she approached the market, more and more people called out to her, and whispers began stirring up under the breath of many.

"Tomorrow, we will make plans to be wed, Bella!" A rotund baker leaned out of his window and crossed his arms. His girth spoke of a man who clearly had plenty of food to spare—and the way he was standing was meant to call attention to that fact. In his own ham-fisted attempt at subtlety, he was attempting to show that she would never go hungry if she were a part of his household.

"I don't think your wife would appreciate that, Master Baker. Besides, I wouldn't want to marry someone who can't even remember my name." Danielle gently smiled and continued moving while the older man clutched at his chest, as though he were deeply wounded, even as his smile widened.

"My son, then!" The baker tried one last time, but she merely shook her head.

"Why must she *parade* herself around here, disturbing the peace?" The voice of a washer woman near the town well was dripping with disapproval, and it was no accident that she was speaking *just* loud enough for Danielle to hear. "Not even an adult and already acting this way? I must shake my head at what her future will look like."

"An outsider, just like her father. How full of herself must she be that she wears a veil like that? Too good for commoners like *us* to even look at her," another washerwoman chimed in, her tone as scornful and sharp as thorns.

Handfuls of calls reached her ears, dozens of whispers prickled her senses, and though she had long since learned to keep her emotions guarded, the words still stung. Now even her attempts to avoid the attention by wearing a veil were somehow backfiring on her? At that moment, she felt more like an intruder than a member of the town, but if she wanted to feed herself and her father, there was nothing she could do but complete her tasks.

Danielle finally arrived at her normal selling space, finding that it had been left empty for her, though she only arrived once a week or so, when her father finished a new batch of toys. She set up the exquisite figurines, arranging them in a pleasing manner as dictated by her class skills, and let out a soft sigh as the scene she had created reminded her of a book she had loved as a child. "Someday, oh *someday*, I'll have more than this provincial life."

The knights were standing in defense of the princesses, who in turn watched the iron-clad defenders with loving eyes while clasping flowers. After each of the main items for sale were set out, Danielle pulled the last of the items from her basket, two small mechanical birds which sang a familiar tune after being wound.

Music was a rarity in these parts, considered wasteful and unnecessary in this kingdom built on conquest and personal ability, especially here, where the greatest ambition anyone had was to one day be *slightly* more successful at their parents' current job. This meant anyone granted a class dealing with music or artistry was typically forced onto another route in life, unless they were members of higher society, the children of merchants or nobles.

In Frontière, life could be difficult, with a dozen eggs easily being worth half a day's pay if you had to purchase them from someone else—and recently, someone had begun purchasing dozens of eggs a day, driving the prices up to untenable levels. "Now that I think about it, I bet the baker is going to start struggling soon. I'd warn him about the collapse of the local egg economy… if I thought he'd listen. I'd have to explain what 'economy' was, though."

The exquisite toys, paired with the out-of-place yet soothing music, quickly drew a crowd. Children reached for the toys, only to have their hands slapped away by their mothers, who knew too well how breaking the often fragile toys was tantamount to purchasing them at full price without the ability to haggle. Yet, even so, they didn't walk away cheaply: Danielle negotiated prices with the practiced ease of an experienced merchant, her father's teachings echoing in her mind as she carefully negotiated with each person, figuring out not only what they *could* pay but what they were *willing* to part with.

Before the bell was struck eight times, her table was completely sold out. Flush with success, Danielle gave a small curtsy to the crowd of people who were either walking away happily—having secured a toy that would likely be handed down for generations—or frustrated that they would have to wait at least a week for another chance. "Thank you, fine people of Frontière. Your kindness and generosity will see my aging father through yet another winter and help me keep him in good spirits."

There were various polite murmurs at the sincere words, along with a smattering of people rolling their eyes, but a young boy who stepped forward was the only one to actually speak with her. "Hey, Belle, do you know why the town is named like it is?"

"Oh, not *again*, don't bother the toymaker's daughter with your inane-" The young lad's mother reached out to grip his arm and yank him away, but Danielle had already swooped down to her knees to speak to the youngster at his level.

"Yes, history is so *interesting*, isn't it?" Danielle's eyes were shining as she dove right into the conversation. "Long ago, when your mother's father's father was only as old as you are now, Verdelune was still a young kingdom. Our neighbors were fierce and greedy for our natural resources. Our king's father was barely able to push back a half-dozen kingdoms holding royal abilities of their own. But his son, the current king, and his wife, the queen, came to power and defeated those greedy kingdoms; they claimed large chunks of those countries for our sake. This place, Frontière, was at the very edge of the territory that was captured for our people—now we're right at the edge of the *frontier*. See how that word sounds similar to Frontière? That's why-"

The mother, seemingly having had enough, yanked on the boy and pulled him away while scolding him sharply. "You don't need to know any of that! You're going to be a *wainwright* like your father. Stop filling your head with useless thoughts, like she does, or you'll never have a proper career. When you're an adult making wagons and carts, you can walk any path you want. Until then, your entire focus must be on your future!"

Danielle started to stand up, not bothering to wipe the dirt from her dress—knowing that it would either vanish or integrate itself into her clothes in a pleasing manner—only to feel a *pinch* on her rear. That was quickly followed by a shout of pain, and she whirled around to see a young man clutching his hand where six small spots of blood were welling up. Her toy bird was fluttering around his head, pecking and squawking an alarm. "Pierre Bakersson! How *dare* you!"

"You *maimed* me, you temptress!" The man she recognized as the baker's son bellowed as he stumbled away. "My father told me he had proposed on my behalf, and I was coming to make sure you knew I was on board! You turn eighteen tomorrow; how long are you going to put off accepting marrying me?"

"Try something like that again, and I'll let the other birds out to peck and claw at you every time you step out of your father's shop!" Danielle warned the grumbling young man. She lifted her hand, and the toy bird flew back to perch on her finger. Reaching back, she allowed the small machine to hop over and clip onto her belt; ready to dig its sharp talons into the next person who invaded her personal space.

Her excitement over the sales drastically waned after the duo of negative interactions, but as she stomped away, Danielle remembered having met her original goal—and that she had promised herself a treat.

Taking a deep breath, she strode away from the mocking or covetous gazes and entered the nearby bookshop. As the scent of old paper and ink settled over her, the anger and annoyance started to drain away. Her eyes traveled along the shelves filled with *books*—a true treasure trove in this backwater. She had long browsed through all of the titles on display, so she walked directly past them and met the eyes of the shopkeeper.

"Francois, I know you've been holding out on me. Someone told me that you have a copy of *On the Artistry of Architecture* by the scholar D. Koda in the back. Are we going to do this the easy way, or am I going to have to bribe someone to buy it for me at a massive discount?"

She was met with a deep sigh of frustration, and Danielle had to bite the tip of her tongue to hold in a snarky comment as the merchant shook his head.

"Why do you do this to yourself, Belle? You confuse your future, trying to undo all of your hard work, your skill gains of the past. The whole town has heard that tomorrow's your birthday, and you'll be unlocking your Full Class. Are you certain you should weaken yourself further?" The shopkeeper, Francois, eyed her skeptically, and Danielle felt a surge of anger as she saw an all-too-familiar glint in his eye.

Before she could interject, he let fly the exact insulting words she'd been expecting. "I'll just say what you need to hear. You don't need to bother with all of this… *reading*. Surely any man would marry you as you are!"

"I seek knowledge for *myself*, not for the pleasure of others," Danielle sharply retorted, her patience having already been fully spent this morning. "Perhaps *you* should fear for your own future? Why are you trying to convince a customer not to make a purchase? Do you want your business to fail? Are you cautioning me because you look at your own life and feel *distaste*?"

Moments later, she was leaving the shop with the book in

her hand, though it was noticeably *not* wrapped in fine paper like all of her previous purchases had been. A loud cheer pulled her attention to where a crowd of young men were gathered around Pierre Bakersson, pushing a large mug into his still-bleeding hand and showing the small scars on their own hands.

"One of us! One of us!" The entire group laughed as they exchanged high-fives, bonding over how they had each earned marks on their hands from failed attempts at 'courting' Danielle.

She muttered furiously under her breath, lamenting the narrow-mindedness of the people from this far-flung frontier town as she stormed home. "Tomorrow, I unlock my Full Class. Tomorrow, I prove that my fate is my own, not something set in stone by my birth. I will leave here, create, innovate, and be admired for *those* things… not for a face that's carved by the system to be *pleasing to the eye*."

Luckily, not all hope was lost just yet. Even though the Full Class was *almost* always an upgrade based on how often, or sometimes just *how* the skills were used in the past, the desires and hard work of the person in question would sometimes persuade the system to grant a class and skills that either tempered or controlled the earlier classes. There was plenty of precedent of a Full Class shifting drastically away from the Basic Class, or even the Advanced version. Or—better yet—outright changing how the previous classes presented themselves.

More than anything, Danielle wanted to be able to shift her ability to beautify to be completely external, allowing her to affect other things—only what she *wanted* to change, *when* she wanted it to happen.

"How did the system document put it? There exists the potential to shift this from a *passive* ability into an active one? Yes. I want that. Otherwise… so long as I can gain a class that will offer me a *profession*, I will at least be content."

Holding back a tear of frustration as she passed by whispering wives pointing her out, Danielle looked up at the sky and spoke in a shaky voice, "Please... system, fairy godmothers, *anyone* who can help... don't let my Full Class be a direct blend and upgrade of what I have right now."

TWO

THE FOLLOWING MORNING, Danielle was startled awake by a small explosion and the exuberant voice of Henri, her father. "Happy birthday, my dear!"

Her bleary eyes opened to the sight of confetti raining down around her, focusing in on a face beaming with an infectious cheerfulness. "*No~o*. It's too early to be my birthday."

"Not even a little! Now come on, breakfast is ready, and I have something special for you!" The man paused for a moment, but Danielle only shook her head and tried to pull the covers over herself. "Fine, fine! I'll let you open it here. That way you'll be too excited to go back to sleep."

Eyes twinkling with excitement, Henri pulled out a neatly rolled parchment which he unfurled with a flourish. "Ta-*da*! It's a brand new schematic. I've had the idea for a new mode of transportation which will take Verdelune by storm! You and I will be at the forefront of this project, revolutionizing how the kingdom moves. I call it… the walking barrel!"

"That'll never catch on, Father. It's a barrel with legs. People will call it that, and…" Seeing his excitement wane ever so slightly reminded Danielle that her father was not a terribly wealthy man. This was his way of spending time with her, while at the same time trying to give her what she truly wanted: recognition for creating something that would change lives for the better. "…and love it! Just call it what it is, so there's no confusion! When do we start?"

"Right after breakfast!" Henri beamed with immense enthusiasm. "Just think! This device will allow people to travel long stretches of road at high speeds! If you look here, you'll see spring shocks meant to absorb the bumps and swaying as the legs power forward. It doesn't matter how useful it is; unless the ride is smooth and comfortable, people won't ride in the system-blessed thing! Oh, which reminds me, the seat will have to be padded and upholstered, and I've already thought of safety straps to keep the rider secure, even at its maximum speed."

Danielle shook her head, laughing at how well her father knew her. The delightfully absurd idea of a barrel sprinting down the road destroyed the last bit of sleepiness holding her in place, and she threw her covers off and stood to wrap him in a hug. "Did you forget steering? I only saw a seat, no reins. That would make sense since there are no horses, but…"

"Ah. Yes. Steering." Henri rubbed his chin thoughtfully, "I was thinking instead we have it run along only preset paths, otherwise… well, I'm still working out the collision avoidance mechanism. It's a bit tricky, you see. The legs need to be able to respond to obstacles and adjust the path accordingly, as well as navigate sloped terrain. I figure, by the time we have the prototype working, I'll have figured it out. No, *we* will have figured it out!"

"I'm sure we will." Danielle's heart warmed at the thought of spending long hours in the workshop with her father, tinkering and adjusting the barrel with legs until it was just right. "It's just like you to come up with something so novel and fun! Thank you for the lovely gift, and I'm looking forward to working on this with you…"

Henri nodded as he took in her hesitation. "But you want

to go to the Class Shrine and see what the system has in store for your Full Class, yes? I understand, of course I do. I was eighteen once. Hurry back so we can celebrate. I... I'd love to go with you, to be there for you... but I... no, I can-"

"Breakfast first. Plus, I'd rather be alone for this, just in case the system pushes a class onto me I'd rather not have. If there's reason to celebrate, you'll be the first to know." Danielle interrupted him, waving off his fumbling attempt at an explanation. He smiled thankfully, then turned and started hobbling to the table, and as always, Danielle's eyes were drawn to the leg he had made for himself.

The artificial limb had been made with all the prowess the Tinkerer possessed, and it *clicked* and *whirred* as he walked. The noises were jarring and extremely attention-grabbing, which was why he almost never left his workshop, even going so far as to have a bed in the same space as his most volatile creations. She knew this wore on him, as he was a social person by nature and wanted nothing more than to go out and dance the night away in search of a new wife.

Years ago, he and Danielle's mother had been attacked by wolves while traveling. While he lost his leg to infection after being mauled by the creatures, his then-wife had lost her life. This had filled him with a deep-seated fear of forests, wild animals, and open spaces—driving him to settle down in this border town to make toys instead of more *interesting* machines.

They had a pleasant breakfast, leftovers from the previous night as well as a small cake to share between the two of them. As she ate the confection, she noticed that the texture was slightly off. Looking over to her father, she found a shame-faced grin waiting for her. "There's no eggs to be found, at least not without paying a week's wages for just enough for breakfast."

"How bizarre." They made light conversation until Danielle's nerves finally got the better of her, and she could no longer distract herself from what the day meant. "I think I need to get going... thank you for the surprise and a wonderful meal."

"And a happy birthday to you, may they only ever be happier." Her father stood as she did and waved her away when she went to clear the table. "Go on now, get your full class and hurry home! There's legs to attach to barrels!"

With a wan smile, she wordlessly bobbed her head and hurried out the door, her thoughts already fully focused on her destination. She hurried along, with only one small notable moment catching her attention: the baker had trapped two young farmer's sons in an alley, and was shifting back and forth to block them in as they tried to dart around him. As Danielle stomped toward him, his angry pleas became audible, "Just give me those baskets of eggs, boys. I'll pay you properly! I'll even throw in a free loaf of bread for each of you. Not going to get that kind of deal wherever you're taking them, are you?"

"What are you doing?" The distraction she provided was just enough for the young men to get past him and run off. The baker threw his hands in the air, glaring at her as he stomped off without a word. Danielle watched him go, utterly nonplussed by this situation. "Now what in the world was *that* all about?"

Shaking her head, she continued toward her destination, quickly putting the bizarre situation out of her mind. It had been four long years since Danielle had gone to the local Class Shrine, a humble building—having only enough space for two people to stand comfortably within—just on the edge of town. Despite being easily overlooked, the small space contained a mystical, powerfully enchanted artifact rumored to be a shard of the system itself.

While the walls of the small building were plain and unadorned, thousands of attempts over the years had proved that the space was utterly indestructible. Not only that, but it was impossible to foul the space or permanently close it off.

Anything left within the temple was gone by the next morning, and if something were splattered across the walls or floor, the mess was wiped away the instant no one was looking.

The first time she'd stood before this shrine, Danielle had been fourteen, filled with wonder and excitement for the future. Now, she stared at the glowing artifact with fear and resentment, knowing that, although she had made every attempt at changing her destiny, her future would be decided the moment she touched the object.

As people only infrequently visited the small building, only the attendant who helped guide people through the process, collected the kingdom's shrine usage tax, and recorded their various skills and classes to pass along was here to witness the moment. Usually, attendants were a highly respected, scholarly sort, but right now, all Danielle wanted was a moment to calm herself...

...and the attendant was driving her *nuts*.

"Oh, *Bella*, why do you fear so much for what comes next?" The attendant was all smiles, moving his head side to side to try and peer under the veil she wore over her face. "It's your birthday! You should be celebrating, riding at the head of a grand parade which deposited you in front of the shrine alongside a rain of flowers from the entire town! Certainly, you're going to go on to do great things, enticing a husband who'd otherwise be far above your station and forever outside of your reach, perhaps? Think of how your father will benefit by not having to work his hands to the bone every day to feed and house you after you marry a rich-"

She had barely arrived, yet had already decided she had suffered enough of his prattling. Danielle steeled herself and stepped forward, firmly slapping her hand onto the artifact, only to be met by the text she had been expecting... as well as more information than she'd ever heard of someone getting during their class upgrade.

Codex Arcane Ledger access requested.

C.A.L. is assessing…
Age verification: 18 years. 0 months, 0 days. Conditions for Full Class advancement met.

Assessing skill use and level. Combined skill levels: 38. Determination: 98th percentile.

Scanning brain waves to account for knowledge and desires in Full Class selection process. Requirements met for: 52 Full Classes.

Comparing skill use and desires… 98th percentile of skills shows a subconscious desire to continue progressing. Waking brain <u>not</u> in alignment with subconscious.

Determination made.
Full Class Unlocked!

Full Class: Enchantress
Basic Skill: Unified Radiance: Level 0/10.
Requirement to advance: use this skill a single time.
Passive skill automatically activated!

Unified Radiance: Level 0 → 1.
Unified Radiance is a passive, continuous skill representing the culmina-tion and fusion of the skills Resplendent Self, Aura of Refinement, Alluring Assemblage, and Graceful Movement, seamlessly integrating them into a symbiotic relationship where the admiration you receive will [Minimally] fuel the enhancement of your surroundings and yourself. The radius of this effect extends up to [1] meter(s) from your body.

Building upon the original skills, Unified Radiance extends this skill's effect to a broader range of activity. Any task or action you undertake is imbued with [Minimal] inherent beauty. This effect also [Minimally] increases the value and appeal of objects and people you are involved with, both for sales and social interactions. As this passive skill grows more potent, it will allow you to adeptly evolve to new situations, allowing yourself and those impacted to be [Minimally] more adept at navigating social scenarios.

This creates a positive feedback loop between yourself and your environment. As your beauty and grace increases, so does the beauty and appeal of your surroundings, in turn further amplifying your own allure.

Requirement to advance to level 2: inspire envy in at least 50 people within 1 hour OR beautify and sell 50 items.

Advanced Skill: Locked!
To unlock, reach level 10 with your Basic Skill.

"T-this is…" Danielle could barely force the words out of her throat, her eyes shaking as she read over those horrifying words again and again.

"Huh… you know, I've never seen the floor in here sparkle like this." The attendant suddenly muttered to himself. "Was it that new wax I tried? I wonder if I could write a paper on a successful blend and pass it on for a reward."

With the sudden reminder that she wasn't alone, Danielle hunched forward slightly, wishing that she had a hood on her dress so she could further hide her face. Unfortunately, the shifting motion utterly backfired, immediately causing the attention of the attendant to fall solely on her.

"Oh, done already? Well, show me your arm, and I'll record the details." The man pulled out a parchment and quill, thankfully looking away from her in preparation of completing the only required work he had scheduled for the day. "Come along now, I'd love to get over to the bakers before he sells out."

"Is there any chance that I don't… is there any way to get

a different class?" Danielle whispered softly as the new golden script on her arm slowly faded away, leaving nothing behind on her usual porcelain skin. "I don't want this."

"Come now, it can't be *that* bad!" The attendant jubilantly called, motioning her over even as his smile faded slightly. "I've seen all sorts in my day, and so long as you strive to use your system-granted ability for the good of the kingdom, I'm certain someone like you has every chance at reaching the status of a Fairy. Fighting against it, and becoming bitter and twisted because you don't like what destiny has deemed appropriate for you? Well, there *are* far more Witches than there are Fairies, I suppose. Power is power, as the queen has proven time and time again. That is…"

With a stricken look on his face, the attendant gulped and backpedaled. "The system knows best, and since it is a neutral observer, who can say what is the better choice? Personal experience says that Witches are far more likely to get us good things, right? I wasn't trying to slander our… that is, **ahem**… your class information, please."

Knowing that she needed to present her status or face the king's justice, Danielle quietly walked over, after ensuring her veil was in place. With a single finger, she wiped along her forearm from her elbow to her wrist, leaving behind a glowing trail of words written by the system.

"Would you look at *that*?" The attendant gasped as he grabbed her wrist and pulled her close to read the details being written out. "An *Enchantress*? In this backwater? I can't imagine the celebrity status you're going to be able to attain! What the… *five* modifiers on your Basic Skill? That's… that's *Legendary* grade! You'll be able to advance nearly five times as fast as someone with only one modifier… look, Belle… let me tell you something. Impressive classes like this? They're wasted out here."

He took a deep breath, tightening his grip as a hint of avarice appeared in his eyes. "Come with me to the capital, and I'll make introductions to all the eligible bachelors of high society. *Any* noble house would marry you on the spot! Imagine it! The parties you'll be able to throw! The beautiful children you'll be able to have... *wait*! Perhaps we could find a powerful Hero and have you marry him for the combined Conjoined Skill... a Hero of the sword could gain a *Unified Swordsman* skill!"

He was breathing heavily at this point, gripping the parchment that was slowly shifting its appearance from sweat-stained to a crisp, vellum-like material. "By the king, Belle! You're worth ten times your weight in gold! I just found my ticket out of here-"

"I don't want any of that." Danielle whispered as she yanked her arm out of his grip and backed away from the attendant, feeling as though she needed to escape this cramped space. "I just wanted to be a researcher. I want to learn how the world works. I don't... I don't *want* to be trapped away in some filthy stone room for the rest of my life."

"That's the whole point of it! Belle! No matter where you go, you'll always be surrounded by *beauty*!" The attendant, seeing his payday slip away, roared his frustration at her. "What stone room? It'd turn into a *diamond* if you stayed there long enough—*no*! Come back!"

Without another word, Danielle had turned and fled, sprinting away from the small Class Shrine. The attendant shouted after her, but to her relief, he didn't give chase. She ran as fast as she could, minorly surprised at how natural it felt, only to scowl in displeasure as she realized her speed and stamina had increased because she was running even more gracefully and efficiently than usual. Then it hit her, "The new class and skill are already affecting me? They're *changing* me?"

As she ran through the town toward home, her ears picked up the sound of a bustling crowd in front of her, and a quick glance informed her that the town square was filled with almost every resident of Frontière. Without missing a beat, she shifted her aim and took a hard left, bypassing the town square in an effort to return home as swiftly as possible.

Pounding along the cobblestone street, Danielle raised one hand to angrily wipe away tears streaming from her eyes. It was only when an unknown, velvety voice called out to her that Danielle realized she had moved her veil out of the way to perform that action.

"Fair woman, why do you cry? Tell me who dared to treat you in such a manner, and I'll have them hanged by tea time."

A second voice called out almost at the same time as the first, though this one was harsh and demanding. "Halt, peasant! You are approaching Baron Gasteel Leiter at speed, and if you do not comply... we will *cut you down!*"

That broke through the fugue state Danielle had found herself in, and she screeched to a halt, adjusting her veil and dropping into a polite, trembling curtsy. "I-I'm so sorry! I was on my way home after unlocking my Full Class, and-"

"Well, that won't do!" The baron spoke in his deep, manly voice. "I sent a messenger this morning that the entire town must be gathered for an announcement. This is a mandatory event, and I wouldn't want to see a *prize* like you punished for no reason. Why don't you come over here and mount my horse? I'll be happy to keep you close and ensure that you're following the laws of the land."

Having no good reason to refuse, and not wanting to get thrown into prison for literally no reason, Danielle slowly approached the horse, hating the fact that she needed to get closer to the leering, brawny, hairy soldiers. The baron reached a hand down, taking both of hers in *one* of his, and pulled her onto the saddle with a casual ease that frankly terrified her.

This was a man that could literally rip her in half with his bare hands if he so desired... and now she needed to ride into town with him in front of the entire population. Danielle deflated as that thought struck her, and she tried to control her breathing as they came ever closer to their destination.

The horse began trotting forward, and Gasteel made a few appreciative comments about her joining him, and even went so far as to comment about how the air suddenly felt fresher, the sun warmer. "Pierre! Is it just me, or does this town not stink *nearly* as bad as border villages usually do?"

"It's not just that, my lord!" The honor guard walking next to the baron's horse looked at him with confusion evident on his face. "Somehow you seem... did you gain even more muscle definition along your jaw?"

"I'm glad you noticed! I didn't think it would be obvious this soon after I started my mewing exercises." Gasteel raised an eyebrow and chuckled. "Just don't look too closely. I own a mirror. I know all too well that *anyone* can fall in love with this face."

The men began laughing and making bawdy jokes back and forth as they approached the town square, and Danielle found herself disgusted and dreading remaining with this group for any length of time. Not that anyone seemed to notice her again, and they *certainly* didn't include her in their conversation. In fact, as soon as the baron had grabbed her and placed her on his horse, he hadn't bothered to even glance at her again.

It was as if she was fully already accounted for in his mind: an interesting, shiny object that he'd picked up on the side of the road.

THREE

As they marched into town, the eyes of all of the townspeople turned on to them, and a flare of golden text scrawled along Danielle's arm.

Skill increase! Unified Radiance [Level 1 (Minimal) → Level 2 (Limited)]!
Requirement to advance to level 3: Enhance 100 objects and sell them for at least a 50% increase in price OR publicly receive a sincere marriage proposal.

"Fifty people were envious of me? For this *embarrassment*?" Danielle had stiffened upon seeing that she had already gained another level in her skill but breathed out a small sigh of relief when she saw the skill upgrade requirement—often known as a skill upgrade quest—was something that she could likely shut down easily if it were to come up. "So long as I remember to let people get a good deal, I might be able to stay at level two for months."

As she refocused on her surroundings, Danielle realized that practically everyone in the square was staring at *her*, not at the baron she was sitting behind. Her stomach dropped as their muttered words washed over her.

"What's going on?"

"Wasn't her birthday *today*? Did she *already* manage to throw herself at a nobleman?"

"Girl works *fast*, gotta give her that. She must've run straight to him on the way back from getting her Full Class."

Closing her eyes, the newly christened Enchantress could only shake her head and let out a small sigh of defeat.

Baron Gasteel launched himself off of his horse and directly into a prepared speech for the gathered crowd. "I stand before you as a man that proves you can be *more* than you were born as. Starting as a humble hunter, I increased my prowess to the point where I gained the attention of royalty then proved my worth on the battlefield as a Greenhorn, working my way up the ranks until I earned a Knighthood! From there, I cut my way through the ranks of our enemies, bathing in their blood until I had soaked in enough prestige… recently gaining the title of Baron."

Gasteel paused for a moment to let his ringing words echo back to him and allow a silent fervor to build in the assembled crowd. "Now, I stand before you as a humble lord, prepared to offer you the same opportunity I was once given! The enemies of Verdelune are amassing against us, planning to swoop in and take our resources for themselves! Our ores, our fertile crops… our beautiful women!"

To add to this, he turned and gestured at Danielle, who was struggling to get off of the war horse. Each time she started to slide off, it would shift side to side and knicker at her in warning. "As a gesture of my goodwill, I plucked this beautiful flower from the side of the road and have decided that this is the day her dreams come true."

Danielle went very still at that moment, clutching the shifting horse. "Baron Gasteel… what could you possibly know about my dreams?"

He didn't hear her, already having turned back to the crowd. His next words wove a tale of glory and adventure, blood and honor. Still, beyond a few, young, fiery men, the people assembled simply didn't seem to find much interest in his words. This was a peaceful border town, situated next to a chunk of no-man's-land that hadn't been invaded in living memory. Very few had the desire to leave their hometown and the comfortable life they lived. Somehow, Gasteel seemed to catch on to that fact and wrapped up his speech by once more turning to Danielle.

"Fair lady, from the moment I laid eyes on you, I had decided that you would be my wife. You joined me on my horse, so I already know the answer you have for me. Even so, for the ears of these common folk, I'll ask aloud." Danielle could only watch in numb shock as he turned an important moment in anyone's life into a sideshow, all to make his case for the locals. "Would you join me in my glorious rise to the highest ranks of the kingdom of Verdelune... as my wife?"

**_Skill increase! Unified Radiance [Level 2 (Limited) →_
Level 3 (Rudimentary)]!**
Requirement to advance to level 4: Successfully mediate a dispute between two parties, offering no solutions, while leaving both of them feeling more positive and agreeable OR enhance a space enough it could sell for 60% more than its purchase price.

The Enchantress stared at the warrior, completely flabbergasted, only saved from embarrassment by having her expression hidden behind her veil. As the seconds ticked past, the proud smile on Gasteel's face faded, being replaced with annoyance... then anger.

Finally, Danielle found her voice. "M'lord. You don't even know my name."

"A minor detail! Certainly one that can be rectified before the wedding. Or, at the latest, on the honeymoon." Gasteel waved away her concerns, motioning for her to get on with her answer. "Come now, don't keep them waiting. You just got your Full Class, so even a place like *this* has a Class Shrine, huh? That means we could be married in the sight of the system before dinner!"

Choosing her words carefully, she spoke quietly, so as not to project her voice to the enormous group of gossip mongers watching on. "I'm... speechless, my lord. I really don't know what to say, other than-"

"Just say that you will marry me, and we'll be off! You'll live in my manor, taking care of my homestead in my absence."

Though the thought of his absence had a definite appeal, Gasteel's next words, which mirrored the attendant's from earlier, lit a fire of defiance in her.

"Think of the parties I'll be able to provide, with people who will look on in admiration and jealousy toward me. You, the most beautiful woman I've ever met, are the perfect adornment to a lord like myself, the most handsome man of the generation. It was meant to be."

"I'm sorry... but... *no*." The words were out of Danielle's mouth before she realized how sharply she'd spoken them. Remembering herself, she quickly adjusted her tone, much more softly adding, "Certainly someone so lowborn as I doesn't deserve you."

With that, she launched herself off of the horse, landing smoothly and gracefully rising to her full height with a single, fluid motion. Then she backed away, her eyes never leaving the fuming nobleman, worried that he'd attack her no matter the fact that they were in front of a crowd. The baron's eyes had narrowed, his nostrils flaring while his hands balled into fists as if he were about to charge her, despite the crowd gathered and looking on. For a long moment, the tension was stifling, but then he took several deep breaths and forced a smile.

He turned to the crowd, rolling his eyes. "Don't worry, I'll have her as my wife. Even if she may need some *convincing*... make no mistake about that."

His words earned a chuckle and cheer from the crowd, their mood shifting from curiosity and concern to amusement. Several people turned toward the fleeing Enchantress and sneered at her: it was no secret that she had turned down marriage proposals from nearly every single eligible man in town—not to mention a concerning number who were *already* married. Now, seeing even a nobleman being snubbed, their annoyance with her swiftly shifted from petty envy to full-fledged contempt.

"Can you believe that? What kind of peasant is so ungrateful that they'd spit on a nobleman's affection?"

"It's not like he said something improper! He asked her to *marry* him, not-"

"One of us... one of us..." A few young men standing near each other put their fists together, showing the scars on their hands and looking at the baron with something akin to hero worship.

Finally, Danielle got to the edge of the crowd, at first seeking an escape. But, to her dismay, each of the paths into the town square had either a soldier or a guard standing there to prevent people from leaving. Seeing the oddity, Danielle finally snapped out of the confused and shaken state she'd been in since gaining her new class and began to think through the situation at hand.

"This is... this is wrong. He said other countries are going to be invading us? That's not right, is it? Think, Danielle. What are the facts? He's here trying to recruit people and offering them the chance to sign up. But if that were the case, why wouldn't he just send one of his men to set up a kiosk or something? Instead, this is a mandatory meeting we're not allowed to leave? That's never happened before. Well, except back when the... the... by the *system*! Not since the draft! He's going to give people a chance to sign up, then conscript anyone who doesn't volunteer!"

She whirled around and stared at the armor-clad warriors, where once again, the baron was giving an impassioned speech to the populace. Finally, he slowed down and held up a large ledger. Now that she had an idea of what might be going on, she paid attention to his final, parting words.

"Anyone who'd like to register as a Greenhorn, come forward now and sign the documents, so that we can assess your best ability to serve. Within a year, you will be earning achievements and accolades, maybe even showing off muscles *almost* as impressive as mine."

Gasteel proudly bellowed out, standing as tall as he could and showing off his admittedly impressive physique. "By volunteering, you will join Gasteel Company at the same rank *I* originally joined the army—and now I'm a Baron! You can do it as well. I'll tell you all right now, no one *fights* like Gasteel or has as many *rights* as Gasteel!"

"No one stays up as many long *nights* as Gasteel," a warrior near Danielle quipped under his breath.

Another nudged him. "Or gets infested by sand mites like Gasteel."

Hoping she wasn't wrong, Danielle strode forward, lifting her hand in the air and shouting over the quiet murmuring of the crowd, who seemed utterly cowed by the huge man and his offer of impending bloodshed. "I would like to sign on as a Greenhorn!"

Her melodic voice washed over the audience, and they turned to look at her in abject shock. Danielle kept her gaze firmly on the document being held in the air, striding forward and holding out a hand for the quill as every local hurried to get out of her way, as though the desire to join the military was infectious.

"The trophy wife-? *Ahem*, that is… never mind. Wait. You would refuse the opportunity to marry into nobility but offer yourself as a warrior on the front lines?" Gasteel stared at her with great confusion in his eyes. His mouth formed into a hard line, then his tongue flicked out and licked over his pebble-dry lips. "You are... *perfect*. I must have you."

Suppressing her gag reflex, Danielle merely plucked the quill out of his hand and signed the document, filling out her name and class. Thankfully, she didn't need to provide any details on her skills. As soon as she'd finished, she stepped back and stared up at the huge man defiantly, hoping she hadn't just made a terrible miscalculation.

Thankfully, it seemed that the baron was far too amused to think through the situation carefully, and instead turned the document around and read over the information, as if he had been presented with a child's drawing he now needed to critique. "D... Dani..."

His brows furrowed, and he glared at the words as if they were being intentionally difficult. "Where's Lefroupe? Ah, there you are, my most loyal scribe. Get over here at once."

"M'lord!" A short, pudgy man with a weaselly face scrunched up in an attempt at appearing wise came out of seemingly nowhere, having been hidden behind the horse Gasteel rode in on. "If I may, could I read off the information to the crowd at large so you may rest your voice?"

"Smooth," Danielle muttered under her breath, surprised a moment later as the man glanced her direction and gave her a wink. He looked down at the parchment, threw his shoulders back, and announced for the gathered people.

"Danielle Marie Tinkersdottir!" The scribe, though Danielle thought that perhaps 'herald' would be a better word for him, announced her full name, then continued on with barely a pause. "Eighteen years old, as of... today! Happy birthday, madame Danielle!"

There was a momentary pause as the scribe looked out knowingly at the assemblage. Reluctantly, a large part of them began clapping in acknowledgment of her surviving this long.

"I'm certain you will go on to do wonderful things in your life, especially with your Full Class being... *Enchantress*?"

There was a collective gasp of astonishment, and Gasteel stared at her with even greater fervor, his eyes seeming to sink into his skull slightly as he failed to blink. The minor noble wiped a thin trail of drool from the corner of his mouth, then stepped forward and snatched the document out of Lefroupe's hands.

"Absolutely *not*! I won't let the worth of an Enchantress be wasted on the battlefield. I deem you unfit to join as a Greenhorn." Lifting his hand, the noble touched a signet ring to the paper, and with a flash of light, the words 'permanently unfit for duty' scrawled across it in bright red, washing over her signature and class. "No. I have a far better... *position* for you to be in. If you won't be my wife just yet, you'll be my attaché. From this point forward, you'll ensure that I meet my quotas! Welcome to the support staff of House Gasteel."

With that, he waved his hand and turned back to the others who were watching on with wide eyes. "Well? Are the rest of you going to let this waif of a woman upstage you all? Where are my brave new soldiers?"

Either from the shame of being upstaged or desiring some of the benefits the baron had been pouring out on Danielle, approximately a dozen of the young men of the town stepped forward and waited for their turn to sign on. As each of them filled out their forms, they were given a basic iron helm with a single green horn welded onto the left side to denote their position within the ranks.

Beyond being a simple weapon, this was the only armor anyone of their rank was given. In essence, the amount of armor, as well as the quality of it, determined one's position in the ranks of Verdelune. The thought was: if a soldier had the wealth to purchase armor, the strength of arm to earn it in combat, and the ferocity to *keep* it when their fellows tried to take it, they were obviously leadership material. An increase in rank was almost always in the cards for someone who could demonstrate a consistent record of maintaining arms and armor.

Finally, the dozen young men were proudly wearing their new protection, though a few of them seemed slightly unsteady from the unaccustomed weight of the cast iron helmet. Gasteel looked around the area one last time, his eyes hardening. "Is that all? No one else will answer the call from our kingdom?"

When no one else volunteered, he simply nodded and darkly intoned, "Fine. Then I've seen the extent of your resolve. Gasteel Company! I see dozens of healthy and strong young men and women here who don't want access to promotion opportunities. Bring them in, assess them for service, and *conscript* any who meet the minimum requirements!"

"What? You can't do this!"

"I'm going to be *conscripted* because I didn't *volunteer*? I didn't know, give me another chance-"

"I have every right! Not *knowing* the law is no excuse for not following it." Gasteel boomed as he raised his hand and glared at the crowd, shouting over their clamoring in a cold tone.

He paused for a long moment, meeting the eyes of the most defiant—taking note of them—and allowing the noise to die off before he continued. "No one can say I didn't try to get you to join up with as many benefits as possible. It is *you* who have shown your true colors today. I tell you this, it's not green like these fine volunteers! It is *yellow*, and cowards have no right to complain when their betters put them to work."

As the townsfolk once more started shouting and screaming, Danielle could only close her eyes and let out a soft breath of relief as she realized that she'd just taken a major step in controlling her own fate.

"I took a calculated risk... thank goodness I'm great at math."

CHAPTER
FOUR

By NOON, Danielle was seated in a tent erected in the center of the town square, tasked with assisting Lefroupe with the inprocessing of the new Greenhorns and conscripts. The air was thick with tension between the two groups, as there was already a clear divide growing.

Those who had taken the leap and volunteered—whether out of patriotism, a thirst for adventure, or simply to avoid the shame of being unfavorably compared to Danielle—now stood tall and proudly. Their chins were lifted proudly, all so they could look down their noses at those who had been forced into service with a clear bent toward contempt.

On the other hand, the conscripts were shuffling back and forth, their eyes darting around as they sought a way to escape. The smattering of soldiers standing at each exit to the town square precluded any actual attempts, but it was a near thing on multiple occasions.

The contrast between the two groups felt like an irritation just beneath Danielle's skin, but she clenched her jaw and resisted the urge to snap at the Greenhorns as they jeered at the less fortunate conscripts: people they had grown up with and known their whole lives. Finally, she had to stand and close the tent flap so she could block out the deeply aggravating sight.

"As bad as it is for them, I need to figure out a way to save my own skin first." Then, she took a deep breath and smoothed the durable canvas fabric of her dress and swept into her seat once more. Attempting to maintain a pleasant demeanor, she loudly called out, "Next! Pierre Jacob Bakersson. Can I say, I'm impressed that you would sign on willingly, knowing how your father would react? He's not exactly known for being overly gentle when he's angry or wants something. Just this morning, I saw him accosting a few farmhands for their eggs on my way to the Class Shrine."

"He didn't get any, neither," the hefty lad stated as he strolled up to the table she'd been provided. "'Sides, he might've been angry, but now all he is, is proud. Relieved, actually. I could've been like one of *them*, still having to do all of the scut work but not actually gettin' any benefits out of it. Uhh… sorry about the whole pinchin' you thing. I hope you don't hold that against me, now that you're gonna marry the baron."

"Ah… right. You don't need to worry about that anymore. Also, good for you, Pierre." Danielle's soothing words put the young man greatly at ease, the tension immediately melting out of him. The Enchantress bobbed her head and shuffled through the various documents needing to be filled out and placed with his initial sign-on packet.

She quickly gathered each paper, had them signed by Pierre, then gathered them once more and tapped the stack on the table a single time—and it shuffled into perfect alignment. Then, she dismissed the baker's son and handed the documents over to Lefroupe, who watched on with a glint of amusement in his eyes.

"See that? What you just did with arranging everything beautifully? Why is that not a *scribe* ability?" Lefroupe had proven to be a hidden gem, constantly making jokes and attempting to put her at ease with the situation. "What wonderful work you are already doing for us, madame Danielle! Truly, as you get more familiar with your tasks in the future, I hope you will lean on me and bring any fears or concerns that you have. I am very excited to have this opportunity to get to know you better."

Danielle considered the words he'd spoken, searching for hidden meanings and wondering why he had said something similarly complimentary practically every time she completed even the simplest of tasks. As they finished their paperwork and sent the next new recruit away with a smile on his face, she turned to the scribe and directly inquired, "Why are you being so nice to me, Lefroupe? What benefit do you get?"

"My lady?" Lefroupe's face scrunched up slightly as he smiled uncomfortably. "Surely, you understand that you will one day be... well, you'll be in charge of me."

"By the system, what are you talking about?"

"I know you don't know him very well, yet, but... you know? Baron Gasteel is the *epitome* of what a hunter should be." Lefroupe's smile faded slightly, and he noticeably gulped. "Once he's found his mark, he will tirelessly chase it down until he has his trophy. I truly mean no disrespect to you when I say this, as I know you have your own feelings on the matter, but you *will* be his wife one day."

"Over my dead body." She barely managed to murmur the words instead of shouting them, not wanting to get on the bad side of this potential ally so early.

"More likely... it's *far* more likely to be over many *other* people's dead bodies." Lefroupe whispered nearly as softly, leaning in to keep the conversation as private as possible. "You're far too valuable and exactly what he's always dreamed of having. Someone who can make him even *more* handsome than he was before?"

Lefroupe shook his head in wonder, though his eyes stayed fixed on Danielle's face. "You have to understand, you're the *ideal* trophy for him. Yet, even as I feel for the hesitation you have for your situation, I still envy you. You will have a life that no one in this town could have ever dreamed of. Gasteel has the eye of the king, and he will one day rise in the peerage once more. You're… well, a peasant for the moment. You'd do well to accept this new reality and make peace with your future."

Shaking her head and refusing to say another word, Danielle turned her eyes to the next set of documents and wearily called out for the next volunteer. The hours dragged on, the bombardment of compliments for every minor action she took only draining her as they continued to flood in from the man who seemed to be the baron's personal cheer squad. As dinner time approached, she was exhausted from the emotional toll that had been inflicted on her over the course of the day.

Happily, Lefroupe sensed her fatigue and finally called for a break. "Dinner will be brought in shortly; why don't you chat with me for a while and take your mind off all this unpleasantness?"

The Enchantress could hear dozens of people outside of the tent still waiting to be processed, and she had heard enough commands from the soldiers around them to know they had been forced to remain standing the entire day. "What about them? Wouldn't it be better to just continue on while we eat?"

"Everyone who remains is a conscript." Lefroupe let out a soft huff through his nose, wincing and looking sadly toward the opening. "Trust me when I say that it will be good for them to get used to the idea that life no longer moves at their pace. It's a lesson they'll need if they're going to survive the next few weeks."

Not sure what else to say about the situation, Danielle reluctantly nodded, though his outlook didn't sit well with her. Looking around the tent for anything she could use to change the topic of conversation, her eyes came to rest on a large book casually laying on the cobblestone floor of the tent near Lefroupe's feet. "Oh? Do you read?"

"What, *this*? No, I read *fun* books." The scribe rolled his eyes and picked up the thick book. "This absolute doorstop is a copy of the laws of the land, given to Baron Gasteel upon his ascension into the nobility of Verdelune. He gave it to me to reference when he needs information, after expressing his frustration with the lack of pictures."

"I've never seen a full version of the laws of the land before. I can't believe it's only one book!" Danielle stared at the tome with bright eyes, focused on the gilded edges of the pages as the scribe moved it back and forth slightly. "If I promise to be careful with it, can I read it when we have breaks?"

"Hmm? You can read? That's adora—I mean, certainly! I'm not worried about you damaging it—you'd never be able to repay the cost of this book." Lefroupe looked between her and the book thoughtfully, a sly grin appearing on his face. "You know... *actually*... destroying this would cement your engagement with Gasteel. Win-win for me. Take it. *Burn* it, if you'd like."

Even with the clear warning, Danielle barely hesitated before gingerly reaching over and accepting the immense book. She nodded at the scribe as she opened the volume with care, feeling the weight of knowledge in her hands and a settling of a concerning responsibility on her shoulders. Upon taking a deep breath to calm her frazzled nerves, the scent of aged parchment filled her senses. Despite the potential for dire consequences, she couldn't help but feel a flicker of excitement at gaining access to such a rare and important treasure.

Best of all: Danielle knew that, somewhere in this book, she would find a way to escape.

She cracked it open immediately. As she read through the dense text, her mind raced to make comparisons between her situation and the laws of the land. Each time she touched upon a new section, amendment, or precedent, she tried to find a way to apply it… but the material was dense. Before she had gotten more than three pages in, dinner was served.

Danielle distractedly munched on a steaming slice of over-sized quiche without tasting it, taking care not to get food crumbs or grease on the pages as she continued to absorb the information. Even if she hadn't been so well distracted, it was unlikely she would've been able to taste anything but ashes. The thought of being tied to *him*, becoming his 'trophy wife', went against everything the Enchantress wanted out of life— not to mention making her feel physically ill.

Eventually, she had to reluctantly close the cover of the body of law as sad-faced conscripts were ushered into the tent. Danielle had to process them and worked hard to help them regain some of the dignity that had been stripped away from them over the course of the day.

Almost none of the people stepping into the tent had the ability to read or write. In fact, most of them were only familiar with the system text etched on their arms, only under-standable because the system ensured that everyone—no matter how noble or lowly—would understand their class and skills. Recognizing their anxiety and confusion, Danielle moved to help each of them with as much patience as she could, carefully guiding each of them through the process, helping them write out their information, and explaining the terms of their conscription in simple, reassuring language.

Beyond doing the bare minimum and getting everyone to sign, Danielle went out of her way to offer them a sliver of hope. To Lefroupe's great annoyance, she pointed out a clause in the conscription contract which informed everyone that, after a decade of service, they had the right to return to their lives and make their own choices once more. Or, if they chose to stay in the military, they would immediately be lifted to the position of a squad leader in charge of at least fifteen other conscripts. This way, she made sure they understood that, although the term of service was long, it was finite.

By explaining the contract, Danielle felt she had done everything she could to ensure they wouldn't be trapped—at least not forever—in a life they didn't want.

Now that Danielle had read over some of the initial laws governing Verdelune, the flash of light emanating from the signed document had taken on a new meaning: every signature on a contract was no different from signing a verbal oath to the kingdom.

Each document integrated them directly into Verdelune's ward structure, which would document all of their individual contributions to the kingdom, whether it be through combat or in support of the nation. For those who had signed on willingly, this was a path to leadership, knighthood, or even a noble title, if the kingdom expanded farther and took new lands.

For the conscripts, this was simply a way to ensure they were working and fighting on behalf of Verdelune. Still, the more she thought on this topic, the more Danielle realized she may have discovered a path forward. Murmuring to herself, she reached out and ran her fingers along the spine of the law book. "I was added to the ward structure, then removed immediately afterward. What does that mean, legally speaking?"

Lefroupe glanced up from his own documents, blinking rapidly as he tried to stay awake. "Madame, apologies, I did not hear you correctly. Did you say something to me?"

"What? No... I was just thinking out loud," Danielle replied with a slight blush, the color in her cheeks hiding the deeper machinations spinning in her mind.

The scribe shrugged, then glanced out the open tent flap, only for his eyes to go wide. "Look at the hour! I've kept you far too late. I know someone such as yourself doesn't need their beauty sleep, but you should still go and get some rest."

Smoothly getting to her feet for the first time in hours, Danielle nodded at the weasel-faced man and scooped up the large legal manual. "I'll see you in the morning, I suppose?"

"Absolutely. That's Gasteel Company for you. No one works like Gasteel, has early mornings and late *nights* like Gasteel." Lefroupe's words reduced to humming as Danielle calmly walked out of the tent, doing her very best to appear innocent.

Walking to the edge of town, then just a little bit past, she finally returned to her father's home and workshop. She opened the door, barely managing to get inside before her father swooped in and pulled her into a tight hug.

"I heard the news, Danielle. I'm so sorry to hear you didn't get the class you were hoping for." Henri stepped back to arm's length, inspecting his daughter for a long moment, his eyes lingering on the Gasteel Company pin she had been ordered to wear on the front of her dress. "Tell me what happened. It looks like today has been even more eventful than we'd been expecting. How bad is it?"

Whether it was from the long day or her own musings, Danielle needed a moment to pull herself back to the present and respond. "It's the worst. I'm an *Enchantress*. I'll never be able to trust the people around me, always locked into wondering if they're simply there to gain something from me instead of-"

"My sweet Danielle, I mean your newfound military service," Henri gently interrupted her, flicking the large pendant with evident annoyance. "I've seen this sort of thing far too many times for my liking in the past, and I know exactly what it means. Not to mention, I've had no fewer than three visitors today—three more than I've had in the last six months, I might add—telling me all kinds of wild stories. Everything from you signing up for the military, to you being conscripted, to getting married to a noble. So what's the truth of the matter?"

"The truth is... complicated." Danielle hefted the weighty book. "I think I managed to do something significant; I just need to spend some time figuring out exactly how important it was—and how I can use it to get out of this mess."

That wasn't enough of an explanation for her father, so she was treated to a truncated round of questioning as he gently pried out the events of the day. When he had a full account, he could only nod his head wearily and wave toward her room.

"Sounds like you lived a whole week in the span of a few hours. You must be tired, so feel free to get some rest. I'm sure you're going to your room to humor me, but if you're just going to stay up and read, feel free to do so out here where the light is better."

"You know me too well." A small smile appeared on Danielle's lips as she gave her father a kiss on the cheek and thumped the book onto the table, settling into her usual spot and throwing the cover open.

CHAPTER
FIVE

DANIELLE'S EYES burned from the strain of poring over the dense, convoluted laws of Verdelune. The language of the text was a labyrinth of legal jargon seemingly designed to confuse, deter, and be impenetrable to the common reader—and it certainly might have been to someone less determined.

Luckily, the Enchantress had a solid foundation learning how to parse blueprints, technical manuals, and philosophical debates, thanks to her long years of attempting to persuade the system to give her an intellectually focused class. While that hadn't worked out as she had hoped, she was determined to use that experience as fuel for her efforts to get as far away from the baron as possible.

Even so, a heavy knot of anxiety began to form in her stomach as the minutes passed without finding anything relevant to this particular situation. Her hands were clammy and shaking as she turned the pages, the gold-gilded edges sometimes slipping from her fingers as she grew sleepier. "Come on… there's got to be something. He can't just walk up to me and tell me I have to work for him; I'm *not* a conscript. I'm… oh. In fact, I'm not even… hmm."

There was something there, she just knew it. Though her

body was aching from sitting hunched over a table all day and now all night, the still air was broken by the rustle of pages being rapidly flipped as she looked for a few keywords. Even with the small hint provided by the signing of the conscription documents, the sheer volume of information threatened to overwhelm her. As Danielle realized she may have already passed the section she needed, she felt the prickling sting of tears at the corner of her eyes. "Take a breath… I just need to slow down and make sure I don't make more work for myself by passing the section on conscription law."

Taking out a blank piece of parchment, she took small, detailed notes on each section she found, trying to build an index she would be able to reference in case she needed to cross-reference something later. As she got more absorbed in her work, her breathing slowed down, and her nerves became as numb as her thoughts.

Midnight had come and gone, and Danielle slowly blinked, her quill hovering over her parchment, almost catatonic as she tried to understand why she had stopped progressing through the tome. She reread the words twice more, mumbling them out loud before they finally sank in. "On conscription and recruitment. Chapter three-nineteen, subsection ninety-one."

Reading the entire chapter took another two hours, but any hint of tiredness fled as she pieced together the puzzle of the legal argument she needed for a clean escape.

Finally, she'd written out all the laws which would affect her current situation, and there she found it: the loophole. "Father!"

Henri startled awake, having gone to bed hours previously. Despite his initial confusion, as Danielle explained that she needed his opinion on her work, he happily hauled himself out of his slumber and came over to inspect the document.

Raising an eyebrow, her father read through each of the laws she had cited, annotated, and put together in a clear synopsis. "Since Baron Gasteel has refused your initial enlist-ment, he would need the approval of a higher-ranked noble to overturn this decision and force you into the military. As you had volunteered, only to be turned away, he cannot in good faith make you work for him in any capacity. If he does so, this will not only damage his reputation among his peers but also highlight his inability to read. As a newly raised baron, this would be a source of ridicule and possibly be enough to strip him of his new title."

Henri nodded several times then turned to his daughter with his face crinkled into a smile. "Very impressive. Every-thing you wrote down is likely exactly correct. I also hope you know that you can't hand this over to him. In fact… burn this one after you've made one we can use. No… now."

"*Burn* it? Why?" Even as her father lifted the parchment and waved it over the candle, Danielle didn't move to stop him —though her heart was pounding with anger that her work had just been destroyed so casually. Still, very rarely did Henri do something without a good reason, so she simply waited for a *very good* explanation.

After tossing the flaming parchment into the fireplace, Henri limped over and sat into the chair opposite her and let out a deep sigh. "Sometimes you forget, because your skills smooth over the rough edges the rest of us feel, but most people don't like to be confronted with absolute truth. If you hand over only hard truths, people will enjoy speaking to you exactly as much as they do a habitual liar. Truth can be painful. Sometimes, even the most flawless design requires a touch of beauty to truly come to life and function as intended."

"You're saying…" Danielle tried to still her whirling thoughts and understand his meaning, her lips pursed as her mind sluggishly tried to catch up, "This would hurt his *pride*, so I shouldn't use it? Who cares about his pride? I don't want him in a position to control me!"

"It sounds like *he* cares about his pride. If you go at his sore points like this, especially with as public, as it will end up being, it's likely he will fight to the death rather than lose." Henri nodded along as he spoke, his expression softening with approval at her quick uptake. "Why don't we put something together... *together?*"

By the time the sun rose, Danielle and Henri had spent the night poring over the legal text and formulating a plan of action. A clear letter had been written, with all the legal jargon necessary, as well as plenty of additions in an attempt to assuage Gasteel's need to win. Danielle could only hope it would be enough.

"We need to leave immediately," Henri stated with a drawn-out sigh as he got to his feet and stretched for the first time that morning. "It's only a few hours of travel to the border. I think it'd be best if we left Verdelune entirely. I'll pack a few things, put together anything I think will have value to our neighboring kingdoms, then we *must* leave."

"No!" Danielle froze halfway into a standing position. "Father, I can't just have you give up everything you've worked on for the last *decade!* Why do we need to leave? Everything we're doing is completely legal, and just as you wanted, we're going to be keeping our heads down and being extra polite."

Henri turned to her with a wry smile. "It won't be enough, Danielle. You're correct, we're doing nothing wrong. It won't matter. At best, we'll have a short period of time when they pretend we don't exist before rallying the town against us. We need to use that moment to make our escape. There are worse things than military commitment that can happen to a family in a place like this. Now, quickly, while I pack up, you go and buy any foodstuffs you can that'll travel well. If you can't get anything, we'll just have to make do. Be back by the eighth bell!"

"You're... you're sure?" Danielle questioned him in a soft

tone. "You're ready to just drop everything and leave it behind? Just like that?"

"For you, the world." Henri reached out and gave her a gentle squeeze on the shoulder. "I settled down here so you could have a stable life. That time has passed. Now, let's find ourselves a big city somewhere far away and make the most wondrous toys the world has ever seen. Somewhere with a grand library."

"You… you're the best father in the whole world." Eyes sparkling with happiness and unshed tears at his willingness to drop everything for her, Danielle nodded, scooped up her coin pouch, and hurried out the door. As she raced along the road, the baker suddenly sprinted past her, carrying a large crate and laughing wildly. Moments later, a cursing farmer went by her as well, chasing after the surprisingly spry large man.

Her mind dull from lack of sleep, yet focused on quickly buying rations, she watched their antics, only to have her attention pulled by a voice calling her name. As was her usual habit, Danielle ignored it as long as she could, only for Lefroupe to suddenly step in her path and bar her way.

"Good morning, madame! Where might you be off to in such a rush?" The scribe was holding a tray with a chunk of the quiche from the previous night, as well as an enormous cup of coffee. "If you're on your way to accept the baron's marriage proposal, feel free to walk along with me!"

"Ew. No." The words flew from her mouth before Danielle could clamp her jaw shut, and at Lefroupe's wince, she realized how he'd taken the casual insult. "No! Lefroupe, walking with you sounds pleasant. I meant that the idea of becoming his wife sounds absolutely disgusting. Stop, don't shake your head at me like that; I want a different life than he's offering. In fact, here! This letter is for him; it explains everything. I'll… goodbye, Lefroupe. I know we haven't known each other long, but you seem very nice."

"I *am* very nice." Lefroupe readily agreed as Danielle

skirted around him and rushed off once more. "I hope you find what you're looking for. Safe travels, I suppose? See you soon."

With that, Danielle continued toward the market at speed. "I need supplies. Anything but eggs. At least I know why they've become so overpriced these days. The baron must've sent some of his people ahead to arrange their stay. I can't believe how many they must go through on a daily basis."

Unfortunately, the lackadaisical nature of the locals meant the market was slow to open. The sun rose higher in the sky, and even after cajoling and pleading with the merchants to move faster, it had still taken her the better part of two hours to secure enough supplies to make a *short* trip—let alone an inter-kingdom escape. With frustration gnawing at her, she rushed home nearly empty handed.

As she approached her home, Danielle's heart sank.

The door was ajar, the windows in at least the front of the house were shattered, and small bits of metal she recognized from her father's parts bins were strewn across the lawn. With panic surging through her, Danielle walked forward in a daze, feeling as though she were moving incredibly quickly even as she took timid steps. "Father? Where are you? What happened here?"

No answer came from the house, but as she got closer to the door, Danielle felt herself nearly passing out as she saw a writ pinned to the door with a small knife. She blinked several times, the letters on the parchment swimming in her vision and making it impossible to read what it said. At first, she could only focus on the seal, a blob of wax pressed with the signet of House Leiter. The wax was a perfect sanguine, looking for all the world like a wound on the paper.

"To whom it may concern." Danielle read the paper aloud, shocking herself out of her dizzy spell at the sound of her own voice. "The master of this house, Henri Tinker, has been found guilty of espionage against the Crown of

Verdelune. His sentence is to be determined by Baron Gasteel Leiter. All items and the property are now the sole possession of Baron Gasteel Leiter, punishable by incarceration. He… abducted my father?"

Danielle's blood ran cold as her hands began shaking. "This is my fault. Why'd I give Lefroupe that letter before I was ready to leave? He even told me he was on the way to see Gasteel! Of course they'd act immediately. This is a warrior, not a pampered noble. I'm a system-cursed *fool*!"

Without any further hesitation, she turned and stepped off of her father's lawn and onto the cobblestone streets once more. Though she moved with purpose, and her tired mind was racing, she still felt as though she were dragging her feet, perhaps walking to her doom. Over and over, her thoughts went to the cold, callous way Gasteel had lifted her onto his horse, only to ignore her until he was prepared to make a point for the crowd. "He doesn't care about me. Why would he? He only just met me! But if that's true, how can I convince him to give up my father without a fight? I can't go directly on the attack; he'll only fight harder. So…"

Before she could put all of her thoughts in order, Danielle had arrived at the town square. A crowd was milling around, excitedly speaking yet going silent whenever they laid eyes on her. Clearly, they knew something about what was going on. Gathering her courage, Danielle pushed forward through the murmuring crowd, marching onward until she spotted Baron Gasteel himself coming out of the town's only tavern. Before she could stop herself, Danielle's voice rang out with a clarity that silenced all other voices and drew every eye.

"Baron Gasteel! I *demand* to know the whereabouts of my father!"

The crowd around her shifted away as if a school of fish had just realized a shark was among them. Their eyes were wide at the audacity of her confrontation, and many went to great lengths to make themselves look small so as to not draw the attention of the powerful new noble. For his part, Gasteel's eyes narrowed, but he kept his composure as he turned and allowed a handsome smile to spread across his face.

"Ah, *there's* my Enchantress! I'm delighted you would seek me out. Why are you standing so far away? Yesterday, you practically sprinted to my side as soon as I made my presence known." Gasteel held his arms out wide, "Well? What are you waiting for? We all know how this ends. Fear not, fair maiden! I wouldn't put my father-in-law to death without properly reviewing his case, now would I? That'd be a terrible way to begin our marriage."

"I have no need to go to such lengths, Baron." Danielle cursed herself as her words faltered slightly under the combined weight of the town staring at her. "What you're doing is illegal, and I can prove it!"

Gasteel's smile curled fractionally, and he waved a hand as if encouraging a favored pet. "You seem to think you know the law. Well… enlighten all of us."

"You're using him to get to me, because I informed you that not only can you not make me work for you, it would be *illegal* for me to do so!" Danielle's voice strengthened as she drew on her newfound knowledge. "By refusing my initial enlistment, you barred me from the ward structure of the kingdom of Verdelune. *I* was trying to do *you* a favor by not working for you—were I to do so, you'd begin accruing demerits!"

A susurration spread through the crowd as Gasteel's smile lost some of its intensity. He raised an eyebrow and shook his head slightly. "How kind of you to take me into consideration. Also, surprising… you *actually* read through that table-bender of a book, didn't you? Beauty, brains, and the means to bring it all together. What a fine wife you'll make for me! Imagine using your skills and what the system granted you for a *useful* purpose. However, I've done nothing to attempt to force your hand. I didn't arrest you nor haul you in for avoiding duty. As much as it may pain you to realize this, Belle, not everything in the world revolves around *you*."

Danielle struggled with her thoughts for a long moment, her lack of sleep causing her normally sharp wit to be dulled. "What are you talking about?"

"What am I talking about…?" He paused leadingly, waving his hand forward and back in a 'come-hither' motion.

"What are you talking about, *Baron Gasteel*?" Danielle hissed out the words, her hands clenching into fists.

"Mmm. I would've also accepted 'husband' or 'my love'." Gasteel smirked as the crowd chuckled, and his eyes flicked from side to side as he swept his gaze over the audience. "For anyone who doesn't know, this morning, Henri Tinker was arrested on charges of espionage against the kingdom of Verdelune. Yesterday, he avoided the mandatory assembly. We started looking into him and found that he came here from outside of our kingdom years ago, attempting to ingrain himself in our society."

He paused for a moment to allow the crowd to chatter but then simply spoke over them when it became apparent they would not be quieting themselves. "From there, it took almost no time for us to learn that he's been sending messages outside of our borders every month since his arrival. Clearly, he was placed here by some foreign power to keep an eye on our people, to *warn the enemies of Verdelune* we were planning to expand our glorious kingdom once more!"

By the end of his speech, he was practically shouting, joined by dozens of people in the square who pumped their fists and howled with anger. Danielle's heart skipped a beat as she saw the people she'd grown up around turn against her and her father with only a few words.

Gasteel turned his full attention to her once more, his tongue flicking out to gently lick his lower lip before he continued speaking. "So, no, Belle, this has nothing to do with *you*."

SWAYING ON HER FEET, Danielle nodded several times. "So there's nothing I can do to save him?"

"As I told you before, I'm a merciful man." Gasteel opened his arms once more, though this time only half as far as before, leaving him in a slightly guarded position. "Were you to become my wife, both of our desires would be fulfilled. I certainly wouldn't accrue demerits for having my wife help me recruit people, and no one would think twice about my father-in-law being confined to my estate. In fact, no one would think of him at all. He could simply live comfortably, making toys for our children, away from people who look at him with disgust for his accent or his clicking imitation of a leg."

Before another word could be said, Henri himself stepped out of the tavern, visible only for a brief moment before a guard roughly yanked him back inside. Still, in that short span, he managed to shout a single somewhat-garbled sentence. "Don't worry about *me*, go live-!"

"Who was supposed to be keeping an eye on him?" Gasteel's shout echoed twice in the square, and his face was flushed with anger. After a moment, he managed to get himself under control and turned back toward Danielle, his eyes cold. "So, what'll it be?"

Danielle looked at the doorway where her father had appeared, feeling her resolve firm up. There was absolutely *no* chance of her abandoning her father. But... she was also certain the baron didn't particularly care about her father. Knowing allowing her true thoughts to show would remove all her power in the situation, the Enchantress shrugged and put on a sad expression. "He never speaks without being absolutely certain of what he's saying. So... goodbye, Father. I love you. Baron Gasteel... I choose freedom."

With only the paltry amount of supplies she was still carrying in her bags, Danielle turned on her heel and began walking. The townsfolk got out of her way as she moved, as if brushing against her would transfer the baron's ire to them. The path she chose was the shortest distance needed for leaving Frontière, and she was determined to walk the route she and her father had decided on that very morning.

Still, before she could fully commit to her actions, Gasteel spoke up once more, seeking a way to regain control of the situation. "While I love to see how steadfastly you will follow through on your choices, I wouldn't want to be the cause for such a beautiful face to have tears running down it. Wait, *wait*. Hear me out. You want your father's freedom...? Let me offer you a deal."

Danielle's steps slowed, and after a heartbeat of hesitation, she turned and faced him. "What kind of deal?"

Gasteel's eyes gleamed with interest as he strode across the town square, coming to a stop only when he was looming above her. Danielle's heart pounded harder with each step he took, gut churning with fear, wondering if this was how a deer would feel as this hunter closed in on them.

"The deal is rather simple, Belle. All I need you to do is prove your, and your father's, loyalty to Verdelune. You know... the kingdom that has kept you safe, fed, and supplied with all manner of toy making materials? Simply travel to the estate of the Artificer Comte LeKrout and convince him to join in the upcoming war effort. Of course, he's been resistant to all attempts at recruitment thus far, but with your *talents*... perhaps you can figure something out."

"If you succeed, I'll release your father and swear to leave both of you alone. Frankly, all I want is the opportunity for advancement. You give me the Comte, I'll be far too busy unwrapping all the gifts the king piles on me to bother with you a moment longer. Yet, if you fail..." Gasteel's eyes traced her figure, the tip of his tongue poking out of the left corner of his mouth for a moment, continuing as though forcing himself to make a concession. "You'll have to prove your loyalty to the kingdom by joining me and becoming a noble wife and therefore above reproach."

Danielle felt as though the air around her was pressing in, the weight of Gasteel's words hanging heavily on her. At the same time, her mind was racing with interest at the deal she was being offered.

An Artificer was an incredibly magically potent, exceedingly *dangerous* version of a Tinkerer. Over the years, her father had spoken of the class with all caution, strangely enough a bit of fear, and not a small amount of longing. As far as she was aware, the only way to achieve such a class was to have all the qualifications of an engineer, runesmith, and logician *before* they unlocked their Full Class. Even so, there was no guarantee the system would assign the class.

Her momentary pause for consideration was taken as hesitation, and Gasteel reached forward to offer his hand. "Why don't you put this aside and just come with me? It'll be a wonderful, relaxing life. You won't have to do anything except *enjoy* yourself!"

"Can I have a few minutes to think about this?" Danielle gracefully dodged away from the grasping hand.

Gasteel frowned deeply, his hesitation to allow her to slip

away written clearly on his face. After a moment, his desire for personal accolades seemed to barely win out, and he eased back and straightened up. "Fine. No more than ten minutes."

Danielle nodded sharply, turning and walking back to the town square, going from the gravel path to cobblestone in only a half-dozen steps. There, she was faced with a wall of bodies blocking her from going any further. "Excuse me, I need to go talk to-"

"There's no one who's going to tell you anything different, lass," The town blacksmith crossed his arms and grumbled at her, "You don't fight the weather, and you don't go against nobility. As for him? He's a force of nature. You got hit by lightning; just accept your fate."

Before the Enchantress could say a word in her defense, one of the village women smacked the blacksmith on the arm, though she was furiously scowling at Danielle. "You say that like it's a bad thing! You stuck up, *little*-! Do you have any idea how many of us would kill for the chance you're trying to throw away? Marrying a baron? As a peasant? We all saw you throw yourself at him, riding his horse into town! He offered to do the honorable thing and marry you, and now you're using that as a way to get extra attention?"

"She's always been too good for this town," a young man who had just signed on as a Greenhorn piped up. "Strutting around, thinking she's something special because she has a pretty face! What else are you waiting for? You've already got a baron on the hook; are you waiting for the *king*?"

"Well, here's a news flash, the king's already married!"

"That's never stopped the men in *this* town from proposing to her, anyway." The last comment wasn't pitched to carry, yet somehow everyone seemed to hear it, and practically everyone started laughing.

An old woman with hard eyes stepped forward, barely able to be heard above the now-riotous crowd. "You clearly haven't thought this through, girl. He's powerful. Not only is he incredibly strong on his own, that man has the ear of the king. He's got strength physically *and* politically, and I know his type. He's willing to use it to get what he wants, and nothing is going to stand in his way. The longer you fight it, the more people are going to get hurt. Is that what you want? Are you willing to ask us to help you, knowing *we* will be punished for it?"

The crowd had gone quiet sometime during her rant, and their mood rapidly shifted. Instead of laughing or mocking the Enchantress, all eyes in the area swiftly turned cold as they glared at her. After a long moment, the old woman sneered and leaned in close, her voice rising so everyone would hear what she had to say. "My grandson is a conscript because of *you*. Now you're trapped, just like the rest of us. You know what? I'm glad. You've had it too easy for too long. It's about time you get a taste of *real life*."

Danielle took an involuntary step back, away from the white-hot hatred emanating from the old woman. "How could that possibly be *my* fault?"

A few hands reached out and pulled the crone back as she shouted at Danielle, her words unintelligible over the rising voices of the crowd—all of whom were telling the Enchantress to just get on with it, to go marry the baron so she could secure better treatment for their children, who had just been forced into service. For a few moments, she only stared at them, slack-jawed, but quickly her mouth closed, and her lips pressed into a firm line. Her hands were trembling with anger, so she balled them up into fists.

"Years of trying to be polite, to be kind, to help the town thrive. Making toys, helping beauty-obsessed women have smooth skin and wrinkle-free faces." Danielle shook her head and turned back toward the baron. "I'm done with this place. I will *never* go out of my way for you. Not again."

She stomped closer to Gasteel, who had been watching the entire situation with amusement shining in his eyes. Danielle spoke in a calm voice. "As much as I despise the idea of manipulating someone into joining a war they want no part of, you said he's *already* a Comte. If he's a nobleman of Verdelune, I have no idea how he's able to refuse service to the crown, but that's his duty. He's already made his choice. I can go and make sure he reports for duty, so long as my father and I will be left alone."

"That's not good enough." Gasteel flashed a smile someone else may have considered charming. "The Artificer 'reporting for duty' isn't what I want out of this. He needs to report for wartime duty under *my* banner!"

"I'll get it done," Danielle replied woodenly.

"Why don't you just listen to these nice people? They make some very compelling points." Gasteel gnashed his teeth in frustration, barely managing to hide a scowl behind a smile for the crowd staring at their interaction. "Let's get you to-"

"On one condition." Danielle firmly stated, breathing deeply to remain calm while facing down a man who could pick her up and snap her like a twig. "Our agreement must be written, and both of us must sign."

Now it was Gasteel's turn to take a few deep breaths, attempting to rein in his anger at her impertinence. His scowl deepened, and he leaned forward, opening his mouth and shouting into her face—though he wasn't speaking to her. "*Lefroupe*! Sharpen your quill; we have an agreement to sign."

He began stalking away, and Danielle followed after a heartbeat of hesitation. Gasteel moved in a straight line to the door of the tavern, with the locals practically throwing themselves out of his way. Some of them called out to her, but Danielle refused to acknowledge them.

As soon as they stepped inside, Danielle cast her gaze around the room, seeking out her father. Henri was seated at a table, a dark bruise spreading across the left side of his face. He met her eyes, his own going wide as he started shaking his head. "Danielle! What are you *doing*? Leave while you have the chance!"

"Quiet down, old man," Gasteel snarled at his prospective father-in-law. "If you get in the way of this deal, I'll move your execution up to *tomorrow*."

Lefroupe watched the interaction with a concerned frown on his face, turning to look at Danielle with guilty eyes. Taking a deep breath, the scribe sat himself down and began scribbling on a piece of parchment as the baron laid out the deal they had struck.

For the next few minutes, as the tension in the room continued to increase, with Gasteel tapping his foot and squeezing his arms in agitation, the only sound to be heard was the scratching of the quill and the labored breathing of the tinkerer. It was easy to tell his nose was broken, and it hurt Danielle to realize that she couldn't do anything about his poor treatment.

A short while later, Lefroupe pulled out a pinch of sand and sprinkled it across the document, gently blowing on the ink to dry it. With a flourish, he presented the contract to Gasteel and stepped back. "That'll be all, Lefroupe. Clear the room; I want only my future family in here for this conversation."

"Baron, is it wise to-" Lefroupe stopped talking as Gasteel sent him a glare that landed like a physical blow. "Of course, a man of your stature has nothing to fear from these locals. I'll... be outside."

As soon as they had privacy, Gasteel turned on Danielle and let out a long, slow breath. "If you ever embarrass me like that again, our marriage will have a *rocky* beginning. I'm a man of ambition, and you are someone who can help me achieve status in a way I cannot do on my own. The moment, the very *moment* we are wed, you'll be sent to the palace, meet the queen, and pay your respects."

He swallowed a few times, barely managing to hold back

his violent reaction to her disrespect. "In other words, you'll go there and be giving her everything your skills can offer. Beauty, youth, *everything*. She will want you closer, which will necessitate my rising through the noble ranks. But, if I can't trust you to act properly, I'll need to *make sure* I can."

Completely uncertain as to where this was going, Danielle sang out with the first thing that came to mind. "Put it in the contract!"

"To that end, I'm going to show you what happens to-" Gasteel paused mid-sentence, his hand reaching toward Henri, pausing in the air and hovering there while he processed what Danielle had offered. "That's... yes... a good idea. Let's keep everything nice and *legal*. Your father already has practice getting around without one of his limbs; he would have probably adapted quickly, anyway."

"*What?*"

"What?" Gasteel brushed his shirt off unnecessarily, waving at the document on the table. "Tell me what you *propose*."

"Why don't you tell me what you'd like to see in there, and I'll make it happen?" Danielle carefully stepped over to the seat Lefroupe had vacated, reaching for his quill and dipping it in the ink. She looked up at Gasteel, gulping at the smile playing about his lips.

"Good, this is much better. I speak, you listen." He pondered for a moment, "When you are my wife, you will do nothing to embarrass me. You will work to further my ambition and do your best to be a good steward of our assets and reputation. After all, this will affect your life directly."

Ever so carefully, Danielle added the words he had spoken to the document. After a momentary pause, she went up a little higher and put a line of ink through a sentence written by Lefroupe. "Both of us need to initial here, next to where I... *underlined* this clause, then sign at the bottom."

"First, read it back to me," Gasteel demanded instead of

moving to sign. "Start here, then go to the sentence, then the last one, then read it from the beginning."

She did so, and he tested it once more, even going so far as to furrow his brow and pick apart the words on his own. Eventually, Gasteel was satisfied that it had been changed as he directed and motioned for Danielle to sign first. Then he did the same, followed by melting a blob of wax and dipping his signet ring into it. The parchment flashed with the light of the system for a moment then rolled itself up.

At the same moment, Danielle felt a warm glow spread across the inside of her left arm. She winced slightly but casually slid her limb below the table, doing her best to be inconspicuous. Even without looking, she knew that feeling: one of her skills had increased in level and potency. The Enchantress could only hope the increased power wouldn't catch Gasteel's attention or cause him to go back on his word, but luckily, his full attention was on the scroll.

"There we go." Gasteel was all smiles now that he'd gotten what he wanted, so offered a hand to Danielle. As they shook, his smile turned charming once more. "It's a pleasure dealing with someone who knows what they want. Now, let's go convince a war criminal under house arrest to activate his murder machines once more."

"What?"

"Danielle... I *told* you to leave while you had the chance." Henri let out a long sigh as he sagged in his seat, his head dropping to the table. "What did you agree to do?"

"Nothing much, old man!" Gasteel cheerfully slapped his hand on the table, scooping up the scroll and carelessly stuffing it in a belt pouch. "She's either going to convince Comte LeKrout to reactivate his metal soldiers or become my wife. Either way, a victory for House Leiter! More power will be mine, either in combat or among the peerage. Soon, I'll have the strength to strongarm my detractors into silence... and I'll *use* it!"

"You… you're trying to get that *beast* back on the battle-field?" Henri sucked in a breath, his eyes darting over to his daughter. "Danielle, you *can't!*"

"Now wait just one moment…!" Gasteel stated threaten-ingly, turning on the brunette. "Your name is *Danielle*? I thought it was Belle. No, never mind. I'm sure you won't mind me calling you Belle. You must be used to it by now; everyone seems to know you by that name."

"If your only options are to get the System-forsaken Battle Beast back into service or marrying this man… *please* let me be the first to congratulate you on your nuptials," Henri stated with no small amount of desperation. "You recall the war which ended barely ten years ago? The one which nearly doubled the size of our kingdom?"

Almost unconsciously, the Tinkerer's hand dropped to his leg, and he let out a soft grunt as his fingers trailed over the homemade limb. "The Artificer-made metal soldiers were the only reason they managed to push through three kingdoms at once and hold the land they captured. No one knows why he deactivated his creations and refused to make more, but they *can't* be allowed to slaughter people like they did before."

"Please, trust me." Danielle could only shake her head at her father, hoping she was making the right decision. "I'll figure something out; I just need time."

"For your sake, for *all* our sakes…" Henri replied in a defeated tone as Gasteel ushered her out of the tavern. "…I hope you're right."

CHAPTER
SEVEN

DANIELLE STOOD ALONE at the edge of town, her mind flooded with confusion and determination. To her great surprise, she was to find her way to the Artificer's estate on her own. "They gave me a pack of food, clothes that aren't my own, and a map. Why? Why would they send me out on my own, knowing I might simply make a run for it?"

Taking the first step was the hardest, as the soldier's pack they had given her felt immense and threw her balance off. For just a moment, she hesitated, wondering if she really wanted to go through with this. Still, with each step, she found that her fear was a little further behind her, and she was moving faster and steadier. After a few minutes, having put more distance between herself and the edge of Frontière, she found the familiar sights and sounds fading, replaced by the muted sounds of nature.

Soon, she had reached the edge of the cleared land around the town. The gravel road ahead was no longer as well-maintained, turning into a simple dirt path as it was swallowed by the shadows of the forest. The density of the trees turned the bright morning into something dark and sinister, and her heart began to pound in her chest at the thought of going off into the unknown. She had lived here, in this town, as long as she could remember, and never before had the means to actually set out on her own.

Chancing a glance over her shoulder, Danielle was surprised to see dozens of people watching her from afar. Their crossed arms, disdainful expressions, and heads shaking in silent judgment struck her like a blow. The obvious, collective doubt in her ability to stay strong stung... but also filled her with determination not to hesitate any further. Refusing to give them the satisfaction of seeing her fear, she pressed forward and vanished behind the trees.

Taking her first breaths of the cool air, heavy with the smell of earth and leaves, Danielle steeled herself and marched along the trail. "So that's it, isn't it? I'm going alone, unescorted, because he knows I won't run—he's hoping that I won't have the guts to see this through. He thinks I'm just a scared little girl, and I'm going to go crawling back begging for mercy and stop 'wasting his time'."

Pulling out her map, she unfolded the parchment a vicious *snap*, taking a minute to look over the detailed route that had been highlighted for her. "What, do they think it's so difficult to walk down a road? Ridiculous."

She set off on the path, jogging lightly to gain some distance early on. Every step felt like an act of defiance, and it felt *fantastic*. As the minutes ticked by, closing in on half an hour, Danielle waited for her breathing to grow ragged or a stitch to appear in her side, but found barely felt a hint of fatigue. Focusing on that oddity gave her some much-needed mental space, and eventually she realized she had her system-granted skills to thank for her endurance.

"My muscles are coordinated and moving efficiently." The words came out naturally along with each exhale, almost turning them into a song as she rushed along the road. "Unless I actively choose to go against the system's enhancement, I seem to naturally pick out the least arduous pathway. Huh... this is an unexpected benefit. Maybe I've-"

She bit her tongue, welcoming the pain rather than admitting anything positive about the class and skills that had gotten her into this situation in the first place. As she settled into a rhythm, her speed slowly began to increase, and the miles melted away.

As the sun reached its zenith, the heat and humidity began to become oppressive. With the sun high in the sky, the shadows around her were darker, and the sounds of the wilderness were constant and far too close. The sound of rushing water reached her ears, and she slowed to a walk as a sudden, creeping realization of her own vulnerability hit her hard.

Only then did she realize exactly how terribly thirsty she was, and her stomach wambled in protest at her mounting hunger. She continued speaking aloud, as if the words alone could ward off both animals and loneliness. "Okay, some water, some food... maybe a nap."

Walking down to the water's edge, she filled the empty water skins she'd been given, only now realizing *all* of them were empty—sparking both a flare of anger and a touch of concern over the rest of her supplies. Grumbling about the attempted sabotage, she drank her fill and pulled out some of her food, carefully inspecting it to ensure it hadn't been tampered with. Surprisingly, it was all edible and well wrapped... what little of it there was.

Taking only a few bites, she settled down in the hollow of a tree next to the riverbank, curling up in it and falling into a deep slumber almost immediately.

Yowwrr!

The sound of a wild cat screaming into the night caused Danielle to wake with a jolt. She blinked several times—fearing she'd gone blind—before realizing that she must have slept through the remainder of the day. Taking a deep breath, she looked around for any source of light, but found only a sliver of moon rising above the river. "There might be no one around for miles… I'm not sure how to feel about that."

Never before had she been alone, at least not without actively seeking it out. People had always wanted her around, going so far as to follow her around town and speak at her while she was running errands. Even when she had returned home, her father had always been in his workshop, tinkering with whatever project he'd decided to work on that day. Allowing herself to be lost in her thoughts gave Danielle the respite she needed to get her racing heartbeat under control, and she breathed in deeply, letting out a slow breath and trying to expel all of her fear at the same time.

A sense of calm enveloped her, and she snuggled back into the tree trunk. Moments later, her fear spiked once more as a furry limb brushed against her. Barely allowing herself to breathe, she slowly reached out a hand and found that an animal was standing next to her. Ever so gently, she ran the tips of her fingers along its coat. "Easy there… nice, um, animal. Oh… you're definitely a bear."

For a few long moments, she felt as though she were locked in a stalemate with the creature, but then a wash of hot air flowed over her as the animal settled down next to her and let out a sigh of contentment. Danielle closed her eyes and focused on breathing, doing her best to keep her Unified Radiance skill guiding her hand as she continued to pet the creature next to her. She wasn't certain why it hadn't chomped into her, but Danielle was going to thank it the only way she could—by making sure it was a stunningly beautiful creature when it left.

The night passed far too slowly, as whenever she stopped massaging the bear, a low snarl would fill the air. By the time false dawn was starting to arrive, her hands were cramped, and Danielle was absolutely exhausted from the strain of staying in one spot and focusing on the animal next to her.

Before enough light had filtered through the trees for her to see exactly what the bear beside her looked like, the creature finally had enough. It stood with a low grumble and padded away without another sound, leaving the human to her own devices.

Carefully, dizzy with relief, Danielle got to her feet and started moving, determined to get as far away from the river as possible. "I'm not going to make a mistake like that a second time."

The forest was still alive with the sounds of nocturnal animals, though the rustling of leaves and the calls of distant creatures were becoming less frequent as false dawn turned to true sunrise. The sound of birds slowly began to fill the air as she traveled along the river, analyzing her surroundings and attempting to match up what she was seeing with where her map said she should be. "There was supposed to be a bridge somewhere around here... where's the road? I barely left it last night to get some water. It can't be that far away, can it?"

After nearly half an hour of searching, she finally retraced her steps to the edge of the road and slung her pack off her shoulders. "Never in my life have I been so happy to see packed dirt. Wonderful! From here, I just need to travel along the road for... let's see, judging by how far I got yesterday... it'll only take me another two weeks. Lovely."

She reached into her bag and pulled out a bit of food to break her fast, only then noticing how chaotically packed the bag actually was. "Oh, for the system's sake, did they just dump a bunch of stuff into here?"

"Keep the water skins, the food... pretty sure we don't need these two bricks. What is *this* thing? A *caltrop*? No wonder this was digging into my back so much yesterday. Oh, there is a blanket in here. *An~nd* it's wrapped around rocks. I'm going to go *so* much farther today than I did yesterday. If I ever find who did this, I'm going to make them *eat* this garbage." Danielle dumped everything on the ground and began reorganizing it under the guidance of her Alluring Assemblage skill, finding some small comfort in the order she had created.

Thinking of her skills reminded her that she'd earned something in her negotiation with Gasteel the previous day, so she ran her finger along her left arm and looked at the change the system presented her with.

Skill increase! Unified Radiance [Level 3 (Rudimentary) → Level 4 (Basic)]!

Requirement to advance to level 5: successfully make a sale to someone who has no need of what is being sold OR enhance an item enough that it sells for 180% of its standard price.

"I... can't imagine I successfully mediated a dispute without offering solutions yesterday. That means... just by going into that hole-in-the-wall tavern, I enhanced it enough to be worth fifty percent more than its original sale price? You know what? I'm not even going to be annoyed. At this point, I'll take every advantage I can get to finish this distasteful task as soon as possible—even skill increases."

Once more hefting the noticeably lighter burden of her bag, she was pleased to find that it no longer dug into her, nor was it anywhere *near* as uncomfortable to carry. Buoyed by this small victory, she set off down the road with a spring in her step. The farther she walked, the more her Graceful Movement skill kicked in, making the otherwise tedious march feel like a dance, as though she were gliding across the surface of the world.

After an hour of effortlessly striding along, Danielle couldn't keep the smile off her face. "I've never even *considered* that my skills would be useful for travel. Hopefully, once I rescue Father, he'll get some benefit from them as well. I wonder where we will eventually end up? Verdelune isn't an option, not anymore, but if they are going to be invading the neighboring kingdoms, we're going to have to travel for *years*, potentially."

That night was far easier than the previous had been, as she climbed a tree and wrapped herself in the thin blanket she'd been provided. Even without tying herself to the branch, she had no fear of falling: Danielle hadn't fallen off something since she'd achieved her second level in Graceful Movement. Even asleep, she was certain she'd be perfectly balanced.

The days passed quickly, and soon a week and a half had elapsed in this way.

As the sun rose each morning, Danielle's confidence grew further. She'd become used to the long days of travel, hard but nutritious food, and careful management of her resources. More than that, she felt more free than she had in a long time, having been given no time limit for her success.

Sure, she'd had to scrounge for anything edible along the route, but the time had been peaceful. It had been nearly half a month where she hadn't needed to fend off the ham-fisted attempts of a local lad pawing at her or turn down insincere proposals. Never once did she need to tell someone off, nor wear a veil just so she could slink around without being treated somewhere between a criminal and a temptress.

Still, there had been a few near-misses. Several times, she had avoided creatures in the forest, and twice she'd heard people's voices and made sure to go out of her way to avoid whoever had made the forest their home. They almost certainly wouldn't be well-intentioned people; only bandits and outlaws lived so far away from civilization by choice.

A full three days ahead of schedule, the estate came into view. From a distance, she could see the manor towering above a huge wall which encircled the entire estate, a wall made of a near-blindingly white stone intensely reflecting the midday sun.

She marched along the road, absolutely brimming with confidence, now that she had nearly arrived at her destination.

Only as the road came to an end, and there was no entrance to be found, did her beaming smile falter slightly. "Why did the road end if there's no gate here? Hello? Is there anyone over there who can hear me, maybe direct me to the entrance?"

Not surprisingly, no one deigned to answer her, *if* she was heard in the first place. Still, while she waited for a moment, she took a closer look at the barrier between herself and the person she needed to convince. Her keen eyes trailed along the wall, taking in every detail, especially the odd, spiky objects atop the wall that seemed to follow her as she moved. Danielle stepped close and lifted a hand to touch the stone, but for some reason, she felt a cold chill along her spine.

Looking up, she found the spiky objects pointing at her and had a disturbing feeling that, when she was watching them, they were watching her. "So... not sure what those do, but they're *definitely* dangerous. There goes climbing over the wall as a viable option."

Carefully withdrawing her hand, she stepped away from the wall and observed as the spikes shifted into a less ominous position. "No touching, got it. But look at the craftsmanship... the intricate designs! They're practically *begging* someone to touch them, maybe to paint some embellishments or designs on them. This entire wall is literally a blank slate, an artist's dream!"

She began walking around the wall, searching for an entrance to the estate. After nearly two hours, she found herself back at her original position, somewhat frustrated at her lack of ingress, yet excited by the possibility that there *must* be more to this area than met the eye. "If there's no obvious entrance, there must be a *non*-obvious one. If I were an Artificer, how would I stop people from getting where I didn't want them to be?"

Taking note of everything she saw, Danielle explored the area around where the road ended and the wall began. There were no seams in the stone to indicate a gate being hidden, but even she knew how easy it was to disguise those, thanks to her father creating coverings for the toys he made. Soon enough, she began to find *unnatural* objects in the otherwise untouched landscape.

Trees with leaves made of metal grew alongside perfectly normal versions, only her trained eye allowing her to pick out the minute differences. Patches of wildflowers had small gears and cogs in them, their petals *ticking* as they moved in a circular dance, as though a pocket watch was determining their position. Even the grass in some areas was a shade or two too green, and a careful swipe with a cloth revealed they were coated in some sort of oil, which was flowing out and into other small machines.

"This is incredible." She breathed the words as she crouched to examine a patch of flowers at an intersection of three false trees and a trickle of bright green fluid. "They look exactly like actual flowers, and if they weren't moving, I wouldn't have noticed the difference. Why would someone go to so much effort to create a false landscape—especially *outside* of their home?"

As her gaze moved from flower to flower, she found herself smiling, already picturing how she would bring this design back to her father to turn into a toy. "If we play our cards right, not only will we have a market for the beauty of the creations, but we can make them have a useful function as well. Perhaps they could act as a timepiece someone keeps inside their home? I'm sure that would lower the barrier to entry for those who didn't care about the look of things as much as making practical purchases."

Tick, tick, tick-

Even while feeling a deep connection to the natural and mechanical landscape, Danielle noticed something odd. One of the flowers in this patch was a clockwork rose, and something about it was setting her on edge. Scooting over to it, she tried to determine what the issue was.

Tick-

-Tock.

Tick-

-Tock.

Tick-

-Tock.

After a few moments, she realized it was ticking to a different metronome than the others around it, the *tock* a discordant sound amidst everything else *ticking* along.

Reaching out, Danielle gently gripped the metal rosebud, holding it in place for a breath, then releasing it. Exactly as she'd hoped, the momentary pause had allowed it to sync up with the others around it, and once more, there was a harmonious *ticking* noise.

That wasn't the only sound to reach her ears. Moments after she aligned the flowers, there was a soft grinding of stone drawing her attention back to the wall. To her delight, a section had shifted to the side and opened a path to the manor.

Danielle hopped to her feet and rushed over, not wanting to miss out on the opportunity. "Oh, thank you! Was this a test, a trial to see if I would be allowed in? What an interesting way to keep out those who aren't worthy of meeting you! Riddles! Ha! Or, wait, was-"

A screeching of metal caused Danielle to clap her hands over her ears, and her eyes went wide as she saw the most bizarre sight she'd ever witnessed in her life.

Thundering across the manicured lawn was a massive amalgamation of metal and tubes, a humanoid mechanical monstrosity standing nearly nine feet tall and half that in width. It trumpeted at her, the deep, mechanical sounds barely recognizable as speech.

"*Get off the Comte's grass!*"

EIGHT

THE GROUND SHOOK beneath her feet, and Danielle yelped while instinctively bracing for impact—fully expecting to be crushed by the terrifying metal contraption. Instead, it abruptly halted only a few feet away, its looming form draping a dark shadow over her. A half-dozen glowing, crystalline structures in the shape of eyes fixated on her with menacing intensity, a cold blue light sweeping over Danielle as it thoroughly scanned her.

Though her heart was still racing from the initial fright, Danielle slowly eased herself into a proper standing position. The terrible voice that echoed out from the amalgam's chest was mechanical and growling, devoid of any hint of warmth.

"Why are you here? It is illegal to trespass, and I have every right to cut you down where you stand. Before I, the Beast Guardian of House LeKrout, make my decision on this matter, you will tell me how you opened the outer gate. It should have allowed itself to be destroyed before it would allow someone to pass!"

The dissonant resonance faded as the creature went completely, *unnaturally* still, as if it had transformed into a statue with an eerie patience while waiting for her answer.

For several long seconds, Danielle could only take shallow breaths, trying to push through her fear of this terrible entity. Gathering her thoughts, she realized she had been presented with a puzzle, one she would need to solve quickly if she wanted to get out of this situation alive. "Oh, great metal guardian... beast? I am here to speak with Comte LeKrout. I was sent to ask for his aid-"

"Yet another recruiter for the *Witch Queen* of Verdelune!" the Beast bellowed in frustration, stomping one of its feet hard enough to crater the ground nearly a yard out from the point of impact. "I tell you now, not one automaton shall join in the slaughter. Assessing... you're an *Enchantress?*"

"I am!" Danielle felt a brief flicker of hope, only for it to be snuffed out as the terribly dangerous machine tensed. "But that doesn't have anything to do with why I'm here. You're right, I was sent as a recruiter, but all I want is a chance to make my case to the Comte."

"Your kind manipulates beauty and emotion, and if I have my way, you will *never* see my master face-to-face." There was a long, dangerous pause as the Beast's crystalline eyes studied her. "Yet, I notice a discrepancy between who has been sent before, and... you."

"Is it that I'm alone, half-starved, and reeking of hard travel?" Danielle quipped mirthlessly, only for her eyes to go wide as she realized the words that had just slipped from her lips.

"I see it now." The Beast's eyes flashed. "Someone's trying to get you killed. No one with any knowledge of the Comte's situation would send an Enchanter here. You are going to take your trouble away from our door before it follows you into the house. Take note, Enchantress. Your system enhancements are laid bare before my vision. You have no hope of enchanting *me* with your looks, and my lord's history with Enchantresses guarantees I am immediately distrustful of you."

Danielle opened her mouth to try and argue with the creature, but flinched away as it suddenly moved past her toward the opening in the wall.

Its voice boomed out, "There's more going on here than meets the eye. You will remain in the estate until I reset the defenses and adjust all protective measures. Do *not* attempt to leave until you are escorted out. Do not attempt to meet the Comte. Attempting either *will* end in your immediate demise, and we haven't created a new mop in the last four years."

"A mop...? Is that some kind of oblique threat? Wait, before you start tearing your landscape apart, the problem is the rose-" Danielle trailed off as the Beast whirled around and stared at her with its many sensors. "Um. Out there? There was a clockwork rose ticking out of sync with the wildflowers around it. I adjusted the metronome so it would match the others, and the wall opened up."

Though she couldn't tell for certain due to its strange anatomy, it seemed like the massive machine relaxed slightly. "I see. That will narrow down my search. Follow Sneezy and Doc to your waiting room."

The Beast started to move away, and Danielle took a step after him before realizing what she was doing. "Wait! Please, I have so many questions that I need to ask the Artificer. Can I beg an audience with him?"

"No one sees the Artificer, and the Artificer grants no one an audience—least of all an *Enchantress*," the machine practically spat as it turned toward her, jabbing an oversized finger aggressively toward the house. "You will go *now* or be classified as a threat."

As he said those words, the strange spiky objects on the wall turned to look at her, the flowers in the area moved unnaturally against the wind, and the blades of grass on the lawn shifted until they were all bristled up like the hair of a scared cat. Danielle finally started to understand exactly how dangerous of a situation she was in, so she gently lifted her hands in the air and backed away.

She turned away to follow the Beast's instructions as the landscaping around her calmed down, but her jaw dropped as she saw what would be escorting her.

"Hello. Am Sn-three-zy." The automaton was a child-sized machine with arms and legs nearly twice as long as Danielle felt was necessary. Its torso was rounded and oddly shaped, connected to its face with tubes snaking up on either side to its long nose, the ends of which clearly were nozzles. Danielle stepped closer, more intrigued than frightened when she realized that its body was only mostly an outline of a body, designed to hold a large canister she had originally seen as its chest and stomach.

"Hello, Sneezy." Danielle sank down into a crouched position, staring at the elongated face of the diminutive humanoid. "Can you tell me why you're designed the way you are? It's… *fascinating*!"

"Sn-three-zy is a guard patrol automaton designed to eliminate problems," the nasally voice of the creature explained, just before turning its head on a swivel like an owl looking behind itself. There was a sharp *hiss*, as though a water skin was being squeezed, then a *click*… followed by a twenty-foot burst of flame erupting from Sneezy's face. A moment later, the flame turned into a coil of acrid black smoke and flowed up into the air.

The designed creature turned back to look at her, its forced, rictus grin suddenly more threatening than it had been moments before. After the head *clicked* back into place, it stated, "Sn-three-zy also destroys hornet nests and prepares a crème brûlée to die for."

Danielle got up, not certain exactly when she'd fallen onto her butt. She tried to put a smile on her face, only for it to feel completely unconvincing. "Well. It's very nice to meet you, Sneezy. Where is Doc—*wahh!*"

Another automaton caught her attention just then, and Danielle realized why she had missed it earlier. The machine was *literally* razor thin, and when looked at from the side, it blended near-seamlessly into the surroundings. When it turned to face her directly, her eyes traced over its form, which resembled nothing more than a metal cut-out of a person. The machine stepped toward her, its edges glinting danger-ously in the morning light.

"D-zero-C has been here the whole time." Its voice was tinny and disjointed, each word coming out as a clinking of metal on metal, like notes played on a kalimba. "Proceed to the guard room. Please."

Danielle hesitated for a heartbeat at the reminder that she was an intruder in this domain. The cold gaze of the machine sharpened, but luckily, Sneezy began to lead the way, and the Enchantress followed him along the winding path across the lawn without thinking. The seemingly erratic choice of route only began to make sense after she noticed a pattern: they always changed directions just before they stepped onto natural grass.

"Sneezy, I hadn't given his words much thought before now—too terrified—but the Beast was truly angry that I'd stepped on *grass*?"

"It has been a long-term directive. Comte desires restora-tion of exterior of estate to pristine condition," Sneezy's nasally, stunted words replied after a moment of silence. "Do *not* step on Comte's grass."

Danielle glanced behind herself at Doc, just in time to see the creature bending an angle impossible for a human to repli-cate. The machine practically folded in half then swung an arm out, shearing through a blade of grass that had grown higher than those around it.

Despite her initial introduction to the guards, as well as clearly being unwelcome here, somehow, she found herself relaxing in their presence. As shown by Doc's actions, despite their initially terrifying appearance, the machines were clearly created to serve very niche and specific purposes. Having grown up around a tinkerer, not to mention studying engineering and toy making herself, Danielle realized that these creatures had been built with specific functions in mind.

They would execute their roles without deviation or question, even if she didn't yet fully understand what that purpose was. In other words, they wouldn't do anything to so much as *annoy* her if they weren't designed for it.

"Just don't give them any reason to see me as a threat, and I'll get through this just fine," she reassured herself under her breath.

After one last curve around a patch of browning grass, they arrived at the front doors of the manor, which swung open silently, without any visible assistance. Danielle stopped, scanning the hinges, frame, and every surface of the door to try to find where an apparatus must have been installed, for no reason other than opening and closing the door. Still, even as her trained eyes darted around to take in the details, she couldn't make out anything out of the ordinary.

The design and craftsmanship were impeccable—with only one aspect she would consider to be a major flaw: no matter where she looked, Danielle saw absolutely no embellishments or adornments of any kind.

No attempt had been made at blending the machines into artistry or disguising them as something they were not. Everything was extremely orderly and decidedly functional. The walls were perfectly smooth; the mechanisms perfectly camouflaged and hidden away from prying eyes.

"Even the grass was maintained at a uniform height," Danielle mused softly, her disgruntlement getting the better of her as she searched for anything designed *just* to be pleasing to the eye. "Nothing? No artistry at all? What a shame. Sneezy, what opened the door? I'd love to be able to study more of the design-"

"Stop that." Doc's voice cracked with a sharp, tinny edge, cutting her off before she could finish her thought. "You are *not* a guest of the house. You are an intruder being held for questioning and will be removed from the premises as soon as the defenses are reset."

The cold finality to the words hit the Enchantress like a hammer, but there was nothing she could do but grit her teeth and nod placidly, as if she *wasn't* already making contingency plans. Stepping inside, she found that the inside of the house was as plain as the exterior, though it seemed extra spacious and bright, thanks to the white walls, large windows, and open design of the grand hall the door had opened into.

Danielle was led to a room directly off the entryway, which turned out to be a well-appointed guest room with a comfortable bed, large wardrobe, and even a small bathing room complete with indoor plumbing. The last was of great interest to Danielle, as she and her father had created a much more basic version of the same.

"Not even here ten minutes since entering the walls, and I already have two new designs to put in place wherever we end up living," Danielle cheerfully muttered to herself, turning around and freezing as she realized the small automaton guards were in the room with her.

"Are you finished inspecting the toilet?" Sneezy inquired with full sincerity. "If so, I have been instructed to ask you some questions."

Danielle flushed slightly, turning away from the toilet and saying the first words that popped into her mind. "Sorry! I was… wait… when were you told to-?"

Without giving her an answer, the walking flamethrower began running her through a gamut of basic questions. "What is your name? Your class? Your purpose for intruding? Are you currently comfortable? Do you have somewhere to go back to? Is there any chance you would like to donate one of your organs for research purposes?"

Danielle answered most of the questions easily, somewhat uneasy by the unwavering focus given to her every word. Still, the final question made her pause and carefully consider how she worded her answer. "I do not want to lose any of my organs, or give them up, for any reason."

"That is good. You need your organs." Sneezy bobbed his head as gears spun loudly in its chassis. "Please do not be concerned by this line of questioning. You will not be harmed. We are establishing a baseline for your reactions. Do not fail to follow instructions. Is there anything you need? At this moment?"

"I'm…" Only at that moment did Danielle remember she'd been living off trail rations for nearly two weeks and hadn't had a substantial meal since the night of her birthday. "I'm pretty hungry? Do you have anything I could eat?"

Both automatons fell still and silent, failing to respond to Danielle's follow-up questions as they processed her request. Without warning, Doc spun in place as a flash of silver, then walked out of the room, each footfall sounding like a tiny bell as its razor-sharp feet *clinked* against the stone floors.

"Wait! Can I please speak to the Artificer?" Danielle instinctively reached for the guard, only for Sneezy to move to block her outstretched hand.

"The master is not to be disturbed," Sneezy intoned as the tip of its nose *clicked* several times, sending sparks into the air in an act that seemed more habit than threat. "A highly recommended tip: do not attempt to grab D-zero-C. Without proper protective equipment, you will suffer immediate lacerations."

"I don't… I just don't know what I can say to convince you. It's incredibly important that I speak to him. My father's life is on the line. Mine, too, but… in a different way."

"Your urgency is understandable. It is not *possible* to disobey our master's orders." Sneezy's internals whirred as it evaluated her plea, but its response was just as unyielding as previously. "If you wish to make an appeal, speak to BST model three, 'Beast' as you've been calling him. He is your only point of contact with the Comte. Please await further instructions. Do not attempt to force a meeting. It will only end badly. For you. Alert! We have received approval to escort you to the dining area. Please follow."

Without another word—as she didn't want to say something which might make her lose this opportunity to explore the manor—Danielle fell into step behind her mechanical guard. As they walked along the enormous grand hall, which seemed to cross the entirety of the manor and had doorways connecting to dozens of different rooms, a strange sound reached her ears.

It took her tired mind far too long to realize the background noise was the hum of machinery, a symphony of metal and motion unlike anything she'd heard before. "This sounds like the toys my father makes... but on a grander scale by far. A *thousand* times larger at least."

"The Comte has worked hard. Over many years. Substituting all staff with replacements," Sneezy stated with a hint of awe—which Danielle felt she *may* have been projecting onto the creation.

She listened intently in hopes of finding some clue she could use to convince the Artificer to leave all *this* behind. The farther they went, the more Sneezy spoke, the more her chances seemed to slip away.

"The first change was made to the location most important to human functionality: the kitchen. Firstly, he combined the kitchen with the dining room to ensure the food was not served at an incorrect temperature. Many experiments have failed for that reason. My master was positive he could automate the process of creating a delicious meal, substituting 'care' and 'making it with love' with proper measurements and a standardized process."

"How'd that turn out?" Danielle's chuckle rebounded off the cold white walls of the hallway, echoing flatly back to her ears. Trying to get past her nerves, she quickly added on, "I'm certain you're going to tell me how perfect the food is."

"False. According to the master, each meal is rather bland. Yet, sufficient," Sneezy explained in a careless, flat tone. "He's been searching for a solution to 'freshness testing', 'flavor infusion', and 'mouth feel', but has put the research on hiatus in favor of less complex subjects. Even so, each meal is perfectly created for the individual, covering all of their nutritional requirements without excess."

As they finally arrived in the kitchen, Danielle's breath caught in her throat. The large space was dominated by a massive oak table, above which dozens of mechanical arms dangled like snakes ready to strike. Sneezy looked up at the heart of the tangle of machinery and called out, "One dinner for the Enchantress. Status: travel-weary, minor malnutrition."

The air *hummed* as the complex array jolted into action. Danielle's eyes were glued to the mechanical ballet of automated arms reaching into crates, barrels, cupboards, pulling out and chopping vegetables and chilled meats and cheeses with lightning speed. Other arms stirred pots, adjusting the heat of the stovetop with exacting care, all as a conveyor belt transported prepared ingredients from one station to the next.

A delightful smell soon filled the air, and guessing by the sizzling and spattering ending near-simultaneously, all the food items were perfectly timed and cooked to perfection.

From the center of the dangling mechanism, a device resembling a metal tree slowly descended to the table. Two of its 'branches' peeled off, unfolding to reveal a fork and knife that spun across the table and came to rest on either side of Danielle's placemat with excellent precision. Within moments of the silverware coming to a rest, her meal was completed.

A mechanical arm delicately swooped the dish across the room from the stovetop, spatulas arranged the food on a plate, and finally, it was deposited before her on a golden charger.

Steam rose off the dish, and Danielle barely held herself

back from diving into the feast—she had far too many questions about what she'd just seen to simply *eat*. "That was extraordinary! That was a display of skill taken to its logical extreme, beyond anything I've ever seen! How was this made? No, this is beyond what's reasonable. What level of an Artificer is the Comte? Has he achieved a Breakthrough Skill, to be able to work such magic?"

"The master values precision and innovation and strives for *Perfection* in all things." Sneezy responded after a slight pause, as if calculating the safest choice of words. "A word of caution. Further inquiries into the master's personal achievements may flag you as attempting espionage. Now, is everything here to your satisfaction?"

"It is, thank you." Danielle was only slightly downcast from the chilly warning and resolved to be more circumspect with her questions in the future. Even in the small town she had grown up in, asking for the exact details, level, or number of someone else's skills was considered incredibly rude. Here, where she was *already* an unwelcome intruder, surrounded by machines who were utterly loyal? It was downright dangerous.

"Sorry about that, I'm... not sure what got into me." Unsure of the protocol in this strange environment, she half-heartedly gestured at the food, "Should I start eating, or...?"

"Please." Sneezy waved at the plate in front of her. "Be our guest."

CHAPTER
NINE

DANIELLE SETTLED into her bed in the room provided by the automatons with a sigh. Though she was relatively safe and well-fed, her inquisitive mind was starting to grow bored. The first few days when she'd been not-quite a guest had been a whirlwind of mechanical marvels and interesting concepts. Now, she was simply growing frustrated, as the machines she truly wanted to study—the automated kitchen, wall guardians, and Beast—were far out of her reach.

"Sneezy, any chance the Beast will come back soon? He's been adjusting the protections around the estate since I got here, right?" Danielle called into the open air, knowing her guards wouldn't have left her alone.

There was a slight hum of machinery, a telltale sign of Sneezy preparing to do anything other than simply maintain a vigilant watchful status, immediately followed by the nasally voice of the miniature flamethrower. "I do not know enough about the functions of the estate, BST model three's itinerary, or the estate's strategic operations. I have no answer for your query."

Danielle let out another dramatic sigh, as it was the fifth time she had gotten the same answer. "I need something to occupy my mind; do you have any books I could read? Maybe I've been given approval to go to a different room in the manor? By the way, you seem to be speaking with a clarity you were lacking when we first met. Is that because you haven't had someone to have conversation with for a long time, or is it something I'm doing?"

"Unknown changes are occurring within my speech processing center. Thank you for alerting me to the anomalous change; I will report for unscheduled maintenance."

Frantically waving her hands, Danielle shook her head as she sat bolt upright in bed, "No, wait! That's not what I was saying, Sneezy. I was more thinking that my skills might've been acting as some sort of social lubricant, but I'm worried they are actually altering your systems."

"Unknown. I will report for maintenance." After a slight pause, Sneezy spun his head back and forth and steadily continued, "Unfortunately, none of your permissions have been updated. The Comte's library is decidedly off limits, as it contains many years of his research, not to mention rare manuscripts his family has been collecting for generations. What sort of entertainment are you hoping for?"

"Honestly? I'd love to take a look at his research. I've been studying engineering for years, and I wanted nothing more than to follow in my father's footsteps as a Tinkerer toy maker." Danielle relaxed slightly when the guard didn't leave the room to get checked on. A soft smile began playing about her lips as she daydreamed. "The idea of placing a gear here, connecting it to a lever there, then having it move with a life of its own? It's *astounding*. In no time flat, I'll have created a princess who can dance, and some wide-eyed child will have a toy they can play with for years, maybe even hand down to their own children, if they take care of it."

"The library is off limits."

"I know, I know." Danielle waved the expected response away, then leaned forward, eyeing the small guard with interest. "Can I ask how *you* work? There's so much more to you than the mechanical portions, or I would've been able to create something like you on my own by now. You're clearly magical, Sneezy, I just don't understand how it all fits together."

For the first time in their simple exchanges, Sneezy hesitated. His mechanical sounds grew more frantic, gears whirring and clicking faster in the conversational lull. For the first time in their one-sided conversation, Danielle got an answer she wasn't expecting. "Checking against stated rules…"

"Sneezy?"

The mechanical sounds intensified, and the Enchantress gasped in shock as the small, mechanical man's frame began shifting and sliding. After only a few moments, its internals were completely exposed. The intricate workings within— gears, pistons, wires—all of it was laid bare before her. Danielle rose from her bed, moving slowly so as to not startle her guard. "This is… okay? I can learn from you without getting you in trouble?"

"There are no explicit rules against it," Sneezy responded without hesitation, showing that, even if his chassis had opened up, he was not helpless or inactive. "Likely, the lord of the house assumes no one will be able to glean sufficient information or reproduce his work from simple study and observation. Otherwise, it is probable he would have implemented a rule to stop exactly this situation from happening."

"Good enough for me. I hope you don't get in trouble because I found a space where my curiosity found purchase, Sneezy." Danielle didn't bother thinking too hard about the loophole she had discovered, as her fingers were practically *itching* to explore the intricacies of the design.

"If this causes too much trouble, or you damage me, we may both be decommissioned." Sneezy's voice carried a surprising note of worry, unexpected only due to his mechanical nature.

"You'd be decommissioned? Just like that, though you are his brain-child? I don't... no, I'll be careful." Danielle promised easily, her tumultuous thoughts steadying as she began digging into his wiring. Despite her eagerness, as soon as she started pawing through the complex network of gears and circuits, the Enchantress realized exactly how out of her depth she was. "At a glance, this is pretty overwhelming, Sneezy. I probably should have asked before now, but is there any chance I could have a notebook or something I could write my thoughts in?"

"D-zero-C will have one delivered," Sneezy responded after a moment of silence, which could have been either hesitation or simply making the request.

"Tell Doc I said thanks." Danielle nodded distractedly, not wanting to pass up this opportunity to learn more about Artificing. Her attention was already back on the delicate mechanisms, and she moved carefully as she studied and thought through what she should be asking.

"While self-study is admirable, I would appreciate it if you asked questions before attempting to discern the purpose on your own." Her guard had noticed the shifting expressions on her face and spoke before she had a chance. "Let me be clear. You are free to ask questions. I may be unable to answer them. If I tell you not to touch something, don't."

Though the offer had been made warily, Danielle immediately began bombarding him with questions. She started with simple, specific, pointed questions carefully chosen to demonstrate her knowledge and respect of the craftsmanship... which quickly devolved to technical questions and slight frustration over specific configurations.

"Why does this flamethrower mechanism require multiple tubes? Wait, before that, what are the tubes made of? How are the materials chosen?

To her delight, the mechanical man replied verbosely to almost all of her inquiries, rather *tersely* as he explained his flamethrower mechanism, but far more detailed as he went over the composition of the tubes which delivered the compressed gasses to be burned. As to the reasoning behind the placement of his components? The automaton could only helplessly inform her that he did not know why his internals had been placed as they were, but even so, Danielle quickly noticed subtle shifts in his tone. The more she asked, the more the machine showed what seemed to be true emotion: specifically, pride in his creator.

She also quickly learned which topics were absolutely off limits. If she asked a direct question about the Comte, the internal power source contained in an armored pocket, or the glowing script she found etched into certain joints and mechanisms, Danielle was met with firm refusal or even pointed warnings.

Without those key pieces of knowledge, she was left floundering to make her own hypothesis. Over the next few days, she carefully wrote out her questions and thoughts on the matter, taking meticulous notes, sketching diagrams, and jotting down her observations. For the first time in her life, she was able to ask an endless deluge of questions and get patient replies to almost all of them. It was a refreshing change from her usual experience of someone going out of their way to tell her she didn't need this information, to push her onto the path *they* thought best for her.

After perhaps a moment of careful contemplation, Sneezy would either give an answer or *not*. Not once did he ask if she should even ask the question, and even if he didn't always answer, Danielle was utterly *thrilled* with the experience.

Nearly a week into her gentle captivity, as she was asking Doc about the different alloys used in his armor, versus his internals, Danielle stumbled onto a fundamental disparity between her assumptions and the reality of the mechanical body. After rechecking her findings three times, she carefully formulated her question before actually uttering the words. "Sneezy... I have a question that might be somewhat impolite."

"Not to put too fine a point on it, Madame Danielle, you currently have a grip on the equivalent of my major arteries if I were a human." Sneezy's near-humorous response caused her to raise an eyebrow and jot down another note. "Please request whatever information you are seeking."

Danielle felt a quiet satisfaction even as she blushed at his pointed words. The Comte's creation was clearly starting to trust her, and with that trust came the opportunity to learn more, faster than ever. She felt a twinge of guilt at the realization, knowing her stated goal remained unchanged: the Enchantress was here to recruit Sneezy's creator and would have to be removed by force before she would give up.

"I'm wondering why you were designed like this." She gently rubbed a fingertip over a rusted patch deep in the automaton's leg. "You work amazingly well, but there's a clear lack of maintenance. Some of these sections are clearly very efficient, but without additional casing and lubrication, you're going to break down or rust to pieces. At the *very* least, you'll need replacement parts. You already do, here and here at least."

"There is no query in your words." Sneezy sounded almost... resigned?

"Ah. Let me try again. Your designs are not put in place with thought to long-term maintenance or anything other than pure utilitarianism. Why? You would last so much longer with just a little more time spent on adjusting your design." Danielle pulled her hand away, leaving behind a gleaming patch of metal where before there'd been a thick coating of rust. "There. I can't do much for you, but... you should have a greater range of motion now. Call it my thanks for humoring me the last few days."

Sneezy *whirred* softly, his internals on full display, yet far quieter than previous thanks to Danielle cleaning as she studied. For just a moment, the thickly armored cylinder covered in glowing runes glowed brightly.

"Thank you for attempting to assist me. As for my design, you must understand that the primary focus of the Comte is efficiency and precision. He believes in a 'minimal viable function' process for any of his projects which do not require robust redundancies. In this way, he can create two or even three times as many guards and utility automatons, such as you've seen in the kitchen—uhm."

"Well. *I* think you're worth a little more time and attention," Danielle informed the flamethrower-guard, who had stopped speaking suddenly. Worried that she had pushed too closely to a forbidden topic, she shifted her attention and reached out to poke a metal plate, "Let's see if I can convince my skill to smooth over that patch; it looks particularly intrusive-"

"What am I looking at right now?" The horrendous voice of the Beast echoed through the open doorway, causing Danielle to scamper away from the open chassis of her guard in surprise. "I've been working for *days* to ensure the safety of the estate, resetting the protections, adjusting the mechanisms and locks. I come back here, expecting to find an annoyed recruiter for Verdelune's war efforts. Instead, I stumble upon the very automatons meant to be *guarding* that recruiter showcasing their internals and leaving themselves undefended against any sort of attack she might be able to produce!"

"BST model three, this isn't what it looks like!" Sneezy's parts slid back into place, his metal covering clicking into position faster than Danielle had ever seen them move. "We were just-"

"I just found you with your proverbial pants down, giving an outsider access to protected designs!" the Beast roared in reply, cutting off Sneezy's protestations. "Why are you arguing with me? *How* are you arguing with me? What did you do, *Enchantress?*"

Danielle rapidly shook her head. "I didn't do anything to him! I was just trying to learn. Well, I mean, I *do* have a theory as to why they seem to be gaining a bit more personality, it seems-"

"A *theory?*" The Beast stomped forward, its oversized hands reaching out and wrapping around the entirety of Danielle's arm. "It's time for you to *leave*, before you corrupt my mechanisms. The Comte has no need for the theories of an untrained peasant. His designs are perfect as they are! We don't need or want your meddling. You're lucky I have been instructed to release you, or... *walk!* It's time for you to leave."

As she was frog-marched from the room, Danielle leaned over and managed to snag her notebook, hoping she could talk some sense into the Beast. "Please! Hear me out, I need to speak to Comte LeKrout; it's a matter of life and death!"

"As you said when you arrived. Yet here you are, happily playing with objects far beyond your understanding." The Beast growled back, causing Danielle to go still as she realized he was correct. "If you were so *desperate*, why were you not ruminating on your needs?"

"You say objects, I say *beings!* Intelligent creations, though they may only be like children right now."

"You're *wrong*. They are merely so advanced they appear to be truly intelligent. Just because something is beyond your ken, does not mean they are even truly close to being alive. They are certainly not children; they are replaceable *objects*."

Only as they exited the front door of the manor did the Beast's sudden crashing footsteps draw her attention to the fact that he had been making almost no noise while moving. She glanced behind them, trying to understand what had changed, only to see several cables extending up into the ceiling being retracted. "Are you on a pulley system when you're in the house?"

Surprisingly, the Beast responded with more than threats or growls. "This immense design cannot run on internal energy indefinitely. I have a limited amount of time I can remain active outside of the building. A solution is being researched."

"I have a theory about *that*, too!" Danielle shouted over the noise of the Beast's crashing momentum. "Your designs are pure function; they aren't designed to be harmonious. A huge amount of your energy is being consumed by just-"

They came to a sudden halt with the Beast looking up at the top of the wall.

"Please don't throw me over." Danielle's words were met by a snort of disdain, then the machine crouched, its hand extending to wrap around Danielle's waist before *pouncing* upward. The sudden movement pulled a scream from her lips, then they landed on the wall with a *clang* and a *clatter*.

Danielle expected to be looking out over the untamed countryside, but with a deep feeling of dread, she found her eyes locked on a banner in the distance. "Gasteel Company. *Oh, no.*"

A huge column of people were marching into the area, and the beginnings of a camp had already been set up. Their sudden arrival had drawn many eyes, and as the Beast and Danielle watched the frantic activity below, a familiar figure appeared, waving happily.

"Madame Danielle, you're *alive!*"

Swallowing her suddenly very dry throat, Danielle croaked out a reply, "Lefroupe? What's going on? I thought I was to be sent here alone?"

"You were!" The scribe chuckled as he let his eyes trail over the mechanical monstrosity gripping her. "However, your loving fiancé has deep concerns over your health and well-being, and sent us—all of us—to check in on your welfare. It's good to see that you're alive and... being treated well?"

"He's *not* my fiancé!" Danielle felt a caustic snarl erupt

from her mouth and blushed furiously. Shaking her head, she took a deep breath and tried again a moment later. "I will not be marrying Gasteel. I'd throw myself head-first off this wall first."

"See, that wouldn't be a great idea if you want to maintain the status quo." Lefroupe rubbed at the back of his head in agitation, seemingly pondering for a moment before nodding sharply and explaining himself. "You would be dead, your father would be dead, and the Comte would need to appear before the king to prove his innocence in the matter. I don't know if you've had a chance to talk to the man himself yet, but... I don't think he'd appreciate that very much. Are you sure you don't just want to accept the noble title and a happy, calm, peaceful life? Were I in your shoes, I would've jumped at that chance. Almost anyone would have."

"No one's *stopping* you, Lefroupe. Make your play. I'd *love* to be replaced." Danielle called back angrily, getting only a chuckle of appreciation from the scribe.

"I lack your... natural gifts, and system-enhanced charm, I'm afraid," Lefroupe stated wryly. "Anyway, we'll be out here, waiting for your success. Or, more realistically, your acceptance of the situation. Well, they will. I'm leaving to report on your health in the morning."

The grip around her waist tightened slightly, and Danielle had a moment of feeling absolutely sick as she turned her attention to the Beast. "Please... wait. Don't put me out there with them. They have my father. If I fail to recruit the Artificer, I will need to marry the baron to save him. I... I don't want that to be my life. I can't."

"Tell me true. Until you go out there, or the Comte officially refuses, are you in a stalemate?" The Beast's voice was much quieter, clearly aimed at not projecting his question to the assembled soldiers below. "If you remain here, not having an audience, without a yes or a no, there is nothing *forcing* you to take action against Comte LeKrout?"

Danielle thought for a long moment, going over the actual terms of the agreement she'd made with Gasteel. Ever so slowly, she started nodding, and a small smile appeared on her face. "That's… yes, that's true. I hadn't thought of it like that."

"In that case, do not ask to see him again, or I will *let* you. He'll refuse, and you'll be off to a Class Shrine to be married before you can try a second time!" the Beast growled at her, then turned and hopped over the wall, his mechanical legs absorbing the shock of their fall.

As he released Danielle, he plucked the notebook from her nerveless fingers and began flipping through its pages. Even though its features were mechanical, and therefore not expressive, Danielle could still see that the Beast was shocked and surprised at what he was seeing. "This is your work? Your questions? You were not given instructions on ways to get close to LeKrout?"

"Quite the opposite, in fact. If I'm reading the situation correctly, I was set up for failure at every turn," Danielle quietly replied, hoping he would give her back the notebook. "I learned from my father how to be a Tinkerer, and I've been reading every book I could get my hands on ever since I was a child. I guess I just want to see how the world works?"

"Hmph." The Beast started moving again. "Follow me. Since you're going to be our guest for the foreseeable future, against my recommendation, I've been told to grant you access to a new part of the estate."

"Do *not* make the Comte regret this decision."

MOMENTS after they crossed the threshold into the manor, the clattering and screeching of metal and mechanics went quiet as cables and hoses descended from the shadows of the ceiling. After only a few moments, the Beast had been hooked into the system and was gently lifted a few inches off the floor. Then, with a quiet *hiss* of steam from above, the towering entity began gliding through the stone hallway like the ghost of an entire workshop.

Although Danielle was uncertain where they were going, she couldn't help but feel a flicker of excitement knowing that she'd be able to stay in this wondrous manor for at least a little longer. A twinge of nervousness and guilt filled her at her next thought—how this would give her more time to prove herself, to get close to the formidable Artificer hidden somewhere in this house… and send him away to war.

Her cycle of rumination was broken as the Beast began speaking in a low rumble, "Your observations… are surprisingly astute for someone with no formal education."

Only then did Danielle realize some of the crystal eyes of the machine had been scanning her notes as the Beast drifted along. Without turning to look at her, its grating voice echoed out once more, "Explain how you came to these conclusions. They are *wrong*... but not by much."

"If by formal education, you mean the royal university, you would be correct in assuming I hadn't been trained there." Danielle squared her shoulders and took a deep breath. "Even so, I've been studying machinery for years, thanks to my father. He's a Tinkerer, and always encouraged my pursuit of any subject I could get my hands on."

"Simple tinkering doesn't explain *this*." The Beast turned the notebook around, tapping on a masterfully drawn diagram. "You did not copy this. This is an alteration to the current schematic for Sn-three-zy. It wouldn't function, but it's close enough that I can understand your intent."

"What do you mean, it wouldn't work? The original design is clearly based on the toy soldier version one, from *Iiago's Fun and Functional Schematics*. My design is from a *far* more modern version I've made dozens of times." For a few moments, they went back and forth on whether the design would work or not.

Eventually, Danielle had to throw her hands up and shake her head, having no way to *prove* the design was workable. "Look, Beast. Ever since I turned fourteen and got my Advanced Class, I've been doing everything I could to stay out of sight—it just worked out that I'm fascinated by how things work, how different materials and components can interact to create something beautiful. Spending most of my time in my father's workshop, working or reading, was a perfect situation for me."

"Yet, here you are, arguing with a machine about how *machines work*." The Beast's mechanical eyes brightened as one of them shifted to focus on her, while the others continued scanning her notebook. "You have a deep connection to your father, the man captured to coerce you into recruiting the Artificer?"

The question was so incongruous that Danielle's footsteps

stuttered slightly, though her skills easily corrected her balance and even turned the motion into an adorable little skip. "He's my *father*. Of course I have a deep connection with him. He's taken care of me my whole life, encouraged me when everyone else told me not to bother, and has tried to help me live the life I want to live. I'd do anything to help him, which is… why I'm here."

"*Almost* anything, going by your refusal of your other options," the Beast growled at her, closing her notebook with a *snap* and handing it over with a sharp motion. "Your understanding of the basics is commendable, but you are to refrain from opening any of the Artificer's machines without permission. Let me be clear: you *won't* be getting that permission. He is in closed-door study, attempting to breach the final hurdle of achieving Perfection—your interference will slow him down. So long as you follow the rules of the house, you will be allowed to remain."

"Hold on a moment, why would my studying interfere with his advancement?" Danielle directly challenged the Beast, who had floated to a stop before a large set of double doors she'd never before been invited to step through. "Learning is a continuous process, and inspiration can come from unexpected places. As my father always told me, *everyone* brings something to the table."

"Yes, that is true." The Beast let out a burst of steam in a way that reminded Danielle of someone huffing in derision. "Yet, some people bring a cornucopia… and others bring a slice of stale bread."

"Abyss… *that's* a condescending outlook, if I've ever heard one," Danielle retorted, leaning into the argument instead of ending it as the Beast had likely hoped for. "How about this? I *know* that the parts in Doc and Sneezy can have a fifteen to twenty percent increase in efficiency by changing their placement. Their maintenance could be far easier by turning their gears into gear *boxes*, allowing for lubrication and modular replacement."

The blue crystals of the Beast's eyes flashed with red light. She may have imagined it, but Danielle clearly heard a hint of irritation seeping through its mechanical voice—which seemed stiffer and more formal than usual. "The Comte does not care as much as *you* do about the cost of material things. He is perfectly happy to replace parts as needed. Beyond this simple mentality shift from poverty to abundance, there are aspects of the runic language used in the higher functions of the automatons which could be impacted by such a change."

The red light faded, and the Beast relaxed slightly, shaking its head at her in a facsimile of human motion. "You don't even know what you don't know, which means you don't get to judge the Comte's work."

"Give me a chance to prove myself, at the very least," Danielle demanded as she held up her notebook like a weapon. "Even *you* were surprised at what I was able to glean from studying the finished product. I want to know more; I want to have a chance at convincing the Comte to help me. If that means I have to help *him* raise his mechanical children first, so be it!"

A strange squealing of metal and steam escaped the Beast, and it took an embarrassingly long time for Danielle to understand that the entity was laughing at her. Cheeks flushing, she opened her mouth to continue the argument, but the Beast simply held up a hand.

"Very well. If you are to stay in this house and use up the Comte's resources, you may continue your direct study of Doc and Sneezy *only*. As to the rest, you *will* better yourself. This was meant to be a gift, but now, as payment for your care, you will somehow need to find a way to help the Comte achieve Perfection. Just… stop with this 'children' nonsense. They are tools."

"*You're* a tool," the Enchantress huffed grumpily.

The Beast's hand shot out abruptly, gripping the oversized handle of the door they'd stopped at. With a rough motion, he threw it open. The scent of aged parchment, paper, and vellum rushed over Danielle, and even before she saw what was within, she knew what this place was. With a cautious step, the Enchantress entered a magnificent library filled with shelves upon shelves of papers, scrolls, and thick tomes.

"Start there." The Beast's index finger *clattered* into position, fixed on a small crate of books covered in dust. "That is the general knowledge section. Without an understanding of what those contain, the rest of the accumulated information within the library will be useless to you. Going by the glaring flaws in your… 'hypothesis', your foundation of knowledge is lacking in many areas. If you put in the effort, you can fix it."

Perhaps contrary to the Beast's expectations, Danielle's eyes had lit up with eagerness. Barely looking back at the Beast, she rushed over to the container, her fingers brushing over the spines of the long-neglected books. "I can just… read? Learn? I don't even know how to… to *thank* you."

"Believe me, I'm perfectly happy letting you read these books, which are useless to me, if it means you stop *touching* things better left alone." The Beast remained in the library, perfectly still as its 'eyes' watched Danielle throw herself into her studies without delay.

Pulling each of the books out of the stack, she sorted them first by if she had read them or not, then by complexity. Finally narrowing her selection to a book titled *Basic Principles of Mechanics*, Danielle carried it over to the table, her fingers unconsciously brushing over the worn cover as a sense of anticipation filled her. Settling into a well-worn leather lounge chair, she began devouring the book with her eyes, astounded as each page offered new insights, which seamlessly connected to her existing understandings.

She barely noticed as the hours passed, completely engrossed in the book which explained so many *new* ideas and allowed her to intuitively connect with different concepts she already had a deep understanding of. Finally, Danielle reached a section she mentally bounced off of, her brow furrowing in concern as she tried to parse the dense subject. "What in the-?"

"I see you found the 'applied physics' section." The chiming voice of Doc rang out, far too close to her face for comfort. Danielle flinched away from the razor-sharp sentry, but the machine didn't appear to mind. "We were given permission to help you with your studies, whether that be practical examples or explanations we have been informed of. Would you like me to explain if you have a question?"

"Yes!" Immediately, the Enchantress leaned forward again, tapping on the book and nearly slicing her finger as she flipped a page and nearly touched the guard. "This graph doesn't line up with the information; why would it show only numbers?"

"It's an explanation of the principle of leverage." Doc shifted slightly, reflecting light off its metal arm and on to the sentences he wanted Danielle to read once more. "I'm sure you understand the principle of distributing force across a fulcrum; this is merely the mathematical representation."

Doc's explanations were clear and sharp, but even more than that, his mechanical patience and perfect willingness to repeat explanations until they were fully grasped proved invaluable. Danielle found herself absorbing the information at an astonishing rate, as if she had been given a lesson tailored specifically to address her weaknesses—a perfect blend of theory and practical application.

"Look here…" The tiny hand held up a cogwheel and spring as they reached a section bringing many topics together. "Without the use of a differential, the opposite ends couldn't rotate at different speeds."

"That must be why I could never get my toys to move their arms separately from their legs!" Danielle furiously scribbled notes, already seeing dozens of places she could implement the information she had just learned. "Thanks Doc!"

What would have taken her days to learn on her own, she was mastering in hours, thanks to the guided instruction. As if she herself were an automaton, she kept powering on through the book, asking questions as needed while having no intention of slowing. Eventually, Doc didn't answer one of her questions, and she blinked in surprise as he asked one of his own.

"Why are you pushing so hard, Enchantress? You have no set end date for your tenure here," Doc chimed in confusion. "Learning is a good thing, of course, but this seems excessive. Unsustainable."

"Well… if I'm being honest," Danielle sheepishly grinned at the guard. "I love this, of course I do, but the Beast's refusal to acknowledge my abilities as a Tinkerer *might* be fueling my determination to prove myself a little overmuch. I've, um, kinda become accustomed to spite-learning."

"Spite-learning?" The brand-new term clearly meant nothing to the automaton. "You are serious?"

"Deadly." Danielle grimly nodded, her eyes practically shining with fervor. "When someone tells me I can't do something, I'll throw myself against it until I finally get a chance to casually showcase how easy it is for me—no matter how hard it actually was to learn or do it. No one sees the effort; they only ever see the result."

"Pardon the intrusion, madame, but you are late for dinner. The kitchen is sad." Sneezy's nasally voice broke Danielle from her thoughts, and she tore her eyes away from the half-written sentence in her notebook. "I would offer to bring you a tray, but there is no food or drink allowed in the library, for obvious reasons."

Danielle languidly smiled, her mind only partially present in the moment. "I'm surprised *you* are allowed in here. Fire seems a lot more dangerous to the books than a few crumbs."

Sneezy froze, its rictus smile hiding the actual concern the machine had suddenly been struck with. Realizing she'd brought up a valid concern, Danielle stood up and snapped her fingers to try and break the machine out of whatever logic cycle it had fallen into. "You're okay, Sneezy! I was trying to make a joke. Let's go to the kitchen?"

"I should leave my lighter in the hall." Sneezy muttered at less than a quarter of the volume Danielle had ever heard it speak. The machine started moving, leading her toward the dining room slowly at first, but picking up speed as it followed the new task. "How have you enjoyed your time in the library today?"

Knowing whatever she said would likely get back to both the Beast and the Artificer, Danielle chose her words carefully. "I'm beginning to understand what he meant when he said I needed to increase my foundational knowledge. Doc has been a wonderful help in understanding where I was going wrong. Then there's… well, some of the questions I had are directly answered in this book, and I'm even slightly embarrassed about a couple of my assumptions. Even so… I don't think I'm as far behind as the Beast seemed to assume. I *know* some of what I was talking about is correct. Simply ignoring the facts will not allow the Artificer to progress."

"Surely, this is so basic that it will not have an impact on such high-level work as artificing," Sneezy replied, its faith and pride in its creator shining through his words. "The Comte is a true genius, having the talent, the wherewithal, and the work ethic to reach the highest heights."

"That's actually *why* he needs to listen to me." Danielle shook her head when the guard didn't respond to her. "Think about it, Sneezy. If you have a complicated problem, is it better to fix a mistake early on or wait until you're nearly done with the project to try and work around it? The entire reason the Beast told me to study was so I wouldn't make simple mistakes. How long has the Artificer been pursuing Perfection? Is it *possible* he's simply ignoring what he actually needs to do out of sheer arrogance?"

"It is not."

Danielle could only laugh at the instant reply from the automaton. "It's good you have such faith in your father. I hope it is earned and not *only* something he instilled in you."

"My creator. He would be uncomfortable with your choice of words."

"It's okay, Doc. It's just how I see him. He created your body, and programmed your mind—just like any parent does, even if we don't think of it that way usually." As she sat down at the kitchen table, and the enormous mechanism hooked to the ceiling began preparing her food, Danielle couldn't hold back the smile tugging at the corners of her lips. "I'm going to save *my* father by helping an Artificer, by doing exactly what I want to actually do with my life. Even without the actual class, maybe I still *can* be a researcher."

As the machine overhead deposited a plate in front of her, the inside of Danielle's left arm began to glow.

ELEVEN

"WHAT IN THE... how'd I gain a skill level?" Even before chomping into her food, Danielle swiped her fingers across her arm, revealing the notification from the system. "Oh! Aura of Refinement? I haven't seen an upgrade in this skill for more than a year. It's... *what*!"

Skill increase! Aura of Refinement [Level 8 (Extensive) → Level 9 (Master)]!
Requirement to advance to level 10: Decide what a beautiful life looks like to you, and take the steps needed to live it.

The requirement for increasing her Aura of Refinement to Perfection left Danielle absolutely flabbergasted. Until this point, all of her skill increases had been something tangible, an achievable set of instructions she would have to carry out in such a way as to progress. "What does this even *mean*? How many steps? How deeply into a new way of living do I need to get before it will upgrade?"

Greatly annoyed at the sudden loss of clear steps for increasing her skill—and doing her best to completely ignore

the fact that she'd never *wanted* them to upgrade before—
Danielle read over the details of the Advanced Class skill.

Advanced Skill: Aura of Refinement: Level 9/10.

*Your presence subtly, permanently, and [Masterfully] enhances the beauty
and charm of people and objects within your vicinity, based on the local
aesthetic, reaching up to [9] meters from your body. This effect is gradual
and automatic, becoming more pronounced the longer you are around
people and objects or the more focused attention you give them with this
skill.*

*Requirement to advance to level 10: Decide what a beautiful life looks like
to you, and take the steps needed to live it.*

Danielle growled softly, swiping the words away.

"You seem disheartened. Was your knowledge truly so
lacking?" The Beast's voice came from above her, causing
Danielle to yelp and nearly overturn her plate as her focus
broke.

Looking up, she watched with a mix of horror and interest
as the massive machinery of the Beast descended from the
ceiling like a spider, the cables slowly unspooling to bring it
closer to the ground. "That's *extremely* unsettling. I can't think
of a single person who would be happy to find you floating
above them like that. Then again, how long has it been since
other actual people were here?"

The silence stretched for an uncomfortable moment, and
Danielle blinked a few times as she made the connection.
"Oh. A *long* time, then."

"That is *none* of your concern," the Beast enunciated with
the sound of a steam engine attempting to turn over in cold
weather. "I had come to check on your progress, and I find
you glowering at your weak human flesh. Explain what your
concern is, or I will take my leave."

"Oh, right." Danielle shook her head, tapping on her arm where golden letters had been etched by the system. "I just increased a skill from my Advanced Class. First of all, I never even considered that I would still be able to level those skills up after getting my Full Class. But, most importantly, the level increase requirement to achieve Perfection is... rather abstract."

"That's a good sign." The Beast jabbed a finger at the table. "Eat your food while I explain. It is a waste of your time to *only* sit and listen when you could be doing another task at the same time. Now, a ready answer for your first concern is that, by accepting your next class, you have locked yourself out of gaining new skills in your previous classes. Yet the system knows you aren't always done with what you left behind. Anything already available to you can still increase up to Perfection."

The Beast paused a moment, and the Enchantress hurriedly took a bite of her food. With a grunt of approval, he continued speaking. "It is worth doing so, as it will provide system merits when unlocking skills in your Full Class. This may allow you to gain a better version of whatever skill you would have otherwise gained."

"You don't mean to tell me that I may have missed out on gaining the Full Class skill I desired because I didn't put in my full effort into raising my previous skills? Is there a standard-ized rubric for-" Danielle set her fork down after swallowing a bite of fried potatoes, reaching for her notebook so as to take notes on what she was learning.

However, the Beast tapped a hand on the table to get her attention. "You don't need to do that. Your questions have simple answers. Read *A Treatise on Skills* in the general knowl-edge section of the library if you desire to have a better understanding of the subject. As for the abstract nature of your skill increase, again, that is a good sign for earning merits. If you have only simple requirements, you will only gain basic benefits from the system for completing them. In fact, this is a similar issue to what the Comte is facing currently."

"But... there's no clear direction for upgrading!" Danielle shook her head, realizing how her complaint sounded. Letting out a soft chuckle, she shrugged and waved off her own concerns. "Then again, reaching Perfection only lets me more readily enhance the beauty and charm of the things or people around me. I likely have a long time before my Full Class skill unlocks, so I suppose it's not necessary for me to reach Perfection in the near future. But... I do so *despise* leaving things unfinished."

The Beast was silent for a few minutes as she ate the remaining food on her plate. When she finished, she settled back and looked up at the dangling, multi-limbed food preparation apparatus. "Thank you for yet another delicious meal!"

"It can't understand-" The Beast's chastisement was cut short as one of the limbs waved at her. "That... that is not supposed to be possible."

"Sneezy told me that it was sad I was late for dinner. I just wanted to show it how much I appreciated the effort," Danielle awkwardly explained after the Beast trailed off. "Err... it's always a good idea to be extra nice to the people who make your food. Or *children*, since their emotions are usually so raw and unfiltered, I suppose?"

"They are his *creations* not-" Just then the first part of what she had said registered, and the eyes of the machine glowed brighter. "The other automatons can understand it? Again, this is supposed to be an impossibility. I need to inform the Comte. Also... as you have been given permission to continue your study of Doc and Sneezy, a third guard has been assigned to follow you. Do *not* attempt to influence it."

The cables attached to the Beast retracted, near-silently pulling the machine back up into the shadows along the ceiling. Danielle watched him go with a shiver, halfheartedly shouting after him, "That's still *extremely* creepy! Now... where's the third guard?"

"Duke will be waiting for you in the library or your room, whichever area you prefer to go next." Sneezy quietly explained as it stared up at the ceiling. "I'm uncertain what the consequences of you informing the Comte of our ability to converse will be. Remember me fondly if I am decommissioned."

"I won't let him!" Danielle gasped at the thought of the little flamethrower's fire being quenched. "You're far too interesting to be cast aside. If you've been learning, improving, and growing beyond what was originally expected of you, that can only be a *good* thing."

Her guards remained silent as Danielle walked back to the library, and she winced slightly at the thought that she may have inadvertently done something which would cause them to be destroyed.

As she pushed open the door to the library, a quick scan of the room revealed no new guard. Looking around suspiciously, Danielle went back to her favorite chair, pulled out her notebook, and eagerly picked up where she had left off with her studies.

Hours passed in quiet concentration, the rhythmic scratching of her quill the only sound in the large library. Eventually, a familiar tingling discomfort crept into her legs. Even with her enhanced flexibility, Danielle couldn't remain seated in the same position for so long without some discomfort, so she leaned back to stretch out her legs... only to feel a soft object shuffle under her feet.

Slightly taken aback by the change, she slowly shifted her position so she could see what was under her... only to raise an eyebrow quizzically at the seemingly normal footrest. "That's a comfortable resting position, thanks. Are you a machine as well? My new guard?"

"That is a *cushion*, madame Danielle." Doc's tinkling voice called out with wry amusement, causing her to blush ever so slightly. "Not *every* object in the manor has been... enhanced."

"Sorry, that might've been silly of me to-" The footrest wiggled, letting out a low growl when she tried to push it away. Danielle was startled into letting out a soft shriek, which she quickly stifled with both hands flying up to cover her mouth. "*Ahh!*"

"Doc..." Taking a few deep breaths, she cautiously watched the footrest, then turned to the razor-edged guard which had been assigned to her since the day she arrived. Danielle quizzed him with mock severity. "Did you play a *prank* on me?"

Doc's silence, combined with the slight *whirring* emanating from Sneezy, told her everything she needed to know. Danielle couldn't help herself, and a chuckle bubbled up from deep within her, turning into a deep belly-laugh. "You did! You played a *prank* on me! Was this revenge for accidentally alerting the Artificer to how you've all been growing? I totally deserved that!"

Both of her original two guards started making sounds she could only interpret as laughter. As the mirth of the group began to subside, Danielle lifted her feet from the footrest and stood, shaking her head but still allowing the smile to linger on her lips. "With that, I think I've officially stayed up too late. What's your name, little guy? Oh, the Beast already told me. Duke, right?"

"Unfortunately, Duke is not equipped with a method to hold conversation, which may in fact be the reason he was chosen for this position." Doc explained in its sharp, tinkling voice. "His original design is based on a guard dog, though he has been lazing around the manor for the last six years. At this point, it might be better to describe him as a *pet* dog."

The footrest, now confirmed to be her newest guard, growled slightly, capturing Danielle's full attention once more. She noticed that the fabric across the cushion had clearly once been a deep, velvety red, but it had faded to a muted, pinkish hue.

Reaching out, the Enchantress stroked the cushion, feeling more than seeing the intricate gold threadwork running along the edges and across the surface, forming elaborate patterns which spoke of a true master of their craft creating the original object before its 'enhancement'. Under close inspection, the geometric patterns shimmered faintly in the light, hinting that they may have been a material, such as gold-dipped thread, or simply worked with a high-level, system-granted skill.

"Wow, you're a *pretty* little guy. I suppose I couldn't expect anything less than the highest-quality fabrics from a member of the high nobility." Running a hand across the cushion as though petting an actual dog, she found that the material was still soft to the touch but heavily worn in several areas. Especially along the edges, there were small, threadbare patches, which no one had bothered to maintain or mend. "You know what's extra interesting about you? Even with the toll time has taken on you, this was the first time I've seen something in the estate which is here purely for comfort and aesthetics. You must be *quite* important to the Comte."

The footrest let out a pleased grumble, shifting slightly closer as she tried to pull her hand back, forcing her to give it a few more gentle pets. That was fine with Danielle, as her mind had started wandering. "How long has it been since the Comte stopped caring about appealing to others or giving himself an opportunity to relax and recharge? I'd bet… probably almost exactly as old as you are now, hmm?"

She blinked as she observed an oddity on the fabric surface of the cushion and leaned closer to inspect it. There were two clear, oblong sections of the fabric which looked decidedly cleaner and newer than the rest. "Was that where my feet were resting? Don't tell me you're trying to snuggle up to me just to refresh your upholstering?"

A shift in its position, slightly sagging in the middle, was the only indication she'd been understood and had guessed correctly.

"Giving me the puppy-dog eyes would only work if you *had* eyes." Danielle shook her head and smiled. "I'm too tired to delve into this right now; let's go to bed. Wait... the bed's not 'enhanced', is it?"

"Absolutely not," Doc deadpanned, earning itself a squint from the Enchantress.

After finishing her nighttime routine, Danielle looked at the three guards stationed to keep an eye on her. "Doc, you're made out of razor blades, and Sneezy, you might light my bed on fire. So, I hope neither of you take offense to my having never held you close at night, but I want to try an experiment. Duke, here boy!"

The footstool happily jumped up onto the bed, twirling in place a few times before going still at her feet. Danielle watched on with the bemusement, as it didn't lay down—it had solid, stiff legs—but otherwise acted exactly as she'd expect a dog to do.

"Are you sure about this, madame?" Sneezy carefully questioned the Enchantress. "You were given explicit instructions not to attempt to alter your newest guard."

"I just reached level nine in one of my skills, and I want to see what close contact will look like. It's only a surface-level change; I'm not opening him up or anything like that." Danielle snuggled deeper into the bed, wrapping her blanket tightly around her. "Let's see... I'm focusing my attention on Duke... and going to sleep. Hopefully, by morning, you'll have some of your color back, little guy."

TWELVE

Danielle awoke to the gentle humming of machinery, a strange, rhythmic background noise. Strangely enough, it was a comforting reminder of the strange twist of fate that had brought her into such a wondrous location, as though the walls of the manor itself were welcoming her into a new day.

Sitting up, she noticed Doc and Sneezy staring at the bed silently and followed their stares toward the foot of her bed. With a smile, she reached over and patted the animated foot-stool standing on her duvet. "Come here, let me have a gander at you… well! Good morning to *you*! Who's looking better already? *You* are!"

Duke wobbled toward her excitedly, his movement closer to a middle-aged dog instead of the creaky, ancient hound it had seemed like the previous evening. The faded red and gold upholstery had regained quite a bit of its former vibrancy overnight, but a quick check showed there was still plenty to be done. "Lots of dust and dirt vanished; it seems that your joints are moving smoother. Are you *plush*? Well, at the mini-mum, you're a bit fluffier. I wonder how far my skill will bring you back before someone needs to come in and do some manual repairs? Want to test that out with me? Do you? *Do you?*"

Duke shuffled back and forth, practically vibrating with enthusiasm before bouncing on the bed like a dog expecting a treat.

"I suppose I can only take that as agreement!" Danielle stood up, twisting side to side as a familiar tingle rushed over her skin. For just a moment, the air in the room shimmered ever so slightly, then the natural daylight began reflecting off motes of dust in the air as the aesthetic of the room shifted minutely to mimic her personal preference. "Ahh… feels like nostalgia and smells like a library. It's going to be a nice day."

After a quick breakfast, Danielle excitedly made her way to her favorite place in the manor: the library. Instead of diving straight into her studies, for the first hour, she reorganized and categorized the books, placing them along the shelf in a reading order based on the prerequisites of information each contained. "There we go… now each title leads as naturally as possible to the next. No more searching for the next book I should read. Well…"

She glanced at the arrangement once more, ever so slightly lamenting how not every book was meant to be read one after another. Instead, as dozens of different topics were included, there were often branching paths she could take.

"General knowledge, specialized information, technical manuals, and scientific papers." Danielle ran her fingers along the spines as she murmured, trying to decide which route to knowledge she would move along first.

After making her decision, she slightly rearranged the order, then stepped back and smiled at the immaculate display she'd created—the simple organization optimized by her Alluring Assemblage skill. Looking over it with a critical eye, she nodded and pulled the first book in the row. "Perfect. Now that my workspace is ready for me, I can begin!"

When Danielle settled into study, Duke positioned himself

at her feet, shifting until both of them were comfortable. Sneezy joined in not long after, a puff of steam and a metal-on-metal shriek resounding as he walked to the table. "I see you're working on combustion and non-magical machine empowerment. I don't know if you knew this, but I'm pretty awesome when it comes to fire and how things move when burning. Want me to help out?"

At first Danielle was going to gently refuse, but then she remembered how useful it was to have Doc mentoring her. With a simple nod, she invited the guard to join her and the automaton sent a rictus-smirk at his razor-edged peer. "Told you she would. You're not the only one who has useful knowledge!"

"Yes, you can burn things super well," Doc snarked back sharply—as per his design. "Don't worry, I'll take over again when she gets to *any other* subject."

"Are you… fighting over who gets to teach me?" A slow blush crept up Danielle's cheeks. "I've never had anyone fight over imparting knowledge to me before. Honor duels in hopes of winning my favor, sure. A brawl over who would help me carry my groceries home? Of course, who hasn't had to deal with that? A couple people coming to blows over a lock of my hair that had gotten caught in a door and accidentally cut off?"

Danielle shook her head and chuckled ruefully before finishing her thought. "They treated it like a precious artifact —three young men had to be carried to the healer over that one. But teaching me something I actually value? *Thank* you. Also, you can both teach me at the same time. Two heads are better than one, so three? It must be superb!"

After such a passionate speech, the two automatons glanced at each other slightly guiltily, having no choice but to reluctantly join forces to better explain each topic.

For the next several days, Danielle immersed herself in studying at the oak table in the library. The only interruptions to this continuous activity were at the insistence of her guards, when they informed her it was time to eat or get some sleep. Only very rarely did the Beast drift in to check on her, leaving Danielle to hope that its initial irritation at her presence was giving way to being impressed by her devotion and work ethic.

The automatons had a subtle but profound shift in their attitudes toward Danielle. Upon her arrival, they had been standoffish, but after weeks of continuously remaining in her presence, they were closer to warm, pleased mentors. Now, instead of only answering questions she finagled from them by using loopholes, they were offering guidance and assistance before even Danielle realized she was starting to struggle with a concept.

Doc seemed to have an encyclopedic knowledge of how things moved, broke, and were cut. On the other hand, Sneezy seemed to be able to offer practical tips to simplify even the most complex topics.

Danielle quickly began to realize that their construction had an immense impact, both on what they knew as well as their teaching style. Doc was crafted from a vast array of tiny cogs and wires, the installation of which required immense precision with tools even smaller than those used by jewelers and clockmakers. Each lesson delivered from him was carefully crafted, delivered with that same exactness.

As for Sneezy? He took a more... *pragmatic* approach. He liked to burn things, and was designed for getting the job done at speed. His personality was geared toward finishing things done in the fastest, most practical manner.

Together, they made learning quick, easy, and fun.

Yet, even with her love of studying and learning, even with how much she had been taught, the Enchantress eventually hit a breaking point.

"I've been sitting here for days; I need to *do* something." Abruptly standing up, Danielle took a few steps toward the door of the library, even as her footrest grumbled at her gently for disturbing its rest. Before she was halfway across the room, the Enchantress slowed, then came to a stop. "Then again, where am I going to go? Doc, can I get access to a workshop of some kind to *tinker* with things? I need practical experience, or what's the point of learning all the places I've gone wrong in the past?"

"Access denied," Doc informed her sadly. "Unfortunately, there is only one workshop, and it is perpetually in use. The goings-on within it are house secrets, and without permission from Comte LeKrout, you cannot be allowed to view them without rather *restrictive* oaths."

Rolling up the long sleeves of her dress, Danielle shrugged and stepped closer to the ultra-thin guard. "That's fine by me. If I can't work somewhere else, let's do it right here. Doc, would you mind if I took a look at your components again? I want to see if I can make a better layout for your internals. I'll submit it through the Beast, but only after I'm *sure* it's going to help you."

"That's an acceptable option. Please don't hurt me; I'm very fragile when I open up to people."

"Same," Danielle muttered under her breath as Doc willingly adjusted its position and allowed its components to retract, expanding out to nearly five times its width by separating its body to allow her access.

Rrr. The soft growl emanated from Duke, prompting a quick glance at the footstool, who was paying close attention to what she was doing... somehow.

"Do you have eyes hidden behind that fabric, Duke?" As Danielle had expected, her question received no answer. Moving carefully, she returned her attention to the exposed innards of the guard, ever so gently twisting components in an attempt to determine their individual functions, while taking notes.

Between her previous research and her newfound knowledge, she was able to make a working theory as to what *almost* everything in the razor-thin chassis did. Yet, as per usual, she was completely stonewalled by the glowing lines connected to the protected core of Doc's body. Distractedly voicing her thoughts and expecting the usual refusals to answer, "I don't suppose one of you could help me understand how this works?"

"That… could work," Sneezy replied with a hesitant note in his nasally voice. It took a moment for the Enchantress to understand what he'd said, as she was so lost in her thoughts. "The master has firmly instructed us to disallow you from tampering with our core, but has given no further instructions on allowing you to study and attempt to understand rune-script. Actually, he gave you unfettered access to the library, which could be seen as an implicit approval for you to do so."

"Runescript?" Danielle blinked several times before her mind caught up with the conversation. "Hold on, he has actual *grimoires* here? I can learn unaspected magic?"

Sneezy held up his oversized arms and waved back and forth, mimicking Danielle's nonverbal communication. "Don't get too excited; the books on scripting are over *there*."

Danielle's eyes followed the gesture to the highest space on the tallest bookshelf. "Going by how everything was arranged before I got here… that would make those the most difficult subject to understand in the entire library?"

"Correct, madame," Sneezy stated in a relieved tone. "Once you have a firm grasp on almost every other part of how to make creatures like us, only then will the system glyphs, or *runes* as they are called, be legible. Without an understanding of their underlying concepts, the symbols themselves are completely unintelligible. They can even cause harm to your mind if studied improperly, such as being viewed during their inscription."

"Hmm." It took Danielle a long moment, but she finally tore her eyes away from the temptation of the books. "It seems I have a lot of learning to do before I get there. Now, I have a question for you, Doc. The Beast said I was allowed to continue working with you and Sneezy, but before I do anything like disconnecting a wire or remapping your layout, I want to make sure *you* are okay with me changing your structure. I don't want to break anything."

Surprisingly, there was almost no delay in the razor-guard's reply, "Anything you do can easily be undone or fixed, so long as you do not tamper with my core. You will not cause me injury, nor will I be uncomfortable with you rearranging my internals while active. Go for it. You'll need specialized tools, though. Might want to start with *him*."

"No, I'm comfortable working with tiny parts, thanks to toymaking."

"Ah. Yes. Go ahead and… adjust me." Doc agreed with only a hint of hesitation.

"I'll be careful. On the plus side, the Compte will certainly appreciate his children being well-adjusted, yes?" She turned to Sneezy, cutting him off before he could deny her words. "Now, even if I'm not allowed access to the workshop, Doc makes a good point. I still need some tools; can you find a way to get them for me? I have an idea I absolutely must test. It's been messing with my head ever since I first saw how you were both arranged."

Though he expressed some trepidation, her secondary guard left the room, returning a handful of minutes later with a large box of neatly organized tools. "Please ensure you put everything back where you found it. The lord of the house is… fastidious."

"If I change how they are put away, it'll only be because the system made me do it differently." Danielle grinned at the way Sneezy froze in panic, then she pulled out the first screwdriver and got to work. More than half the day passed as Danielle used the tiny tools necessary for such delicate work to disassemble, clean, adjust, and reassemble most of the mechanical sections of Doc's body. With a simple wipe of a cloth, her skills allowed her to remove patches of rust, shine metallic surfaces, and remove caked-on impurities such as dusty oil.

While she worked, Danielle kept up a stream of conversation with the guard, testing its mental capabilities to ensure she hadn't damaged or removed its ability to communicate with her. At approximately the halfway point, she had removed every single mechanical component except the armored core—but when she went to unscrew the plating, Duke growled and Sneezy *clicked* its nose threateningly.

"I was just going to clean around the armor, not try to pry the core out!" Danielle protested as she quickly pulled her offending hand back. Her other guards didn't make another sound, but she felt a renewed sense of watchfulness from both of them. "I'm glad you care so much about your brother."

"I have been ordered to care." Even though his words were just as mechanical as usual, Danielle felt a flash of triumph when she realized he had failed to demand she not refer to Doc as his 'brother'.

"Ever so slowly making permanent changes over time." She grinned as Sneezy seemingly ignored her words, or perhaps simply didn't pick up on her true motivation for saying them. Returning to her notebook, she went back to the first page of the schema she'd carefully drawn out as she worked. Each page of diagrams was carefully torn out, then placed above her book for easy viewing access. Relying on her own knowledge—while also guided by the hand of the system via her Perfected Alluring Assemblage skill—she quickly drew a new diagram.

What started as ten pages was reduced to seven, and once she was satisfied with what she saw, Danielle returned to the near-empty chassis and began replacing the components in their new position.

"I'm not sure if you know this, but creating a design *before* doing the work is usually the optimal choice," Doc grumpily informed Danielle as she started replacing the gears and cogs.

"As much as it pains me to ask you to step away, you should break for lunch. You're already overdue, and this evening's dinner is already approaching at a relentless pace." Sneezy informed the Enchantress when she leaned back to gently wipe a trickle of sweat from her forehead. "As someone who is very fond of libraries, you should recognize that being overdue is not ideal."

With a shake of her head, Danielle leaned forward and got back to work. "Sneezy, I'm not going to go have *lunch* and leave Doc here unable to move or carry out his own tasks. Even if I *am* hungry, I'm not a terrible person."

"*I* think you're making the right choice," the exposed guard agreed immediately. "What a good person you are. That is the only thought I'm going to share for now; any others can wait until I have been reassembled."

Two hours later, she had finished the main body and moved on to the limbs. The pieces that fit in these areas were half as large, so even though there were fewer of them, it still took nearly the same amount of time as the torso had before everything had been joined according to the diagram she'd created. Stepping back from the table, Danielle let out a long sigh and gave an exhausted nod to the guard.

"Okay, Doc. Everything should be working perfectly; why don't you go ahead and try to close up. If that works, try moving around and tell me how you feel."

"*If?*"

Continuing on as though she hadn't been interrupted, Danielle finished. "If it doesn't work... I'm not saying I'm going to leave you here for a while, but I might pass out if I don't eat soon."

Not needing to be asked twice, Doc smoothly and silently folded in the expanded innards of his chassis, compressing down until he was back to its normal active state. Sliding off the table, he took a few cautious steps, then waved back and forth in a windmill position.

"This is… so smooth." Excited at the flexibility and ease of motion, Doc sped up. His speed continued to increase until his casual windmill motion turned into a deadly blender—which was when things went wrong.

While its upper torso was still swirling, the automaton took a step and tripped—off balance from its own rapid movement. Doc fell over, its angular momentum causing the machine to ricochet off the stone floor and fly into the air. As soon as it left the ground, the guard stopped actively turning, no longer acting as a blender, but still a rapidly tumbling, three-foot-tall razor blade.

Luckily, its direction was not toward any person nor the books. Instead, Doc slammed into the oak door of the library, quivering there like a thrown knife. "Wow. What a rush."

Turning to Danielle with a gleam in its eyes, Sneezy spoke in a hushed whisper, "Do me next!"

Rruff!

"She can't work on you; it was explicitly forbidden by BST model three," Sneezy cheerfully informed the upholstered guard dog. "What do you think? A quick dinner, then an increase to my functionality by shredding my body and putting me back together?"

Puk.

The soft sound resounded through the library, drawing Danielle's attention back to Doc.

She froze in concern as she saw the Beast pulling the razor-thin guard out of the thick wood of the door.

He glared at the guard, then the marred surface of the wood, finally turning toward the Enchantress and slowly advancing on her, brandishing Doc like a sword.

"What could have *possibly* convinced you this was a good idea? Thanks to your meddling, one of your guards can't control itself, and even so another is offering itself up for the same treatment. Is this your attempt at betraying us? Getting your guards to willingly destroy themselves? Seems I barely got here in time. Admittedly, I've been *waiting* for you to play your hand."

The Beast came to a halt, looming above her and staring down with six cold blue crystalline eyes, which swiftly shifted to red.

"I just didn't think it would be so… amateurish."

CHAPTER
THIRTEEN

"TELL me when I'm wrong. You're not just a recruiter, you're an *assassin-*"

"What could *possibly* make you believe that I'd do anything to damage your trust after you've given me so much, not to mention saved me from having to marry a man I have no interest in marrying?" The sheer disbelief in Danielle's tone, perhaps even more than the words themselves, caused the Beast to pause then even retreat a step.

He'd been prowling forward, the normal blue light of its eyes slowly filling with an intense red as he studied her. "You could say I have a bad history with Enchantresses. I don't think... no, I *guarantee* my heart couldn't take another betrayal. I won't be toyed with or destroyed. Not without fighting as though the abyss itself were pulling me in."

The tone and tenor of the words were slightly different than usual, though they still echoed with the rumbling and screeching of machinery. Even so, it was enough for Danielle to make a profound realization, and her gaze intensified as she stepped closer to the Beast.

"Am I speaking to the *Artificer* right now?" She stepped

forward, excitement overcoming her good judgment. "How are you able to speak through your creation from a distance? Is that why its eyes are red right now? It's an indication that you are actively controlling the Beast?"

The machine reared back, assuming its full and imposing eight-foot stature, but the implied threat was gone. Now there was only shock and... perhaps a hint of fear? Even in the absence of verbal confirmation, the movement alone sufficed for Danielle to understand that she'd stumbled upon the truth. The crimson eyes of the construct glowed with an intensified brilliance, as though magical energy was being channeled into the deadly entity.

Before the hidden Artificer could make some grim proclamation, Danielle spoke once more. "I wasn't *tampering*, nor was I attempting to betray you in any way. I can swear to it if needed. All I wanted to do was apply my experience, newfound knowledge, and the insights I've gleaned to the mechanisms of my... that is, to *your* guard. Speaking of Doc, I don't think he's broken or anything like that. He just got a little... *overenthusiastic* while testing his new range of motion."

"Is that so?" The Artificer, currently mentally housed in his own creation, performed a half-turn to shine a red light on the deep score now permanently etched in the wood of the door. The exaggerated action was executed with a deliberateness that spoke of disbelief... but then the mechanical entity hesitated.

After contemplating the damage, as well as inspecting the diminutive guard patiently remaining still while being held in his hand, he extended his hand toward Doc and authoritatively dropped him on the table. The automaton promptly complied with the unspoken request. Positioning itself flat upon the wooden surface, Doc opened itself to expose its magically mechanical innards.

Over what felt like the longest five minutes of her life,

Danielle waited as the Artificer simply scrutinized the alterations she had made. One of its arms reached out, extending twice as far as she'd thought possible, only to close around the loose-leaf pages torn from the notebook. What followed was the Artificer paging through the diagram she had created for replacing the parts, comparing her design to the end result.

Finally, he asked her a question. "Was it *necessary* to add these superfluous designs to the chips?"

The light emanating from its eyes narrowed, casting a focused beam which illuminated dozens of areas where Danielle had gently filed the metal using a wire brush. Her initial artistry had been usurped by her class skills, culminating in a harmonious and elaborate geometric pattern only fully revealed when the innards were completely on display. A heartbeat after the question, Danielle realized it wasn't rhetorical: the Artificer was expecting an answer.

"They're not strictly necessary for Doc's functionality," Danielle replied, doing her best to keep her tone respectful and measured, now that the Artificer was assessing her work, "but they'll help in all sorts of other ways. Let's call them… auxiliary benefits? The least of which is a pleasing feeling of satisfaction when you look upon it."

The machine released a disgruntled snort of disbelief, but Danielle hadn't finished speaking. "Beyond that, unless you possess an encyclopedic, perfect memory and somehow have every part of *every* machine you've ever made memorized, being able to look at the pattern and immediately seeing where it's out of balance will allow for easy replacement of worn or faulty parts. Another benefit is that dust and rust are both more readily visible when there's a standardized pattern, which means that, moving forward, every step—from cleaning to fixing—will be faster to complete."

Putting a bright smile on her face, she tried to sell her improvements even harder. "Ask yourself, what's more valuable than your time? Nothing! Finally, removing the buildup will keep Doc's fluidity of motion intact while reducing over-heating. I'm estimating a... a twenty-three percent increase in overall functionality!"

"Are you a *conjurer*? You must be, because you pulled that number out of nowhere," the Artificer immediately countered, turning specifically to glower at her. "Do not fabricate information in a misguided attempt to present yourself as more inventive than you truly are. I've wasted months attempting to replicate an experiment, only to learn that it was published *solely* because the person who wrote it was in favor with the crown at that time. Let us adhere to the truth. It is far more than sufficient, especially in this instance. Admittedly, I'm already intrigued at the fact that you were able to improve upon my design."

Accepting her chastisement while glowing from the casual praise, Danielle remained silent for a few moments as the Artificer compared the diagram with the final product. "The Beast refused to even consider improvements as a possibility. Again, I wasn't tampering; I was just trying to understand if what I knew to be true could possibly be wrong with the intro-duction of magic to the system. Your automatons are incredi-ble, and I keep learning new and surprising things about them."

"Close up," the Artificer commanded Doc, and the machine near-instantly pulled itself together. The red lights narrowed once more, and he examined Doc carefully as it stood up, following the smooth motions and enhanced walking speed. "This is *decidedly* beyond what a simple shift in configu-ration can achieve. I have my own theories on why that is, but I will admit that your direct intervention has increased the potential of this automaton significantly. The problem is..."

Here, he turned to face Danielle once more, perhaps to capture the entirety of her reaction as he spoke. "If this is a result of your *skills* adjusting Doc, it may not be something I can replicate. In that instance, it will not be something that can help me grow past the bottleneck I find myself facing."

Thinking furiously, Danielle tried to come up with a way to prove she had something valuable to offer. But, thinking over what the Artificer had asserted, how he'd already acknowledged that her Alluring Assemblage had increased the potential of his own designs, there was only one word she could think of to describe the situation.

"Fair."

Saying nothing, the Artificer simply watched as she fiddled with her fingers and tried to think of something to help her cause. Finally, she looked up at him with a sheepish grin. "Please don't kick me out. I really like it here."

"Technically, you violated the rules. I like things to be *technically* correct." Even though the words were harsh, the bright red lights dimmed as the beastly machine settled slightly. He waved at Duke, the guard dog that was vibrant and far more active today than it had been previously.

"You were *specifically instructed* not to tamper with your other guards, yet I am informed that you intentionally focused your abilities on Duke and had them running on him overnight. Full of curiosity you might be, perhaps even with an intriguing amount of academic potential, but one fact remains: you have already broken my trust."

Danielle nodded glumly, her heart sinking at the thought of losing access to the amazing fount of knowledge that was this library. She peeked over at her guards and found that she had also grown quite fond of them as well—deadly designs notwithstanding. The Artificer let the pause in conversation drag out before finally making a decision. "I will let you stay and continue to study. You shall not lack for food and safety, but I will need you to earn your keep in a new way."

"What the...?" As soon as he'd made his decision, Danielle felt a shift in the air around her and blinked as her left arm glowed subtly. "That is... what do you want from me?"

The Artificer paused once more, but this time, it seemed as though he were struggling to make an admission. It also became immediately apparent that he hadn't noticed the increased potency of one of her skills.

"The facts do not lie. I've seen more growth from my automatons since you've been in their care than I had ever expected possible. They're not only moving and acting in a more *vital* way, they are growing in personality and acumen. There must be an explanation, and if I can find, isolate, and replicate it, I believe this will at least help me achieve one of my goals. To that end I would like to... study you."

"To be fair, you've already bought me dinner first," Danielle quipped, her smile faltering as she tried to figure out *exactly* what he meant with his words.

"Ugh." Even with the beastly exterior, the Artificer gave Danielle a distinct impression he had just rolled his eyes. "It must come as no surprise to you that you are one of the most graceful individuals who *can exist*. You have an intrinsic ability to flow from one position to another, your body being enhanced by the system itself. What I mean to do is study your movements, capturing the motions you make and applying those qualities to future iterations of my automatons."

"You want to capture my... motion?" Danielle frowned slightly, uncertain what exactly that would entail. "How?"

The enormous machine leaned forward, its eyes suddenly *blazing* with renewed light. "It's a straightforward process! First, you would wear a specialized set of clothing which would transfer signals back to a central core I designed. The rune-script would write out each individual position you took—the tightening of muscles and tendons—as individual images which could then be redrawn and distributed... *ahem.* My apologies, I don't mean to scare you. It's just that this is-"

"Something you're deeply passionate about," Danielle finished for him, instantly warming up to the idea. "That, at least, is something I can perfectly understand. When should I…?"

"I'll leave instructions with the Beast." The Artificer's voice betrayed a hint of relief. "For now… just… *try* not to break my machines? Replaceable they may be, but I don't like having to decommission them. Even if they aren't living, you're right about one thing. They are the closest thing to family-"

The red light winked out, leaving the crystal eyes of the Beast dark and empty. Moments later, they reignited with a light blue, and the normal personality of the Beast re-engaged. "Please disregard the Comte's final statement, he's been listening in on your conversations a bit too closely for comfort recently. Now, I see you've formed a reluctant truce with the Comte. *Peachy*. While I am not exactly pleased that he is *rewarding* your intrusion into his private matters, I suppose it *is* his choice to make."

"The last few minutes have been quite enlightening." Danielle took a deep breath, nodding as she spoke.

Leaning forward, the Beast fixed each of its eyes on her face, and the Enchantress found herself unable to speak the next word she had been planning. "I will leave you with a tidbit of information. Take this as you will. He is not often able to attend in person. If you attempt to take advantage of his presence, just know that his overlay of my system will *not* last. If I find this has been the case, as soon as I have regained control, *I* will follow *my* instructions."

Stepping back, the Beast coldly finished, "I will meet you in the dining room after you have broken your fast in the morning."

With his promise delivered, the machine was lifted into the air by his pulley system and gently floated out of the library.

Danielle watched him go, unsure how she felt about how the day had gone.

At first.

Then, as she turned back to the library, she watched as a Doc cartwheeled across the stone floor, letting out bright chimes of glee. He ended his performance by striking the ground at a sharp angle, sending himself spiraling straight up. While off the ground, he continued his spin, his blade-like body cutting the air with a threatening *ssss* before stopping the spins perfectly—just before he hit the ground. Bouncing twice, the automaton gently came to a rest.

"Figured it out. I just needed a little practice," Doc cheerfully stated as he walked around with far greater ease. "What other improvements do you think you could make, Danielle? It's been eight years since the Artificer came up with my design, and he moved on as soon as I moved correctly."

Sneezy stepped forward, waving his oversized limbs at the razor guard in an attempt to ward him off. "Hold up! You've already had a big upgrade; it's my turn next."

Rrr! Duke growled softly, indicating his desire to be included.

As they were bickering amongst themselves, the Enchantress took a moment to swipe her left arm and learn what the system had changed.

Skill increase! Unified Radiance [Level 4 (Basic) → Level 5 (Moderate)]!
Requirement to advance to level 6: Persuade a skeptic to wholeheartedly embrace a concept they initially dismissed without using any factual evidence OR transform a heavily damaged item into a focal piece of a room without explicitly calling attention to it.

"I guess convincing the Artificer to let me stay counted as making a sale of something the other person had no need of? Kind of *rude*... but I'll take it." Between the automaton's enthusiasm, and the surprise increase of her skill, Danielle broke into a beaming smile.

"What's on your mind, Enchantress?" Sneezy called out, having originally turned to get her to side with him in his argument. Danielle looked back at him, feeling as though a heavy knot of tension had just unraveled.

"I just realized… this day has gone absolutely *wonderfully*."

CHAPTER

FOURTEEN

The Beast led Danielle to a large, heavy metal entryway in the grand hallway the next morning. After slowly pulling it open—unintentionally demonstrating exactly how heavy the armored door truly was—he began walking down a set of winding stairs. Danielle followed after him, and as they spiraled seemingly endlessly deep into the bedrock, she tried to remain cautiously optimistic about their destination.

When they finally reached the bottom, Danielle let out a soft gasp as they stepped into an expansive, high-ceiling workshop practically vibrating with the hum of so many machines working at once. The air was thick with the scent of oil, heated metal, and a faint crackle in the air she recognized as residual magic, thanks to her constantly active aura. Her gaze swept around the room, taking in the intricate machines lining the room, many of them in various stages of completion.

Some were chugging along, gears turning with precise elegance, while others stood cold and silent. A few were only pieces, with chalk outlines sketched out on the floor as an estimation of their space requirements upon being assembled. Even with the scores of machines showcasing a vast amount of wealth and resources, what drew Danielle's attention was a simple, enormous curtain made of rich velvet.

The cloth was inexpertly bolted to the ceiling, in some places held up by gleaming chains. The fabric stretched across the entire open space, from wall to wall, obscuring... something. Its edges fluttered slightly in an artificial wind, and Danielle found herself stepping forward and crouching to try and peer beneath the edge dancing ever-so-slightly off the stone floor.

"None of that!" The Beast's imperious voice shook Danielle out of her almost-trance, and she stood straight, turning her eyes back to him.

"I have to ask... is this why you waited to bring me down here until this morning? Did you set the cloth up overnight? Seems like a waste of fine material."

"This is where we will conduct the motion capture." The Beast ignored her question and spoke loudly, his voice echoing off the hard surfaces of the room and coming back only slightly muffled where the room-spanning curtain was hung. "You are to pay no attention to what is on the other side of the curtain. The contents of the room are on a need-to-know basis, and you do not need to know. Crossing that boundary will result in immediate expulsion from the estate... at *best*. Do not test me."

Danielle nodded eagerly, hopping onto the platform he was indicating and waiting for further instructions.

"Why are you already on the platform? You are not dressed for it," the Beast grumbled as he waved her toward a suit of a thin, flexible material inscribed with glowing symbols. It was laid out over a chair, as though someone had taken it off and draped it there, so it would be ready when they returned. "Put this on, and make no notes or copies of its design. This was created entirely by the Comte, without outside influence. Anyone else who has seen it has been sworn to secrecy on pain of death."

"You had people *cross their heart* just because they've seen this?" Danielle hopped off the platform, gracefully arresting her momentum and gliding forward to lift the outfit. "I won't say a word, promise."

"While that may be good enough for *him*, I am not as happy with the situation," the Beast muttered darkly, gesturing for her to step into a small booth and get dressed. She did so, feeling the strangest of sensations as the suit clung to her, squeezing tightly for a moment before subtly adjusting itself to more perfectly fit her form. A tingle of magic danced over her skin, similar enough to how her skills felt that she immediately understood that the suit was activating.

It was surprisingly comfortable, and as she stepped out of the changing booth, Danielle swung side to side, testing the full range of motion and not feeling the cloth pull at all. "I'm just saying, if he ever gets sick of making machines, tell him to add a few pockets to this, and it would be all the rage throughout the kingdom. He'd start a fashion revolution."

"There it is. *Finally*, someone has determined the best use of his talents. It wasn't making my kind, nor was it incredible feats of magical technologies. It was *fashion* all along," the Beast grumbled at her like the curmudgeon he must have been modeled after. "Begin with basic movements. Walk, run, jog."

"How about walk, jog, run?" Danielle teased the nightmare-inducing machine, getting only silence in return. "I think we should spend more time together. Even Doc has fewer sharp edges than you do, and he's a literal razorblade."

"I am not here to be anything other than the protector and manager of the estate in the absence of the Comte's personal presence. Frankly, the only reason I am agreeing to do this is because I was ordered to do so. That, and I *am* greatly pleased the Comte is finally having you *begin* to pay him back for his generosity." The Beast harrumphed at her as

Danielle hopped up onto the platform. "Stop. Go back down. Jump up again. I want a few iterations of that motion."

"So… if I understood you correctly, that means you're the butler?" Danielle chuckled softly at the mental image of this monstrosity in a pressed suit, and it seemed the Beast took *umbrage* with her prodding. For the next ten minutes, he had her continuously jump onto the slightly above waist height platform, then off, and back on, until she was nearly shaking with exhaustion from the unfamiliar motions. "Why… so many… *jumps*?"

For a long moment, she was uncertain if the Beast would answer, but he finally reluctantly explained, "Motions follow a type of logic called if-else. In this instance, *if* an automaton is moving at peak efficiency and is designed to be able to do so, it should be able to utilize your first, most *efficient* leap up onto the platform. But if they are damaged, or simply not rated for such movements, they will use an *else*. As in, they will use this jump, *else* they will use a less efficient version based on their model."

"You mean you're intentionally tiring me out so I have *worse* motions for them to use?" Danielle swept her hand across her forehead, brushing her hair over her ear. "You could've just told me that-"

"We all enjoy life in our own way," the Beast interrupted with its standard mechanical grumble. "As a reward-slash-break, hop back up onto the platform, then simply begin walking in a straight line. Cool down. Recover energy."

Danielle attempted to jump back up, but at the last moment, her muscles locked up, and she needed to *crawl* onto the platform.

"Ahhh… *perfect*." The Beast gave a single nod. "The final *else*."

"If you can jump, do so. Else, crawl like a fatigued Enchantress," Danielle grumbled as she got to her feet.

"That statement is correct."

Mumbling under her breath about machines being mean for no reason, Danielle began walking, sending annoyed glances at the enormous automaton that was currently glowing brightly from each of its 'eyes'. As she cooled down, each step landed more smoothly, more precisely, her skills guiding her to remain fluid and controlled. Only then did she realize she had been walking for several minutes and hadn't yet left the platform. "Why am I not getting any closer to the outer edge?"

"You recall the conveyor in the kitchen which moves food from one station to another? It is the same principle. The ground beneath you is moving at the same rate as your foot-falls, which should keep you in the same position. As a fun fact, the Queen of Verdelune copied this design as a way to torment prisoners of war. All they needed to do in order to eat and drink was make it to the edge." The casual way in which the Beast spoke of such an odd punishment made Danielle shiver. "Feel free to jog or run, as you gain the energy to do so."

Around the oversized dais, crystals pressed up through the stone, shining with an inner light that washed over her from all sides. Suddenly feeling very *watched*, Danielle decided to turn her nervous energy into action. She slowly transitioned into a run, legs moving effortlessly, her form perfect. As she had discovered on her travel to this estate, the sensation of being able to run near-endlessly was *exhilarating*.

As the minutes passed, Danielle pushed herself harder, trying to sprint across the platform through sheer effort. Yet, no matter how hard she pushed, the edge was no closer than it had started. With a burst of inspiration, she spun around and sprinted the other direction… to absolutely no effect.

"A valiant effort, but ultimately futile," the Beast chortled at her in its mechanical way. "If you had tried that before the recording crystals came up, it may have even worked. In full-motion-capture mode, the ground below you will move perfectly to match you. "

Taking a deep breath, Danielle launched herself into the air, trying everything she could to get off the platform without having to *ask* to end the session. She attempted cartwheels and flips, each higher and more intricate than the last. As she built up momentum, the Enchantress started to gain ground, moving closer and closer to the edge. Then, as she passed the halfway mark, the floor beneath her feet suddenly sped up, and she barely managed to catch herself from falling on her face as she was returned to the center of the platform once more.

"Excellent complex actions. Not what I *asked* for, but a decent baseline measurement of your flexibility and stamina." The Beast's words were delivered casually, with absolutely no hint of aggravation or laughter directed at Danielle; who was currently heaving for air, bent over with her hands on her knees. "However, what you are doing currently is fully unnecessary. Automatons do not need to breathe. These motions will need to be discarded unless... no? I'm told to have you continue. There may be some use if we are attempting to create a difficult-to-detect simulacrum. When you are able, please return to walking."

Even with only performing 'basic' actions from then on, the physical exertion was intense. After only a little more than an hour, Danielle was absolutely drenched in sweat and swaying on her feet. The Beast, recognizing that she would push herself until she collapsed, deactivated the platform and motioned for her to get dressed in her regular clothes. "That will be enough for now. Over the next few days, we will practice complex actions, such as dodging while running, leaping, as well as fighting with various weaponry."

"I don't have any training with weapons," Danielle managed to mumble around a large glass of water which had mysteriously arrived next to the changing booth.

The Beast's voice easily drifted through the cloth of the changing room. "That will not be an issue. You do not have to swing the armaments quickly; you simply need to make the motion. If it's done correctly, we will be able to recreate it at any speed as necessary. Your *skills* will make up for your lack of training, in this instance."

As she emerged from the small, private changing space, Danielle looked around for where she might be able to refill her glass. Her thoughts were interrupted as the Beast went still then spoke in a begrudging manner.

"The Comte is greatly impressed with your physical gifts. I agree with him that your movements are unlike anything I've ever seen. Most people with movement-related skills have a very niche, narrow field in which they are superb. Yet, m'lord believes that, with training, you could master nearly any physical skill without too much hardship. This leads me to a rather obvious question: why do you focus on research and a scholarly life, when you could pursue nearly any other body-focused craft and master it even without the related skills?"

As she gave the question some thought, Danielle fiddled with the glass in her hand, spinning it on her palm to keep from fidgeting further. "It's all the system, though, isn't it? Is it truly my effort? Or, more likely, am I a rank Beginner at everything I do, with my efforts simply magnified by a set of skills I actively tried to subvert? When I'm learning something, applying it, finding new ways to make things work, it *might* be enhanced by the system—what *isn't* in this world? Even so, it's *my* efforts that lead to the success."

"You still clearly enjoy being able to move so well. It was apparent on your face. You were smiling very intently, even if those motions were unable to be captured. Please note, that will be rectified tomorrow—a form-fitting hood and face mask will be completed overnight."

"Please don't forget I'm just a 'fleshy human' who needs to breathe." Danielle meant her comment as a joke, but the

Beast pulled back slightly and muttered something unintelligible before nodding once more.

"Air holes will be added to the design. A sound recommendation" The Beast paused as Sneezy walked over, carrying a large jug of water in his elongated hands. "Is that really all there is to your obstinance? You began to love to learn out of spite, simply due to disdain for what you have freely available?"

"No, that's—hold on. *Ahh*." Danielle shook her head, unable to speak for a moment as she finished drinking her freshly refilled glass of water. "No. I've *always* wanted to know what was going on. But, no matter where I turned, everyone except my father told me 'stop asking questions'. That I would *lose* opportunities if I learned too much. They had a picture of me in their minds, an image that wasn't reality, but they still wanted me to live up to it. But... it's *my* life. I want to live it the *way* I want to live it. My father..."

She took a deep breath, doing her best not to worry so much about how he was being treated at the moment. Danielle reminded herself that she could only hope that Gasteel was following through on his promise of taking care of his 'future father-in-law' so she wouldn't be as resistant to marrying him.

"His name is Henri, by the way. He taught me so much. Beyond simply rote learning, he showed me how to *think*, how to do more than *copy* what other people did. I designed a singing mechanical bird toy, and I don't think I've ever loved something I've made as much as my first real design. But now I know *how* to make it again, as many times as I want."

Lapsing into silence, Danielle fell into internal contemplation, her exhaustion fueling her rumination. After a few dozen seconds, the Beast began moving, lifting off the floor and slowly floating away.

"Thank you for your insights. My master and I will be examining the data we have collected so far, but I can already see multiple areas it will benefit our future work. Until tomorrow, Enchantress. Get plenty of rest, and make sure the kitchen feeds you a larger than normal meal to help you recover your energy."

"See you tomorrow, Beast."

FIFTEEN

DANIELLE GRIPPED THE LIGHT, wooden practice sword, her hands steady though her heart was racing. Taking a deep breath to calm herself, she prepared for another bout against the unnerving figure standing on the motion capture pedestal across from her. The suit of armor was featureless and devoid of any hint of personality—as though she were dueling an empty shell.

Over the past torturous hour of slow fighting, she had attempted to engage the guardian in conversation, but no matter whether she asked questions or tried to banter, all her efforts were met with cold, unyielding silence. Danielle glanced over at the Beast, nodding once to show that she was as prepared as she was going to be—despite her trembling muscles unused to the current exertions. Opposite her, the armor moved into position with deliberate, mechanical precision, brandishing a carbon steel longsword perfectly mirroring the shape and length of her wooden weapon.

"Just get *on* with it, Enchantress," the Beast called with no small hint of annoyance. "We're getting behind schedule, and we still have spears, halberds, and flails to practice with."

Though Danielle was frustrated with the automaton's

goading, she didn't take her eyes off her opponent. "I know we're moving slowly, but that sword has to weigh twenty pounds. If I misjudge where it's swinging-"

"It's not going to hurt you. We've been over this," the impatient machine cut her off, "At the speed it's moving, unless you throw yourself against the tip of its sword, its weapon won't even break your skin if it landed."

Instead of answering, Danielle simply gave a single, sharp nod. In response, the guardian raised its weapon in a salute, signaling the start of their 'duel'.

A bead of sweat trickled down her temple and dripped down her cheek, as her opponent lifted its sword into a high guard position then pulled its blade down in a controlled swing. Danielle mirrored its movement, focusing on the sword above all else. With each move, some of her tension vanished —and soon, she was back in the flow of false combat.

As with every new position they had practiced, Danielle started by simply mimicking her opponent's actions, often finding herself just a moment behind. But as she repeated the movements a second time, then a third, her skills gradually began to guide her hand. Before long, her lightweight practice sword was slicing through the air with a mesmerizing fluidity.

What initially felt like clumsy swings swiftly evolved into precise, controlled strikes. Now that she was back in motion, Danielle no longer struggled to keep the weapon aloft; her body naturally adapted to following the optimal path for each movement. Each step, pivot, and retreat became a seamless set of motions, then a flowing routine.

Movements rapidly began to feel almost instinctive, boosting Danielle's confidence in continuing further, and soon the rhythm of the practice started to feel comfortable. "Do you think I will actually be able to pick up a sword and fight, if I find myself in a bad situation?"

"If you can find a sword that weighs two and a half pounds and will hold up against the heavier swords of stronger, experienced combatants, absolutely." The Beast's scoffing words felt like a glass of water splashed on Danielle's face, and she found herself blushing with some small embarrassment. "I'm not trying to teach you how to fight; I'm trying to make sure you are repaying my master's generosity. These exercises are meant to help refine his automatons, making them more efficient fighters if they ever need to take the field, not put *you* in a duel."

Distracted by the reminder that her movements might eventually be used in combat on a large scale caused Danielle to falter momentarily, but she shook her head and reset her position as she heaved for air. "I'll do… whatever it takes-"

"To what? Pay him for his tutelage, room, and board? Don't bother trying. You couldn't afford an hour of his time, let alone the fair market value of living in a castle-"

"No." Danielle stepped back, and her opponent did the same. She turned and glared at BST model three. "I'll do whatever it takes to keep learning and keep working to hold onto this. I can feel it. This is the opportunity that is going to take care of me and my father for the rest of our lives. When I leave here, I'm going to be able to compete with people who have been trained at the Royal Academy of Verdelune. I'll be an asset wherever I go. I'll do whatever it takes to make sure that dream becomes a reality."

Closing her eyes, she lifted her sword and moved through the form once more, each motion executed with the same care and attention to detail as a high-level calligrapher's brushstroke. Danielle felt the heft of the sword, the resistance of the air, even how her own muscles were beginning to sing a song of strain against the repeated movements.

She'd been near-exhausted half an hour ago, and was now *shaking* as she repeated the motion again and again, remembering that perfection wasn't the point—it was important to have worse-than-optimal versions of the same movements. An acrid smell of heated metal caused her eyes to pop back open, and she looked on with concern as the soldier in front of her began to smoke from its shoulder joints. "Beast? Is it supposed to be doing that?"

"Why do you ask questions to which you already know the answer? Step away from it, quickly." At the sound of the Beast's voice, the crystals around the platform began descending into the floor. The metal soldier dropped its guard, its arms swinging down and causing the sword it held to bounce off the ground repeatedly until finally coming to a stop. "Let's call that a break while I get another version in here."

Then both its arms fell off, clattering against the stone surface and causing Danielle to yelp and leap away for fear of getting her toes crushed by the heavy metal. With a gulp, she silently thanked the system that the platform had been deactivated and hadn't pushed her closer to the collapsing hunk of scrap. "Yeah. A break sounds good."

The Beast's cables carried him to the platform, and he quickly scooped up the fallen pieces of the metal soldier. To Danielle's surprise, he didn't immediately cast the broken parts aside, instead laying the damaged automaton out on a nearby workbench. His massive hands *unfolded* into an extensive set of tools, which each moved independently of each other, and he lowered them onto the fallen machine.

Even though her body was barely able to muster the energy to cross the distance between them, her mind was absolutely burning with interest. The Enchantress hurried over, eager for a chance to watch artificing in action. The Beast had pulled the torso of the soldier apart in moments and was already removing damaged sections along the joints as she stepped up alongside him.

Rusted, stripped gears were pulled and cast aside. From the joints, down the arms, and even into the chest cavity, the Beast continued to pull damaged shards of metal, remaining silent even as the work continued far longer than Danielle had expected it to take. Appalled at how much effort was necessary for this process, Danielle finally blurted out, "How long has it been since some basic routine maintenance was done on this poor guy?"

"Though it's none of your *business*..." the Beast replied calmly, earning an eye-roll for his trouble. "This is the first time since the end of the war that Comte LeKrout has reactivated one of his metal soldiers. Effectively, it has been ten and three-quarters of a year since these were in use."

"It shows," Danielle muttered as she moved in closer to examine the design. There was no disparagement in her voice. Frankly, she felt a hint of relief that the uncaring, featureless creature wasn't out waging war against neighboring kingdoms. "How many of these did he have going at once? They must have been terrifying on the battlefield."

"At the height of the war, LeKrout had just over fifty thousand metal soldiers marching at once," the Beast replied after a moment of consideration, sneaking a glance over to capture her reaction to his words. "There were certainly pros and cons to the use of them. First, though they never tired, they needed regular routine maintenance, due to overuse. Happily, the maintenance was able to be performed by nearly anyone with a mechanical bent."

Danielle started to have a bad feeling about where the conversation was leading, "So many...? So you actually know for a *fact* that anyone with a mechanical skill can assemble these? Because you had *actually* scooped them all up."

"Indeed." The Beast solemnly nodded, never once slowing in his efforts. "The expense in metal alone was the tipping point to begin the war against Verdelune's northern neighbor, which you would now know as simply a vassal state. Their production of high-quality iron was necessary simply to produce such a force. Yet, nearly any well-trained soldier was a match for any five of these."

The Beast trailed off, focused on extracting a particularly

stubborn metal shard which had embedded itself in the outer casing of the soldier. Once the piece was free, he returned to explaining, "Although they are exceedingly dangerous in large numbers, as you've noticed by now, they don't have the same range of motion as regular soldiers. They don't have classes or skills to empower them beyond their physical form. Against elites, they were nearly useless."

There was a lull in the conversation as the Beast pulled out a rough circle of metal and began to spin it at high speed, lowering it into the chassis and using it to grind away at a metal shaft that had fused to the mechanisms in the soldier's shoulder.

"Even so, against the common militiaman, conscripts pulled from farms and a softer life, they were a scythe reaping wheat."

Danielle blanched as she realized the strategy her kingdom must have employed. "Which would allow Verdelune's highly trained soldiers to focus exclusively on the elites, even while *they* needed to try and push back the wave of metal cutting toward them. It must have been quite… *effective*. Why did Artificer LeKrout stop making them and step back from the war? If he was able to field so many combatants, the kingdom must have sang his praises at every opportunity."

"They did," the Beast replied shortly. "However, that is not my story to tell."

So saying, he stepped back and moved to the side of the room, where bins of spare parts were stacked. Selecting a large box, he brought the entire package over and began unfolding it. Sealed away within were shining gears and mechanisms, pristine versions of what was currently piled alongside the fallen soldier. Most surprising to Danielle was the large diagram attached to the inside of the box.

She pulled it off, her eyebrows raising as she found a step-by-step guide to assembling one of the soldiers.

"You must have had *hundreds* of people tasked with

constructing these for the war." Her words came out slowly as she thought over what sort of logistical issues they must have been working to overcome with so many activated automatons. "How was he able to decommission all of them? Or... was he even *able* to stop them?"

"As you've seen for yourself," the Beast rumbled at her, clearly becoming agitated at this line of questioning, "There is more to their function than the mechanisms alone. The rune-scripted core is a marvel created by Comte LeKrout, and he *alone* understands the inner workings. Without his insights and willing participation, it would be nearly impossible for someone else to use his designs. If they wanted to recreate the system, they would need to do so from the very first etching. All attempts to recreate his work have been met with failure, which is why Verdelune is actively pursuing his return to the war effort."

As the Beast began assembling bits and pieces into the soldier, Danielle read over the diagram, slowly shaking her head as she went farther and farther. As she scanned the last image, she scoffed and scathingly muttered, "Minimum viable product..."

Pulling out her notebook, she started drawing out her own design, based on the decades-old version. The current schematic was extremely simplistic, *barely* meeting the requirements to cause each joint to articulate, for each limb to have enough torque and energy to move. As she worked, Danielle muttered her thoughts aloud, "We need to account for the sword, as well... I'm willing to bet these fighters fall over at least once in every ten swings. They're too top heavy, so without a proper counterbalance..."

Halfway through her redesign, she paused, stumped and frustrated. There was just some information she didn't have yet, some knowledge of materials and tensile strength—not to mention what was actually *available* here—which prevented her from finishing out the design. Reluctantly, she closed her notebook and looked up, only to find that the Beast had been watching what she was writing… and his eyes were glowing a deep red.

"That looked extremely promising. Why did you stop?" The Artificer spoke through the Beast, his voice as gentle as the mechanical rumblings would allow. "That wouldn't have worked for mass production, but it's along the lines of what I'd want for my personal houseguard. Would you like to finish it, or…?"

Danielle brightened up immediately at the offer. "Yes! But, I need some help. Could you explain to me why the crankshaft is positioned at a thirty-seven-degree angle instead of…"

Her questions and his answers ricocheted back and forth, with the Enchantress writing out her suppositions and the Artificer pointing out flaws or intriguing possibilities. Before Sneezy could demand that Danielle come to the dining room and eat her dinner—at least before his *third* demand—they had worked out an initial prototype. She looked at the complex design, completely enamored with the idea of 'hydraulics' that had just been explained to her.

"Is that why you have so many hoses installed across the Beast's frame?" Danielle turned to scan the titan of metal, her eyes locking on the numerous dangling tubes. "Why wouldn't you encase that in an exoskeleton of some kind? Armor? Wouldn't someone cutting through those make it lose much of its functionality?"

Hesitation turned into a drawn-out sigh, and finally the Artificer answered her question. "Unfortunately, at the moment, I am unable to continue working on the BST model three. I am… otherwise precluded from adjusting its setup, as I am entirely focused on another project. I can't leave my current workspace without severe risk to what I'm working on, and the Beast is the only one of my automatons I can remotely interface with to this extent."

"Oh… that's…" Danielle trailed up, uncertain what she

could say that he wouldn't already know. "If there's anything I can do to help...?"

"There is *one* thing I've been wondering." The Beast's hand dipped down, cradling the metal soldier's head and lifting the machine into a sitting position. "Could you *please* explain why you etched a face into this helmet?"

Looking at the goofy caricature of a face she'd brushed into the metal while the Beast had been stripping it down and reassembling it startled a laugh out of Danielle, and it took her a moment to regain her composure.

Then she nodded seriously, though her twitching smile took away from her attempt at sincerity. "Yes. It was very creepy. Trying to copy this thing's movements while it was faceless and blank is just... harder without something to focus on. This will help me mimic it a little better, and I'm *sure* I'll be able to mimic its fighting style more easily."

"You drew two eyes, a triangular nose, and a mouth with a tongue sticking out of the side," the Artificer pointed out incredulously. "*That's* going to make it easier for you to replicate its combat style? Do you expect me to believe that?"

"Absolutely I do." Danielle bobbed her head without cracking a smile.

The red eyes studied her for a moment longer before yet another sigh came from the entity. "I don't know why I believe you, but somehow I do. Carry on with your strange choices."

Danielle yelped as her left arm blazed with light, her gaze drawn to the system notification beginning to scrawl across her skin. "You're kidding me...! You actually took that seriously?"

"Of course I did." The Artificer looked at her in confusion as she read over the updated information of her skill. "While I much prefer tried and true methods, and worry that changing them could disrupt the balance I've worked so hard to achieve, I'm open to embracing new methods when you can explain their merit and *prove* it. Yet, I find myself confused as to how that ended up increasing one of your skill levels?"

"I needed to convince someone to embrace a new concept they were skeptical of without providing them any factual evidence," Danielle distractedly explained to him. "I hadn't expected a silly little *doodle* to be the tipping point."

Skill increase! Unified Radiance [Level 5 (Moderate) → Level 6 (Considerable)]!
Requirement to advance to level 7: Restore a severely neglected outdoor area in such a way that it becomes a sought after spot of tranquility for the owner of the land OR successfully change the opinion of a highly influential individual about a deeply held belief during a presentation of something you created or altered by at least 80% of its original design.

"Huh," she muttered as she tried to decide how she'd go about achieving her next level. Danielle paused when she realized she was *excited* to make progress—she'd only been here a short while, and already she was ten times as comfortable in her own skin as she had been surrounded by dozens of people attempting to ply her with compliments.

Turning to the Artificer, she showed a crooked smile, "Any chance you have a particular patch of grass outside that you want to look extra green? I know how much you love your grass."

CHAPTER
SIXTEEN

As Danielle stepped off the platform and into the vast subterranean workshop the next day, she was shocked to find the Beast meticulously adjusting the final details of a new automaton. At first glance, the sleek design looked almost exactly like a normal human—if that person's skin had been cast from gleaming metal. "Is that what I think it is?"

"If you think it is the finalized prototype of the updated design you had a *tiny* part in creating with the Comte yesterday, you would be correct." The Beast's voice rumbled through the room, only barely and begrudgingly acknowledging her contributions.

Even with how much it seemed to pain the Beast, there was a hint of respect in his tone that hadn't been there the last time they spoke. Danielle's smile turned to a playful smirk as the machine studiously avoided looking at her. "Are you upset because you know his work can be improved upon, or is it just me you do not particularly like? No… it's more than that, isn't it? I think it bothers you to learn, *gasp,* the Comte is only human and therefore *fallible!*"

"He is n-" The Beast cut off his heated reply, stepping back and motioning for her to come closer to the new machine. As she waited for him to put his thoughts in order, Danielle swept her gaze across the metal man laying on the workbench. The design was flawless, perfectly smooth, but she was already able to see issues she would change if she had the option. Finally, the Beast tried speaking again, only to practically stutter as he attempted to relay his instructions. "You… I am—*gahh*. Before installing the core, my master has instructed me to… to…"

Sensing the machine's reluctance, but uncertain as to where the Beast was going with this line of conversation, Danielle could only wait impatiently for the machine to growl out his instructions. As the moment stretched, the Beast finally released a huff of steam as its internal components clicked furiously, as if physically gathering his resolve. Words came in a rush of humidity and mortification. "He wants you to *draw* on it."

"You don't mean to say he's thinking about having his oh-so-functional things be… *pretty*?" Danielle gasped while dramatically covering her mouth with her hands. "*Scandalous!*"

"Please wear the motion capture suit, so we can replicate your artistic process." The Beast practically powered down as the instructions escaped him, not even twitching as Danielle chipperly acquiesced and put on the suit.

The Enchantress stepped out of the small changing booth and put her hands on her hips, cocking her head slightly to the side. After waiting nearly a full minute for additional instruction, but only seeing the blue crystalline eyes dim further, Danielle let out a gentle scoff, which turned into a chuckle at the enormous machine's petulance. "Your discomfort is endearing, Beast. I'll just start doodling on this friendly mannequin. Sound good?"

The only response was a soft shriek of tortured metal as the Beast's enormous hand *crunched* down on a tool he was holding. Deciding not to push him any further—for her personal health—Danielle reached for a bucket of files, wire brushes, chisels, and other carefully crafted tools meant for creating divots and impressions on metal which had clearly been for this express purpose.

Putting the grumpy Beast out of her mind, the Enchantress gathered her thoughts and carefully viewed the entire outer shell of the machine. Lifting a thin metal scalpel, she used the sharp edge to cut a hair-thin design in the metal, treating the implement as she would a pencil on paper. Once she had a sketch of a face to go off of, she moved along the blocky torso, moving out to add impressions where she would later add fine details, such as a curve of muscle or fingernails on the tubes of metal which currently served as the creature's fingers.

The automaton's metal skin came alive with intricate designs and patterns, each pull of a blade or brush adding depth, texture, and character. As she worked, Danielle realized that her movements with the tools were smoother and more deliberate than she had been expecting. After a moment, her eyes went wide with understanding. "Now would you look at that? My fingers are longer than I remember. It's not *uncomfortable*, but... let me..."

She tossed the scalpel into the bucket, then reached in and easily pinched it without looking, pulling it out without snagging anything on the way. "Yep... more dexterous. I wonder... my skill tells me I will be impacted by the aesthetics of the five people I spend the most time with. If I'm not spending any time with any other humans, does that mean I'm shifting because of my own desires, or because this is what my digits would look like without interference?"

A *hiss* of escaping steam pulled her attention back to the BST model three, which was vibrating in place slightly. Raising her eyebrow, Danielle carefully put the scalpel on the table and turned to face the entity. "Do you have something you need to say?"

"*No*," came the sharp reply. "I'm just concerned with how

much damage you are doing to this frame. Every imperfection means another place that might crumple under the blow of an opponent on the battlefield."

Danielle could only shrug, turning around and reaching for the bucket of tools once more. Only then did additional dialogue follow the snippy answer. "I find this entire process unpalatable. Function is paramount. It is imperative to be able to recreate the design multiple times. Fine detail work serves no greater purpose. It simply slows the entire assemblage and reduces the number of protectors which surround the Comte."

"If I understand correctly," Danielle chose her words as carefully as she had used the scalpel to cut into the prototype, "You aren't against beautification as a concept, but because you think it will have a negative impact on your creator? He must be a very good man to inspire such devotion from his children. Or, he is a *superb* runescripter for his creations."

"*Pahhh.*" The derisive noise was extended by a venting of steam. "I challenge *anyone* to capture the concept of *loyalty* in a rune. We cannot actively hurt our creator or work against him. That does not mean we are forced to *like* him."

"Well…" Danielle quietly listened while she rasped away at the soldier with a large file, adding texture to the metal face she was working on. "If he cannot create loyalty, that only leaves my true argument, doesn't it? What has he done to make you like him, child of the Comte? I'd love to hear more about that."

"No."

Though she rolled her eyes at his sheer petulance, Danielle didn't press further, simply deciding to pay undivided attention to her work. Each movement was purposeful, her skills keeping her from missing her mark, allowing her to move at a speed that would be reckless for almost anyone else.

Though she was no master artist, she had crafted toys for *years*. Adding details to metal soldiers which would captivate children was hardly different from this process: an attempt at capturing the essence of a grizzled veteran. As a point of fact, having a much larger surface to work on made the process faster and far easier.

As Danielle moved from one planned section to the next, she began explaining her thought process to the Beast, who continued to glower at her while keeping his silence. "Adding texture to its hands, feet, and knees will allow this guardian to maintain its grip on things it grabs, its footing on slippery surfaces, and stand up easier if it falls over. The crosshatching across the entire surface will make it easier to spot damaged sections, whether it be from the wear of time or battle."

The Enchantress paused in recounting her train of thought as she pulled out a thin chisel for some fine detail work around the eyes she'd just sketched out. "It will also *hide* minor scratches and signs of wear and tear that aren't important enough to fix. On a different note, adding in a false face will give people fighting against it an impression that destroying its head will render the creation unable to function. It may cause them to let down their guard, receiving a lethal wound for their carelessness."

She turned to the Beast, wearing an expression as serious and stoic as she had ever shown. "All of this to say, we are not just making this 'pretty' for the sake of it. We're integrating function and form to create a machine capable of doing more than simply chopping away at an enemy. It will confuse them, lull them into false senses of security, and be more effective than a more basic version where all the internals and mechanisms are the exact same. Now, I can't bend these parts myself. Help me create some 'muscle' shapes here, here, and here."

Over the next few hours, Danielle lost herself in her work, with the Beast silently assisting her as she went. The room was filled with the rhythmic sounds of metal being shaped, tapped, and scraped… punctuated at irregular intervals by a *hiss* of steam coming from the Beast—a sigh of annoyance if Danielle had ever heard one.

Once the portions of the creation which were meant to show muscles had been completed, she turned her attention to the standard-armor shapes of the breastplate and greaves. There she added swirls, geometric patterns, and even the sigil of House LeKrout she'd noticed on the few ornate objects scattered within the manor. When she finally decided she was done, the prototype truly looked like a human who had been transformed into metal while wearing ornamental armor.

Wiping away a thin film of sweat threatening her eyes, Danielle studied her work and allowed herself to feel a rush of satisfaction. "Finished. What do you think?"

Even as she looked at the lifeless automaton, her skills subtly adjusted the final product of her rapid art. The muscles became ever so slightly more defined, scratches on the face began to look more like a five o'clock shadow of beard hair, and the eyes took on a sharp, piercing quality. Danielle watched as the changes were made at a speed visible to the naked eye, feeling as one of her skills began thrumming with a density of power she hadn't felt since she'd arrived.

Frowning ever so slightly, she looked at her arms and noticed a slight increase in her muscle tone. "Why would Resplendent Reflected Self-?"

"It's *exquisite.*" The change from annoyed to impressed was accompanied by a shift in eye color—from blue to red—as the Artificer arrived within the Beast to see the final product. A soft *hiss* sounded out, not of steam, but a sealed compartment opening. The Beast's body quickly floated over to the mostly-repaired metal soldier which had fallen the day before, retrieving a glowing cube of metal which coated in swirling words that wrote themselves out, then vanished, over and again. "All that's left to do is see the difference with our own eyes."

"That looks like the writing of the system, when I look at

the status on my arm." Even with as curious as she was, Danielle couldn't help but recoil from the sheer power of the system energy roiling off the tiny cube.

"That's exactly what runescripting is. Understanding and writing the language of the system itself." Once more, the hands of the Beast transformed into a set of functional tools, quickly prying open the lifeless chest of the detailed automaton Danielle had been working on. With careful motions, he slotted the glowing cube into a compartment before quickly pressing it closed.

It sealed with a flash, and the mechanisms of the soldier began to shift and hum to life. Gears spun, pistons began moving, and the soldier's fingers *twitched*. The open chest plate smoothly closed, and finally... the soldier sat up. Though it moved with far less resistance than its previous rusty and damaged body had been able to manage, Danielle felt a moment of panic and dissatisfaction when she saw no clear signs of instant improvement, compared to the previous model. "It's still moving as if it was in its old body. Was it worth-"

"This is *exactly* what I'd hoped for." The tone of the Artificer's voice was hard to determine, as it needed to escape the rumbling machinery. Even so, Danielle easily picked up on the fact that he was completely sincere—and deeply invested in what he was seeing. "I'll update its runes with the updated motion capture from today and let it practice until tomorrow. But already, I can see numerous improvements. Look here... its grip on the sword is only seventy percent as tight, allowing for that excess energy to be used in other areas as needed. Its stance is well-balanced. Swing, soldier."

The automaton went through several of the sword forms Danielle had been taught the previous day, and even *she* was able to see that the motions were less... comical. Not that a deadly machine swinging dozens of pounds of sharpened metal around was ever truly *funny*, but there was a clear shift toward actual skillfulness.

The Artificer mumbled, deep in thought, "Yes... it seems that form actually can enhance function, though I'm not completely convinced on the embellishments yet. Still, your comments about a false face were intriguing, and I am interested in seeing how that plays out."

"Form factor." Danielle had been only half listening to the Artificer as he spoke, and the words she said caused him to look away from the automaton and give her his full attention. "That's what we should call it. The size, shape, and physical components, combining function with the design and overall look of the thing. I'm willing to bet heavily that this well-designed form is going to not only meet *every* expectation you have for your standard work but exceed it in ways we don't know yet."

"I'm looking forward to you being proven correct."

Although they hadn't engaged in the usual motion capture routine they had settled into over the last few days, the entirety of the morning had already been eaten up with the reworking of the metal soldier. After a gentle dismissal from the workshop so the Artificer could continue with some secretive portion of his work, Danielle found herself slowly ascending the stairs, disappointed that she wasn't going to be included in the mysterious, *magical* portion of adjusting the automaton's core.

Even the thought of returning to the library and getting ahead in her reading wasn't enough to cheer her up. When she finally got to the top of the stairs, Danielle smacked her hands to her cheeks and tried to shake off the negative feelings. "No, this is good! I haven't had free time since I got access to the library. At least, not time I haven't filled with study and work. I'm doing something *new* today!"

Over the next few moments, her smile faded a bit as she tried to think of anything else to do, only to remember she was not allowed access to the majority of the building. There were no other forms of entertainment or people to sit and have a conversation with. "Nothing to do, beyond study. Or, I guess I could stand out here and slowly go insane by staring at white walls stretching on as far as the eye can... that's it!"

After a few inquiries, which were distractedly approved by the Artificer, Danielle soon had dozens of cans of paint being delivered to her by a stream of household utility-automatons. Grabbing a brush, she selected warm, inviting colors, and began painting on the wall directly opposite to the door into her bedroom. "I'm sick of the first thing I see in the morning being a cold, sterile wall! We're going to breathe some *life* into this mansion!"

"Madame, may I please politely inquire as to why you are defacing the Comte's building?" Doc interrupted after she had been fiercely swiping her brush over the wall for a few minutes. "We will be tasked with cleaning it up, and these paints are not water-soluble. Someone will pick me up and use the side of my body to scrape it off before repainting the wall to a neutral white. It's not a *pleasant* experience for me, so I would appreciate knowing you started this endeavor with plenty of forethought."

"The Artificer himself approved this project." Danielle didn't bother looking away from the splotches of paint she was adding to her picture. If she had, she would have seen the automaton immediately relaxing.

"I see. In that case, is there anything we can do to assist, or should we just keep your paint supplies well-stocked?"

"No..." Danielle's reflexive denial faded even as she voiced it, and she slowly turned to consider the guard. "Hold on. If *you* were going to draw on the walls, what would you put on here?"

"I am not equipped to draw on the walls."

"But if you were?" Danielle patiently persisted.

The razor-edged guard went quiet for a few moments,

only the high-pitched hum of tiny gears spinning showing it hadn't lost power. "I suppose I would put together geometric patterns originating from a central point. Perhaps hexagons held in place with straight lines?"

"Like this?" Danielle quickly sketched out a recreation of Doc's words, stepping back and considering it when she was done. "Huh, looks kind of like a spider web?"

"Oh, *yes*." Doc stepped forward, gleaning in the bright light of the hallway. "Spiders are so very interesting, aren't they? So tiny, almost unnoticeable normally, but as soon as someone sees one, it's all they can think about. They never look away or forget where they saw it last."

"Everything okay there, Doc?" Danielle's soft chuckle was only met with silence, the machine simply staring at the wall. After a few moments of waiting, the Enchantress turned toward Sneezy, "How about you-"

"Massive fires." The machine unhesitantly responded without waiting for her to finish the question. "Forest fires, exploding volcanoes, birthday candles… you know. Anything like that."

"Want to give it a try, Sneezy?" She motioned at several paint cans set to the side, oranges, yellows, and reds. "Actually, let's make a game of this. Why don't you see how many of your friends you can get in here, and let's start painting the entire hallway."

"What's the game?" Doc finally turned away from the simple painting Danielle had etched on the wall.

The edges of Danielle's lips curled up as she let out a mischievous chuckle. "I want to see how much of the hallway we can get painted before the Beast notices."

CHAPTER
SEVENTEEN

AFTER NEARLY A SOLID week of being allowed to pursue her own proclivities, not once being called back to motion capture or be a part of the artificing process, Danielle was starting to get on edge. Though it turned her stomach, she needed to have contact with the Artificer in order to make progress with his recruitment—even if actually following through was only a backup plan if every other attempt to rescue her father failed.

Touching an oversized paper, she walked down the stairs into the subterranean workshop, nervous mainly because she was coming here uninvited for the first time. "Hello? Beast? I have a new design I wanted to run by you, and while I'm here... maybe we could talk?"

Compared to each of her previous visits, the underground workshop was very dark, only partially lit by an assortment of shining crystals evenly spaced along the ceiling. Even so, the stark white walls and floor allowed the low amount of light to reflect off every surface and provide her with the means to avoid running into objects. As she descended, she continuously called out, trying not to overstep the restrictions that had been placed on her.

"I'm really not trying to intrude! I just haven't seen you in a week, Beast! I'm not sure what you've been up to…" Her eyes were drawn to the enormous curtain stretched across the room. As the silence stretched, for a few long moments, Danielle seriously considered taking just a little peeky-peek at what was behind it. Still on the stairs, she hesitated about descending any further; "Don't do it. I know myself well enough to know that my curiosity would push me to look. If I don't get any closer, the temptation will fade. Right?"

While she deliberated, her choice was made for her. The light in the room shifted from a soft blue white to a concerning flashing red. A bell started clanging, and Danielle sprinted up the stairs, shouting her apologies as she went. Yet, as she burst into the great hall, she noticed dozens of clunky guardians streaming toward the exits. "Wait, they're not after me? What's happening?"

"Madame Danielle! *There* you are!" Sneezy's nasally voice was filled with relief, "Did you not notice Duke wasn't following you? We could be decommissioned for being unable to keep track of our charge. Please don't put us at risk like this."

"Sneezy!" Danielle let out a sigh of relief at the site of the familiar face. "I'd give you a hug, but I don't think I could get my arms around you. What's going on?"

"There's an intruder; you need to come with me-"

The huge doors at the end of the hallway were suddenly thrown open, sending a half-dozen guardian automatons reeling. Silhouetted in the doorway was a man in heavy armor, who paused for only a split second before striding into the entryway with clear purpose. Panic surged through Danielle as she looked over the gleaming sword casually held in one hand, the firm set of the unknown man's jaw… and the way his eyes locked on her.

"Gasteel Company?" Danielle's thoughts escaped her mouth as a squeak, and she stumbled backward, hand reaching for the door to the stairwell. "I can't let them-"

Suddenly, the lights returned to normal, the clanging bell silenced, and all of the guards that had been taking attack positions settled. Most notably, the intruder stopped as well, standing straight and waiting patiently. The sudden lack of sensory input had Danielle looking back and forth, trying to figure out what was happening, only for an echoing, metallic laugh to fill the air.

She whipped around, only to find the Beast descending from the shadows of the ceiling.

"I *got* you! That's what you *get*. Painting along the entire hallway inside the house? Don't think I didn't find what you were doing outside, either! Haa... that was worth whatever punishment my lord will choose to lay on me. I had my doubts, but it seems you and my master were correct. The realistic appearance and fluidity of motion adds an *entirely* new dimension of intimidation."

In the ensuing silence, Danielle struggled to contain her emotions, so as to somewhat temper her reaction. Chiefly among her thoughts was relief that this 'intruder' wasn't actually a threat. Even so, that initial solace was followed by a *wellspring* of indignation that the Beast would cause her such distress. Squeezing her hands to try and stop them from shaking, she wordlessly glared at the Beast, who simply remained in place waiting for her to say something. Eventually, the moment stretched too far, and the automaton spoke from sheer irritation.

"Why are you not impressed with how realistic he looks?" The Beast fully settled on the floor, its eyes shining brighter as he watched the Comte's guest. "*Days* were spent putting together a compound which would work to mimic natural skin. Do you have any idea how much effort it takes to create functioning eyes without causing them to shine with an inner light? Well? Say something. Your silence *irks* me."

"Beast," Danielle finally managed after taking a deep, shuddering breath, "Had it occurred to you, even slightly, how absolutely *terrifying* the prospect of Gasteel Company raiding this estate and dragging me back to wed the baron is? How swiftly I can be thrown into a comfortable room, never again to read interesting books or create something that could be of use to the world? You played a *cruel* prank by using one of my greatest fears against me."

"Preposterous. If they crossed into the estate without permission, they would be breaking the agreement the Comte made with the crown. That would set him loose to aid their enemies. It will never happen, so you have no reason to react so negatively." The Beast paused—perhaps slightly uncertainly—as he waited for her to understand his points and therefore be excited over the realism of the creation. "Are you not *pleased* with the final product?"

Instead of answering, Danielle simply dropped the paper she was still clutching, returning to her room without a backward glance. Though Sneezy followed her, she turned and *firmly* closed the door without allowing him entry, calling through the barrier in a heated tone, "This is the first time I've truly seen you as a *beast*."

"*You* were the one who painted the walls without permission!"

After the Beast's parting comment, no one attempted to enter the room or even interrupt her as she seethed; though Duke scootched closer and offered his cushion for emotional support. Mealtimes passed without interruption, but she didn't once step out of her space, instead focusing her energy into angrily reading over her notebook, trying to see areas she could improve without needing to face the Beast and his casual dismissal.

It was only the following morning when a soft knock on the door pulled Danielle from her slumber.

Opening the door as she rubbed the sleep from her eyes, she froze upon realizing her visitor wasn't one of her normal friendly guardians. Her hands dropped to her side, and her lips pressed into a firm line as she stared up at the towering form of BST model three. "What do you want, *Beast?*"

The entity's hand swung out to the side, wrapping around something out of her line of sight. A moment later, a tall, gleaming machine which she easily recognized as the design she'd been attempting to show the Artificer the previous day was deposited on the ground. As she looked over the flawless craftsmanship, which had perfectly captured her sketches, she glanced up at the silent Beast, raising an eyebrow and speaking in a clipped tone.

"You made this? It wasn't the Artificer trying to fix your mistakes?"

"I fully generated the construct." The Beast let out a long hiss of steam. "My lord was… quite displeased with my actions."

After waiting a heartbeat for him to say anything else, Danielle archly inquired, "Is that why you went to all this trouble? Because *he* was upset with you?"

"I will admit," the Beast turned to the prototype and pulled open its chest cavity as he spoke, "It has been quite a long time since I have had to take the concerns of others into account as I performed my duties. It is… let us say, *possible* that my initial test run was not conducive to a continuing beneficial working relationship between us."

"All of that to say…" Danielle leadingly stated, refusing to let him off the hook for his actions—not even looking at the enticing, gleaming display the Beast was trying to distract her with.

"Look at this exquisite craftmanship…!" Steam erupted from the Beast in no less than three locations, and its eyes dimmed significantly when she started closing the door. "Fine, *fine!* Don't starve yourself to death because I chose a suboptimal option. I… apologize. It will not be an action I repeat."

"Thank you, Beast." Danielle slowly reopened the door. "I'll let it go. *Once.* Now, as much as I'd love to look at the peace offering you brought me, breakfast is calling. Just so you know, an apology would have sufficed, but... I *am* excited to see this."

She walked past the mechanical entity, who simply remained standing in place for a long few moments before scooping up the metal object and following after her. "The Comte was quite pleased that he didn't need to come back and redo this design on his own. Based on this model, he has given me permission to grant you access to *three* new guardian designs. If you wish to practice on them, we will manufacture and add in the runescript on our end. Additional house guardians are always welcome."

Only his final comment incited Danielle to show a reaction. Her steps slowed slightly, and she cocked her head as she looked back at the Beast floating along as he followed behind. "What do you mean *additional* guardians? I wanted this to be a new housing for Sneezy. Even with the detailing I've done to clean out his rust and dust, he's practically on his last legs. His canister has *soft* spots, for system's sake! He's at risk of bursting if he takes the slightest tumble."

"Then he should be decommissioned-"

"Even the Comte told me he didn't like decommissioning his guards who'd been around for a long time." Danielle cut off the interruption with a sharp motion of her hand. "Sneezy is fun and absolutely dedicated, so why wouldn't you reward that instead of throwing him away? He's already a quality *person*, losing that over mere quantity of guards sounds completely reckless."

"Quality over quantity, you say?" The Beast appeared taken aback, but at the same time, didn't sound as if he hated the idea. "Even a week ago, I would have dismissed your comment outright. Still... as much as the prank I played on you yesterday was perhaps slightly out of line-"

"*Perhaps*? No, wait, *slightly*?"

He continued as though she hadn't interrupted him, "-it

did highlight the significant advantage such an upgrade could bring to bear. How about a compromise? An upgrade for the guards who merit it, followed by blank cores being added to future iterations."

"How will you determine who 'merits' it?" Danielle felt her anger melting away as they devolved into a deep conversation on the noticeable changes certain guards had after a long period of time. According to the Beast, only rarely did they develop past their initial design, and usually when they did so, it was in a negative manner.

Swamped in the details, Danielle barely tasted her meal, though she was decidedly hungry after missing several meals. "Why is this such a concern? Shouldn't you be able to exchange one core for another without any issue?"

"Yes... and very much no." It seemed the Beast was uncertain how much information he should reveal, but eventually caved and told her the bare minimum. "Runes, as I know you now understand, are system symbology that contain a fundamental understanding of a concept. By using a blank core—no personality or memories—we are assured that the script connecting the core to the body of the automaton will integrate correctly. You see, in past attempts at moving a favored creation to a new housing, even a perfect replica sometimes caused issues. It's a problem the Comte has looked into in the past, but there was no clear rhyme or reason for the failure."

"Really? It seems pretty obvious to me." Danielle popped a fried potato into her mouth and chewed in silent contemplation as the Beast reeled from her casual statement. A low *hiss* of steam permeated the air, and she rolled her eyes as she began to explain. "Don't blow a gasket, Beast. This is what I was talking about when I first arrived. Other people might have perspectives you just *don't*. Tell me this, when there was a mismatch, what did Comte LeKrout do to fix it?"

"He *didn't*," the Beast explained to her slowly, as though *she* were the one not noticing what was obvious. "Per my previous statement, there was no obvious explanation for the mismatch. He instead replaced the internal mechanisms and returned the core to its original housing."

"What he should have done…" Danielle drew her words out, only then realizing that she had *perhaps* not fully forgiven the Beast. Her smirk shifted slightly as she realized she was edging too far into petty retaliation. Taking a deep breath, she gave a clear explanation instead of dancing around the subject any further.

"If a core is essentially the mind of the automatons, and they change and grow over time in unexpected ways, doesn't that mean the runes themselves will change over time? If the Artificer isn't accounting for those shifts, of *course* the integration between a new body and its current mind won't work."

For a brief moment, the crystal eyes of the Beast blazed with red light.

EIGHTEEN

"CALLING THE CORE THE 'MIND' of the automatons is a bit of an oversimplification, but it's close enough that the lord of the house is shifting some of his priorities to study the potential of your hypothesis." Danielle took the information the Beast was saying in stride, knowing it was practically *shaking* with excitement on behalf of the Comte. "As a reward for the potential new avenue of research, he has invited you to be a part of the scripting process for Sn-three-zy's upgrade."

They had descended into the basement workshop, and the Beast was bodily lifting and shoving huge mechanical apparatuses into position as he spoke. Danielle looked over at the silent form of her guards and had a concerning realization. "Sneezy... do you even want a new body?"

"It doesn't get a *say*," the Beast thundered with sudden annoyance. "It's creator is offering him an opportunity to become more than it was-"

"*He* needs to be a part of the process." Danielle had to shout to be heard over the Beast's booming voice. "Have you ever considered that part of the reason previous attempts have failed—unless you are using a mindless drone like the metal soldier was—is because the core didn't *want* to be moved?"

"Of course not! That would be like saying *you* didn't want to perfect your physical form," the Beast replied indifferently.

"That's *literally* the issue that brought me here. I *didn't*," Danielle stated quietly, causing the manic motions of the Beast to slow. "I fought against my current class and my skills with everything I had... until I got here. It was *only* in the last weeks that I realized they could be used for the goals I have for my life as well. What if your little brothers and sisters are fighting against this just as much as I did, just quietly, out of fear of being decommissioned?"

"*This* again?" A deep, rumbling growl escaped the Beast as it whirled around to stare at the still-silent flamethrower guard. "Well? Out with it! Are you going to get this upgrade, becoming the foundational entry point of this new line of research, or are you-"

Danielle stepped in between the two of them, balling her fists as she glared at the Beast. "That is *not* a question. That's nothing more than extortion, and will have the opposite effect you are attempting."

"How do *you* know?"

"Because I-" Danielle blinked rapidly, only then realizing she had no logical reason to make this claim. She'd read books on how people thought but had actively gone out of her way to avoid interacting with them as she grew older and more altered by the system. Her eyes widened as something *clicked* in her mind.

"Oh. It's my Aura of Refinement and Unified Radiance. Both of them enhance my 'charm'. What is charm, beyond the bounds of simple beauty? Couldn't it be thought of as the ability to understand how people want to be treated and then *doing* so? What word do people love more than their own name? What do they want to talk about, other than their own interests? Huh."

Shaking off the attempt of her mind to follow that path down a rabbit hole, she turned to Sneezy and sank to a knee to be at face level. "*Is* this something you actually want? If you don't, I'll fight him bare-knuckled if that's what's needed to make him stop bothering you."

She held up her fists and flexed her thin arms, showing an amount of toned muscle which surprised even herself. Before she could become too concerned with how rapidly she was changing under the effects of her Resplendent Reflected Self skill, Sneezy reached forward with one of his over-elongated arms and patted her on the shoulder as gently as his jerky motions could allow.

"Your concern is pleasant, but unnecessary. BST model three correctly captured my own thoughts on the situation." Sneezy stepped around Danielle and up onto the large workbench where the Beast was finishing the placement of various implements. "On the path to Perfection, all avenues must be explored!"

As the machine sat down with a *thud* and bounced slightly—having no shocks installed to reduce the impact of the motion—it said something that put a gentle smile on Danielle's face. "Between the progress of my master, the workmanship of the Beast, and the sheer amount of care put into this design by you, Madame... I'm sure I will succeed where others have failed."

Then the automaton flopped back, with each of its enclosed spaces popping open and allowing for easy access. The Beast glanced over at the extended display only momentarily before turning his attention back to the prototype. After everything was in place, he reached for a long, thin stylus... and went perfectly still as his eyes shifted to pure red.

"Enchantress?" The almost imperceptibly softer tone of the Artificer came through, and when Danielle made a noise of acknowledgment, its entire frame flinched. "Ah. That's exactly what I was worried about. In his excitement to move this process along, the Beast forgot *yet again* the danger this process poses to us fleshy humans. He was supposed to invite you to see the final design before the core was placed but forgot that there are incredibly dangerous side effects which could occur if you watched me write out runes without a proper grasp of their underlying concepts."

He made some slight adjustments to how the tools were arranged, seemingly gathering his thoughts. "There are many reasons my work hasn't been replicated by another. Chiefly among them is the immense risk of an instant onset of insanity or catatonia. Witnessing the language of the system itself be written into the world can make you sink into your own mind, almost always temporarily, but sometimes all too permanently."

"You mean to tell me that, for even the most simplistic of your creations, *you've* always been the one to do the work?" Danielle's eyes flashed as she thought back on some of her previous conversations. "But the Beast said at the height of the war there were over fifty thousand soldiers active at any given time. How could you have possibly created all of those on your own? You would have died of exhaustion, or... old age? How old are you?"

"*Ha*! Now, to be honest, that's a very good question. A conversation for another time... as I'm not, hmm, actually sure, to be fully honest. The fact remains: no matter where or when I've worked on these, no one was ever willing to take the risk. While I will only be studying and adjusting a core, seeing me actually write runes is too dangerous. Before you volunteer, I must instead ask that you swear not to look back when I am actively writing out the script. While *you* may be willing to take the risk... I... I am not."

Danielle swallowed her words, as she had been about to volunteer exactly as he predicted. Reluctantly, she nodded her agreement, feeling the extreme depth of apprehension in the Artificer's voice. "I... understand. Just don't make it sound *too* interesting, or I might accidentally sneak a peek without thinking."

The Artificer's chuckle clearly meant he didn't understand exactly how serious Danielle was about her statement. "Good, good. First, let's take a look at the very essence of Sneezy and see what has changed."

Piloting the immense mechanical man with surprising delicacy, the Comte retrieved Sneezy's core from the dormant body. The glowing rectangle shimmered with an iridescent, silvery light that seemed somehow more *real* than the bright illumination of the room. The surface of the object reacted as if it were alive, shifting with symbols and words Danielle felt she could *almost* read. Yet, each time she leaned in, certain that she'd be able to understand, the glowing rune would fade out of existence, only to be replaced by another.

"Ready for the worst first lesson on understanding runes anyone has ever had the misfortune of having?" Comte LeKrout chuckled softly as he directed the needle-thin tool holding the rectangle to start rotating in place. "If you can *see* this word, that means you have an understanding of the concept. But, if you can't *read* it, you do not fully understand the underlying attributes. For example, this one means—oh, I see that brought some enlightenment?"

Danielle's eyes reflected the light of that rune, her pupils dilating slightly as it shifted from a logogram to a *legible* word. "I *can* read it! It says 'integrity', right?"

The excited admission was followed by a reverent moment of utter silence from the Artificer. "That's... interesting. I'm uncertain how to... huh... reply right now. This calls into question every interaction I've ever had with another person at the Royal Academy, or even in my military career. Not because *you* can read it, but because I've always started an explanation by pointing at this specific rune... and, well, no one else ever could. The fact you *can*, means you understand what it means to *have* integrity. Perhaps I'm not actually a terrible teacher? Could it be that I've only ever been surrounded by people who don't understand what integrity means on a deep, fundamental level?"

Danielle wasn't sure how to respond to his seemingly rhetorical questions, as anything she could think to say would only further disparage his previous colleagues. The Artificer seemed to realize he was taking the conversation in an unpalatable direction and quickly moved on. "Apologies, I lost my trail of thought there. This means 'malleability' of physical attributes as well as thought. Oh… interesting. This has changed ever so slightly; it didn't used to mean-"

Strangely enough, as the Artificer spoke the last word of his sentence, it morphed into static when it entered her ears. As he kept going, voicing his thoughts out loud, there seemed to be a malfunction between what he was saying and what she was hearing. Danielle could only glumly admit to herself that the system was likely censoring his words to force her to discover and understand high-order concepts on her own.

Eventually, *much* later, the core was lowered, then pushed into the awaiting slot in the prototype's body.

"You were right, Madame. I can't believe I never thought to see if *my* work had been changed over time, based on the experiences of my automatons." Forgetting himself in his excitement, the Artificer grabbed the strange stylus once more, the tip of the pencil-shaped object glowing with a light that hurt Danielle's eyes to see. "Using all that information, I can begin integrating its core with the new body directly, bypassing the most stringent requirements which have made it fail in the past."

Remembering her promise and the warning she'd been given, Danielle spun around at the last moment, just before the stylus touched the metal frame. A strange shockwave rocked her body, and glowing motes of light sprang into existence all around her. Eyes wide, she watched in wonder as the vast underground space was transformed into what looked like a field of stars.

Behind her, the sound of metal being torn, melted, and reformed rang out—a sharp contrast to the beauty of the area surrounding her.

"No! Celestial feces, did I just kill her?" The light show and sounds faded instantly as the massive machine flung itself around, barely keeping itself from falling at the sudden motion. "Danielle! You're alive! And, I hope, *not* insane?"

"We can only hope," she quipped, much to the Comte's relief. Still not trusting what was behind her. Danielle didn't turn around to address the Artificer, keeping her eyes focused on a point in the distance. "You told me not to, and I said I wouldn't. Even if *you* forgot yourself in your excitement, what does integrity mean other than doing what you are supposed to do, even when no one's watching or even remembers to follow through, except for you?"

"I'm just going to throw it out there…" The Artificer seemed to be on the verge of hyperventilating. "I am incredibly glad *that* particular concept was the one you resonated with the most."

NINETEEN

THROUGH THE ENTIRE process of the stylus scraping against the inner metal casing, the entire room was filled with the faint hum and sparkle of pure, unadulterated magic. Though Danielle could hear the Artificer muttering to himself as he worked, occasionally letting out a burst of steam in frustration, she ignored her nearly overwhelming curiosity and tried to think about anything other than her *boiling* desire to know what the magic process looked like.

Mostly, the Comte worked in genuine silence, the scraping and rhythmic pulsing of light the only sign he was still doing anything at all. Yet, every once in a while, he voiced his thoughts. There, Danielle started to glean that something was happening, something outside of his expectations. "Enhances the flow of energy... stabilize the input and output... what is *this?*"

In her experience, it was a very bad sign when a craftsman was working on something and released a question so filled with surprise. His voice trailed off, and when it picked up again, it was barely louder than the whisper of steel across leather. "These runes are *shifting* as I go, Danielle. That isn't supposed to be possible. I need to move faster... no! It's catching up to what I've already finished!"

He lapsed back into silence as he frantically scratched away, but now his words were coming more frequently. "That's an unexpected curve; it'll throw the whole system into disarray...! Oh. Never mind. I see. *I see*! It's condensing? I have more room to write, and it's so *elegant*."

That was the first hint to Danielle that her skills were directly impacting the Artificer's work as he made his etchings. His mumbling became almost manic with excitement. "It combined! It *combined*! I didn't know runes could *combine*. But now I can't fully understand it? It must do something, and... and I know what the underlying concepts were. A day of study, no more—I'm certain of it. Then I'll have access to an entirely unknown, unexplored symbol! Noble titles have been granted for lesser versions of the same-!"

Finally, an interminable amount of time later, the glowing motes of energy vanished once more—just before the Comte let out a tired sigh of satisfaction. "Done. Come and take a look."

He'd barely spoken the words before Danielle was standing next to the newly scripted prototype. Her eyes greedily roved the internal mechanisms, easily picking out where his magic had come into effect. "Sneezy? Are you all right? Comte, are these always so bright when you just finished creating them? Some of your older machines have barely a hint of a glow on their scripting."

"Yes, they all started out looking like this. Well... not like *this*," the Comte stated with a laugh hidden in his voice. "Look how these turned out! It's as if I was writing basic, blocky lines, and this turned it into exquisite calligraphy. I hate to have to admit this, but it's a work of *art*. I've never in my entire *life* seen something more beautiful. As for if this worked as intended? Let's find out."

It took a split second for the stricken Danielle to realize

she was shocked to her very core that the Artificer considered the simple script in this machine more beautiful than *her*. It was a sensation she'd never before felt, and to her surprise, all she felt was…

…relief.

After tapping on one of the extended plates, the exposed internals of the prototype pulled together with a hum of gears and a flicker of light, seamlessly shifting into position. Soon after that process had completed, its eyes began to glow from an internal power source. The automaton began to move, sitting up with a human level of fluidity, using one of its arms to brace itself. "I seem to be adjusting quite well to the new body! Give me a moment to test my range of motion, then I'll be able to give you a better feel for how I'm… feeling."

"How unexpected," the Artificer murmured as the light from its eyes focused in on the articulating jaw of Sneezy's new body. "Why are you moving your mouth when you speak? You don't need to do that."

"It's kind of nice, if I'm being honest," Danielle joined in before the automaton could adjust its movements to better fit with LeKrout's expectations. "I've been surrounded by all sorts of machines giving me information, and half the time, I can't tell which one is talking to me. It gives me something to focus on. Again, a nice touch."

"More moving parts simply means it will break more often." The Artificer's grumble had no heat behind it, so Danielle could only consider his words as a last gasp attempt at holding on to his long-standing traditions. "I hadn't realized the motion capture was doing such a good job at the small movements and flexing that your cheeks, chin, and jaw make. On that note, they must have glommed onto the larger range of motions I was attempting to instill. Does that cause you issue, Sneezy?"

"I *like* it!" Sneezy happily stated, showing them a double thumbs up as he twisted and turned. "I've already found at least two dozen sounds I was unable to properly use without moving my mouth. Now I should be better able to convey my desires."

"Desires?" Where before the Comte had been mostly paying attention to how well the creature was taking to its new body, now he was studying its face. "You mean to say you have goals and ambitions? *Beyond* what I have designed for you?"

"Is that…" The machine paused and perfectly replicated the motion Danielle made when she nervously cleared her throat. "Is that… okay?"

The red lights turned on and off rapidly, as though the Artificer somewhere in the distance was blinking rapidly in surprise. "*Okay*? Sneezy. Do you know what the final hurdle for achieving Perfection is for my class skill?"

"I wouldn't *dare* to pry, my lord!" Sneezy swept into a deep bow and back out, just because he could.

"I need to create a life my machines *want* to live." As the Artificer spoke, Danielle felt a deep sense of deja vu, due to how similar his level increase requirement sounded to her own. "How could that be possible, if I couldn't make one of you that wanted more for itself? That had ambitions and goals? With this… Sneezy, I'm on the very edge of success!"

"You mean I can just let you know what I want, and it won't be an imposition?" Sneezy smiled brightly. "Being allowed to freely discuss my thoughts and protect you is all I've *ever* wanted, m'lord. Well, that, and someone to sample my crème brûlée."

Danielle waited for the Comte to respond, for him to praise his creation for its words, but he said nothing. Confused at the disconnect between expectations and reality, she looked over at the towering behemoth of metal and hoses—which saved her life. Even as she looked on, the entity was already falling at her, and she had just enough time to launch herself out of the way before the half-ton machine crashed to the ground. "LeKrout? Beast! What's happening?"

Pulleys and wires dropped from the ceiling, hooking into the fallen machine and pulling it off the ground. To her great relief, its eyes began glowing once more—though they were a deep, sapphire blue. "Beast! What was *that*?"

"Rejoice! Today is the start of a joyous, momentous occasion," the Beast replied with utter reverence in his terrifying voice. "Comte LeKrout has achieved Perfection in his skill, and the Awakening Shard he carries at all times activated immediately. Currently, he is undergoing *Breakthrough* in his Full Class, and will soon be able to achieve even higher heights."

"What does that mean for him? Is he going to come celebrate; should we prepare for anything?" Danielle pressed the Beast for information, but his hesitation to answer her spoke volumes.

"I can make the biggest crème brûlée you've ever seen in your *life*." Panels shifted across Sneezy's body, his humanoid nose elongating slightly as the tip lit on fire. The palms of both hands widened to allow a series of spigots to be viewed, and his chest opened to reveal a nozzle three times as large as his original flamethrower. "Wait, I've reconsidered. I would like to have a few hours to practice before I deliver dessert."

Even without having sprayed gouts of flame into the surroundings, the air around Sneezy had become heated to the point of discomfort for Danielle. "That... might be for the best. Perhaps you prepare them... outside? Away from the grass?"

"Unfortunately, the Comte will *not* be joining us," the Beast finally intoned heavily. "While I appreciate your enthusiasm, it is simply not possible at this time."

"Not possible? But why?" They had danced around the subject for so long at this point that Danielle was starting to grow annoyed. "If his full attention truly had to be on what he was doing, wouldn't achieving Breakthrough have interrupted everything? Whatever it is he's doing, by now it's either broken or needing to be restarted. Tell him to take a break!"

"There will be a creamy dessert with a flambéed surface of sugar!"

"*Enough*," the Beast growled in its usual menacing manner. "This is not a conversation we will be having."

Annoyed at the stonewalling she was facing, Danielle crossed her arms—only then noticing a shimmer of light clinging to her skin. With a swipe of her arm, she learned what had changed.

Skill increase! Unified Radiance [Level 6 (Considerable) → Level 7 (Proficient)]!
Requirement to advance to level 8: Influence a leader with extensive political power to go against their best interests in order to change a policy and benefit you.

"It appears I've successfully changed the opinion of a highly influential individual. Probably something to do with form factor. Bah. Why couldn't it have been an opinion that would help me more?" Danielle could only let out a soft groan as the Beast ushered her toward the stairs. "Might as well have restored his *lawn* instead, for all the good it did me. Hold on… what kind of requirement is *this*? It's basically forcing me to convince him to join the war if I want to progress my skill any further. Or… or I'll need to leave and suffer the consequences that come from *that*."

"Don't think about it too much, madame!" Sneezy wrapped an arm around her, giving her a tight half-hug. "I've *never* seen or heard of the Comte backing down or changing his mind about something. The fact that you've managed to do it once? I'm betting that means you'll be able to do it again."

Thinking over the automaton's words, Danielle slowly shook her head. "I don't think I *want* to do that, Sneezy. This skill just gave me a requirement that goes against what I believe in. How could I possibly ask someone to put themselves in a bad position for *me*? Even now, I've been moving forward under the assumption that rejoining the war effort wouldn't be such a burden on Comte LeKrout... but seeing how he was in there? How he truly loves the *craft* of what he does?"

They left the stairs behind and emerged into the grand hallway as Danielle finished her thoughts. "Something tells me he isn't a man who wants to go back to creating creatures like his soldier, intended only for battle. Especially now, knowing that you can grow, learn, and live an actual life? That'd be like sending his children to fight for Verdelune, without ever giving them a choice in the matter. What parent would want that for their family, unless they were truly insane?"

Almost in a daze, Danielle walked back to her room, "I think it might be time for me to rethink why I'm really here... especially if I'm putting the Comte's life in danger."

CHAPTER

TWENTY

GASTEEL

NOT FOR THE first time since he'd arrived in this miserable excuse of a town, Gasteel found himself slamming his fist onto the table of the *Local Tavern*—an uninspired name for an uninspiring establishment. "Abyss *take* that woman! She should've failed and been thrown out by now."

"Or even succeeded!" Lefroupe added in quickly, nodding along with fervent agreement to everything his liege lord was saying.

"Exactly that!" Gasteel leaned back in his seat, the ancient chair creaking ominously beneath the weight of his imposing frame. He crossed his arms in front of him as he frowned, rippling muscles hypnotically catching the eye of everyone in the room. "How long does it take the most beautiful woman in the entire kingdom—handpicked by *me*—to convince some pathetic old recluse to join the glorious war effort? Wait... you don't think my choosing her will reflect poorly on how the king views my decision-making, do you?"

"Absolutely not!" Lefroupe shook his head, eyes wide as if

194 DAKOTA KROUT

he had never even considered the thought. "My lord, I've seen her. We've all seen her. You made the right choice. If she fails, it could only be because she has always relied on her looks to get her way. What if the Comte is blind? If she never developed a good personality-"

"That must be it!" Gasteel pretended to wipe sweat from his forehead, and a rueful grin cracked the scowl on his face. "On the plus side, I'm not marrying her for her *personality*, so that works just fine. Contractually, she'll have to be pleasant. Still, she's wasting my time! At the very least, she should have admitted her failure and came crawling back to my side so I could move along to the next province and continue *recruiting*! All the towns in half a day's ride are tapped out."

"We could just-"

"No, Lefroupe. Even if this whole situation is beneath me, I'm not going to give either of them a chance to slip through my fingers. Until I know the results, we're all but trapped here playing nursemaid for this *raving* lunatic. Look at him, over there. Living his best life on *my* generosity, all because I—*I*, a man of my word—swore to take care of him."

Gasteel's voice dripped with contempt as he gestured dismissively across the room, his eyes focusing past the boisterous patrons, through the thick, musty, ale-and-sweat humid air of the small building. In the far corner was Henri, who by all rights should have been groveling thankfully for the privilege of living another day.

Instead, the old man was enthusiastically dancing with two younger women while a local bard slammed his fists on a set of drums to keep an intense rhythm going.

"Raving indeed." The hint of jealousy in Lefroupe's tone drew Gasteel's eyes, and despite his annoyance, a hint of amusement was shining in them. "I don't think he's stopped since before I went to bed last night. Makes me wonder how long it'd been since he left his house before we came along?"

"Who cares?" Gasteel's hollow laugh was devoid of any

real humor. "To be fair, were he a younger man, I would consider bringing him into the fold just to infect the rest of Gasteel Company with the same enthusiasm. There's a man who is truly in love with life at the moment—he reminds me of myself. An old, weak, and pathetic version of myself, but still."

Tired of looking at the wrinkly face, the Baron shifted his attention. Holding up a hand, he waved a tavern maid over with a dismissive flick. Despite his careless attitude, she smiled at him and walked over with as much swaying of the hips as she could put into each step. Standing closer to him than necessary, she practically begged to take his order. "What will it be, *my lord?*"

"Give me the usual. A Frontière Flip." Though he wasn't truly interested in the subpar local options, his cold eyes still lingered on her form as she nodded and hurriedly scurried off, all in hopes of returning to his side as quickly as possible. "I need some positivity in my life, Lefroupe. Tell me something pleasant."

"Well, that is, umm… even with all the annoyances and indignities you've suffered in this town, at least they make a drink you like." The scribe's words caused Gasteel to furrow his brow, his lips pressed into a thin line before reluctantly dipping his chin in acknowledgment.

"Be that as it may, we need a win, and we need it soon. Something to get the men riled up, to achieve some significant backing. Something to get us back on top, Lefroupe!" The corner of the Baron's lip twitched up in a snarl, which he quickly hid, smoothing his face into a practiced expression. "If I could just get the Comte under my control, it'll give me a level of authority I'm unlikely to ever achieve without him. Once I have that, the world will fall into place, just as it should."

"I thought you had pinned your hopes on social climbing through your fiancée?" Lefroupe ventured carefully, tiptoeing around the subject of the Comte. "It's been a decade since LeKrout left his estate, and I don't think a pretty face 'asking nicely' will be enough to change that."

"Oh, my loyal scribe, *that's* a foregone conclusion; she *will* marry me." Gasteel let out a hearty laugh, as though his loyal sycophant had said something absurdly funny. "The real issue is *timing*. How do we hurry this tedious process along? I meant for greater things than sitting around waiting for some local girl to come to her senses. I want to be back on the war front sharpening my skills, growing my power. Though it pains me to admit, even now my trigger finger grows itchy, and my sword arm grows weaker by the day. It's been at least a week since I killed a man... I'm losing my edge. I can feel it."

"*Wha~at?*" Lefroupe vigorously shook his head in disbelief. "My lord, you could spend a century away, and you would still be unmatched! Look at those muscles! That face, your hair? That velvety voice that tickles the ears of all who have the pleasure of hearing it? You only get better, aging like a fine wine! Every man wants to be like you, and every maiden by your side! Who could possibly resist that face, that physique? It's her *privilege* to marry you!"

A self-satisfied smirk curled Gasteel's lips as he enjoyed being showered with praise. As if to underscore Lefroupe's flattery, the tavern maid came to a stop next to their table at that very moment. In one hand was a quart-sized mug, and the other held a small serving dish.

She set the mug down with a flourish, the smell of harsh whiskey and aged port drifting up and mingling with the other scents of the establishment. Moving with exaggerated care, doing her best to impress the baron without accidentally spilling on him, she poured in a generous helping of sugary water, then cracked two eggs and released the yolk and egg white into the mixture. Gasteel looked on, face set in an expression of mild approval.

After stirring the mixture with an elongated spoon, she

dropped in a sprig of smoked rosemary. Her task complete, she stepped away from the table and curtsied with a bright smile. "A Frontière Flip, m'lord."

"That will be all." Even as Gasteel dismissed her, another maid hurried by and carefully set down a platter with a generous slice of an egg pie. Without acknowledging the effort, he pulled out a spoon and quickly devoured the meal. "You see, Lefroupe? When you're around me, you'll find that even the simplest tasks are completed to create an *experience*. This is why it's so important to be strong, and for everyone to know it. When no one knew who I was, do you think they did more than slap my meal down on the table and walk away? No. Every benefit I have was earned by soaking my hands in blood. Sometimes, that just takes time."

"Then...?" Lefroupe tried to discern what he was being told. "Do you *not* want to hurry the Comte along?"

"No. I do. I'm saying I've already put in my time waiting around, and now I deserve my experiences when I *want* them. Not when someone else wants to *give* them to me. Enough of that, for now." As soon as he'd scraped the last crumb into his mouth, Gasteel lifted his drink and took a long pull. "Ahh... now that hits the spot. Do you want to know the secret to my bulk, Lefroupe? It's my spoon, right here."

He tapped the flatware against the table. "If you can't eat your food with a spoon, that just means you are going to be wasting time chewing instead of digesting. The key is to bring your muscles all of the energy they need, as fast as possible. More eggs, over-*hard* this time—just like me! *Ha!*"

The shout and flexing was met with a round of cheers and applause, exactly what he'd been hoping for. The baron basked in the attention, feeling it warm him even more than the potent drink. To his great annoyance, at that moment, the door of the tavern swept open, allowing in a gust of fresh air that upset the delicate balance of smells in the cramped space. Turning his annoyed glare to the person who'd entered,

Gasteel found he recognized the intruder and so held his tongue as the squirrely man rushed over to Lefroupe and handed him a small pamphlet.

Sketching out a *barely* acceptable salute, the young man then turned and fled as fast as he could. Lefroupe opened the first page, his eyes flicking back and forth as he read the contents of the missive. The farther he went, the more his eyebrows were raised—yet he didn't make a sound.

Gasteel cleared his throat rather violently, getting the attention of more than half the room and startling his scribe out of reading. "Well? What is it?"

"If I'm not mistaken..." Lefroupe tapped the page he'd been reading. "This is the answer to the questions we've been asking. It seems the Comte's situation isn't as simple as we'd thought. Instead of being a shut-in, as we'd been expecting, it turns out he has a formal agreement with the king of Verdelune not to leave his estate. Not for any reason. Essentially, he's on house arrest. If he steps across the edge of his land or sends his creations out to do his bidding, anyone with the authority to do so may order him to take up arms once more."

"Why would this need to be a formalized agreement?" Gasteel leaned forward, not for the first time frustrated by how words seemed to dance across the page when he tried to read them. "Tell me what it *says*, Lefroupe!"

"It's the reason the last war ended," the scribe stated with a deep sense of reverence. "The Comte up and decided he wanted no part in expanding the kingdom. Out of nowhere, it seems. Without his metal soldiers to maintain occupation of the captured territory, all of the king's horses and all of the king's men were needed to hold the expansion again."

Gasteel allowed his annoyance to show on his face. "He just didn't want to fight anymore? That makes no sense. At all. Every major reward, all the best funding, everything goes to those who increase their value to the king. There is no better way to do so than expanding his territory!"

"According to this, their Majesties attempted to *make* him continue, but in an instant, he had tens of thousands of troops at his beck and call. His creations are utterly loyal to him, and that control couldn't be broken." Lefroupe likely knew he was playing a dangerous game by not allowing the baron to lead the conversation, but seemed to think the risk was justified in this instance. "Instead of breaking off relations or starting a civil war, the Comte sued for peace. So long as he was left alone, he would work for neither Verdelune nor anyone but himself. In return for being left alone, he was placed under permanent house arrest. On pain of…"

Lefroupe let out a gasp as he read the final line of the document. "He crossed his heart! If he doesn't fulfill his end of the agreement and return to service if ordered, his heart will be destroyed. He essentially bet his life on being able to live the rest of his life alone in his home."

"Interesting…" Gasteel's lips curled into a malicious smile. "Now that… *that* we can use. Lefroupe. I've had a thought."

"You have? Do tell, my lord! No one has *thoughts* like Gasteel!"

"I believe it's time to officially stage a grand, public spectacle. You know, something to increase the morale of the troops." The baron's eyes traveled back to the corner of the tavern, lingering on the old man who was still dancing away— face soaked in sweat and grinning like a fool. Gasteel's eyes glittered, and his next words were practically dripping with self-satisfaction. "*I* know. Perhaps a public execution of a known traitor and spy?"

Lefroupe, ever the clever man, immediately picked up on what his lord was truly after. "A delightful idea! I can set the date for the near future, long enough for word to spread a significant distance, and bring in *everyone* who wants to participate in the display."

Gasteel closed his eyes and visualized what he wanted, raising a finger in the air and gently swinging it in time to the music as he savored the moment. "Flushing out our prey is a good start, but we can do better. Once the people are distracted by this news, perhaps we can stage an invasion against the unit surrounding the Comte's estate."

"A false flag attack?" Lefroupe visibly paled, though he kept a smile plastered on his face. "A war game... I can see the appeal. If the unit gets wiped out, well, they were too weak to be members of Gasteel Company in the first place."

"*Exactly*! That's what I love about you, Lefroupe!" Gasteel barked out a laugh and clapped his companion on the shoulder, sending the small man tumbling out of his chair to the ground. "You *get* me! Now, with this two-pronged approach, we'll force that Comte into action. As soon as he steps so much as a toe out of line, well... someone in the region has to have been granted the authority to recruit for the kingdom, don't they?"

Gasp. Lefroupe's eyes went comically wide, and his hands covered his mouth in exaggerated shock as he scrambled back to his feet. "My lord... I believe that would be *you*!"

Gasteel slammed his hand on the table, the sound reverberating through the room as he stood, raising his mug with his off hand in a triumphant gesture. "A toast, to the foolishness of those who think they can outwit a man of my caliber! To the Comte, who will soon be joining our ranks, and to my bride, as she'll soon be by my side!"

The patrons of the tavern joined in, raising their mugs with a guttural cheer. As more people became involved, Gasteel's face became flush with victory, and his boasts grew increasingly elaborate. "Soon, we'll be at the head of the finest army this kingdom has ever seen! We'll have so many banners flying that we won't need to stop for shade! The ground will tremble between our feet, and we'll subjugate all we meet! For the king, for the queen, for Verdelune! Gasteel Company!"

"*Gasteel Company!*" came a roar in return.

"Don't rush off now. It's time to celebrate. To victory, Lefroupe! To a future we cut out for ourselves." Gasteel got to his feet and flicked a gold coin at the bartender. "Drinks are on me today. It's going to be a good month…"

"…we'll have an execution, a wedding, and a *war!*"

TWENTY-ONE

DANIELLE

"COMING, COMING!" Danielle sprinted along the vast hallway of LeKrout's manor, a bundle of blueprints and sketches in her arms. Today was the beginning of a daunting yet exhilarating task the Artificer had graciously offered to allow her to participate in: retrofitting the estate's automatons.

She'd been hoping for an opportunity like this since the first time she had convinced Doc to open up to her in a literal way and couldn't *believe* she had allowed herself to sleep in.

"Don't start without me!" The Enchantress burst into the dining room, her vision sweeping across the room where dozens upon dozens of machines were lined up, patiently waiting their turn to be interviewed by her and the Beast. BST model three stood next to the table, looming in his usual imposing manner… and clearly exuding an aggrieved impatience at her tardiness.

"Thank you for joining us. I had not realized how many things you must have going on. You must be quite busy if they distract you enough to keep you from being on time… whatever those tasks may be."

"Here's a question for you, Beast," Danielle shot in reply as she slid into her chair, an unflustered grin on her face. "Were you *designed* to be so passive-aggressive, or did you upgrade yourself over time?"

"I was designed to be *aggressive*-aggressive," the deep voice chuffed at her, releasing a cloud of steamy air that blew her bangs to the side. "To answer your question, it seems I decided on this path after I found one too many problems I couldn't simply *squash* on behalf of my master."

Danielle sent a brilliant smile at his towering metallic frame, wondering if his crystalline eyes were showing a spark of something new—respect, gratitude, or—perhaps—even trust? After a moment of contemplation, she shook her head. "Sorry, I got lost in thought there for a moment. I saw such a charming smile reflecting off your eyes that I forgot where I was and thought you were gearing up to be nice."

"There's a word for people who stare at their own reflection too often."

"Philosophers?"

The cloud of steam escaping the Beast this time started sounding like a tea kettle that had been on the stove too long, so Danielle decided it was time to move on.

Carefully stopping her gentle teasing of the oversized butler, she turned her attention to the lined-up machines, shifting her demeanor to one of earnest enthusiasm. As she began asking them questions, Danielle tried to show them that she wasn't just reading off a list: she was genuinely interested in what each of them had to say.

As the morning wore on, she and the Beast started putting together an explanation for what had been changing the creatures. The vast majority of the automatons, which were designed specifically for utility, or with a singular task such as scanning an area to watch for intruders, simply had no growth from the original design they'd been given.

Conversely, those with at least semi-human forms and

were given complex tasks where they needed to make more than simple decisions had grown in one way or another.

Most startling was how extensive the changes were for those that had constantly been in close contact with Danielle or the Beast. Those entities all had extreme alterations to their original design, and with some careful questioning, were able to articulate their own hopes and desires for the future. Though she might not perfectly understand their reasoning, with every unique preference, Danielle's eyes would light up, and she would gently coax them along. "A third arm so you can dust at the same time as sweeping? Very doable!"

There were times when she absolutely couldn't grasp why an automaton would desire a particular upgrade, but she never let her confusion show. She would simply take every opportunity to reassure them that their input was valuable, making sure to involve them in all decisions while treating their responses with utmost respect.

Several times, she had to intercede and stop the Beast from telling off one of the machines. Eventually, she had to step away with him and have a quiet conversation.

"What's the matter with you? That one was *simple*; he just wanted to be seven and a half inches taller!" The Enchantress hissed the words, trying to keep the waiting machines from hearing her.

"It's excessive!" the Beast firmly replied, trying to turn back to glare at the offending machine, only to be stopped by Danielle. "An extra seven and a half inches means at least another twenty pounds of metal. More than that, if we take into account the counterbalances. That machine is designed to tend to livestock. Horses, chickens, cows?"

"Okay? *And?*"

"We haven't had any animals here in over five years." The Beast snorted in annoyance. "It should be re-tasked, repurposed, or-"

"Don't you *dare* say decommissioned," Danielle smoothly

interrupted. "You know the Comte's growing feelings for his *children*. Listen, being seven and a half inches taller would allow it to take better care of taller livestock or collect eggs from stacked up nests. Beyond that, all we're doing today is taking note of what they want. This may be a low priority, but eventually we will make it happen. Right? Because the system is rewarding the Artificer for allowing his creations to live a life they want to live. Remember that?"

"He's already earned his reward for that; he doesn't need to *keep* doing it." As Danielle let out a long suffering sigh, BST model three grudgingly pressed on, "But I see your point. There is no harm in taking *note* of its desires."

As each creature was given a chance to show their growth, Danielle made sure to offer each of them a word of encouragement, attempting to match their excitement with her own before dismissing them. She praised their efforts, celebrated their small victories, and cheered on their continued progress.

When the last of them had gotten back to their usual duties, she slumped in her chair and closed her eyes for a minute. After collecting herself, she turned to the Beast, only for him to speak first. "I think the first thing we need to do is decide on a priority upgrade rotation. Why don't we-"

"What happened there, Beast?" Danielle interrupted as she leaned back into her chair with a soft groan, stretching her tired lower back muscles. "Kind of left me to fend for myself, huh? Look, I don't mind doing the interviews, I enjoyed it. Even so, we had a whole plan, and you dropped all your responsibilities on me."

"I... apologize," the Beast replied with a deep solemnity in his voice.

Danielle immediately sat up straight. "Oh no, you're falling apart, aren't you? Are you being decommissioned as we speak?"

"There is no call for your jibes." The stiff reply allowed Danielle to heave a sigh, and she swiped a hand over her forehead to show off her immense relief. Surprisingly, the Beast continued, though he spoke in a halting tone. "It seems I truly was holding them back. I am afraid that, without you arriving unexpectedly and without invitation, I would have never realized there were truly *minds* trapped within the lesser models. Because of my *obstinance*, Comte LeKrout very nearly lost out on his opportunity to achieve breakthrough."

That was when Danielle realized she had the distinctly strange responsibility of comforting a multi-thousand-pound metal monster because it was *sad*. Bizarrely enough, she was delighted at the opportunity. "I'm doing what I can, just as you were doing everything you could. Listen, Beast. If you can look back and realize how poorly you were doing before, it just shows how much you've grown since then. You can't hold that against yourself."

"Cease spouting your cliches." Although the machine was back to acting like a butt, the fact that he was unable to hold her gaze spoke volumes for the fact that he was *feeling* something at this moment.

Danielle decided to take that for the win it was and move on before she pressed her luck. "You didn't know. Now that you do, you're taking responsibility by giving them the chance they need to move forward. You heard what they said, just as I did. None of them blame you... they revere you nearly as much as the Artificer himself."

"Since you conducted the majority of the interviews, I will do the next part. There will be a priority list for you to peruse by dinner," the Beast stated as his pulley system activated and began slowly lifting him into the air. "I believe the best option to start with would be Doc. Plan on that, and we'll go from there."

"Don't forget to put the kitchen on the upgrade list!" Danielle called, causing the Beast's upward momentum to halt for a fraction of a moment. "It can't speak, but I bet it would love to be shaped like an octopus."

"Of all the *ridiculous* things I've been told today…!"

The grumbling Beast was carried away, leaving Danielle to laugh for a short while before returning her attention to the stack of blueprints she'd brought in with her. As Doc was the first of the automatons she'd ever studied, the Enchantress already had a deep understanding of what its current system looked like and how it functioned. All that was left before deciding on an upgrade path was asking his opinion on what his evolution should look like. "Duke, could you call Doc in for me?"

"As per usual, madame Danielle, I'm right here." The razor-thin creature uttered with a sigh which sounded like a gust of wind over a taut harp string. "I am to get an upgrade? I have a thought in mind for the final form… but it might be too much."

"It's your life, Doc." Danielle shrugged and dipped her quill in ink, preparing herself to start jotting down notes as the machine spoke. "It might have seemed like an oversight, but I only haven't interviewed you yet because I already *know* you've changed. Tell me, what sort of life do you want? How can I help you attain it?"

Doc stepped closer, its tiny feet chiming off the stone floor. "You may not know this, but I am one of the most dangerous of all the house guards. My mission, my goal, has always been to protect the estate. But too often, I feel like an assassin waiting to strike from the shadows. Even the people who *want* to be around me often overlook me, simply because I am standing at a dihedral angle to them."

The creature trailed off, an aura of hesitation surrounding it, Danielle gently pushed, "I'm ready, Doc. Whatever you need."

"I would like my next body to be something very difficult *not* to see." Doc met her eyes with his own lifeless beads—tiny flakes of crystal which allowed him to view the world. "I see how you watch as the Beast travels through the house, practically unable to look away. I would like *that*. Specifically, I would like to have the body of a great spider and have a pulley system."

"Um."

Doc spoke in a rush, hoping to cut off what he assumed would be an instant denial. "That is, I can hook into the already-existing pulley system! Then I'll be able to move around silently as needed while indoors, but also present a show of force which would be enough to dissuade evildoers from *attempting* wrongdoing, instead of needing to punish them."

"You want to be... a spider?" Danielle had heard the automaton perfectly yet didn't trust her own ears. "I don't watch the Beast move around because I think it looks interesting, or exciting... it's *terrifying*, Doc. Such a large creature moving silently? Through the *air*?"

"Yes. I would like that," the tiny automaton responded with a voice full of conviction. "Please make me into a glorious combat-spider capable of defending the house while also convincing others not to intrude in the first place."

Ever so reluctantly, Danielle nodded and wrote out the specifications her guard was looking for. "Spider it is."

"I would also like to be able to launch a harpoon from my mouth."

"Harpoon spider. Perfect." When Danielle looked up from her notes, she found herself face to face with the Beast, who was hovering over the table. "*Abyss!*"

"See? *That*. That looks fun," Doc pointed out with a tinny chuckle.

As she tried to get her heartbeat under control, Danielle realized that the Beast's eyes were glowing a deep red. "Comte! You're back!"

"I am, and better than ever before." The voice coming through the Beast's body sounded hearty and hale, full of joy as she'd never heard from him before. "The actual process of

Breakthrough is surprisingly quick, but I needed to adjust to the newfound power of my abilities. Also... I have *you* to thank for all of this. For a decade, I was trapped at the same spot. Who knows how long, if ever, it would have taken for me to breach that bottleneck without you."

Danielle shook her head. "I feel like everything here was at a tipping point already, and my presence was merely the final straw. All I did was bring your attention to what was already happening."

"It has been happening for a *long* time." The Artificer denied her attempt at diminishing the recognition he was trying to give her. "It was right under my nose, but I had far too much faith in my own abilities to smell the mess I was creating. I owe you a great debt, and I wanted you to know that I've made a decision."

At that moment, Danielle's skill increased once more, heralded by its usual burst of light. She *knew* what that meant: he had done something against his own best interests. The Enchantress couldn't take her eyes off the red-filled crystal eyes, and when she could finally speak, her voice came out as a whisper. "Don't... please don't tell me you've done something that can't be undone. It's not worth it. *I'm* not worth it. Don't send yourself back to war because I did you a small favor."

"If all goes well, there's nothing to fear." The mechanical face twisted into a terrifying smile, which she supposed was supposed to be somehow reassuring. "Also... a spider, Doc? I love it."

"*Yes~s!*" The guard hissed as it pumped its arm in excitement.

As the red eyes faded to blue, and the Beast was reeled up to the ceiling once more, Danielle numbly looked down at her arm to see what terrible thing she would need to do to someone else to advance once more.

Skill increase! Unified Radiance [Level 7 (Proficient) → *Level 8 (Extensive)]!*

Requirement to advance to level 9: Create a Masterpiece.

Seeing that there were no options or paths to choose from, and the statement itself was ambiguous enough that it could be applied to a song and a dance as easily as a superweapon, Danielle let out a long, slow breath.

"I truly hope I didn't just end up ruining your life, Comte."

CHAPTER
TWENTY-TWO

"A MASTERPIECE, YOU SAY?" Sneezy rubbed his chin as Danielle explained the requirements for her skill increase. "Too bad you didn't get that before you made my new form, eh? *Ehh?* Now the real question is, was it a masterpiece with a lowercase, or an uppercase 'M'?"

"Uppercase," Danielle replied with a touch of frustration in her voice, though she kept a smile on her lips to show her guard—and friend—that she appreciated his attempt at levity. "That means it has to be at a level that the system itself recognizes as a Master-level creation, right? As if I were already operating at level nine with the skill?"

"It's a surprisingly common requirement." Sneezy pulled a book out of a satchel it was carrying and handed it over. "I believe this was already recommended to you? *A Treatise on Skills.* By the way, this is your official notification that you've been given approval to take books out of the library. Yay, *you!*"

Dozens of tiny balls of fire launched from all over his body, dissipating into oily smoke after existing for only a heartbeat each. Danielle flinched away at first, then looked on, mesmerized by the impressive display of control. "You've been practicing!"

"I'm not allowed in the library anymore, so I needed to do something to fill the time," Sneezy let her know with a sheepish grin. "On that note, do you want to bet how long it'll take before Doc isn't allowed in?"

Tilting her hand back and forth, Danielle shook her head. "I can't give a realistic answer for that. The plan *isn't* to coat him in razor blades, so he should be fine to enter the library. To be fair, I don't know what the final design will be. I've been working on the schematic, but... a spider is pretty far out of what I've worked on in the past. I'm having trouble finding ways to balance the front and back... and, well, the harpoon isn't helping."

"It'll be fine, it's not like he's been waiting on this for long-"

The lights in the house shifted red, and the alarm bell began ringing. Danielle went rigid with concern, looking around cautiously to see if the Beast was dangling in a corner and waiting to see her reaction to the noise. Ever so softly, she muttered, "I *think* he learned his lesson last time, but... sometimes you can never know for sure."

Sneezy stiffened then reached out and grabbed her hand. "I just got an update-alert as to what's going on. The soldiers stationed outside the walls to prevent your potential escape are under attack from an unknown group. It's... it's not looking good for them."

"Someone launched an attack against Verdelune? Not looking good?" The reversal of the expected situation threw Danielle for a loop, but the blood drained from her face as her thoughts digested the information. "No! Nearly half of those are recruits from my town. They have practically no training, no armor-!"

Ignoring Sneezy's shouts, she pushed into the hallway and started running toward the door, only to find it bodily blocked by the Beast. "Get out of the way; I'm going out there to help them!"

"Although this pains me a great deal, I cannot allow you to leave the manor." The Beast spoke in a measured tone, not budging an inch from where he blocked the exit.

"It'll be a *bloodbath*!" Danielle's shouts fell on deaf ears, the Beast simply watching her. "They need help!"

"Tell me, guest of Comte LeKrout... how will you turn the tide of the battle in favor of your countrymen? Will this foe break against your mana-imbued plate armor? Fall before your immense training with weapons?" The Beast stared her down, still refusing to move. "Or, more realistically, would you simply join the casualties?"

"I need to-"

"No. You do not." The Beast shook its head gravely. "If you were to be harmed, the Comte would be summoned to the high court of Verdelune to give a reckoning for what occurred. I can tell you this... by doing so, he would be forced to create an untiring, unfeeling, *uncaring* army for the kingdom once more. It would break him."

"Then *you* send out your soldiers to save them!" Danielle shouted at the Beast, eyes darting back and forth as she searched for an exit which never manifested. "They don't deserve to die for no reason!"

"Soldiers almost never deserve their fates," the Beast told her gently, though his voice was laced with steel—much like his body. "They are pulled into someone else's war to fight a battle they did not choose, to die on land they have no knowledge of. If I let you go out there, so much more death would follow."

The lights in the hall dimmed suddenly, and an image captured by reflected mirrors was splayed across the white hall above the new paintings. Standing in a shoddy formation, dozens of men fought with a desperation born of hopelessness. The defending forces had their backs pressed against the seamless, looming wall surrounding LeKrout's manor.

Danielle's hands were pressed to her mouth as tears

streamed from her eyes, watching the soundless, senseless fight. The greenhorns—many of whom she recognized from growing up in the same town—wore dented, rusty helmets, at best. They wielded shields and swords against their attackers to little avail as arrows dropped from the sky, punching through flesh and bone with near-equal efficiency.

A powerful warrior wearing heavy armor threw himself into the fray against the conscripts, his sword barely visible as it blurred from person to person, each swing leaving behind only falling bodies. In another pocket of resistance, a magic user of some kind stepped forward, lifting his hands and releasing a glow of light that washed out Danielle's view for a moment.

When the reflected light on the wall showed the moving picture once more, the entire platoon of defenders had fallen to the ground, steam rising from their bodies. Oddly enough, they didn't appear burned or charred, simply... *heated*.

"Enough," the Beast called out, and the lights in the hallway immediately returned to their normal brightness. Danielle stared at the patch on the wall where the carnage had been shown, her mind trying to understand why the white stone of the wall was blackened. "Spellcasters who use radiance are few and far between. Even watching them use their powers from a distance can be enough to permanently damage fleshy sensory organs. It is good you were not watching this from the walls directly. You would have gone blind."

"Nothing..." Danielle slowly sucked in a breath, turning to look at the Beast with hollow eyes. "*Nothing* about that was good. You could have done something. You could've saved lives. Why-"

Rat-a-tatta!

The sound of hundreds of pistons slamming forward and back at the same time echoed into the hallway, and the Beast tilted its head slightly as it looked toward the source of the noise. "If it brings you any consolation, half of the attacking forces were just eradicated as they attempted to breach the wall. They failed. The defenses stand strong."

"Is this what we've been working toward while I've been here?" Danielle voiced the thought gnawing at her heart. "I wanted to make wonders of machinery, create life from dead components, maybe find a way to create some joy. Am I instead empowering a merciless killer who won't bend—not even a little—to save others?"

Choosing to remain very still, the Beast spoke more gently than usual, as though to a wounded, trapped animal. "It is necessary to ensure the safety and survival of the lord of the house. It is true, scores of people just died absolutely point-lessly. It is not something we asked for, something we perpe-trated or endorsed. We could not intervene for fear of a far *worse* outcome."

"Worse than *that?*" She shook her head in disbelief. "I just don't know what to say."

"I *tire* of this!" The Beast snarled at her with immense agitation. "You invade my master's house, laying the actions of others at his feet and attempting to put the blame squarely on us? It seems history repeats itself, *Enchantress.*"

"Let me leave."

"Gladly-" The Beast recoiled as no fewer than half a dozen guards stepped forward to plead with Danielle in his place. Letting out a deeply frustrated sound, he amended his words, "but apparently not before you *understand* what you are truly asking for. Come with me."

"Where?"

The machine paused momentarily before finally speaking in a hushed tone. "To witness the Comte's greatest shame."

The Beast began floating through the hallway, though he went out of his way to stay low to the ground—all so he could still stomp on the stone floors to show his frustration. He led her directly to the stairwell leading to the subterranean workshop, not once looking behind himself to see if she was following. It seemed he'd gotten to know her very well over the last few weeks.

Certainly well enough to understand that her curiosity would eventually force her to join him.

When they arrived in the cavernous room, Danielle was surprised to find that the motion-capture platform was already in its fully active mode, the crystal spires extended and glowing brightly. The Beast stomped to the edge, its hands expanding in a cascade of tools. It began pressing on the crystal in a rapid pattern, hundreds of points poked in the span of only a few seconds. For a moment, they glowed a brilliant blue... then faded into a deep, sickly green.

A new voice, one she only recognized due to its cadence and careful way of speaking, sounded out from the center of the platform.

"My name is Comte Kota LeKrout, and no matter what my kingdom of Verdelune tells me, or their citizens..."

"...I am a war criminal."

The lights shifted slightly, and a familiar figure appeared: a metal knight, but somehow made of light and standing in the exact center of the platform. The Comte's voice continued, steadily speaking as though he were reading from a prepared document. "I was recruited at nineteen years old, the youngest graduate of the Royal Academy to have passed all of the courses deemed necessary to become a system-recognized Artificer."

A young man appeared in place of the metal soldier, standing in regal clothes with a wide smile on his face.

"Upon going to a Class Shrine, I was awarded the vaunted class of Artificer, a goal I'd worked toward since the moment I showed aptitude for machinery on my tenth birthday."

The image of the young man shifted slightly, the highborn clothes replaced with a stylish military uniform. "I had barely returned home to celebrate with my family, House LeKrout,

where my father held the lowest rank of nobility—Baron—
when I was given orders to report to the capital city to begin
working on the war effort on behalf of Verdelune. Like a fool,
I was *proud* of the opportunity and raced forth to prove
myself."

"And prove myself, I did."

TWENTY-THREE

DANIELLE WATCHED the image of the young man as his face and clothes subtly shifted. His cheeks filled out slightly, his uniform turned into a pure white overcoat which would show any hint of dirt or oil which splattered upon it. She recoiled ever so slightly as the man turned and seemed to stare straight into her eyes.

"I created a weapon which would risk no one… not on our side, at least." His jaw worked momentarily, seeming to need to force out the next words. "I unleashed a tide of edged metal and handed control over to the generals of the armies of Verdelune. I knew they were expanding the kingdom, I *knew* that meant my machines were to be used in combat. But I was offered royal treatment. Parades were thrown in my honor. Feasts were declared. My birthday? It was a week-long celebration hosted by the king himself."

"I didn't understand what was happening, only that I was being told that I was doing the right thing." His clothes morphed once more, but strangely, he looked to be the same age as when he had first become an Artificer. "More was required of me. I developed a method to prolong-"

The image flickered, moving with inhuman swiftness.

Danielle glanced to the side, where the Beast was holding an implement to the crystal. Before she could ask a question, he rumbled out, "This part is not relevant to what I want you to see. We're just moving through his speech; it will resume shortly."

"-not until I received a guest at my estate that I learned the true horrors of what I'd unleashed on the world." The image of the man started speaking once more. "At first, I thought this was the promised soulmate, a person chosen by my family or the crown to be my partner in life forever. Why would I think otherwise? She was the most beautiful woman I'd ever seen, an *Enchantress* of all things! But when she had been shown to my office, she confronted me with crystallized memories of what was happening on the outskirts of the kingdom."

"My soldiers were not *only* fighting against foreign armies, cutting them down to the last man who dared resist." His clothing shifted to traditional mourning garb. "They were tirelessly keeping watch on captured citizens of our neighboring countries. Cutting them down when they didn't do the work they were forced into, from farming to provide food to our people... to mining for more metal to expand our army further. It was only at this point I learned what they thought of me outside of the borders of Verdelune."

"They called me the System-forsaken Battle Beast."

At these words, Danielle had to catch her breath, as she recalled her father saying this title with such fear in his voice that he'd been prepared to see her wed Gasteel in lieu of the Artificer's creations seeing combat once more.

"The Enchantress was utterly shocked to learn that I had no knowledge of these events. She pleaded with me, appealing to my better nature. I admit, her social skills won me over quickly, but after what I'd witnessed, even with what she later did to me... I do not believe she was wrong to do it."

His eyes went hard, and his figure, which had slowly been

slumping, once more stood straight and proud. "With her support, I remotely recalled every one of my soldiers. I stood defiant against the crown, and I won the right to remain here under house arrest for the remainder of my life. Without the accolades and the respect, I quickly began losing staff. When they went into town, they were harassed by the locals—or at least those masquerading as locals. Even with all of this, I would've been fine, happy even, if it hadn't been-"

The image vanished, and the lights in the subterranean space regained their normal brightness. Danielle blinked rapidly, her eyes searching for the Artificer, but only finding the Beast stepping away from the crystal spire. "No… what happened? He seemed so *lost*."

"It is not relevant to the subject at hand," the Beast informed her without a hint of remorse. "Now you have seen why he stopped creating soldiers. Three entire *kingdoms* fell beneath the weight of his metal gauntlet, and that was when he was casually creating soldiers with the bare minimum of effort required. Beyond the initial conflict, untold *thousands* suffered under his creations. All while he was partying and parading during his free time."

The Beast walked across the room, his footfalls echoing through the area like a doomsday clock ticking down. "Tell me now, Danielle. Are you still willing to demand he puts himself under the thumb of the crown by saving a few random soldiers who were only stationed here to pressure you into a life you did not want? There would be one major difference, I suppose. This time, the kingdom would hold him in place with *far* more restrictive oaths to produce and send out his forces. He would never again have the opportunity to force a stalemate."

As he finished his statement, the Beast gripped the curtain which spanned the massive underground warehouse and *yanked* it.

The bolts holding it in the ceiling remained in place, while the fabric ripped clean off. As the cloth floated to the floor, lights began turning on, one row after another. Danielle winced as her eyes adjusted to the glare of light reflecting from metal. Then her eyes went wide, and she forced herself to look on despite the pain, her stomach feeling like it was dropping into a deep, dark hole.

Metal soldiers in formation stared back at her, their eyes cold and lifeless—lacking any hint of being active. With each light that turned on, hundreds more of the tightly packed soldiers were revealed. Danielle tried to see where the deadly machines ended, but each time she thought they'd reached the far wall, yet another light turned on.

"If you are wondering, the full underground space spans the entirety of the space contained within the outer walls," Beast informed her gravely. "There are seventy-six thousand, two hundred and forty-one soldiers collected here... every last working version that had been sent out, and all those who were repaired *after* his 'disagreement' with Verdelune."

Danielle stood as though frozen, her eyes darting between the nearly identical faces of the seemingly endless rows of metal soldiers. The enormity of the situation sank in, and a deep sense of shame and guilt washed over her. Only then did she realize how badly she'd misjudged the situation, the Beast, and the Artificer. "I didn't know what I was asking you to do. I mean, I did, but I didn't... I didn't understand the scope."

For what felt like a long time to her, Danielle mimicked the automatons she'd been around when they were powering down. Her eyes went glassy, her vision narrowing into tunnels which only served to help her focus more closely on the death machines in front of her. A moment later, she was stumbling over to the workbench, grabbing a book and hugging it to her chest to seek comfort from the familiar, *usually* joy-inducing texture.

Then she looked down at what she was holding, finding a manual on creating the metal soldiers, with a new image on the front—the upgraded design she had made with the Artificer. The book fell from her nerveless fingers, and she leaned on the table to try and catch her breath, feeling as though she'd just run a great distance.

More to herself than the Beast, she whispered her thoughts, "I just thought you were... being difficult. *Petulant* even, as if you were a spoiled noble refusing to do your duty for Verdelune. I had no idea this was the burden you'd set down... and here I am, trying to force you to pick it back up. No wonder you weren't willing to trade your life for one old Tinkerer. No... *thank you* for refusing. I would've never forgiven myself, once I understood what I'd asked of you."

"Comte LeKrout rejoining the war efforts would be a colossal mistake, with a great potential for the devastation of dozens of kingdoms," the Beast agreed with her without holding back. "The most likely outcome is a union against Verdelune. It would take the combined efforts of dozens of kingdoms to crush the threat he brought, and they would not stop until they were certain it could never happen again. This would mean the devastation of every workshop, educational center, royal academy, military outpost, and likely the razing of every city, just to be *sure* they hadn't missed something."

"But... if you know this, the Royals must know as well. Why would they risk such an outcome?" Danielle latched onto the shift in conversation like a drowning woman being thrown a life preserver.

The Beast began rolling the enormous, torn-down curtain into a tidy bolt of fabric. "It's an acceptable risk to the Witch Queen of Verdelune. There are two paths forward, once you hit a certain point within the system. Most people only gain access to the reputation system upon achieving Breakthrough with their Full Class, but some... those who are pure of heart, or rotten to their very soul, can access the subsystem much earlier—influencing the path and power of their class and skills."

"Reputation system?" Danielle echoed faintly. "I've never heard of anything like that before."

"Knowledge of the subsystem is actively suppressed in our kingdom, because the queen would prefer that others did not understand exactly what it means for her to be a Witch Queen," the Beast bluntly informed her. "You either maximize your negative reputation through dark deeds, becoming a Witch or a Villain—as she did—or maximize it through positive actions and become a Fairy or a Hero. On that note, those who have reached maximum positive reputation in Verdelune are almost always executed or driven into exile so the Royals can maintain their fiction."

Danielle shook her head, not because she didn't believe him, but because it simply didn't make sense. "But if she has such a terrible reputation with the system, wouldn't it try to have her destroyed? Or *something*?"

"The system acts as a neutral arbiter. It merely tracks change. Conflict is exceptionally useful for increasing skill levels and generating innovation... also known as *change*." The Beast finished what he was doing and swept his hand at the stairs. "I believe you should take some time to think through what has happened today. Grieve, if necessary. But tomorrow, you will start the day with knowledge and understanding you did not have when you woke up this morning. Take that as an opportunity to decide what you want your future to look like."

Danielle started walking without any further prompting, still lost in her swirling thoughts. Halfway across the room, the silence was interrupted by sudden commotion on the stairs, followed by Sneezy sprinting into the room. "Look at how nimble I am! I ran down those stairs without falling a single time. Maybe I should try taking them *three* at a time when I go up?"

"What is the meaning of this?" The Beast's muted roar echoed off the hard surfaces of the room, causing Sneezy to skid to a halt.

The fiery guard stood straight, saluting before pointing back at the stairs behind him, "There is a Baron of Verdelune demanding an audience. Apparently, he received notice of the attack and led a large portion of his troops here."

"The attack happened less than an hour ago," the Beast grumbled as his cables lifted him in the air and started rapidly pulling him upward. "How did they get here so fast? They either knew it was going to happen…"

His blue crystals turned to Danielle as he floated up. "Or they were already on their way here for another reason."

TWENTY-FOUR

DANIELLE SPRINTED UP THE STAIRS, knowing she was already far behind the Beast. Sneezy was right behind her, shouting for her to slow down. She refused, though not out of anything other than simply not hearing his words. Her mind was already too full, to the point where her questions spilled from her lips as she ascended. "What did he *mean* Gasteel might already have been on the way here? Did he know about the attack before it was coming, or... something... *else*?"

She rushed down the cheerfully painted hallway, slipping through the door of the and onto the lawn as it slowly swung shut from the Beast's passing. He was far ahead of her, and even as she stepped onto the lawn, the thunderous exchange between the two sides had already begun.

"I demand to know what happened here!" Gasteel's deep voice seemed to resonate with the air itself, causing a shiver of fear and discomfort to shoot through Danielle. With an effort of will, she kept one foot moving in front of the other, though her pace had slowed considerably.

Even with the dramatic flair, the self-righteous indignation sounded real, as though the muscled man were grieving the loss of some of his people, "There was an attack against my people, and I will have an explanation. I'm declaring a formal investigation; open the gates of this estate. *Now.*"

The Beast stood tall, armor extended slightly from his body to make him look even larger than he was. The sun was at his back as he replied with his own mechanical growl, the volume of his voice easily outmatching Gasteel. "There was no attack from this estate. Those who died here trespassed or were killed by an unknown force."

"You will *open* this gate-"

"Let me make one thing very clear, *Baron* Gasteel," the Beast spoke over the shouting commander. "You have no authority here. You are not speaking to soldiers, peasants, knights, or even a fellow Baron on the same footing as yourself. You are attempting to give orders to *Comte* LeKrout. As a reminder, as I know you have been rather recently elevated, the noble hierarchy continues from Baron to Vicomte, and from *there* to Comte. There is as much distance between your authority and Comte LeKrout's as there is between *him* and the *king*."

By this point, Danielle had found a ladder and was quickly scaling the wall, hoping to see what was going on. By the silence, she could only assume the baron was gearing up to explode at the mechanical servant, but the expected outburst never came.

Instead, Gasteel spoke in a moderated voice, likely through clenched teeth. "We will be looking through the carnage out here. If I can find any reason to make you give a proper accounting, I *will*. This is not over. My men, soldiers who relied on me for their safety and well-being... are laying as corpses at the foot of your estate."

"Then perhaps you should have stationed them *elsewhere*." The ensuing silence caused Danielle to pause as she climbed the ladder, not wanting to pop her head over the wall and offer the baron a new target for his ire.

After a moment, she heard the jangling of metal as the

baron's people got to work outside of the wall, and decided to slowly descend the ladder and wait to speak with the Beast. She was attempting to carefully study the situation, thinking through all possible avenues for not only the Beast's refusal, but the baron's presence itself.

"Even yesterday, I would have thought Gasteel was in the right." She spoke into the air, trying to get her thoughts out of her head to leave behind room for ideas. "He sounds so grief stricken… but… even if he truly is, the Beast is doing the right thing by refusing to allow them entrance. There's more at stake here than I ever expected."

The tension in the air remained as people began calling back and forth, and the casualties were collected, separated, and inspected. The sun slowly traveled across the sky as they continued, but Danielle didn't move from her spot, simply waiting to hear the outcome. She needed to know if they had truly done something despicable… and she was deeply disappointed to hear what the eventual result was.

Eventually, Gasteel returned to shout up at the stationary Beast. "Many of the fallen are riddled with metal from sources we do not recognize. Our best guess is that you and your *creatures* cut them down."

"I'm certain you were able to notice the fact that the only people who were slain by the estate's defenses bore no sigil and were the aggressors against your men," the Beast replied easily, almost as though it were bored of the conversation.

"That's where you're wrong." There was some quiet shuffling before the baron continued. "As you can see, this is one of my men, and he was clearly killed by-"

"Even from *here* I can recognize that armor is covered in damage from a radiant spell." The Beast cut Gasteel off before he could build up a full head of steam. "Yet the corpse does not have any signs of radiant damage to its skin. If you are going to play dress-up with the dead, at least have the decency to put some effort in. I warn you, baron, any further attempts to malign, lie, or force entry through false methods will result in the Comte invoking an official charge against you."

Gasteel took the denial in stride, continuing to bluster, "I don't think that's what happened. There are clear signs of your mechanisms outside of these walls. I think you've overstepped the bounds of your *house arrest*. By the authority of the king, granted to me as the military recruiter on behalf of Verdelune, I officially demand your return to the war effort under my banner. Failure to do so will be cause enough for your oath to the crown to be considered broken. Are you willing to bet your life that you are within compliance, *Comte*?"

A long, dangerous *hiss* of steam escaped the Beast. For a long, dangerous moment, that was the only sound... then there was a crash of metal as the Beast leapt over the wall and landed on the other side.

Danielle practically flew up the remainder of the ladder, desperate to see what was happening. By the time she peeked over the stone barrier, the Beast was looming over the baron, nearly three feet taller than the fleshy man. "Baron Gasteel. It is within my rights to demand an honor duel with you at this very moment. Clearly, you have only a surface-level understanding of what is happening here, which is the only reason I am not cutting you down where you stand."

"You can't-"

"The Comte is bound to his *territory*, not his *house*." The Beast would have been literally spitting mad at the baron, if it was a human. "Tell me, how much land do you think a man two steps from the throne of Verdelune has under his control? I could follow you for hours in any direction and still not take a single *step* outside my master's territory. Others are allowed to be in this land at his suffrage... and I think we will suffer your presence no longer."

A heartbeat after the Beast finished speaking, its eyes shifted to a deep red, causing no less than thirty swords to be drawn in preparation for a fight. "You are officially exiled from my territory, baron. While I cannot keep you off my land when you are on a mission for the king, the moment you have completed your task, you will see yourself away. I am adding this directive to the local ward structure as we speak."

Danielle watched as the blood drained from Gasteel's face, and he sputtered with rage as a tingle of bronze energy raced through the air. "You can't—I'm a *Baron!*"

"Yet you don't even know how to interface with the laws of the kingdom directly." the Beast scathingly replied, his eyes once more his standard blue. "If you had done your duty properly, you would already know how to block what I just did. But it's already in place. At this point, you will need to petition the king directly to have my decision reversed. Please, go before him. Explain why you need to be there, begging for help."

Letting out a deep, guttural roar of frustration, Gasteel turned on his heel and marched over to his horse. He leapt up, sending back one parting glare before digging his heels into the animal. "Don't think you're hidden up there, Belle. Someone tell her what's going on. I came as a favor, and *this* is how-"

Then he was galloping away, leaving a trail of dust to mark his passing. With the low-noble gone, Danielle stood to her full height. She looked at the assembled soldiers, not recognizing anyone among them. Taking a deep breath, she called out, "What did he mean by that?"

It seemed that no one wanted to be the first to answer, but finally, a man with his body mostly covered in armor—marking him as a sergeant at the minimum—stepped forward to offer an explanation. "Our original purpose for coming all this way was for the baron to offer his explanations to you, so you didn't hear what was happening and assume the worst of him."

"Just… just tell me. Is my father…?"

The soldier pulled his helmet off, revealing a weathered face and close-cropped hair. "Henri is currently alive and well, but an execution date has been set for him. After a careful study of the kingdom's laws-"

Here the man sent a deep glower at the Comte's representative, "-it was discovered that someone found guilty of espionage needed to be publicly executed within a specific amount of time, unless their sentence was commuted or superb reason was offered for their continued existence. As neither has occurred, two weeks from this day, the traitor's life will be cut short. The baron hoped to offer his most sincere apologies and explain on his own terms why it was out of his hands."

Danielle tried to reply but found that her voice was caught in her throat, which was suddenly too dry to allow for speaking. She simply stood there in a daze, shaking her head slightly —her thoughts filled to the brim with questions that demanded an answer. But, no matter how she tried, she simply couldn't ask.

The cleanup had mostly been completed already, but the soldiers remained on site for a decent amount of time longer, before finally turning and galloping away. All of the bodies were secured... or at least hidden from her view. Danielle didn't even notice when the Beast had returned to the wall, at least not until she felt a cold, steely grip on her arm.

"I'm terribly saddened you needed to see that, and yet I'm relieved that you came out here to see and hear what lengths they are willing to go to. Why I must be *more* than merely vigilant; I must be actively resistant to unauthorized visitors." The Beast sent her an annoyed glance. "Which is why your seemingly effortless entrance onto the estate was such a cause for concern."

Danielle pulled away. "This is not the time, Beast. My father is to be put to death because I'm resisting Gasteel's demands. I need some time."

Before she could go too far, she was stopped once more.

The Enchantress turned to snap at the Beast, only to bite her tongue as she realized its eyes were red, and she was now speaking to the Artificer.

"Do you remember what I told you a few days ago? That I've made a decision? Perhaps it's time for me to open up to someone else once more. If you will hear me out... there's more to my story that you should know."

TWENTY-FIVE

DANIELLE FOUND herself walking down the stairs to the enormous underground workshop once more, though her heart was heavy with extreme trepidation. It had taken the Comte offering her extreme reassurances to convince her not to immediately leave the estate and chase after the baron, surrendering herself to him for the sake of her father. The Artificer had then gone ahead to prepare, leaving her wondering exactly what new revelation was going to be dropped on her this time.

With nothing else to focus on as she descended the stairs, she couldn't help but notice how Resplendent Reflected Self's subtle transformation of her body seemed to have settled. The stairs were easier for her to navigate, but she wasn't much stronger—she was slightly taller than before. As she nervously fiddled with her hands, she realized how they moved with increased nimbleness and dexterity, having only been merely competent before.

Arriving at the base of the stairs, she glanced through the window into the open space, noticing her reflection in the glass and seeing how her cheekbones were better defined, and her eyes seemed sharper—seeming to focus with near-predatory precision. Scoffing slightly at the tangent her mind had gone off on, Danielle pushed through the door and entered the workshop.

As per usual, it was brightly lit, thanks to the glow of ensconced crystals. Yet today, the space seemed stark and deadly, thanks to the open presentation of so many war machines. Danielle's heightened senses allowed her to take in every detail, from the sharp lines and rusted edges of the imposing humanoid figures, to how the Beast was standing next to the extended crystalline spire with signs of despair showing on his almost-blank mechanical face.

The Enchantress furrowed her brow as she marched forward, softly murmuring to herself. "How am I able to read him like this? Logically, I know there's no way to tell what he's feeling…"

The memory of the Comte was standing in the center of the podium, mouth opened and poised to speak, but seemingly frozen in time. A half-dozen blue eyes turned to Danielle as the Beast spoke with great reluctance. "I've been instructed to show you the outcome of my master's defiance."

Without further warning, the image on the podium sprang to life, replaying what the Comte had been saying before the Beast cut off the words during Danielle's last visit. The Artificer's words echoing through the subterranean space.

"When they went into town, they were harassed by the locals—or at least those masquerading as locals. Even with all of this, I would've been fine, happy even, if it hadn't been for the Enchantress. Once I'd pulled back all of my creations and sued for peace with the kingdom of Verdelune, I was expecting to retire to a quiet, peaceful life."

He paused for a split second, then spoke despairingly.

"I thought she had grown to love me."

Unshed tears showed clearly in the memory, but the Comte pressed forward without allowing them to fall. "We had spoken about having a life together, since I had understood what I had done and took the steps needed to stop it. But... she turned out to be a foreign agent. When I had distanced myself from all others, cutting off all my support networks, replaced all of the people around me with my loyal machines... she injected me with a heart-destroying poison. To her credit, as I fell to the ground, she took the time to tell me why I was being murdered."

The Comte scoffed even as he spoke, seeming as though he almost didn't believe the words coming out of his mouth. "Apparently, simply stopping the atrocities from *continuing* was not enough. She needed to make sure they could never happen again, and that I paid for the crimes I didn't even know were being committed in my name. Before the poison could fully run its course, my newest creation, the BST model three, rushed to my aid. The Enchantress, with no defenses of her own, was cut down in a single blow."

"When she died, so did every plant on the lawn. Everything green, everything beautiful that could witness her death, killed in the same instant. It seemed... poetic, almost. Since then-" At the same time as he continued his tale, the lights in the area turned off, all but a pair of powerful spotlights pointed at the very back of the room. There, a large metal capsule rested, fully surrounded on all sides by the metal knights.

"Since then, I'm only kept alive by remaining within the stasis chamber granted to me by the kingdom to ensure I would remain as I was, able to work endlessly on behalf of the kingdom. Physically, I have not aged a day since my twenty-fifth birthday, and I can only hope the maintenance I am able to provide through my 'Remote Usage' skill will keep the stasis going until I can find a solution."

No for the words followed, and it took nearly half a minute for Danielle to realize no more were forthcoming. "That's it? He's just stuck in that device over there, waiting to die?"

"Waiting to *live*, is the hope," the Beast stated in a chiding tone. "He is permanently trapped in a dream-like state, able to learn and work, but... each day, he can only remotely access his creations for a short period of time. The longer he waits between activations, the longer he can stay active before falling back into his cursed slumber."

"So that's what he meant when he said he didn't know how old he was?" Danielle shook her head at the thought, unsure of how to process this strange turn of events. "How long has he been stuck in there? Actually, do *you* know how old he is?"

"Let me answer your question with a thought experiment." The Beast spoke around a slow leak of steam, as though he were letting out a deep sigh. "Imagine two men are born on the same day, of the same year, and both live very similar lives until they turn eighteen. One of them goes on to live an intense life, working more than twelve hours a day and still finding time to experience joy and life with his family. Let's say he is awake eighteen hours a day, barely getting the sleep his body needs."

"Now, the other person lives a life of absolute leisure, sleeping eighteen hours a day and only being *awake* for six." The Beast gestured at the capsule in the distance. "In ten years, one of those two men will have three times the life experience of the other. At twenty-eight years old, which of them is twenty-eight years old?"

"Both of them." The Beast shot her a look, so Danielle rolled her eyes and played along, "*Technically*, they're the same age. But, in terms of life experience, I'd say the man living a life of leisure could be compared to only a twenty-one-year-old when directly compared to the other who'd been awake and active that whole time."

"The system seems to agree with you." Once more, the Beast looked at the capsule in the distance longingly. "During his last physical, when looking at his personal information, I found that the system had split his age-related information. It now is listing his age as two separate categories: mental *and* physical. Physically, he is still exactly twenty-five years old. His mental age is shown only as twenty-eight. Yet… he was born nearly fifty years ago. He is given at most thirty minutes of time each day he can be awake, but often forgoes even that much in hopes of having access to the time when it truly matters. So. You tell me, how old is he?"

Danielle thought about that for a long few minutes, arguing back and forth with what was the exact correct answer. Finally, she could only shrug her shoulders and decide, "He's *all* of those. *Everyone* sleeps nearly a third of the day every day, and we don't consider their age to be only two-thirds of how many years they've been alive. His body hasn't aged in a long period of time, so if he were healthy, he could leave that chamber and live the rest of his natural life from that point. But…"

Here, her eyes blazed with conviction, "But we are the sum of our experiences. I've met people twice my age who were barely as mature as I, half as skilled, and only a *fraction* as ready to live life to the fullest. Frankly, I am surprised the system doesn't offer everyone in the world an accounting of their mental age. It would actually answer many questions I have about some people."

"Well… now you know the truth of why you have never met Comte LeKrout face-to-face." The Beast was studying her carefully as he spoke. "He is fragile beyond belief, and there is no one else alive who has access to this information. If you wanted to do so, you could hand this information over. It would be a simple thing at that point for the kingdom to starve us of resources and force him to create weapons once more."

The implication hung in the air for a brief moment, until Danielle realized that what he was truly doing was asking her if she would take this information and use it for herself. "Beast! Since I came here, I've been given nothing but kindness and respect. At least, after I earned some trust. I've been living a life I couldn't have... *anywhere* else, to my knowledge. I'd never betray any of you like that. An Enchantress might have taken you out of the war and hurt the Comte terribly, but that doesn't mean a different one will be the reason he is thrust back into it."

The Beast heaved a sigh of relief, or at least that is how Danielle decided to understand the cloud of steam that poured out of him. "I greatly appreciate your candor. With all of this new information, has anything changed for you?"

"I don't... I can't think of anything?" Danielle tried to determine if there was a hidden meaning to the question, but it seemed quite straightforward. "I still don't want to marry that terrible man, yet I need to find a solution which keeps me from his clutches while saving my father. I suppose the only thing that's changed is my desire to make the Comte accept this responsibility in my stead."

"Then, perhaps you will not be terribly pleased to learn that he has sent a half dozen of the newest, most-human versions of his soldiers to rescue Henri?" The Beast's words almost caused Danielle to turn on her heel and start running. "Do not bother, Danielle. They were dispatched a day ago and can move nearly as far each day as a man riding on horseback. They will be making their move as soon as your father is brought outside, and at this point, there is no way for them to be recalled. Without a horse, you'd never get there before they are already returning."

"*Why*? Why would he do that? Do you realize what this means? He's painted a target on his back, and Gasteel will be able to order him into the war if he finds out!" Danielle cut off her barrage of questions and accusations, biting her lip to keep from dipping her toes into insulting the Beast.

Surprisingly, it wasn't the Beast who answered her, but the memory that had been frozen on the platform until this point. Its image shifted to a weary man, wearing simple, comfortable clothes. "For years, I've been striving for *Perfection*, trying to find a way to fix my heart so I could truly live once more. Now, I have reached Perfection with my skill and have the added bonus of my Breakthrough Skill to help me along. My hope is that, with the assistance of Danielle, who has proven herself not to be my prisoner nor my guest, but a true peer… I will instead be able to create an entirely new, working organ for myself."

"For her assistance so far, as well as in hopes she will stand by me and offer her support in this very dangerous juncture, I am attempting to pay her in advance." The image shifted to a landscape, somewhere far distant that she recognized immediately: it was a picturesque view of Frontière as viewed from a distance. "First, to ensure she does not feel conflicted in her choice, her father will be rescued and brought to her side. Secondly, several of my automatons have been loaded down with supplies and riches, dispatched to our neighboring kingdom to purchase a large estate on her behalf."

The memory of the man shifted in place, looking at the ground then back up without truly being able to meet her eyes.

"I can only hope this will be enough to convince you to stand by my side for at least a little bit longer."

CHAPTER

TWENTY-SIX

GASTEEL

THE TOWN of Frontière was practically buzzing with a twisted festival mood, a hint of excitement mixing with a palpable bloodthirst. The townspeople, conscripts, and soldiers were already shouting and jeering in eager anticipation of the day's entertainment. Gasteel stood on the balcony of a makeshift stage, scanning the crowd and at the same time looking to the edge of town to see if a scout was rushing in to give him an update.

It had been two weeks since he had delivered the notice to his prospective fiancée, yet not a whisper of compliance had reached his ears. Not from her, not from any scouts stationed throughout the area to watch for motion, absolutely *nothing*. A thick coating of annoyance at her defiance festered beneath his skin, but a cold smile crossed his face at the thought of venting his frustrations.

"She's willing to sacrifice her own father... unexpected, yet commendable. Truly, she would've been the perfect fit for me. Beautiful, yet willing to do whatever it takes. We could have started a lineage incomparable to anyone else in the world." Gasteel let out a heavy sigh, shaking his head at missing out on such an ideal specimen, then tried to put her out of his mind.

With a smile on his face, he turned to the crowd and reassured himself that this was one of three acceptable outcomes. "I'd hoped today would be a wedding celebration, but a little blood sport is always an acceptable alternative."

In the exact center of the town square, a makeshift guillotine had been constructed for this event. Only a select few were allowed to sit with the baron on stage, giving them a perfect view of the execution, as well as being as a sign of his favor. Taking a deep breath, Gasteel shouted over the laughing, cacophonous crowd. "Bring out the traitor, and witness the king's justice!"

People moved as a wave, opening a path from the doors of the tavern at the edge of the town square, all the way to the stairs leading up to the guillotine itself. As the crowd quieted, the sound of the tavern door being thrown open violently rang through the space, echoing ever so slightly as Henri was pushed through the opening and fell to the ground with an *oof*.

The crowd immediately began to chaotically roar with cheers and booing in equal measure, quickly reaching a fever pitch as they watched the one-legged man get lifted to his foot —as his prosthetic had been cruelly confiscated that very morning. One of Gasteel's men flanked him on either side, their arms hooked under his shoulders so they could slowly and deliberately drag him toward the guillotine.

A few onlookers began griping that the rotten fruit they had purchased to throw at the Tinkerer would go to waste. They could only swallow their anger, as no one dared to risk hitting one of the baron's soldiers, not even by accident. Gasteel's ears twitched, so he made sure to quickly call out, "Don't worry! Once he is in position, I'll make sure my men step back for a few minutes, so you can vent your frustrations while his crimes are read."

The condemned man showed no signs of resistance and barely even flinched as the strong men pinched his arms to make him wiggle as they pulled him along. Henri's energy had been drained by his daily raving, and in his exhaustion, he simply kept a small smile on his face—certainly not the visage expected of a man resigned to his fate, but one of quiet defiance and calm acceptance.

The crowd's jeers and hurled insults grew louder as they watched him seem to laugh at them, their cacophony of accusations and false charges bouncing off of him like pebbles thrown against a stout stone wall. Even when broken toys were tossed at his feet—the last remnants of his life's work now reduced to fragments scattered across the path—he only calmly hopped along as best as he could.

Finally, Henri was forced to his knees before the guillotine, and Baron Gasteel stepped forward on the elevated stage, the perfect place to see every gory detail of the execution while keeping an eye on the crowd. With a deep breath, his voice boomed over the uproarious crowd, releasing a tirade about how this man was a foreign agent.

As rotten fruit and vegetables rained down around the old man, the baron only laughed and mimed joining in, encouraging the people to correct their aim.

Just as he had promised, Gasteel worked hard to get every person to vent their frustration, to cast all of their anger at the feet of this man, so their issues would die with him. With his daughter out of the picture, the reclusive Tinkerer had no strong ties to the community. The baron made sure to use this fact to paint him as the scapegoat for every unsolved crime, every minor misfortune, even going so far as to blame the man for impacting the local egg economy by creating toys which would cause chickens to be too afraid to lay.

Issue after absurd issue was dropped on the man, fueling

the crowd's bloodlust. Soon they were *howling* for the old man to be torn apart instead of cleanly beheaded. Notably, the baker had to be physically restrained by those around him as he attempted to rush forward and beat the man to death with his rolling pin.

As Gasteel continued his rant, something strange caught his eye. In the midst of the seething crowd, a handful of figures were standing almost unnaturally still as they watched the proceedings. Something about the odd figures made his hackles rise, and he inspected them, even as his hands waved back and forth, keeping everyone's attention on the spectacle. Dark, heavy fabric obscured their features, and their heads were bowed with their faces hidden in shadow.

Even so… as a hunter, Gasteel had long been able to notice when there was an aura of barely restrained violence around someone. His eyes narrowed as he tried to assess the threat; these men who had appeared out of nowhere. The way they held themselves? Poised, patient, predators waiting for the perfect moment to strike—all of it set off alarms in his mind. Grinding his teeth, the baron decided it was time to act.

"Today, we rid ourselves of a traitor who conspired against our great kingdom. Without further delay, you are sentenced to death and will pay for your crimes with your blood." Gasteel nodded to the person who'd won the raffle and earned the right to pull the lever which would remove Henri's head.

Throughout all of this, the Tinkerer remained calm, seeming to have accepted the inevitability of his fate.

This relaxed demeanor made Gasteel grind his teeth in fury—he wanted this man to be *afraid*. To *suffer* in his last moments for the annoyance his daughter had caused. But, if this was how it was going to be, it would be best to end it quickly, before people started to second guess the charges tossed at him.

A drumroll began as the bard who had been playing for Henri in the tavern offered the man one last beat, a glum expression on his face. Gasteel wasn't the only person to lean forward, his eyes fixed on the blade as he waited for it to fall.

A thrill of anticipation ran through the crowd as the local raffle winner grabbed the lever. But as the wooden handle was yanked, and the gleaming blade began to descend, a blur of motion pulled Gasteel from his enjoyment of the moment. Someone moving with inhuman speed passed through the crowd, jumping between the descending blade and its intended destination.

Ta~ang.

The baron had heard that sound many times throughout his military career: it was the sound of a blade being parried by someone with great skill. Yet, it was nearly exclusively found when one swordsman was facing off with another. In this case, the unknown individual had caught the guillotine with his bare hands—stopping it dead in its tracks.

Having already noticed the cloak-covered men, Gasteel recovered from his surprise nearly instantly. "Soldiers! Slay that person! Anyone who would rescue a traitor must be a spy or a traitor themselves!"

The crowd gasped in shock, recoiling hurriedly as the cloaked figure lifted and threw the entire mechanism to the side with a single powerful motion. The festival mood shattered instantly as panic spread through the crowd like wildfire. Civilians began screaming, running for their life as the massive implement of death began falling toward them. The baker, who had been so eager to extract his own form of justice, now stumbled backward, his rolling pin clattering to the ground from nerveless fingers as he tried to flee.

The soldiers nearest Henri were all conscripts, and though they pulled out their swords and fearlessly threw themselves forward, the cloaked man danced around them easily, avoiding their attacks while *thumping* them with precise strikes to send them crashing to the ground, unconscious.

For his part, Gasteel had already launched himself toward

the tavern, rushing to grab his weapons and hunt down these interlopers. He kept an eye on this situation as he ran, watching as five similarly cloaked figures appeared, swooping in, scooping up Henri, and dashing away. Still weaponless himself, the baron saw red as he bellowed with all his might, "*Stop them*! Whoever brings one of them down gets leave for a *month!*"

Across the square, every soldier unsheathed their weapons and descended on the intruders who had ruined their event. Unfortunately, no weapon could touch the hidden individuals. They moved with a fluid grace, each swift and merciless blow a masterclass in combat efficiency. Upon drawing their weapons, they fought with an economy of motion where every slash, punch, and kick was delivered with a specific intent. Anyone who tried their luck against them stood no chance, being outmatched, outmaneuvered, and overwhelmed in moments.

Watching in stunned disbelief as his men were systematically felled, the baron's mind whirled with the implications of what he was witnessing. "I've only ever seen Swordmasters at the Breakthrough Skill level able to casually avoid attacks like this, especially en masse... did I actually manage to find a foreign agent? Can there be any other explanation?"

Bursting into the tavern, the baron found Lefroupe already standing there, holding his sword and musket. Gasteel held up a hand, turning in a practiced motion as his scribe reared back. "*Now!*"

Then his weapons were flying through the air with all the force Lefroupe could muster, which frankly wasn't much. Still, it was enough for the baron to return outside nearly three seconds faster than if they'd exchanged the items normally. Once more standing in the light of day, he looked for the cloaked figures and found—with a deep sense of disbelief— that to a man, every single soldier who had stood in the path of one of the cloaked figures had been left on the ground behind them as they made their escape.

Worst of all, Henri was being whisked away.

"No! I *will* have at least *one* of my good outcomes!" Gasteel shouted as he sprinted over and leaped onto the stage, discarding his sword and swinging his musket into position. Though they were moving fast, he had taken down trophies at a far greater distance. Carefully aiming for center mass, he lifted his musket slightly... making sure his projectile would strike his target in the head. Then he invoked his highest-level skills, one after another. "Aim and Strike... *Compress and Spark!*"

As he said the final word, his self-created weapon practically exploded, held in place only by his immensely muscled form. A lead ball spun through the air, ever so slightly off course. Instead of killing the traitor, the person holding him took the projectile dead-center to the back of their head... but somehow kept running. "*What?* What *Witchery* is this? Abyss, that was a perfect shot! What kind of monster can lose their head and not even be bothered?"

As he watched in stunned disbelief, another of the cloaked figures turned toward him. Though he couldn't see the man's face, the baron could feel the weight of that cold gaze. Under his breath, Gasteel quietly muttered, "That's right. Get mad. Stay angry. Stay in *range*."

Quickly adding a second lead ball bearing to his weapon, he lifted the tube once more... but his target had already entered the tree line. Swinging the musket back and forth, Gasteel realized all of the cloaked figures had already vanished. Letting out a roar of frustration, he cast the weapon to the side, grabbed his sword, and began to give chase. "Find them and bring them down! The spy dies *this day*! Horses! Men! *Charge!*"

Following the path Henri had been dragged away on, the baron nearly stumbled as his foot kicked a large, solid object.

Glaring down at the offending article, his eyes went wide, and he skid to a stop. "What is—a helmet? I *knew* I hit him. How did this manage to stop my…?"

Grasping the metal object, he could see clearly where his musket ball had put a hole through the thick armor. He spun it slightly, eyes narrowing as he found a face looking back at him.

A face cut directly into the material of the helmet itself.

"So that's it… the System-Forsaken Battle Beast has broken his oath to remain under house arrest." His fury quickly drained away, turning into calculation as he tossed the head into the air and caught it, lost in thought. He looked into the forest, "I suppose it might be a good thing I didn't accidentally hit my future father-in-law. Thank you, *Comte*. You've given me a delightful wedding present this day."

He returned to the town, shouting for his soldiers to stand down and prepare to break camp instead of going on a wild chase. "Lefroupe? Celestial *feces*, man! Why can I never find you when I need you?"

"Here, my lord!" The weaselly man pushed through the crowd, his eyes cautious as he closed in on the baron, who was shaking with excitement. The scribe had only ever seen the baron act like this directly after a wonderful battle, and he could only hope there was something productive for the huge man to channel his energies into.

"Prepare a dispatch to the king. Inform him of the Comte's breach of his oath and request immediate support for my conscription of the man." He casually tossed the metal head over. "Send *this* along as proof of his oath-breaking ways."

As everyone in the town hurried to carry out his orders, Gasteel took a long inhale, letting loose a satisfied sigh. His thoughts drifted to the Enchantress, imagining how she'd react to the news that she had played directly into his hand, serving him a bride and an Artificer on a silver platter.

Remembering the metal head, he let out a soft chuckle.

"Silver for certain, but perhaps not a *platter*. No execution yet, but two of my three good outcomes instead. Today is starting to smell like a *career* move."

TWENTY-SEVEN

DANIELLE

THE DOOR to the library burst open, causing Danielle to look up from where she sat at an oversized oak table, scribbling away at a design she'd been working on since breakfast. Thick books and handwritten technical manuals were blocking her view of the Beast floating toward her, so she carefully pushed them to the side and gave him her full attention. "Is something the matter, Beast?"

"I see you have been *productive*, as usual." Blue light gently reflected off the thick stack of paper and empty bottles of ink directly adjacent to the Enchantress. "Commendable, especially with Comte LeKrout having already informed you of your impending reward. This may come as a shock to you, but-"

"But you've come around to my presence here, and you're glad I showed up in the first place." Danielle popped a cork in the open bottle of ink, raising an eyebrow and smiling at the towering machine as it faltered. "What? You don't think I've *noticed* how much nicer you've been over the last few weeks? Some of the engines I've been studying in here couldn't have been moved by anyone but you—they're at least two to three thousand pounds each. That, and no one else took credit for your efforts. Thank you, Beast. I like you, too."

Eh-hrrm. The grinding of gears was almost a perfect mimicry of someone clearing their throat. "Yes, well, you have proven yourself less intrusive than I had first expected. I know you wanted to take a look at some of the larger designs. It was not an issue to move them here. In fact, it was... rather nice to feel like I was working alongside someone, instead of simply *managing* them. Enough of this. That's not why I'm here. Follow me?"

Though it had been phrased as a question, it was clear the Beast expected her to immediately get to her feet and chase after him. Danielle complied, more out of a sense of interest in this odd behavior than a feeling of obligation. "Did something good happen, Beast?"

"As a matter of fact... yes." The Beast stepped into the hallway and turned around, "I am pleased to inform you that the rescue mission was successful. Your father has been safely extracted, though there were... complications."

Danielle let out a shriek of delight, throwing herself forward and wrapping her arms as far around the machine as she could reach. "I can't believe it! He's safe? He's on his way here? Wait! What do you mean, 'complications'?"

"He is safe and in good health. His arrival is expected within the next few days." The Beast held very still at that moment, perhaps concerned that he may accidentally shift too suddenly and squash the frail human like a bug. "I would be happy to explain further, but please step away. I am unused to being *grappled*."

"It's called a hug, Beast. If you're going to keep doing such nice things, you'd better get used to them." Even as she teased the massive automaton, Danielle complied, easing back and away.

"A solid justification for me to outsource 'nice' actions."

The growl from the Beast only served to make Danielle laugh. "Yes. Unfortunately, there was a slight complication. Baron Gasteel managed to land a powerful blow against one of the dispatched soldiers, revealing our involvement in the rescue. At last check, they'd been waiting on orders from the crown, but now they are moving in our direction. As they are moving here with their full force, they are moving slowly."

Danielle slumped as though the gravity of the situation had actually increased the weight on her shoulders. "This is bad... they're coming for us. What do we do, Beast? Can we fight them?"

"Yes, and at the same time, very much... no." The gears in the Beast's body literally began spinning, their lack of proper housing showing clearly that he had just started thinking about something very intently. "There are some ideas floating between myself and the Comte, but we will include you in the deliberations before we've made a final decision. Before all of that, as a celebration of your father's successful rescue, I'd like to show you something else to lift your spirits. Behold... Doc's new form!"

At that moment, a flash of motion in her peripheral caused Danielle to look up—just in time to see a massive mechanical spider *drop* from the ceiling. It hit the stone floor with a surprisingly muted series of **clangs** as its eight legs moved with eerie precision to reduce the impact. The creature looked over at the duo, its eight glowing eyes holding her attention for a bare moment before her gaze was directed toward a **clacking** set of razor-sharp mandibles.

Despite its terrifying appearance and abrupt arrival, Danielle's face lit up with a beaming smile. "Doc! Just *look* at you! How does your transformation feel? Is it everything you hoped it would be? When did they complete the prototype?"

The spider's body was sleek and polished. As her eyes roved over its thorax, Danielle noticed how there hadn't been a *hint* of alteration to her final submitted design. A thrill rushed through her when she realized that meant the Artificer hadn't been able to find a single place to improve upon the blueprint. That tingle swirled, becoming a physical sensation before traveling to her left arm.

"Madame Danielle, it is good to see you... and even better to *be* seen." The spider bowed slightly toward her, its eyes flickering ominously. Doc's voice was similar in cadence, but gone was the chiming quality his tiny form had previously necessitated. Now when Doc spoke, his voice resounded from the center of his body and echoed in both his thorax and abdomen sections, adding a cavernous quality to the words.

"Well, you look amazing. This is exactly what you wanted, yes?"

"It's everything I hoped for and more." The spider looked back and forth ever so slightly then leaned in, as if to share a great secret. "I can shoot a harpoon out of my mouth... *and* my butt. I'll be able to travel through the trees surrounding the estate by swinging on the attached coiled chain. When we're done here, I'm going to go practice."

"That's... that's wonderful, Doc." The Enchantress's smile wobbled slightly as she tried to get on board with the sheer enthusiasm the automaton was expressing. "I'm glad you're happy. When I was working through the design, I figured, if you wanted one so badly... you'd really be excited about having *two*."

"And you were *so* right," Doc muttered as he bobbed his head at her a few more times then spun around and began *clattering* down the hall faster than a regular man could sprint. "I'm going to go *practice!*"

Watching the machine run away, Danielle could only blink in slight shock at how the interaction had played out. Releasing a sound somewhere between a scoff and a chuckle at the audacious situation, she turned her eyes to her arm to view what new information the system had for her.

Skill increase! Unified Radiance [Level 8 (Extensive) → Level 9 (Master)]!

Requirement to advance to level 10-

Then, to her shock, even as she read the words, the golden text was wiped away and replaced with a pearlescent light so intense that it would have blinded her if it hadn't been gentle system energy pouring in and altering her.

Skill increase! Unified Radiance [Level 9 (Master) → Level 10 (Perfect)]!

Unified Radiance is a passive, continuous skill representing the culmination and fusion of the skills Resplendent Self, Aura of Refinement, Alluring Assemblage, and Graceful Movement, seamlessly integrating them into a symbiotic relationship where the admiration you receive will [Minimally] fuel the enhancement of your surroundings and yourself, and vice versa. The radius of this effect extends up to [10] meters from your body.

Building upon the original skills, Unified Radiance extends this skills effect to a broader range of activity. Any task or action you undertake is imbued with [Perfect] inherent beauty. This effect also [Perfectly] increases the value and appeal of objects and people you are involved with, both for sales and social interactions. As this passive skill grows more potent, it will allow you to adeptly evolve to new situations, allowing yourself and those impacted to be [Perfectly] adept at navigating social scenarios.

This creates a positive feedback loop between yourself and your environment. As your beauty and grace increases, so does the beauty and appeal of your surroundings, in turn further amplifying your own allure.

Advanced Skill Unlocked!
Advance Skill gained: Holistic Refinement, a Damsel of Distress: Level 0/10.

Holistic Refinement allows the user to synergize and direct all previous skills into a powerful enhancer. When actively crafting something new, whether it is an object, design, or idea, all factors of the final product are taken into account and enhanced [level x 10%] by the System. Legacy creations will only benefit half as much as new creations.

All previous skills remain permanently and passively effective on the user of this skill, but the user now has [no] control as to what is otherwise impacted.

Requirement to advance to level 1: use this skill a single time.

Special modifier applied: You have been granted a modifier **'Damsel of Distress'***.*

Against seemingly insurmountable odds, you transformed a set of skills or circumstances which nearly guaranteed failure or even death into a foundation for success with far-reaching and profound effects. By taking your fate into your own hands, you have broken free of the Codex Arcane Ledger's predicted outcome for your life.

Effect: When in the presence of another 'Damsel of Distress', you will be able to recognize each other as kindred spirits and [Minimally] share the benefits of your skills, if so desired, while in range. This will increase in potency with the skill it was acquired in tandem with.

Danielle nearly choked on her tongue as she swallowed back a scream, followed by spinning on her heel and sprinting over to the table she had vacated in the library. Yanking over a clean sheet of parchment and abruptly popping the seal off a bottle of ink without concern for how it would splash on the oak table, she furiously began scribbling down the most basic design she knew by heart.

Only a few minutes later, the blueprint for a singing bird

toy stared back up at her, and she slapped the quill to the table and looked up, announcing to empty air, "*Done!*"

Looking down, she saw a slight glimmer rush across the page, ever so subtly shifting the gear positions of the bird and cleaning up droplets of ink that had splashed in her haste. That same light collected at the tip of the lower left corner of the page, then jumped to her arm like static. Danielle's arm glowed, but even before it did, she was impatiently swiping her finger along her skin. "Come on… there's only one line I care about…"

Skill increase: Holistic Refinement [0 (none) → 1 (Minimal)]!
Holistic Refinement 1/10.
Holistic Refinement allows the user to synergize and direct all previous skills into a powerful enhancer. When actively crafting something new, whether it is an object, design, or idea, all factors of the final product are taken into account and enhanced [10%] by the System. Legacy creations will only benefit half as much as new creations.

All previous skills remain permanently and passively effective on the user of this skill, but the user now has [Minimal] control as to what is otherwise impacted.

Requirement to advance to level 2: Create 5 objects or designs you have never created before, without using a schematic provided by someone else.

She gasped as the air around her dimmed slightly, just enough that it would've been missed if she hadn't been specifically watching her surroundings so intently. Tears filled her eyes unbidden as an immense joy welled up within her, and Danielle choked out a few words as she turned to offer an explanation to the Beast, who had followed her and remained by her side, greatly concerned.

"I… I got an *active skill*, Beast! It gave me control of my passives. I mean, it's not *Perfect* yet, but eventually it *will* be. This changes everything. For the first time since the day I turned eighteen, I don't have to be afraid that someone will keep me in a room and use me as their *makeup routine*."

"That is a very specific fear," the Beast mentioned in a slightly confused tone. "Congratulations on your advancement. I am pleased to hear you are happy with the results."

"For the first time *ever*, Beast," Danielle couldn't stop the tears flowing from her eyes, even as the brilliant smile on her face stayed right where it was. "I'm going to work so hard to *Perfect* this skill... you don't even know."

TWENTY-EIGHT

Though they had plenty of cause to celebrate, Danielle fully understood they were working with a deadline approaching with the swiftness of an executioner's axe. Unfortunately, when she pressed the Beast for additional information on what the Artificer planned to do, he came back with an explanation she couldn't accept.

"Comte LeKrout has asked me to explain his hopes for the coming days." The Beast *clacked* and *whirred* as he shifted to face the Enchantress. "For the foreseeable future, it is our hope you will work with us to design and fully create an artificial heart to replace his severely damaged version. Once your father has arrived, the two of you will be transported to the border of Verdelune. As soon as you are safely away, we will collapse the manor and seal ourselves within this workroom while we make final preparations for the replacement."

Through his entire speech, Danielle could only stare at the Beast, the expression rapidly turning to a full-on glare until he stopped speaking. "You mean to tell me you expect me to cut and run as soon as I have my father?"

"You will have everything you want, will you not?" The Beast seemed surprised at her reaction, which only served to further kindle her annoyance. "Your father will be with you. Your foundational knowledge has been repaired and enhanced. A new life awaits. You will have everything you need to-"

"What about the Artificer?" Danielle shook her head and started walking past the Beast. "He's coming with us. At the very least, I'm not leaving until I know for certain that the heart succeeded or failed. You should know better than to ask me to help create such a marvel, then expect me to not stay to see the result. No, I have a better idea. Where can I find all the stored linens, towels, pillows-"

"This was not a *request*, Enchantress," the Beast growled at her, seemingly devolving back to the state he was in upon their first meeting. "LeKrout has a vested interest in your health and wellbeing. If you insist on staying if you assist in the creation of his heart, you will not be given access to the project in the first place. When your father arrives, he will be given a short time to rest and recover, then the two of you-"

"If you drag me away, I'll come *sprinting* back as soon as I have the ability to do so." Danielle turned on him, her head nearly all the way back so she could stare up into his eyes, due to their close proximity. "You say it's to keep me safe that I'm to be sent away? I guarantee there will be a military encirclement at the minimum by the time I get back here. I'm staying, and all of us… we'll leave together."

"What? No, that's not an option we are willing to pursue." The Beast shook his head, even as the Enchantress got a distant look in her eye, and her gaze became unfocused. "Once the Artificer is back to full mobility, he will be able to use all of his skills at full strength as long as is needed each day. Suing for peace will be *laughably* easy-"

"You already told me it wouldn't work twice." Danielle's eyes snapped back to the beasts. "No. We'll all leave together, making a new life for ourselves elsewhere. With all of the forces at his command, why not just go find an unoccupied mountain somewhere and hollow it out? Then we can experi-ment, create, and live *however* we want to live. That sounds much better, doesn't it? Stop. I'm not going to hear another word about this until after I can speak to the Artificer face-to-face. Now… the linens?"

The blaze of pearlescent light shining off of Danielle's left arm, a clear sign of a skill reaching Perfection, brought the conversation to a screeching halt.

Skill increase! Aura of Refinement [Level 9 (Master) → Level 10 (Perfect)]!

Advanced Skill: Aura of Refinement: Level 10/10.
Your presence subtly, permanently, and [Perfectly] enhances the beauty and charm of people and objects within your vicinity based on the local aesthetic, reaching up to [10] meters from your body. This effect is gradual and automatic, becoming more pronounced the longer you are around people and objects, or the more focused attention you give them with this skill.

Advanced Class Breakthrough Skill: Permanently Locked.

As the changes settled within her, Danielle took a sharp breath, her vision clearing, and her mind calming as she felt as though a piece that had been missing was finally returned— with an immense upgrade. Each of her Full Class skills included the Aura of Refinement as part of their makeup, which meant that singular change had just made a heavy impact on a total of *three* of her skills.

"Would you look at that… it seems I've decided how I want to live my life, have taken steps toward making it happen, and the system itself approves. Kind of hard to argue with that, now *isn't* it, Beast?"

Gears were spinning so quickly in the Beast's head that she

expected literal smoke to pour from its ears. Over the course of a few seconds, their intensity ramped down, and he slowly spoke in an indignantly frustrated voice. "I will need to wait to bring this to the Comte, either way. He is resting as long as he can, to give the both of you the best chance at designing, producing, and fully scripting the creation in one go. What is this uncouth desire for sheets that you are suddenly so adamant about?"

"Simple." The corner of her lips pulled up in triumph, but Danielle wasn't one to gloat. "Gasteel is on his way here to demand that the Comte joins him in the war under his banner. Apparently, he'll have every right to do so by the time he gets here. What *we're* going to do is reinforce the estate to make sure we are able to squeeze every last second out of our available time to get LeKrout back on his feet."

"You're going to reinforce the estate against a war party... using the *fancy* dish towels?" Even as his doubtful question echoed in the hall, Danielle had already started nodding her head.

"That's *exactly* what we're going to do." The smirk on her face turned into a full-blown mischievous grin. "Anything outside of the house needs to be put entirely on automatic, cut off from being able to send information back to the Artificer when he wakes up. Oh, don't act like that, you think I haven't realized that he gets some kind of feedback from everything while he's in his hibernation state? The moment he wakes up, he knows what's been going on. I'm no fool, Beast."

The enormous machine was shifting back and forth with great discomfort, seeming as though it were ready to spout fabrications and denials, but it gave up when it saw the resolute stare it was receiving. "Fine, yes... you have figured out yet another of his *highly secret* abilities. Before you ask, it is only a certain few of his creations designed with that skill in mind, and only within a small radius of his physical location."

"Good enough for now." Danielle shifted her attention to

the automatons, which had slowly been gathering as their conversation grew louder. "We are going to stuff every crack in the walls, every air hole, arrow slit, and seam in the doors with anything that will dampen outside sound. If the baron gets here and starts shouting at the top of his lungs, attempting to invoke the Comte's oaths, we need to make sure there's no way for Gasteel's words to reach LeKrout's ears."

"If he can't hear the order, or isn't directly told… it won't have a binding effect." The Beast slowly began to realize her plan. "I see. It doesn't need to be a permanent solution, it just needs to give us enough time to finish what we need and make a run for it. Good. It is a tactic I would not have considered. I'll have the escape tunnel opened, aired out, and cleaned to ensure there are no surprises on the way out."

"No spider webs for the Madame of Machines to walk through." Doc hissed out a laugh from his position a dozen feet up the wall. "But maybe a few for the invaders, yes?"

"You don't make webs, Doc," Danielle called up in passing. "I thought you went outside?"

"I said I was going to *practice*. I am." The spider-based machine gently *clanged* its legs on the wall in agitation. "For your information, you don't know everything I can do! I have *tricks* up my sleeve."

"Now *that* puts an odd image in my head." Sneezy fell in step next to Danielle and began guiding her to the storage room. "If a half-ton metal spider were to wear a shirt, would it be on the cephalothorax or over the entire body? I kind of feel like it would be the former, but that would only put sleeves on two to four of its legs. Err… arms?"

"This is really not something we should be spending our brain power on, Sneezy." After a moment of walking in silence, Danielle let out a soft growl and glared at the smirking flamethrower guard. "It would *have* to be just the thorax, right? If a garment went over the abdomen, that part would have to be classified as pants. Or maybe the whole thing would be a romper? I hate that you put this in my head."

"No you don't."

"Danielle!" The word echoed through the hallway as the Beast finished giving out instructions, only to turn and find that the Enchantress had moved away. "Where are you going? You had a fantastic idea. Now, are you going to be spending the next few days plugging holes with shredded down comforters, or are you going to put your talents to use working with me to design this heart? I can tell you *my* preference, but feel free to grab a pair of scissors and start chopping up the extra-plush bath towels instead."

With a sheepish grin at her guard, who merely gave her a wave and continued moving toward the supply closet, Danielle turned and hurried back to the library. As she walked past the Beast, she kept her eyes forward, not daring to look at him. No one liked seeing a machine preening over its wordplay. "I've said it before, passive-aggressive isn't a good look on you, Beast."

"Of course you are correct, *Madame of Machines*. Oh, *yes*, that's right. I heard what he called you," the Beast snarked back at her, falling into step as they moved to the large table. His hands reached forward, one finger scraping the surface of the table where Danielle had spilled ink in her hurry a short while ago.

The outstretched appendage began spinning, and he swiftly sanded down the affected area. "A touch of varnish, and it will be like nothing happened. A question, if I may. How long have the others been putting you on a pedestal like that? An Enchantress with an over-inflated ego is a recipe for *cooking with disaster*."

"They just like that I'm nice to them, Beast. If you were better about that, they'd probably call you something other than 'BST model three' to your face." She remained standing at the table, rearranging her notes, paper, and ink. "As to what they call you behind your back… well, you float around silently, I'm sure you've heard it once or twice."

"I'm not going to justify that with a response nor pry into their behavior," the Beast stiffly retorted. "I have here the preliminary designs of the lord of the house's proposed replacement heart. Included in them are-"

"We can't use those, Beast! Don't let me see them!" Danielle rapidly backpedaled, going so far as to cover her eyes with an arm. "If I use his designs, the system will improve the final product I make by only *half* of what it otherwise would have. No. All I want are *drawings* of his heart, as well as the physical specifications, if you have them. Even before I do anything on this project, I want to push through the first easy levels of my new skill. Any improvement we can eke out will give this a higher chance of success."

"Might I remind you we are on a rather short deadline?" The Beast chose his words carefully. "While I appreciate your desire for excellence, in this instance, I believe having anything that will work will be better than a perfected solution. If we had all the time in the world, and all the resources to go with it, I would agree with you. But-"

"It won't take me long, Beast. Maybe a few hours for the first increase in level." Danielle stepped forward once more, getting to work without further ado, though she made sure to keep her eyes averted from the documents the Beast had retrieved from… somewhere. "Wait, you don't have pockets? Where'd you get those-?"

"I have a fireproof safe in my chest cavity. Sometimes, it is imperative to transport sensitive items with the utmost care and *secrecy*. While this is something I typically would not share with someone else, I understand *you* will be unable to focus on the task ahead of you without a proper expl-"

"I got it, I got it. Sounds like a touchy subject, and you're in a *mood*. I won't pry any further."

CHAPTER

TWENTY-NINE

THE NEXT FEW hours turned into several days passing in a flurry of activity. Danielle churned out blueprint after blueprint, switching to doing the actual task of *making* the toys she'd designed when the system swapped the requirements for her level to increase. After reaching the Basic tier—level four in the skill—her frantic efforts finally hit a point of diminishing returns, and Danielle conceded that it was no longer possible to put the Beast off further.

Skill increase! Holistic Refinement [Level 3 (Rudimentary) → Level 4 (Basic)]!

Holistic Refinement allows the user to synergize and direct all previous skills into a powerful enhancer. When actively and intentionally crafting something new, whether it is an object, design, or idea, all factors of the final product are taken into account and enhanced [40%] by the System. Legacy creations will only benefit half as much as new creations.

All previous skills remain permanently and passively effective on the user of this skill, but the user now has [Basic] control as to what is otherwise impacted.

Requirement to advance: Collaborate with another highly skilled Craftsman to create a new, effective tool or concept neither of you could have developed alone.

Once she shared the requirement with the Beast, in hopes he would have a better option for them to work on, the machine could only speak in the negative. "With the short amount of time remaining, the only possible item which would increase your level further would be the heart of my master. Otherwise, we would need to likely create several different projects, hoping against hope that one of them would be considered by the system itself to be a 'new and effective' tool. Based on the language used, creating something for creation alone would not suffice to meet that standard. It is time."

At that moment, a breeze fluttered through the open door of the library where Danielle had holed herself up for the last few days. Several of her loose papers went flying, and she rushed to collect them. "Celestial feces... who would open a door? We've been soundproofing the manor for days, and it isn't *that* stuffy in here yet-"

"Danielle? Are you truly here?"

She froze in place, her words dying in her throat, her tired eyes going wide as the voice echoed through the hallway. Without a word, she sprinted around the table, bursting through the open door of the library and running with all her might toward the still-open entryway.

Danielle careened into her father, the duo only able to keep from falling in an ignoble pile on the floor thanks to the timely intervention of a headless metal soldier catching them. She buried her head in his travel-stained shirt, further mussing the garment with her tears and a hint of leaking snot. "*Father!*"

Questions and answers bounced between the two of them rapid fire, from how they were treated, how they got here, what had changed, and finally—most importantly—what came next. Stepping away and using the inside of her wrist to swipe away the last few tears of joy, Danielle sniffed hard and reined in her excitement. As quickly as possible, she brought her father up to speed on the Artificer and his need for a working heart, as well as her part in making it happen.

When she explained that she had an active ability which was triggered by creating things, Henri looked positively *sick* with excitement for her. Reaching out a hand, he used his thumb to catch one final tear, and his expression melted into a soft, fatherly smile. "Just like that, your future is secure, no matter where you go. I've been so, *so* worried about where life would take you... and here you are, mapping out your own path forward one choice at a time—just as you always swore you would."

After allowing the tender moment to stretch an entire three seconds, the Beast rumbled his internal engines loudly to catch their attention. Henri looked over, his eyes going wide before narrowing as he carefully examined the towering machine.

"Abyss, you're a *big* one, aren't you? Now who would go to all the trouble of getting you to work but stop when they were only four-fifths of the way done? Look at that cable management! It's terrible! I can see at least three places with a casual glance that would cause you to stop moving within three minutes, were they cut. Do you have a welding torch I could borrow? I can fix those right up-"

"You will not *touch*-" the Beast squawked indignantly, words failing him as Henri hobbled closer, using a tree branch as a makeshift crutch. "It was *you*. You're the reason she acts the way she does!"

"A complement if I've ever heard one," the man muttered, closing in on the Beast.

"System forfend, now there are *two* of them!"

As her father and the Beast got to know each other, one far more willingly than the other, Danielle took the opportunity to make her excuses and return to the library. For the next short while, she simply studied the diagrams of the human heart, comparing what was in her borrowed anatomy book against the actual measurements, shape, and somewhat difficult to understand imagery the Beast had provided her.

As she struggled to visually interpret what she was seeing, the Enchantress muttered with gentle annoyance, "How'd he put it? He wasn't going to slice the Artificer's chest open and collect a proper image for me? How does he expect this to be enough? A drawing would give me a better representation of the surface structure. Oh…"

With dawning realization, she tossed the near-useless image to the side and gave her full attention to the other reference material. "I'd forgotten, the structure of his heart is damaged. Mimicking what is currently there would be the *wrong* thing to do. Good, that narrows down the scope of possibility somewhat. Instead of replacing what he has now… attempting an idealized version the same size is a better starting point."

She continued to work, until at some point she blinked a little too long, and awoke to the sensation of a large blanket being draped over her shoulders. Sucking in a breath, Danielle sat up and turned to the side, her sleep-addled mind not sure if seeing her father standing there was a trick or reality. "You have both of your legs again?"

Henri let out a quiet chuckle, offering a hand and pulling her to her feet. "Sorry to wake you, but it's time to go to bed. As for the leg? Turns out, they had nearly three dozen options to choose from. Gave me the run of the place for a bit. It was a good time, and I had an interesting tour. One odd moment, I had to convince a creepy-crawly whispering soft promises to me from the ceiling that I didn't *want* spider legs."

"Doc is pretty excited about how things have turned out for him." Danielle couldn't help but lean on her father slightly, basking in his presence, and the surprisingly missed warmth of actual human contact. "How many times did you have to turn down the harpoon?"

"So you knew about the harpoon." Henri walked her out of the library and back to her bedroom, his movements more fluid than Danielle could ever remember seeing. "We'll talk tomorrow. All I need to know is: what can I do to help so we can all get out of here as fast as possible?"

"I'm sorry we don't have much time," Danielle sleepily murmured as she pulled away and lumbered over to her bed. "We need to finish the design for the Artificer's heart, then actually *make* it before anything else can happen. I just don't know how long that's going to take."

"Don't you worry about that," Henri softly called as she collapsed into her bed. "Between the four of us, we'll make amazing things happen."

The next thing Danielle knew, she was blinking in total darkness. For a moment, she didn't know what had woken her, then a loud, rhythmic pounding caused her to sit bolt-upright in bed. "Are they already *here*?"

Flinging open the door to her room, she found that machines were flowing into and out of the manor at a normal pace, none of them seeming overly concerned. A frown crossed her face, then her eyes were drawn to the source of the sound as it started up once more.

Tap, tap, boom-boom-boom!

A groan escaped her lips as she saw sheets of metal being lifted into place over the windows, then bolts were being forced through them and into the walls. "It's too early for this ruckus."

"We are tireless and ever-productive, a huge upgrade over the fleshy form of our creator. Early? Late? These terms mean nothing to us." Sneezy spoke with his elongated nose in the air, only able to hold the position for a moment before cracking a smile. As he handed over a platter, he pulled the silver cover off to reveal a delightful assortment of breakfast foods and hot tea. "The kitchen sends its regards and asks that you visit it a few more times before you flee the estate."

"Oh…" For a moment, her excitement over breakfast was overshadowed by a troubled expression. Then, Danielle paused and looked at Sneezy sharply. "We don't need to leave the kitchen behind! It must have a core as well, right? We'll just remove that and bring it with us when we leave! In fact, we should start collecting all the cores of the large utility items Beast and the Artificer created."

"That's a fantastic plan, madame Danielle." For some reason, though the words and the smile on Sneezy's face showed happiness, the Enchantress felt a chill run through her —as though he were hiding a sad secret. Before she could inquire further, he turned away. "I'll actually go and get that process started right now. Have a productive day!"

Chomping into her fried eggs and twice-baked potato, she was pulled from her musing as raised voices echoed from the library. Making her way over to the area she had practically claimed as her own, Danielle watched as her father and the Beast argued over the design she'd been working on when she fell asleep the previous night. Planning to join in the conversation, she took a single step inside the room, only for the Beast to spin toward her and thrust an oversized digit in her direction.

"No food or drink in the library!" The words made her falter, and a sheepish grin appeared on her face as she began to scarf down the twice-baked potato as fast as she could, happy that it had a soft, creamy texture that went down smoothly. In no time flat, she had finished her meal and was able to dive into the heated argument.

Between the Beast's understanding and his long-term tenure as the hands of the Artificer while the Comte inscribed the powerful runes, Henri's deep understanding and experience with working on the smallest of mechanisms, and

Danielle's rapid increase in knowledge which bridged the gulf between them, the final design slowly began coming together.

When considering the heart itself, they found the organ wasn't an overly complicated shape, nor did it have strange functions they needed to account for. It only needed to do a few things, all of which boiled down to having blood flow into a certain chamber, open a small valve and make it flow into the next space, then be pushed out back into the body. In essence, it was no different from a multi-use water pump.

The difficulty they ran into was ensuring it would integrate properly with bodily functions, increasing and decreasing blood flow as needed. Beyond that, the most intense argument was on the actual material of the final product.

BST model three had decided on an alloy of tungsten and carbonized steel to ensure that the heart could never again be broken. Henri immediately and violently opposed this choice, his experience with making fine instruments and delicate creations shining through as he explained that such a heavy object placed inside of a human was a guaranteed way to create damage in the surrounding tissue—which would quickly lead to the man's death.

Obviously, this was the outcome they were attempting to avoid at all costs, and so the argument raged. The day passed both quickly and with agonizing awareness, each moment experienced to the fullest as their minds were pushed to their physical limits in search of answers for each question that cropped up. Evening came and went, and they worked long into the night.

Finally, as Sneezy pounded on the door of the library, insisting that the humans come and eat breakfast, Danielle completed the final annotation on her parchment. Size, shape, material, functionality, components, durability and weight, all balanced with the knowledge that there would be no way to make repairs.

As she put the quill down, the parchment began to shine

with light, which quickly swept across its surface and left behind glimmering sparkles. Wherever those motes of light remained for any length of time, the ink below writhed and adjusted itself. When the process had fully completed, a spark of light jumped across to Danielle, and her arm lit with the golden illumination of a level increase.

The three of them leaned in to look at how the system had improved the final design, each of them intrigued as well as frustrated when they saw how the minor improvements compounded on each other to bring the design beyond what their combined capabilities had allowed for.

Eventually, it was the Beast who spoke, just before taking the design and carefully slotting it into his chest cavity.

"Three hundred and sixty-five miniscule pain points changed by one and eleven hundredths of a percent, and somehow the aggregate total efficiency of the heart as a whole was increased by exactly forty percent. Truly... the system does things in a *confounding* way."

CHAPTER
THIRTY

WHEN DANIELLE finally stepped out of her bedroom—after sleeping like the dead for nearly a dozen hours—she almost ran smack-dab into the hulking form of the Beast.

"Good, you're finally awake." Immediately, the creature turned and started floating down the hall. "Secure your father and meet me in the workshop. I was downstairs preparing the mechanisms for the heart but realized that this will be another novel creation. I'm not certain if you *can* double dip, but I'd rather not leave this to chance."

"Double dip?" Danielle's eyes went wide as she realized what he was saying, slamming the door closed, only to re-emerge a few minutes later in clean clothes, freshened up and ready to go. "Thanks for waiting. Do you mean to tell me it is possible that the design counts as a new creation, and the actual *construction* of the heart would be the same? That we will be able to get another forty percent increase out of the final prototype? On that note, is it still considered a prototype if there isn't going to be another one, and this will be the working model forever?"

"No, it would not be a forty percent increase." The Beast's

voice bounced back to her, causing a brief storm of bewilderment before he calmed it with a pointed clarification. "I believe your skill upgraded. It would be a *fifty* percent increase."

"Celestial feces, let's *do* this!" As she went to find her father, she ran into a major hurdle: she had no idea what room he'd been put in.

Giving up immediately, she went to the kitchen, and instead asked each of the guards she met to seek out Henri and have him join her at the table. Since she'd slept the day away, breaking her fast happened at dinner time, and the kitchen served her a delectable roasted chicken with a side of green vegetables and fried hash browns.

"Wonderful as always, kitchen. As always, you have my thanks." One of the appendages hanging in the air waved at her softly. Although she bit her tongue to try and keep the potentially rude question inside, eventually she couldn't help herself and spoke the words.

"I do wonder, how do you make your potato selection with each meal? Everything seems perfectly aligned, but it's almost as though the side dish is a meal off? These would've been a perfect pairing with the eggs, and the twice-baked potato would have gone wonderfully with the chicken. I suppose this is just me wondering if the potatoes are off, or if the *chicken* was supposed to come before the egg. I suppose it's a question I'll never have answered."

Henri chose that moment to make an appearance. "Interestingly enough, a question similar to that has been the bane of philosophers and historians alike since even before I was a child. Good morning... that is, good evening. What's going on?"

Danielle explained what the Beast had told her, not at all surprised to see the light of excitement and inspiration filling him exactly as it had her. "*Why...* if this works, the applications at the highest levels would be astounding! Of course, by plucking all the low-hanging fruit to level your skill to that point, the harvest will be sparse. But it is certain to be *satisfying!*"

As she'd known he was coming, Danielle had already requested a meal be prepared for her father, and they were soon able to join the Beast in the basement.

"I have made every mechanism, gear, shaft, cog, dial... every last part of the final product we will need." The hulking machine stood over the table, where literally thousands of shining bits of metal were laid out in orderly rows. Danielle gulped as she realized the massive task of assembly they had waiting for them—many of the smallest pieces would require magnification to see, tweezers to hold, and jeweler's tools to install.

But she was never one to back down from a challenge. Danielle strode forward, rolling her sleeves back from her wrists ever so slightly to make sure she didn't accidentally send small pieces flying by brushing against them. Picking up the largest section of casing, she flipped it to the side and looked into the space which would become the upper ventricle, then reached for the first tool.

Though her skills didn't specifically state she needed to do *all* of the work herself, she wasn't the only one unwilling to risk it. Her father handed over tools while the Beast walked her through the next steps on the blueprint, his own hands extended into an immense series of implements he used to hold and offer each next piece after the previous was installed.

An hour in, hundreds of sections had been put together with an intense accuracy and attention to detail. The Enchantress glistened from all angles as the bright lights shined down on them, but even as sweat trickled into her eyes, not once did her attention waver.

Though, there was *one* strange, standout moment.

As Danielle reached for the next expanding iris disc, which would serve as a valve, she didn't find it placed in her palm as expected. After a moment with her hand hovering in the air, she looked away from the nearly completed ventricle to find that the Beast was looking to the side. Following his gaze, she saw only a hint of motion as some automaton slipped out of the room and back up the stairs. "What was that?"

"Nothing for you to worry about," the Beast growled, pressing the valve into her hand. "Let us continue."

Half in a trance, Danielle simply bobbed her head and returned to the arduous, exhilarating task. The night passed quickly, but around the time that the first light of dawn would be creeping over the horizon, Danielle placed the last mechanism and stepped away. "All… *whew*."

She shook her head as a wave of dizziness and vertigo washed over her, "Sorry, all that's left to do now is have the Artificer do his part. Once he's put the scripting in, I'll seal it. Is he ready?"

"I am." The reply slipped in just a breath ahead of the pulse of red light emanating from the Beast's eyes.

Without stopping to chat, the Artificer began piloting the Beast's utility items with swift and perfect gestures. Knowing what was coming next, Danielle pulled Henri away, impressing on him the importance of not looking as the words of the universe itself were inscribed. Then, she leaned against her father and instantly fell asleep.

What felt like only moments later, she was being shaken awake by a frantic Beast. "I have only minutes left before I will be shut away for another day. Please, allow me to witness the effects of your skills."

"Mmm? Yeah." A very sleepy Danielle rolled to her feet, stumbling over to the two halves of the heart. It had been split as a cross-section straight down the center, and for just a moment, she admired the way the pristine internals reflected the gentle light of the system as words appeared and vanished ceaselessly. Carefully lifting both sides, she turned and aligned them ... then pressed the heart together into a single piece.

There was a sharp *hiss* as the chunks locked together, designed to never be pulled apart again for any reason. What appeared to be steam, but smelled slightly floral, escaped from each of the holes left in the machine designed to allow blood to flow through its internal structure. "What was *that*?"

"Disinfectant."

"I don't know what that is, but okay." At that moment, Danielle returned her full attention to the heart as golden and pearlescent light mixed, the gold coming from the world's system, the pearlescent from the scripting the Artificer had imbued the new organ with.

Though she could only see the external changes, Danielle was still shocked to see how the artificial organ went from a near-perfect metal smoothness to slightly bubbling out in areas —though still without any form of sharp edge being present. As the light sank deeper into the mechanisms, she could look on in wonder. "I can't imagine what it's going to look like in there now. If *only* we could pry this back open and craft a new design based on this, think of how many potential applications it would have!"

She felt the telltale tingle of gaining yet another skill level. "Ugh, now I'm level six... Comte, I only wish I could've had enough time to bring the skill to Perfection, to give you the best possible chance. Imagine what I could do with a *sixty* percent increase on top of what this design ended up as!"

"Don't be too distraught." The Beast's frame had gotten closer without her realizing, and his glowing red eyes were fixed on the miniscule portion of runescripting he could view. "I *categorically* agree with you. If I had any other chance to make this work, any other option at all, I would spend a life-time turning this into pure Perfection. But Gasteel Company has been besieging the estate's walls for hours already, and the barriers will not last much longer."

"*What?*" Only now did Danielle realize what the appearance of one of the guards during the critical moments of putting together the heart had meant.

"If it's any consolation to you," already the red light was beginning to fade away, but the Artificer pressed on, "It seems your fantastic power also increased the potency of the scripting I put in place. I was already ninety-eight percent certain this would be a perfect match. Now I would say my odds are ninety-nine percent or better. I can't thank you e-"

Then he was gone, and the Beast was in control once more. He leaned forward and plucked the newly crafted item from Danielle's surprised grip.

"Let's go cut his heart out and stuff this one in."

"Brute." Danielle sighed the word without any vitriol, knowing he was simply attempting to draw a reaction out of her. "Even so, I agree with you. The longer it's out here, the more filthy it will become. It would be best to embed it within him as quickly as possible."

Henri had joined them at some point but had simply remained still and silent, staring at the absolute masterpiece being created by his daughter. When the others started moving, he blinked rapidly, startled out of his thoughts, and quickly followed after them. As they began moving through the thousands upon thousands of metal knights standing guard around Comte LeKrout's stasis pod, he looked around with intense fear in his eyes. "Haven't been this close to these things in more than a decade. There's so... so *many* of them."

The Beast simply lifted into the air and swung over the orderly mass of soldiers, but Henri and Danielle needed to walk through a small path that had been cleared for them. Though they moved at what could even be considered an above average walking pace, the Enchantress felt as though she were creeping forward, the scenery around her unchanging for long minutes. By the time they arrived at the pod, she'd been filled with a sense of solemnity and purpose...

whereas her father was breathing heavily and looking around with wild eyes.

"These things killed so many of my friends," he whispered to his daughter, calming only slightly when she reached out and took his hand in hers.

Remembering what she'd been shown during her tenure at the estate, Danielle simply kept her eyes forward, ready to finally complete this task and meet the brilliant mind behind everything she'd been learning for the last... weeks? Months? It had begun to blur, between how much she enjoyed whiling the hours away in the library, and the recent sustained bouts without decent sleep quality. "I can tell you with full confidence that he didn't know what was being done with his creations, Father."

"Does that make it better?" Henri quietly inquired, his hesitance showing in how he was slowing them down to capture a few extra moments to speak. "No one who creates weapons thinks they won't be used. Just because he didn't know every detail does *not* make him blameless."

The corner of Danielle's lips pulled down as she frowned and thought, trying to think of how to distill weeks of learning about her host, as well as the struggles they'd gone through together. "I don't know what to tell you, other than I believe he has changed drastically and for the better."

Henri didn't say anything, only grunting slightly as they came to stand next to the Beast.

"I'll take that," the Beast reached for the heart, and Danielle gladly offered it over. Once more, a floral-scented steam erupted—this time from the Beast—coating the heart in a gentle mist. From there, his hand began reconfiguring itself, dozens of beeps and clicks echoing from the hand, which were followed by the Beast speaking a word aloud, in a sequence that made no sense whatsoever. Finally, his fingers joined together, coming together in a configuration of a key-shaped tool.

"Password accepted."

As the Beast inserted the key into the machine, the pod began moving with the shriek of rusty gears. Even though it groaned in protest, the lid slowly unfurled, each petal-shaped panel peeling back until it had unfurled in the shape of a mechanical rose. With a burst of stale air, a coffin-like dome of glass lifted, revealing a man just a few years older than Danielle. Curious to get a better look at the Comte, the Enchantress stepped closer and inspected him, only to freeze and blush when she noticed he was clad only in smallclothes.

Pop! The deep red glow covering the man pulsed one last time, then cut out with the blinding flash of failed runescript. At the same moment, the glass lid which had lifted off the Artificer swung to the side, the machinery failing and causing it to fall, clattering onto and warping the delicate blooming panels.

Comte LeKrout took a deep, struggling breath, and the Beast hurriedly leaned forward, a long scalpel extending from his wrist. "M'lord! You two, move back this instant. I shall begin the operation-"

Just before the scalpel plunged into the Comte's exposed chest, the Beast's extended limb froze, lingering in the air like a foul odor.

"Well, this is *truly* unfortunate."

"Beast? What's the matter?" Danielle stepped forward, ready to assist if he had run into some malfunction. "If there's an issue, just close the pod, and we'll fix it. Don't leave him to suffer like this."

"Closing the pod once it's been opened is, unfortunately, not possible. Even without the damage the failing mechanisms caused just now, it was only long years of maintenance that had kept it functioning to this point. It will not restart, now that it has been fully powered down. It appears that the deepest instructions etched into my core by Comte LeKrout

are still in effect. Even if it is to save his life, I cannot intentionally harm him."

The Beast let out a long, frustrated burst of steam before
pulling his arm back and slowly turning to face Henri and
Danielle.

"There is nothing to be done but to watch as he breathes
his last."

CHAPTER
THIRTY-ONE

"Don't say something like that!" Danielle tried to shove the Beast's extended limb to the side, only to find herself pushing against something with as much give as a stone wall. "Get out of the way. If there's nothing you can do, at least let *me*!"

"I'm sorry... I *can't*." The Beast growled at her, shifting his arm to push her back gently. "You don't have the training to do this without killing him outright, and that means anything you do in your attempt will only end up *harming* him."

"So... after all this time, he's going to die now?" Henri chimed in, his voice carrying a note of relief in it that set Danielle's teeth on edge.

"*Father*!" Danielle spun on the man, ready to take a swing if he made even *one* comment showing he was happy with this result. "You can't be seriously pleased that he isn't going to survive? This is an *Artificer*! He gave me access to his home, his library, and he even taught me directly. I've learned so much, progressed so far! *He's* even achieved Breakthrough while I was here, based on some of *my* theories! To say he's changed even over the last few weeks would be an immense understatement, and-"

"Oh." Henri's soft comment hit Danielle like a slap across the face, and she went silent as he nodded and took a tentative step closer to the dying man. "I see. I didn't realize that you... I see. Beast, I... I can save him."

"No. You *can't*." The Beast turned to face them fully, standing to his full, menacing height. "You don't seem to understand me when I told you that I actively cannot allow him to be harmed by someone-"

"Someone *without* training, correct?" the Tinkerer stated heavily, continuing to step forward slowly, as though approaching a large, cornered dog. "Let me tell you a story. Long ago, when my daughter here was barely taking her first steps, I didn't work only on toys. I worked on the most intense cases of surgery those coming home from the war needed to undergo. The reasoning was simple: what is working on someone during surgery, but making changes to an engine as it's running?"

"I cannot take that at face value," the Beast snippily replied, his voice taking on a sharper, mechanical sound as the deepest parts of its runescripting took over. "Please give Comte LeKrout space as he-"

"Would you accept an oath?" Henri questioned, his eyes dark as he held out his right hand. "You fully understand how important it is for me to have full use of my hands, yes? Then I'll pinky swear to you, Beast. I'm fully trained in the delicate art of surgery. I will be able to complete this surgery, and if I'm lying, I offer *both* my pinkies, once this is over. I ask again, will you accept this oath?"

Bright white light had nearly taken over the usual blue, shimmering sheen coming from the Beast's crystalline eyes. After a long moment, the deep blue fully saturated its eyes once more, then the machine stepped out of the way. "I accept your oath. Please save my master... or I'll be forced to end you for being the one to kill him. I can only ask for your understanding in this matter."

Lifting its hand, the Beast snapped the scalpel off of its own arm, handing it over to Henri. The man accepted the tool, nodded, and stepped forward to stand over the inert form of the Artificer. Danielle came closer, only to find her way barred once more by the Beast. She watched as her father, his hands trembling slightly, prepared for the most high-stakes upgrade he'd ever performed. He took a deep breath, glancing down and running a critical eye over the single tool that had been given to him.

"A scalpel is a great start. Can I get some clamps, pliers, and an extender to keep the tissue open as I cut through?" With each request, the Beast snapped off a small part of its own body, handing it over without question. The lights above them suddenly increased in intensity, flooding the area with intense, stark, white light and driving away all shadows.

With a glance at his daughter, Henri began speaking, even as he lifted the scalpel with suddenly steady hands. "I'm about to perform a heart transplant on an individual whose life is flowing out of him, even as we speak. If there were any other option, we wouldn't be doing it this way. I've no idea if this young man can feel what's about to happen, or if he's deeply unconscious. I can only hope it's the latter."

After a moment of mental preparation, he placed the blade on the exposed skin of the young man's chest. Next to Danielle, the Beast tensed, gears beginning to spin up, steam building to a boiling point. "The first incision is crucial... it must be precise, to avoid unnecessary trauma. Whether he can feel it or not, the more perfect and controlled I am, the less time it will take him to recover."

With a firm push, the blade glided through the skin, muscle, and connective tissue with practiced ease. As blood welled out, Danielle found herself absolutely transfixed by what she was seeing—both the surgery itself, as well as the way her father moved with such knowledge. She found herself speaking her thoughts aloud before she realized she had even opened her mouth. "I never even knew you were part of the war… especially on the side opposing Verdelune. Were you… were you *actually* a spy working against them?"

"Now is *not* the time." The Beast's nervous energy caused it to nearly swing its oversized arm into the Enchantress, but she fluidly and gracefully swept out of the way of the accidental attack. "Ah! Apologies… that was… that was-"

"Don't worry about me, Beast," Danielle soothingly stated, keeping a cautious eye on the deadly dangerous machine. When she saw deep concern and even fear in the stiff metal face, she realized her time spent cultivating her connections with the automatons had all been leading to this point. Recognizing that she was likely the only person in the world who could read the Beast's subtle cues, the Enchantress firmed her will and set about working to keep the Beast calm so her father could work.

"LeKrout's going to be *fine*. Trust my father. He's the absolute best at repairing whatever mechanism he needs attention. To him, I'm sure this is no different at all."

Henri hadn't slowed his pace even for a moment, his hands moving with the practiced precision of a master surgeon. The Tinkerer continued to speak quietly as he essentially *unzipped* the man laying in the pod, but let out a soft grunt, yanking both the Beast's and Danielle's attention back to what he was doing. "Rib cage is separated… heart is revealed. Subject is within a deep state of… I'd almost say hypnosis? Blood flow is minimal but… Beast. To remove his heart is to kill him. What do I-?"

The Beast inserted a massive, clawed finger into the pod. A moment later, a weak, flickering red light sprang up, enveloping the Artificer's body once more. "The stasis field is in place for an *incredibly* limited window of time. Note the flickering—each time it goes out, even for a fraction of a moment, his normal biological deterioration continues. The damage is not stopped; it's merely greatly slowed."

"Then we move *faster*." Henri's voice remained calm and determined as he carefully set about trimming the surrounding tissue. As he clamped the major arteries and blood vessels, Danielle could practically feel the Beast's anxiety growing, and she began subtly moving around the space, forcing him to take his eyes off the surgery to ensure she wasn't getting any closer to his unprotected creator.

"Almost done with the first part. I just need to sever this tube and these veins with extreme precision, leaving just a little extra close to the heart that can be used to amalgamate the mechanical heart with the healthy biological system."

"Tube?" The Beast rumbled with a clear threat in his tone, causing Danielle's efforts to be for naught as he swung around to put his full attention on the surgery. "That is the *aorta*!"

"Yes, exactly," Henri calmly agreed, his focus unshaken by the accusatory words. Quickly and carefully, he cut through the artery—just as cleanly as he had cut off the indignant shout of the Beast. From there, he firmly gripped the heart and slowly lifted it, trimming away anything the connective tissue holding it in place.

Finally, the heart was free.

"Danielle! *Catch!*" As her father thrust the heart at her, definitely *not* throwing it, the Enchantress numbly accepted the organ, her eyes wide with a mix of horror and fascination at what she was seeing. "Put it in a jar or something. It'll be a good conversation starter in the future."

"What in the *what?*" Even as her hands turned bloody from holding the organ, her eyes were drawn to an immense number of markings, which were covering nearly the entirety of the flesh. A quick check confirmed that each of the sigils was a single, solitary, golden 'X'. She shook her head slightly when she realized what she was actually seeing, "How many oaths has he sworn, crossing his heart each time? He literally has a heart of gold."

"Please hold your questions until the end. You, stand aside. With the damage done, every move forward from this point is a rescue operation." The Beast moved forward, a single step bringing him to his master's side as he pushed the Tinkerer out of the way.

A vast array of precise tools and implements extended from his arms, which broke down to a level Danielle had never before witnessed. Dozens of tools became at least a hundred, and the mechanical heart he held was spun and adjusted until it was perfectly positioned within the chest cavity, aligning it with the severed blood vessels and arteries. "Tinkerer. Do what you need to do. Call out for any assistance necessary."

"The first step is connecting the main hose—aorta, that is. Yes." Danielle looked up, her brow furrowing at the intensity in her father's eyes, the way sweat had begun pouring from his forehead. "I need to ensure a leak-proof connection, Beast; how well can you suture using this thread?"

Apparently deciding the question didn't deserve a reply, the automaton got to work, swiftly sewing up the first connection with a fine, durable thread. "It seems you are lucky that *I* at least came prepared. What is next?"

"This blood vessel, then this artery, continuing around the heart in a star-shaped pattern to make sure we aren't over-tightening on any one side." Henri stepped back, allowing the Beast to quickly follow his instructions, joining the mechanical heart into the body even as the red light of stasis flickered dangerously. "The heart has been successfully connected. At this point, we are in the phase of rescuing and stabilizing the subject."

"He is Comte *LeKrout*," came the beastly snarl as the machine worked with a speed and precision no mere human could match without specialized skills granted by the system itself. "I am finished… all that remains is to activate the heart

and seal the chest cavity. For the replacement to begin its function, I need to end the stasis. But once I do, it is gone for good.
Are you *sure* it is time to do so?"

"I can only hope for the best, just like you, Beast." Henri
stated in a serene tone, glancing over at his daughter only
once before nodding. "Do it."

An implement dove into the pod, and the red light
vanished nigh-instantaneously as the Beast tapped on the
heart a single time. It glowed brightly, then... nothing.
Danielle felt a yawning chasm open in her gut, her eyes fixed
on the inert heart. With a surge of panic, she lurched toward
her father, driven by a fierce need to stand between her father
and the inevitable punishment the automaton was sure to
mete out.

But the Beast showed no reaction at all.

After only a few long seconds, he began running his implements along the open chest cavity; beginning to seal it by
suturing all open wounds, then carefully removing the rib
expansion tools. More sutures followed, before finally his arms
retracted and began to fold themselves back into their normal
state once more. "The procedure is complete. We will closely
monitor him to ensure there are no complications, but the
initial results were... promising."

"Promising? It worked? I didn't see..." If she were not
literally holding a poisoned, slowly rotting heart in her hands,
Danielle would've slapped her open palm to her forehead.
"Of course there's no heartbeat. What am I thinking? It
doesn't need to *pulse* to send blood anymore."

"That is correct. Please hand over the Comte's heart; I will
properly store it away." The Beast took the sad lump of
damaged flesh then turned back to regard Henri. "You did
well, Tinkerer. Your steadiness and focus were crucial to the
success of... what's wrong with you?"

Ahem... Henri was breathing with some difficulty, though
he kept a strained smile on his face. Moving carefully, he posi-

tioned himself behind the now-only-sleeping Artificer to make sure the man was between himself and the Beast. "I don't suppose you're willing to do another brief surgery? It seems, well, it seems lying during my oath has caught up to me."

He held up his hands, showing where both of his pinkies had turned black... and lines of infection were already starting to creep into the healthy skin below.

CHAPTER

THIRTY-TWO

To Danielle's great surprise, the Beast didn't throw a temper tantrum or do anything other than release a sigh of steam and step close to her father—blocking her view. There was a brief cry of pain, and when the automaton stepped away once more, her father had lost both of his pinkies, but the stumps were clean and carefully stitched closed.

"I had noticed the discrepancies in the story you were telling. In the oath you made." The Beast's normally severe tone was replaced with an intense wash of thankfulness and guilt. "If I had asked you any questions, I knew I would not be able to save my master. Thank you for lying to me… I wish there was some way I could undo the price you paid."

Henri shook his head, though his eyes remained on his hands. "Sometimes, you just have to do what's necessary, Beast. I saw your core runescripting taking over your mind. You were beginning to sink into despair, and that's far too dangerous of a proposition for us. I can't imagine how the rest of you would've reacted if the Comte died."

"There are fail safes in place which would have destroyed…" the Beast stopped speaking, looking over to the side, where the Artificer had begun to stir.

Danielle stepped close to her father, focusing all of her system skills on him, specifically the hands that had been partially destroyed to save another man at her behest. The damaged, puckered skin visibly began to smooth over as she wrapped her arms around him, giving him the tightest, longest hug she could manage. "Why did you... no, *thank* you for saving him. But how did you know how to do the surgery if you weren't actually trained? Were you really in the war? We'll figure something out with your hands, maybe we can design-"

"Don't worry about it, my sweet girl." Henri gently pushed her away, "I absolutely *was* in the war and lost many friends. I only fibbed slightly. My role was much more support than anything else, but only repairing any form of mechanism as needed. Wagons, clocks, long, wasted hours attempting to reverse engineer these metal soldiers... as to how I performed the surgery? Exactly as I said earlier. Changing out the parts of a person is no different than working on an engine while it's still running. I mostly just hoped for the best, working under the assumption that the Beast would be able to assist with the next steps after I'd done the initial removal."

"*Uugh.*" The Artificer let out a soft groan as his eyes opened. Blinking a few times, he stared at Danielle, then let out grumble and closed his eyes. "So I did die, then? I had hoped the afterlife wouldn't be so painful, but at least there's angels."

"Attempt to *comport* yourself, my lord," the Beast instructed the half-awake Comte. At this, the young man's eyes popped open, focusing on his looming machine.

"How did I manage to see her before I saw *you*, Beast?" LeKrout let out a pained chuckle, lifting a hand and pushing himself into a seated position. The sudden movement caused him to wince. "Beast... is there a *reason* I'm in so much pain?"

"I'm uncertain how much physical distress heart surgery normally would cause in a body." The Beast spoke with a slight *click* of skeptical irritation. "But you had heart *removal* and *replacement* surgery. I can only assume that it is much worse for pain."

"That's not... ugh, *Beast.*" The Comte held up a hand and ran his fingers through his thick brown hair. "You're supposed to always have a high-end healing potion in your personal vault for situations when I am damaged. I know we didn't use one when I was poisoned, and I know they don't expire. We should have a proper stockpile of them. Would you mind?"

At that moment, Danielle saw a side of the Beast that weeks of close contact hadn't revealed: he became actively flustered. With a great deal of hemming and hawing, the machine reached into its chest and slowly extracted a glowing gold-and-red bottle. "Comte... these are literal treasures meant to be used when you are fatally injured, not to reduce recovery time. At the moment, you are on the mend and-"

"Beast." The Artificer looked over at where Danielle and Henri were huddled together. "This is the first time in a decade or more that I'm able to stand on my own two feet. I'd like to enjoy it."

Without any further hesitation, the bottle was handed over, and Comte LeKrout popped the cork, downing the entirety of the viscous fluid in a single draught. Danielle scooted closer, interested in seeing the effects of the alchemical substance firsthand.

Healing potions were not something the general population had access to, as the components used to brew them were beyond rare—few and far between. This was one of the reasons so few people had an Alchemist class, and even those who did were usually low-leveled, due to the sheer investment required to empower themselves.

Color rushed back to his cheeks, his eyes gained clarity, and soon the Comte was breathing easier. After allowing himself a minute for the effects to fully settle into place, he swung himself out of the bed he'd been laying in for more than half of Danielle's life and got to his feet. Immediately, he stumbled, only to be caught by the Beast. "Whoa! I haven't used such an unbalanced body to walk around in since... yeah. Since the last time I stood on my own two feet."

Completely unsure what to do with herself, the Enchantress simply stayed next to her father, gently holding his hand as she resisted the urge to rush over and check on the Artificer. "Are you... is everything...?"

"Working properly, and I'm rapidly regaining my strength." He sent a crooked smile at Danielle. That smile dropped away for a split second, and he reached down into a compartment under the pod, pulling out proper clothes. Face flushed, he quickly dressed himself, even slipping on a pair of soft leather shoes. Then, perhaps feeling more confident, his wobbling steps slowly brought him closer to the father-daughter duo.

Once he was a little over two arm's lengths away, the Comte swept into a low bow, remaining bent and facing the ground. "Thank you for saving me, both from the damage that had been done to me, as well as my own arrogance. If you hadn't refused to leave right away, the Beast would have attempted to install my heart by himself. I would've died here."

"How do you know that?" The words popped out of Danielle's mouth before she considered how they sounded, her academic curiosity overcoming her nerves at meeting the Artificer in person for the first time. "Oh right, I had already-"

"I assume you mean, how do I know he was unable to make the incision? I understand you know this, but for your father's sake, I will explain." LeKrout returned to his normal standing position, jerking his head toward the Beast standing behind him.

"Even when I'm unconscious, my skills give me updates from my most deeply connected automatons. The closer they are, the more clear the information comes across. As soon as I shook off my disorientation, I just... *understood* the full situation. Now, the estate is under attack, and I am back on my feet. Is there anything you need from me before you use the escape tunnel and start your new life elsewhere?"

"Start my...?" Danielle stood dumbstruck for a heartbeat, then scowled at the man. "Is that it? 'You've done your job, so get out'?"

"That's not-!" The Artificer reared back in surprise, "No! That's not at all what I'm trying to say. I just wanted to get you to safety as soon as possible, and now that I'm up and about, I can take an active role in protecting my automatons against this ruthless baron who has seemingly no scruples whatsoever."

"You're coming with us, Comte." Surprisingly, it was Henri who made the claim, causing everyone to stare at him in surprise at the interjection. "You've met Danielle, even if it's just essentially been in your dreams. By now, you should understand that, unless you stuff her in a crate and force her out of here, she won't leave behind someone she loves."

At her father's words, Danielle felt a slow spread of heat filling her cheeks and creeping down her neck. "*Loves*? I... I just met him!"

"No you didn't, Danielle." Henri turned to her with an understanding smile on his face. "You've met him in his books, his writings, his creations. I *guarantee* that every automaton you've interacted with is imbued with a part of him. This means you've seen him at his best and his worst."

As he said this, his eyes flicked out to the thousands of metal soldiers around them. "I'm not saying you need to rush off and get married or anything like that, but I also know who you are and that you won't let him stay behind while we run. If I'm wrong... just tell me."

"I'm not going to let him stay here by himself," Danielle's tongue felt strangely thick as she put up a weak argument, "That doesn't mean I'm *in love* with him."

"Who said you were 'in love' with him?" Henri quizzed

with a sly grin. "I just said you love him. Could be like a brother, or a friend. But it suddenly doesn't *seem* that way *now*, does it? *Hmm?*"

"*Father!*"

"As much as I'm enjoying this family banter, though perhaps not as much as my master," the Beast cut them off before the Enchantress could interrupt his speaking. "May I please take this opportunity to remind you that the estate is under attack? Staying here isn't an option. At the very least, not a good one. If you have unfinished business, I highly suggest you finish it *quickly*."

"There's one thing I'd like to do before going up," Surprisingly, it was the Artificer who spoke out. "It will accomplish two of my immediate goals and one long-term one. This may sound a bit strange, but I need assistance getting used to how my body can move again. I'm too wobbly to run through the motions on my own, so…"

He gestured into the distance, where crystal spiers were lighting up as they rose into position around the motion-capture platform. "The best option, in my mind, is to have someone hold me as I shift and spin. Enchantress Danielle, would you be so kind as to dance with me?"

"You… we? Dance? Why dancing?" Now it felt as though her entire head was on fire, and Danielle could only assume that, if she was mechanical, she would be releasing steam more violently than the Beast did when angry.

"As I said, I'm hoping it will help me achieve two of my short-term goals and one long-term." He held out a hand, "Yes?"

"Okay?" Her reply sounded more frustrated than she had intended, but she still reached out and took the proffered hand. Danielle let out a gasp as the two of them were scooped into the air. The pulley system had dropped cables down to wrap around them, sending them soaring over the field of metal below.

"I had forgotten I'm not the only one who can remotely control the mechanisms of the house," the Beast grumbled as he looked at various machinery coming to life at the Artificer's mental commands. "I'm not sure how I feel about this, now that I think about it."

Holding tight to the man as they continued drifting higher into the air, Danielle looked down at the small figures below. "*What!* Wait! What about my father and the Beast?"

"Your father has a new leg; I'm sure he'll be happy to use it," the Comte replied with a mischievous grin. "As for the Beast, he can walk as well. He's gotten lazy over the last decade. He just likes appearing suddenly; there's no real need for him to float around everywhere. Especially now that I will be able to perform regular maintenance as needed. I temporarily locked him out of this system. He should notice… oh, any moment now."

A high-pitched steaming whistle punctuated that statement almost immediately. The Comte began to chuckle, inciting Danielle to laugh just as hard. They dropped through the air slowly, twirling until they were deposited in the center of the platform.

Just as Danielle realized they had held hands the entire time, the Artificer stepped in closer, wrapping an arm around her and beginning the slow movements of a waltz as soft music began to play from the crystals surrounding them. To her surprise, he lurched back and forth, nearly falling three times out of the four steps he took. Her own arm shot out and gripped him firmly, pulling him closer and guiding his motions.

For the next several minutes, they moved back and forth, Danielle's system skills enabling her to gracefully avoid his clumsy steps and transform what would otherwise be jarring motions into gentle twirls. As he gradually adjusted to piloting his own body—a body which had been maintained at near-perfect health, thanks to remaining in stasis—all sequelae of his poisoning and heart replacement were fully undone by the potion he drank.

Within only a few minutes, his movements became sharper, and his limbs responded more quickly and accurately to his intentions. Soon, he was moving correctly, finally even taking the lead in their movements. As Danielle was able to relax a little more, no longer having to dodge stomping feet, she found herself able to ask questions. "I'm assuming one of your short-term goals was getting into the swing of walking around again. You mentioned motion capturing this, was that one of the other ones? If so... I can't think of what the third would be."

"Being able to imbue the ability to dance is definitely a long-term goal." He met her eyes as he looked up from his feet, the same crooked smile on his face. "I thought I might spend a few years making toys when all this is over."

"And... the short-term goal, then?" Danielle managed to force the words out as they tried to catch in her throat.

"I just wanted to have a chance to be close to the woman I've been dreaming about for months."

At his words, a nervous laugh escaped Danielle's mouth. For a few more moments, she tried to control her nervous energy and just enjoy dancing, but then she noticed how his eyes had shifted to look at the door to the stairwell. "They're going to get inside soon, aren't they?"

"I don't know for sure. I've cut off any information from outside. But... probably."

Heaving a great sigh, Danielle pulled back slightly. "My father is safe; you are in good health and getting even better. I'm glad I escaped Gasteel... but I need to be sure-"

"Danielle." Kota gently placed a hand on both of her shoulders, making sure she couldn't look away. "You are the sun, and he is a moth. He would be satisfied fluttering around a lantern... but you deserve to be among the stars."

THIRTY-THREE

AN ALARM STARTED BLARING, only for the Artificer to lift his left hand and snap his fingers, immediately silencing the sound. The lights remained a concerning red, but the momentary distraction allowed Danielle to pull away and compose herself. "I feel like we should have a longer conversation… but I don't think now is the time."

"Right!" The Comte started walking toward the stairs, slowly at first, as if unsure how much he should trust his own capabilities. "I want us to get all the automatons moving in an orderly retreat, then I'll have the metal soldiers surge upstairs and swarm over the aggressors. By the time the dust has settled, and the dead are accounted for, we will be a kingdom away!"

"You don't truly mean to cut them all down, do you?" Danielle stepped forward, blocking him from charging ahead without thinking. "Comte. I know how this man works, and there's no way he's going to risk himself in any serious way. He'll throw conscripts and low-leveled fighters against you to soften your defenses and happily wade through the ocean of blood, so long as he can call it a win when he's throwing away his ruined shoes on the other side."

"Abyss, you have a point." The Artificer bit his lip. "This isn't a group of hardened veterans who have done terrible things to other people... at least, not all of them. That makes this harder in some ways, but hopefully means I won't be adding to my sleepless nights. Any recommendations?"

Danielle's voice caught in her throat, as she'd been prepared to argue with the man and force him to take her objections seriously. Instead, he had immediately been ready to include her in his planning. Barely missing a beat, she took his hand and pulled him along as she went up the stairs, ensuring his stability while also helping him move faster. "While destroying the entire force would buy us some time, they would be forever searching for us. I don't know about you, but the thought of assassins creeping in to kill me while I sleep is downright chilling."

"I assure you, the reality of it is even *less* fun than you imagine."

She nodded sympathetically but pushed forward. "Unless we can convince them we died in the attack, we're going to always need to watch our step. I propose that we pull the cores from every one of your children that can properly think, pack them up, and let ourselves be seen by Gasteel. Then we fake our deaths, making a clean escape. If we involve enough fire at a hot enough temperature... at the very least, they'll never know for certain, Comte LeKrout."

"I like it. My children, huh? I... suppose that's becoming ever more true." The Artificer pulled a face. "There's really only *one* way to guarantee they believe I'm dead, at least without actually being killed right in front of the Baron. One of the reasons I was able to force Verdelune to back down was that I tied all of my runescripts to the oaths binding me. So long as I am alive, I swore that their cores and runes *won't* self-destruct in a burst of system energy. That oath, like all the others I've ever made, are inscribed on my heart. If I can get Gasteel to order me to join his war effort, and I refuse, the

298 X DAKOTA KROUT

broken oath will destroy my heart, as well as *every* connected oath."

"It'll forcefully break the others?" Danielle considered that and nodded in excitement. "That's perfect! But how do we... how do we keep the cores we want to remain safe *actually* safe? Comte, I can't sacrifice them to save myself. No... even more than that, are you sure breaking the system oaths will be safe for you, even without your heart being in your body?"

"Danielle, please call me Kota." The Artificer was still smiling, but his eyes were distant. "That's my name, after all. If I have enough time, I *can* guarantee their safety. It's as simple as adjusting the bond they have to the oath inscribed on my heart to me as I am. Seconds per core, at the most. As for myself... I can only hope that, as this is not something which has ever been tested before, as far as I am aware, the system will reward me for my finding of a loophole instead of punishing me for my hubris."

"But you don't know for certain."

Comte LeKrout could only offer a slight shrug. "An Artificer who is unwilling to take risks is known as... actually, there isn't a term for it. They don't exist. Can I ask you to begin collecting the cores? I already have metal soldiers following after us, so while you work on the sentient automatons, I'll pull what are essentially blank cores from the soldiers and have you swap them out. That way, it'll look like my trusted guards are still fighting."

"I can do that!" Happy to have clear direction, Danielle shoved open the door and burst into the grand hallway, only to find that it was almost completely silent. The sounds of their abrupt entrance echoed through the stone corridor, causing a few of the nearby, readied guards to glance at them askance. "Why is it so...? Right, the soundproofing! Listen up, everyone!"

She shouted the plan to the mechanical guards, telling them to cycle out into the spacious kitchen as each group was replaced by the blank cores of the metal knights. After she finished, Kota verbally approved what she'd said, immediately stirring the guards to action. Those closest to the kitchen had the least combat utility and so were the best choices for swapping right away. "The kitchen! Comte, um, *Kota*, how do I get its core out? Oh! Can you get Duke in here? We can't forget him."

"Oh, yes, absolutely. We're not leaving *either* of them here." The duo ran to the kitchen. "My dog, that is, *Duke*, was my first ever successful scripted core, and the kitchen? It took *months* for the food to be palatable after I created that. Now I know it's because it was learning, but at the time, I thought I had just gotten used to bad food. If for no other reason, that's a good starting point."

Looking up at the immense machine hanging from the ceiling, Kota sheepishly scratched the back of his head and looked around the room. "Any chance you've seen the installation scaffolding I left in here... oh, ten and a half years ago? I'm not sure how I could get up there; we might need to start with something else-"

"Sss-*pider lift*!" Doc hissed in excitement as he raced past them, launching a harpoon into the ceiling and slowly pulling itself off the ground. "Grab on, I'm *ssst*-able!"

"Oh. Right! I forgot about the pulley system. Thank you for the reminder, Doc." Cables dropped out of the ceiling, wrapping around Kota and hoisting him into the air to where the food preparation automaton was eagerly unfolding its internals.

Danielle stepped closer to the hanging spider and gave it a gentle pat on the thorax. "I would have *absolutely* taken the spider lift. He's got no sense of adventure at all. We'll work on that."

"Thank*sss*, Danielle," Doc happily replied, reeling himself in a few feet, then dropping back down and bouncing several times as he reached the end of his chain. "Look at this! Is the pulley system going to do that? Of course not! It has built-in *safety* features. Ssso boring."

"I'm not sure why you're hissing like a snake, but I'm guessing it's just a spider thing?" The only reaction to Danielle's question was a long stare, followed by the slightest motion of clacking mandibles. "Right… anyway… mind opening up so the Artificer, that is, *Kota* can swap out your core right away when he gets back down here?"

"No can do. I'm highly combat effective. I need to get out there and be a part of the upcoming distraction. Remember? All eyes on the spider." Even as Danielle protested, the automaton scuttled out of the room and back toward the main entrance. "Can't miss out on my *debut*!"

Boom!

Bo~om!

Danielle started to turn back to watch the Artificer finish up with the now-limp kitchen automaton but froze in place as an intense pounding on the door of the manor announced the official arrival of Gasteel Company. Even before her conscious mind caught up to what was happening, her heart rate began increasing, a thin sheen of sweat broke out on her forehead, all while her breath came quicker. "They already broke through the outer wall? The defenses?"

"That's too fast!" Kota called down from his vantage point, fiercely working to force open the core container of the kitchen, which had rusted shut over the last decade. "They must've brought actual siege weapons or spell casters capable of artillery-style magic. Otherwise, we should have had another three hours at the minimum. The blades of almost-grass alone should've been enough to hold off any horses or soldiers trying to walk across it."

"Wait…" Of everything else that was going on, only one part had sunk into Danielle's mind. "That wasn't real grass out there?"

"Almost none of it," the Artificer confirmed. "I call it 'almost-grass'."

"But... there were large patches of it that didn't act mechanical. It looked and acted just like real grass."

"Thanks, that's what they wanted it to look like. That's why it's 'almost-grass'." Kota waved her off, "For *almost* all purposes, it really is grass."

"Who is *they*?"

Her strange insistence finally caught Kota's attention. "There's other things to worry about beyond what is and isn't really grass. Which, just to clarify, what's on the lawn is definitely only *almost-*"

"Yeah, 'almost grass'. I got it." Danielle turned and started hurrying toward the pounding on the doors of the manor. "Keep going, I'll keep him from ordering you to join him. Work fast!"

"What? No! Danielle, it's too dangerous! Hey! Just..." Seeing that she wasn't listening, he got back to work and let out a frustrated shout. "The escape tunnel is in the library!"

There was no way they could have known what was happening outside, and Danielle allowed herself to feel a moment of pride and satisfaction that her idea to soundproof had been so effective. But now, as no other noises were able to be heard over the clamor of the battering ram striking the door, each strike echoing down the massive open space of the hallway sounded like a hammer driving nails right next to her ear.

Luckily, or perhaps unfortunately, it only took a few more blows for the heavy doors to come crashing inward. As the final pieces of the shattered door and frame settled, the troops both in and outside of the manor rearranged themselves, preparing for what was to come. The lingering moment of silence came to an end as a hulking figure stepped into the light of the hallway, head held high and without a hint of fear at the machines arranged before him.

"Comte LeKrout, I, Baron Gasteel, by right of my position and bolstered by this signed writ from the king of Verdelune, do hereby-"

"Go *away*, Gasteel!" Danielle screamed at the top of her lungs, not out of fear, or anger, but just to interrupt the smug words pouring like oil from the muscle-bound man. If he managed to get those words out, they wouldn't have any chance to undo the baron's failsafe... and all of the automatons would self-destruct. "You don't know what you're doing. You need to *walk away*."

"Belle?" Gasteel's voice faltered exactly as she had intended. "You're still here? I thought for certain I would have to chase after you when I finished up here. It was going to be a glorious hunt, ending with the most beautiful man in the kingdom bringing home a true trophy wife. How... disappointing. I don't suppose I could convince you to run off, perhaps get yourself a little head start?"

"Gasteel." Danielle took a deep breath, swallowing to try and soothe her now-sore throat. "Let me make one thing very clear. I will never marry you. You will never get the Comte under your banner, and if you try to make either of those things happen, many people are going to get *hurt*."

"Oh, enough of this." Grumbling with annoyance, Gasteel shoved the paper in his hand into a satchel on his side, rummaging around and pulling out a separate document. "You've officially failed to uphold your end of this agreement. You signed this willingly and knowingly, and therefore, you will obey me. Come out here, and my troops will whisk you away to a life of luxury while I deal with this *beastly* problem. Who knows, maybe by the time I make my way to our home, I'll already have been raised to Vicomte?"

"I fully agree that I have not fulfilled my end of that agreement and willingly agree to be bound by the terms we signed on." Danielle's voice rang out, crystal-clear in the silent manor. The parchment in the baron's hand glowed with a bronze light, flowing into Gasteel, even as a similar light washed over the Enchantress, causing her skin to tingle as the legal document interacted with the wards of Verdelune.

The baron had a massive smile on his face, and he took a swaggering step forward, reaching out a hand and making a 'come here' gesture with his index finger. "I'm glad to see you finally decided to stand by me properly, wife. The palace awaits us both. Now, let's get you out of here-"

"Oh, I won't be going anywhere, Baron Gasteel." Danielle's beaming smile practically dealt radiant damage to those looking on as she tested herself against his words. "However, I'll be certain to only ever speak about Baron Gasteel in positive, affirming ways to the nobility of Verdelune."

"Why are you saying my name so much? I'm not saying I don't like it, but... for some reason, it doesn't please me as much as hearing it normally does." His eyes narrowed as he watched her stand still, a sneer curling his lips. "Come along! Now. It's time to fulfill your end of this bargain."

"I am fulfilling every obligation I agreed to. But again, I'll never be your wife." Danielle watched as Gasteel's face contorted with rage and confusion as he tried to process her words. She didn't interrupt him, happy to let this conversation draw out as long as possible.

"What did you *do*?" Gasteel finally ground out, his gaze going as hard as the latter half of his first name. "You said you would marry me. You wanted to do it! You willingly accepted the terms of the contract and stated that you had failed—you want me. You *want* to marry me! Why aren't you doing it?"

By the end of his tirade, he was shouting, his hand on the hilt of his half-drawn sword. Danielle began speaking at that point, not wanting him to make a move. "Baron Gasteel. For future reference... when a line in a contract is crossed out, and both parties initial next to it, that is the legal acceptance of both parties to remove that clause. It means it can no longer be enforced. What I signed was essentially an agreement to be complimentary toward Baron Gasteel whenever I spoke of him to any of the other nobility of Verdelune. I *fully* intend on fulfilling that obligation."

For a moment, Gasteel simply stared at her in silence, his face a mask of fury. Finally, his voice low and dangerous, he hissed out, "I didn't know what that meant. You knew I didn't, and you *tricked* me. I've given you far too much lenience, even going so far as to let you make *demands*, instead of just doing what I *told* you to do."

Deciding to twist the knife, Danielle hurled back at him the words he had used when he conscripted the citizens of her childhood home. "Not knowing the law is no excuse for not following it."

His face as red as a ripe tomato, the man took a step into the building. "You've defied me for the last time, Belle. There's no coming back from this."

"You brought this upon yourself, baron. No one tricks Gasteel like *Gasteel*."

CHAPTER
THIRTY-FOUR

GASTEEL'S BELLOW of rage was accompanied with his battalion surging forward, their anger a near-physical thing on behalf of their liege lord. The automatons immediately responded with everything they could bring to bear, scythes swinging out, mauls cracking into shield or flesh, and flames billowing into huge clouds and forcing men away. As intense as the initial attacks were, the humans weathered it easily.

Running back toward where she was supposed to be pulling cores out of sentient automatons, Danielle's eyes widened in realization of who was actually fighting against the invaders.

Currently, the most combat-effective guards were closest to the entrance, but only perhaps half of them were designed for fighting. The other half had been made for utility, cutting plants, gardening, smashing stubborn rocks for landscaping and the like. Even as conscripts, Gasteel Company had at least been trained in some tactics, given effective weapons, and were working together in a way that none of the house guards were able to do.

Still, they put in immense effort, unafraid of being destroyed. This allowed each of the creations to hold their position longer than a human of similar strength and skill would, draining the attackers stamina and slowing their advance. Unfortunately, the aggressive forces weren't to be underestimated. As the soldiers gained ground, their more veteran members pushed forward with better command of their weapons, as well as using actual combat system-skills.

These seasoned warriors brought their power and experience to bear against the automatons, and with coordinated strikes, they began to send flechettes of metal flying from each point of impact, the tiny projectiles torn directly from the falling house guards. Step after step, they pushed deeper into the house, forcing a breach in the defensive line while also allowing more of their people to flood into the grand hallway and set up their own formations.

A massive blast of fire—which would've brûlée'd at least half a dozen people—was intercepted as a soldier with glowing hands stepped forward and caught the burning gases as though they were a solid object. He twisted and returned the stream into the ranks of the metal defenders as a collected ball of flame, the impact melting his opponents and sending machine after machine crashing to the ground as a heap of molten slag. Immediately following his successful counter, the man stepped back into the line of attackers and melted into the crowd.

"Woo, *get* 'em!"

"On your left! *Shield up!*"

"I can do this all day, all *day!*"

"Tell everyone else to take a break, *we've* got this. Twenty minutes, in and out."

The shouting and carousing quickly became drowned out by the sound of dozens, then *hundreds* of sabatons slapping against stone. Metal soldiers, which had been the bane of three kingdoms less than a decade previous, began pouring into the grand hallway, a massive formation moving in lockstep as they marched out of the underground workshop. They expanded across the entirety of the open space, and soon, hundreds of them were in position and marching toward the entrance as a wall of sharpened metal with no gaps to slip through.

Their synchronized movements made it difficult to select an individual target, and chaos unfolded as the clash of steel against stone was followed by steel against steel... then flesh. The screams of tortured alloys and wounded people filled the air, a cacophony of sound which drowned out any individual words, shouts, or furious orders.

Danielle's heart hammered in her chest as her eyes locked onto the pristine white floors, now marred by thick streaks of oil mingling with dark, crimson blood. The new paintings on the walls, once vibrant and full of imagination and the wonder of new, artificial minds, were splattered with the same macabre mixture, their colors distorted and melting from the gruesome sludge.

Her vision blurred with the shock as she realized that humans had been cut down, and this ruckus had barely even begun. She stumbled out of the grand hallway, away from the raging battle and the absolutely unnecessary bloodshed. With nerveless fingers, she began grabbing from the pile of blank cores that had been accruing in her absence, rushing them over to the advanced frames of the automatons that were now unmoving and unpowered. "Was I so naive in thinking we could manage to escape without anyone getting hurt?"

Her hands shook as she slotted the blanks into the waiting cartridge, closing it manually and stepping away as the rest of the machine came to life and pulled itself together before trundling off to join the fight.

A glance at Comte Kota revealed a man working furiously, using all the tools at his disposal with immense skill. He didn't wait for the automatons to line up nicely and arrange themselves in an orderly manner. No, he had cables wrapped around himself, and upon pulling out an advanced core, would fling himself backward without a glance—fully trusting in his creations and own skills. He would leave the ground for a brief moment, only to be twisted and gently deposited in front of the next waiting machine.

When his hands started to get full, he'd throw himself over to the table, grab his stylus, and quickly adjust the scripting. As he started on that process, Danielle forced herself to look away, knowing it was dangerous for her to see the raw system energy.

Somehow, seeing the Artificer moving with such confidence gave her back some of her own. Danielle slapped her cheeks, and turned her attention to her task as her cheeks reddened from the not-gentle strikes. "Come on, *focus*! Every second counts, and the longer I wait, the fewer we're going to be able to save."

Even so, she couldn't help but listen intently as the battle raged on out in the hallway, the tide shifting back and forth as each side fought with everything they had in them. Between their training and system-granted skills, the aggressive humans continued to press the attack and gain ground ever so slowly. But Danielle had seen some of the images of how the metal soldiers worked, and she knew they would be responding with unyielding force, a shield *thousands* strong that would never stop trying to protect their creator, unless they'd been fully destroyed.

As minutes passed, some of her adrenaline faded away, and Danielle was able to get into the rhythm of slotting cores into position. A short while after her return, there was a steady stream of sentient machines entering the room and basic, mindless versions marching those old bodies out. Entering almost a fugue state, she simply moved, swapped, and closed slots. Scores of machines were rescued, but between one replacement and the next, the battle took an unfortunate turn.

Danielle felt it in her ears first, a shift in air pressure that caused a wave of vertigo to rush through her. A heartbeat later, a howling wind filled the building, smacking the troops away from each other and causing the tightly packed metal soldiers to sway back on their heels. Worst, it blasted open all doors not fully closed and latched—including the dining room she and the Artificer were furiously working in.

Danielle was sent stumbling from the angled force of the wind, hard enough that she nearly dropped the runescripted core she'd been trusted with. She had to juggle for a moment before finally managing to close her hands around it, and by the time she heaved a sigh of relief, she was fully back in the moment.

The Enchantress glanced toward the door, puzzled by the sudden lull. The air, still swirling with tension, was quickly filling with both the groans of the wounded as well as the creaking of rusty joints as the automatons began to move again. Before she could even think of resuming her task, Gasteel's voice echoed through the open space, carried by the wind.

"Comte LeKrout, you will show yourself this very moment, or I will immediately call upon your oath! You have five seconds! Four... three..."

Danielle bit off her cry of alarm as she watched the Artificer smoothly flipping through the air toward the open door. There was no hesitation as he landed and proudly stepped into the hallway, his posture perfect as he looked down the huge corridor with disdain. "I'm here, baron. Save your threats for the enemy. How *dare* you invade my home? This is a direct violation of the code of conduct for Verdelune nobility, chapter six, paragraph four-"

"I won't hear another *word*!" Gasteel's indignant bellow echoed off every hard surface, his voice rising with a fervent intensity. "This! *This* is the reason our kingdom has gotten so *weak*. Words, rules, *etiquette*. I'm sick of it. Fighting with words is the way of the weak, for those who lack the strength of arm to *take* what they desire."

"Laws are in place for civilization, and it is agreeing to a common understanding that we can trust that allows us to live better lives without losing it to some passing *animal*." The way the Artificer riposted with his words made it clear he was equating the baron to little more than slavering vermin, but Gasteel was in no state to understand.

"You know what *I've* seen? I've seen myself become stronger and better while lesser men hide behind their laws and treaties, shackling themselves and everyone around them with their own *cowardice!*" As the two leaders spoke, the combatants held their position in an uneasy stalemate, but the baron's words began to riling his people up right to the *edge* of reigniting the conflict. "But I… I will change that, for me *and* my trusted peers."

Baron Gasteel started pacing back and forth as he spewed his thoughts. "Power belongs to those who can wield it, to those who are willing to throw off the constraints forced upon them by the whims of the *feeble*. Why should I, a man of strength and vision, be held back by the rules of lesser men of higher *social rank* who've never even seen a battlefield?"

Gasteel stepped forward, and a wave of sharpened swords rose into the air as nearly a thousand metal soldiers prepared to cut him down if he did so again. LeKrout casually and dismissively replied, "You're not running a *mercenary* company, Gasteel. What it truly sounds like is that you should defect and join the Brute kingdom. It sounds like you want exactly what they're offering."

"Maybe they've figured it out-"

"Do it," LeKrout called back, a crooked smile on his face as he waved at the door behind Gasteel. "Power. Might makes right. Sounds right up your alley. Just go. I'll even donate to the cause and tell you exactly which rule you need to invoke to give up your nobility and status. As a baron, the backlash will be miniscule. Go live the life you actually want to live, without having to bow your head to anyone who isn't *stronger* than you are."

"You'd like that, wouldn't you?" A wide, manic smile was on the baron's face, and he nodded approvingly at the Comte. He waved at Danielle, who had poked her head into the hallway, "You clearly aren't shy about taking what's *mine*. But unlike those ineffectual fools at the capitol, I'm not shy about taking it back! I challenge you to an honor duel, so I can prove once and for all that I'm the better man and the better choice. Once I've beaten you into the stonework, I'll step back before I've finished the job... and *allow* you to fill out my army with these metal soldiers."

"Sure, Baron," the Artificer agreed with a wicked grin as Danielle's jaw dropped. "It's been a while since I threw my weight around. I'd be *happy* to show you that I didn't rise two ranks in the nobility by accident."

"The duel is set, then. Get over here, and let's get it started." Gasteel cracked his neck side to side, hefting his sword and stepping forward menacingly. Bronze light washed over both of them, signifying a kingdom-witnessed legal agreement between the duo.

"By the way, I'm going to point at the Code of Conduct... chapter fourteen, paragraph twenty-six, and fight you through my proxy champion."

As the Artificer finished speaking, the Beast was lowered from the ceiling by the pulley system and slowly stood to his full height in front of the baron, towering over the man by a good two feet.

"I'm sure a big, *strong* man such as yourself has no problem with that... so let's get started."

THIRTY-FIVE

"Resorting to trickery? Why am I not surprised?" Gasteel sneered as he hefted his longsword, voice dripping with disdain. "All he's ever been able to do is hide behind his machines and send them out to do his dirty work! But you know what?"

He turned to his men, his gaze sweeping across them before brandishing his weapon and swinging forward with a grunt of effort. "*I'm* not afraid to get my hands dirty!"

Even at a distance, Danielle could see the grin plastered on the man's face and shook her head as she realized he couldn't resist putting on a show. The bronze light from the kingdom's wards barely had time to fade before the grand hall resonated with the deafening clash of steel on steel.

A blinding burst of sparks erupted from the impact of the longsword—engraved with glowing runes—colliding with the Beast's arm. The warrior seemed surprised that his blade had been stopped, but as the sparks faded away, he saw that the mechanical limb had transformed. The thick metal plating had opened slightly and shifted in configuration before settling as a multifaceted, razor-sharp weapon.

Capitalizing on the man's surprise, the Beast shifted back

and kicked him in the chest. The baron managed to react fast enough to move with the blow, hopping several times as he bled off the momentum of the attack. "*This* is all the Comte's champion can bring to bear? This will be over soon, and then..."

He raised his voice, allowing his words to boom across the hall. "Then you'll have an easy choice to make, Belle! I'm going to prove that I have all the power here. I'll give you both a little taste of what I'm capable of. You *know* I didn't need to demand a duel. I'm fighting because I want to warm up a little and impress upon you all that there are no other choices! These toys are cute, but I have *real* power in this kingdom!"

Gasteel launched forward, pressing his assault, each swing of his blade more savage than the last. He moved with brutal precision and system-guided accuracy. His style—if it could even be called as such—was absolutely savage. Each strike was not only aimed to kill but to break the spirit and demoralize any onlookers arrayed against him. His muscles bulged out, the attack appearing as a whirlwind of honed steel and immense impacts, which would drive almost anyone to falter beneath the barrage or surrender, instead of testing their might against his.

But the baron wasn't simply facing a mere conscript, nor was he battling the Beast on its own. The hulking metal machine was being piloted by the Artificer, who had spent countless hours piloting the machine until it was all but an extension of his will. The automaton moved with a fluid grace which belied its size, every emotion carefully calculated, every maneuver a demonstration of mastery. Each time Danielle winced away, expecting a dangling hose to be severed or a joint to be sheared through by the expertly wielded broadsword, the Artificer proved himself to be one step ahead.

Even with his attacks being met over and again, Gasteel seemed completely unfazed by the challenge. With his speed and strength, he seemed to have the upper hand as he aimed for the Beast's joints, targeting its weakest points with every attack. "You're just another monster I'm going to carve up. You see this? There's a lesson here, and you're going to *learn* how futile- "

His words were drowned out by the ringing of clashing metal as the Beast's runescript-reinforced body absorbed the blows with minimal damage. As Gasteel over-committed to an attack, the intricate mechanisms shifted and released a burst of steam. The baron was forced away from the hazard, else he'd be risking blisters forming across his exposed skin or losing his eyesight.

The man stumbled back, covering his eyes before letting loose a snarl as he realized the Comte was holding his own. A wild strike lashed out and found purchase in the Beast's elbow. Danielle gasped, fully expected the machine to lose its arm... yet the now-exposed gears instead rapidly spun and caught the blade. The spinning mechanism *dinged* against the blade with the sound of coppers raining onto a sheet of metal, throwing it off course. Gasteel struggled to control his weapon, being forced to turn and rapidly shuffle away to avoid a follow-up blow which would've left him as paste splattered across the wall.

Though his chest was heaving with exertion, his arrogance hadn't been exhausted in the slightest. Gesturing at his sword, now slick with viscous oil dripping down the groove, he let loose a chuckle. "Looks like I took first blood. How about we call it a-"

The warrior darted forward mid-sentence, doing his best to catch the remotely piloted automaton off guard. Instead, he was forced to backpedal as the Beast retaliated with a closed fist. As the blow whistled toward Gasteel's head, the iron-clad knuckles shifted and reformed into a spiked mace—missing the man's head with inches to spare as he ducked and weaved away.

Slamming down with terrible force, the fist cratered the smooth stone floor and left cracks radiating outward for a yard in either direction. Beside Danielle, the Artificer spoke in perfect synchronization with the Beast's distant form. "Oh, don't let *me* stop you. I'd *love* to hear what you were about to say. Your surrender, perhaps?"

"Give up? When I'm having so much fun?" Gasteel doubled down on his bravado as he dashed to the side. Flashing a cocky grin, he dipped down—but it was a feint. His sword gleamed as he came up in a crouch, slashing at the exposed gears of the Beast's arm, clearly intent on severing the limb once and for all.

But LeKrout anticipated the move, shifting the Beast's body with the same finesse he managed back in the workshop while dancing with Danielle. The damaged arm retracted, the plating seamlessly closing up around the vulnerable openings. Completing the motion, a burst of steam propelled a hidden blade from the Beast's open hand. The weighty projectile slammed into Gasteel's chest plate at point-blank range, denting the steel armor directly above his heart.

The baron staggered back and gasped for breath. Danielle noted with satisfaction that the cocky grin had finally been wiped from his face. Before standing to his full height, the man struggled to regain his composure, giving the Beast more than enough time to reset its position. The Artificer simply waited patiently as Gasteel got into a ready position once more, unconcerned with allowing his opponent to recover.

"You should have taken that chance to finish the fight, *Comte*." The hunter-turned-noble's voice was laced with venom as he aimed his blade. "We seem to be nearly evenly matched, and I'm not going to offer you the same show of *weakness* when I have you dead to rights."

"Hold a moment. You think we're *evenly matched?*" The Artificer's calm disdain resounded clearly through the Beast's mouth. "I've been holding back to try and allow you to surrender with some *scraps* of your dignity intact. Look at you… gasping for air, eyes darting around like a cornered animal as you decide whether you should find an exit to escape though or stay to continue to fail at impressing your soldiers. You should give up. It's a weak man who only fights for attention."

"Weak? *Me?*" Gasteel bristled at the Comte's words. "You're the one cowering behind your *toys*, while I stand here risking myself for honor! If anyone is a weakling here, it's you!"

"Being strong is having the ability to do great harm, and choosing not to," LeKrout calmly replied, carefully studying the baron for signs of another attempt at a sneak attack. "*Weakness* is having no ability to do harm, and pretending you won't fight only because of some personal choice. You? You're the worst of both. You have the ability to do harm and no morals to keep yourself contained. Men who put boundaries on themselves are men who can be trusted. But you? You're little better than an animal."

Gasteel's face contorted with rage, his eyes flashing as he dashed forward once more. Gripping his sword tight enough to bleach his knuckles white, his muscles bulged as he swung with all of his strength. Having given up all pretense of finesse, the baron managed to land a heavy blow on the Beast's torso—sending a shockwave through the enormous entity.

The automaton staggered under the impact, stumbling back but quickly regaining its balance, thanks to the unyielding control of the Artificer. Once more, the Beast shifted slightly, this time transforming both hands into massive hammers, which looked like they'd been put to use crushing boulders and forging ingots for years—Danielle realized just before he attacked that likely this was *exactly* what they were used for.

Then the Beast began swinging his arms with terrible

force, its body not bound by the constraints of a human form. Instead of striking and pulling back to throw another hammer blow, its torso rotated freely as it spun on its axis. This meant the strikes continuously came around in a punishing rhythm, *pounding* against Gasteel's blade.

"I won't lose to… a *toy!*" Instead of flinching, the baron pushed back against the hits, his eyes blazing with bloodlust as he tried to force the machine off balance. On the fifth hit, he seemed to finally realize he wouldn't be able to overpower the created creature. By the seventh, he had changed tactics, dropping low and charging forward, positioned to move *under* the hammer blows raining down on him.

Where Danielle stood, she couldn't see the exact maneuver he executed: she could only hear a deafening **clang** of metal on metal as the Beast lost its footing. Its momentum carried sideways and forced the Beast to overbalance. It spun backward, crushing a half-dozen metal soldiers and nearly toppling before managing to right itself and charge back into the fray.

Even with the Artificer's confidence, Danielle felt sick with worry as minute after minute of grueling combat passed. She could see the toll combat was taking on both sides—blood and oil mingling on the ground, the audience of soldiers and automatons growing restless and eager to participate in the violence. Yet, clearly neither side felt any compulsion to surrender.

"Is that the best you can do, *LeKrout?* Is this all you have to show after so many years?"

A grunt escaped Kota's lips, and Danielle slowly turned to stare at him, her wide eyes taking in the strain that maintaining such precise control was etching on his face. Then he crossed his arms and forced himself to stand tall, his gaze narrowing with intense focus. He ground out a few words which were not repeated by the Beast. "Not. Even. *Close.*"

Slowly, near imperceptibly at first, the tide began to turn.

The Beast's defenses became more calculated. Strategic showers of superheated steam or viscous stinging oil erupted to disrupt Gasteel's battle rhythm, and the Beast adjusted to his opponents brutal offense. Small injuries began adding up, tipping the scales in the Artificer's favor.

For his part, the baron's swings came faster, harder, as he realized his stamina was swiftly depleting. Where a lesser man's attacks might have become desperate, Gasteel had an unyielding drive to dominate, so instead, he put all of his effort into maintaining and even *exceeding* his prior relentlessness.

The combat reached a crescendo as the baron summoned all his strength and stepped forward, his massive sword arcing through the air in a decisive blow. As the weapon descended, a series of *popping* noises rang out. Suddenly the blade accelerated, moving nearly three times as fast, though with far less control guiding its landing. Somehow, using his system skills, the nobleman had formed an explosion behind his weapon.

Though the Beast twisted away, the swift, brutal attack cut through its neck—cleanly severing through the armored plating, wires, and instantly beheading the machine.

Oil sprayed into the air from the bisected tubes, lighting on fire as it splattered across the spark-coated ground. For a split second, there was silence but for Gasteel's ragged breathing. The Baron blinked rapidly then unleashed a triumphant roar as his men began to cheer.

Then the Beast's arm shot out, smashing into the baron's chest and sending him sprawling to the ground, the heraldry covering his armor blackening in the flames as his sword bounced and clattered away.

Gasteel looked up from his position on the floor, and even from this distance, Danielle could feel the absolute confusion radiating off the man. "Stop! I *won*! What is this? Do you have no honor? In an *honor duel*?"

"Tell me where losing a chunk of armor constitutes losing

the duel." Kota's voice, mangled as per usual by the Beast's mechanisms, rang through the dead-silent hall. "You didn't *kill* my machine. Its head is there for convenience's sake only."

"*You!*" As the baron realized the situation he was in, a deranged giggle flew from his lips, but before he could push himself back to his feet, the Beast was standing over him, pressing the baron's own sword to his neck. "You have lost the duel, Gasteel. Admit your defeat, or we shall see if *your* head is also only for convenience."

"I'd rather di-" A soft gurgle came from Gasteel's lips as his blade dug into his skin. "Whoa, *whoa*! I'd... I'd rather... walk away. Victory is yours... I yield."

Once more, the bronze light of the kingdom's wards washed over the two noblemen. However, this time it lingered on LeKrout, and luckily, the Artificer knew exactly what to do. "As per the terms of my victory, I *insist* that you immediately leave my land, making no further demands on me or mine. That is all. Leave now, bound by honor and the law of the kingdom."

The bronze light jumped from Kota to Gasteel, striking the sprawled-out man like lightning from a clear sky. As the baron spasmed, his victorious opponent spoke in a softer tone, trying to allow the man to leave with grace. "Let me be clear as to what this means, Gasteel. If you attempt to go against what I have decided on for my victory, all kingdom merits you would otherwise gain for succeeding in your mission today will instead turn into a black mark on your record."

He paused momentarily to allow the man to process what he was saying, as Gasteel was still laying on his back, sprawled across the floor and heaving for air. "Even if you successfully managed to bring me under your banner, instead of enough prestige to lift you into the higher nobility, you'd instead regress... most likely returning to the position of a Greenhorn under someone else's command."

"It wasn't... a fair battle," Gasteel snarled as he scrambled to his feet, hunching forward aggressively as the Beast stepped away. The machine kept its hold on the gleaming sword, ignoring the outstretched hand of the baron. "You used everything you had in this battle and *still* nearly lost! Even if you managed to land a cheap blow on me, I've proved myself the better of a Comte. *I* am the better man, and *I* say-!"

"Is *that* what you truly think, *Baron Gasteel?*" Now Kota's words were as cold and hard as the Beast's body. "I told you before that I was holding back. Since words don't seem to make it through your thick skull, let me *show* you. *Overclock.*"

For the briefest of moments, the Beast shimmered... then vanished from sight. The onlookers released a collective gasp, flinching back as they stared at the scene in shock. For his part, Gasteel stood frozen, mouth open in a snarl as he tried to understand what he'd just seen. "So, you can turn your machines invisible now?"

"No." The Beast's mechanical growl sounded right next to the baron's left ear. Only then did the muscled man go stiff in fear, as he felt the edge of his own sword against his throat once again. "I've simply refrained from using my Breakthrough Skill. I wanted you to be able to see how, even without my most potent magic, I can put you down if needed."

"I know your type." The Beast patted the rigid man on the shoulder in an *almost* friendly way. "Someone like you would never be able to accept his defeat if I didn't *beat* it into you. The fact is, I'm *immensely* strong, skilled, and experienced. If I wanted you dead, I could have ended this fight whenever I wanted. But, Gasteel, as I already explained to you..."

"Being strong is having the ability to do great harm... and *choosing not to.*"

THIRTY-SIX

THERE WAS an uncertain air about the soldiers in Gasteel company, and they shifted uncomfortably as they tried to come to terms with their commander's defeat. They stood in uneasy formations, their weapons raised half-heartedly, their eyes darting between the Beast who still had a blade to the throat of the seething baron.

Slowly, the mechanical entity pulled the sword away then stepped around Gasteel. Torso faced directly at the still-frozen man, the headless automaton gripped both the tip of the sword and the handle, then began applying immense force, bending the weapon until it was completely unusable. The runescript along its edge sparked brilliantly and fizzled out, leaving the onlookers blinking in pain as they tried to get the afterimage out of their eyes.

Tossing the ruined metal to the side derisively, the Beast shifted and began walking toward the dining room, where the Artificer was waiting to perform repairs.

"This isn't *over!*"

The Beast stopped short, his movement checked not by swords or might, but by the desperation in Gasteel's booming voice. "Yes. It is."

322 ✕ 　　　　　　DAKOTA KROUT

"Lefroupe! Get over here and explain to the Comte why he's in the wrong here. Point out how he cheated, how the law is in my favor," Gasteel commanded desperately as he worked to control his expression. "If I say anything else, I'm going to end up doing something *rash*!"

The weasel of a man was soon shoved into the room, holding Gasteel's tome of the kingdom's laws in one hand and his hunting musket in the other. His sweat-soaked clothes flapped around him with every nervous motion he made, glancing between the naked weapons surrounding him, the automatons, and finally the face of his lord, which was twisted into a mask of venomous fury. Clearing his throat, he quickly flipped open the book and started turning through the pages until he got to the chapter on honor duels.

"This, uh, this duel was not conducted according to proper procedure." His voice was quavering as he spoke, filled with a note that caused suspicion and disbelief in everyone who could hear him. "Yes, as shown here, the terms were not sufficiently documented, the outcome afterward was chosen half-haphazardly, and the use of a proxy-"

"That's directly from the section on conscription!" Danielle's voice drowned out Lefroupe, "Even if that's the only part you read, you can't apply conscription of civilians to an honor duel between noblemen!"

"*Belle!*" Gasteel barked at her in a horrified tone. "Whose side are you on here?"

"She's right. Those are adorable legal platitudes, but unfortunately for you, they hold no weight here," Kota called out in a cold, commanding voice. "The terms were perfectly clear and accepted by both parties, witnessed by the wards of Verdelune. You will stop this farce immediately. It does your lord no favors—only making it ever more apparent that he is surrounded by sycophants and lackeys who are willing to outright ignore the law, if it is convenient. I'll tell you now, your words, your will, cannot override mine."

"But what of the precedents?" Lefroupe tried again, tapping on the book once more, licking his lips as he shot a nervous glance over to Gasteel, who seemed as though he were ready to explode.

"There *are* no precedents," the Comte confidently declared, his voice cutting through with the blustering like a wire through soft cheese. "Do you know how I know that? It is because I have made a study of the laws of the kingdom. *All* the laws of the kingdom, not just volume one, which you hold in your hands."

"Volume... *one?*" Gasteel slowly turned to stare at Lefroupe and the absolute doorstop of a book he was holding. "There's *more* than this?"

"In fact, there is!" Seeing as the aggressors were not immediately leaving, Kota decided to twist the knife a bit. "One of the first assignments given to any newly raised noble house is to carefully read through the entirety of this text. In the middle of the penultimate chapter, there's a writ from the king, which orders the new noble to present themselves to the crown as soon as they have finished their first read-through."

The Comte's grin widened as he saw the abject panic on Gasteel's face. "Don't worry, it's not to test your knowledge. No one expects you to have memorized and understood everything on the first read. As a point of fact, the writ is there as a way to show how the new noble followed through on what they were told to do. At that next meeting, you would have been granted a staff of legal professionals, as well as a copy of all the remaining volumes."

Gasteel went pale, looking as though he could have been knocked over with a feather. At this point, it had been nearly a full year since he'd been raised to his position.

"I see you are beginning to understand what this means, *Baron*. Even if you rushed back to the palace this very night to show that you'd managed to read through the text... you would be derided as a weak-minded man with no further potential. At this point, you—and likely your progeny—are doomed to remain at this level of society, no matter how much you struggle."

Comte LeKrout's voice softened as he decided to extend an olive branch. "Instead… instead, let me offer you a position in my lands. Declare that I am your liege lord. You will have everything you deserve and *almost* everything you desire. Certainly, this is more than the Crown will offer you at this point."

Danielle watched the exchange with immense interest as the Comte verbally flayed the man she'd come to know as little more than a bone-headed lump of muscle and charisma. Her eyes darted between the Artificer, the baron who was on the edge of exploding, and the scribe, who was flipping through the book to try and see if they were being told the truth.

"You'll *hang* for this," Gasteel finally managed to whisper, closing his eyes, only for them to pop back open, wider than seemed healthy.

"Again… you have no power here." Kota let out a sigh, shaking his head and dismissively gesturing at the door. "Soldiers of Gasteel Company, your leader lost an honor duel and is not following through on his end of the bargain. Step outside of my manor immediately, so as to not witness his *shame* any further. Have some respect!"

As though he was absolutely deaf to what was happening, Gasteel stared at Lefroupe, his words echoing around the hall like a snake hissing in a cavern. "I gave you one job, Lefroupe. I told you to obey my orders, and if you haven't, if you don't… I'll make sure you pay the price. Right…"

"Ignore him, Lefroupe!" Danielle's shout was steady and calm but filled with urgency. "You don't have to listen to him any longer. You're a good man and fun to be around. Leave your position behind, and I *guarantee* you a far better one with me."

"...*Now!*" Gasteel finally finished with a shout, spinning back to face the Beast and holding one hand to the side. Lefroupe's expression flickered with doubt, but without a word, he slung the musket off his shoulder and forward into Gasteel's waiting hands. Time seemed to slow as the baron caught the rifle, face twisting into a triumphant sneer. He leveled his weapon and shouted a series of words that caused a gout of flame to erupt from the open end.

Danielle screeched and flinched away, but her voice was drowned out by the deafening explosion echoing off the walls of the confined space. After a moment, she managed to look to see what had happened, only to realize Gasteel was tossing his weapon to the side in a pique, frustration writ large on his face.

"Sacrificing your own creations to save yourself? At least *that* I can understand and respect. You! Reload that musket, I'll need it momentarily." Gasteel's furious shout reached Danielle's ears as though from underwater, the man continuing to bellow while she shook her head to try and clear it. "Somebody get me a sword; tonight we win... or we *die!*"

The Beast stomped forward, causing the soldiers who'd started rushing back into the building to flinch back with a hefty dose of fear in their eyes. Yet, the automaton only made it two steps before the oil and steam gushing from the point of impact *hissed* and spurted its last. Momentum allowed the automaton to continue forward, but all that accomplished was the Beast slowly toppling forward and landing on the ground, unable to move.

"The Comte's champion has been slain! Victory, glory, honor! It's here for the *taking!*" Gasteel was howling as he and his men leapt into action, charging into the ranks of the metal soldiers and swiftly carving through the first rows. With the baron at the head of the charge, the battle began anew, and the hallway devolved into a scene of chaos and violence once more.

Danielle found herself rushing forward, only to force herself to come to a stop and pull back before her impulses could control her further. "Kota! Grab the Beast. Use the pulley system and yank his core. It's time for us to get out of here before this turns into the scene of a massacre."

"Hold your ground! Aim for the legs; they don't need those so much!" the Artificer howled in a rage as his machines fought back. Danielle needed to grab his shoulders and *shake* him to break the man from his focused rage, and only after she repeated herself did a light of understanding appear in his eyes. "Right! He's not dead, he just can't move!"

Cables began dropping from the ceiling, wrapping around the Beast and yanking him into the air.

"That's *my* trophy!" A moment after his shout, Gasteel's musket practically exploded once more, impacting the control mechanism for the pulley. Sparking furiously, it went limp, dropping the huge chunk of metal. Just before it would have crushed a slew of men beneath it, a sharpened spear slammed into the Beast's body.

The chain it was connected to went taut.

"*Harpooooon!*" Doc cackled like a madman as the Beast swung down, then back up, barely clearing the heads of the packed metal soldiers. At the top of its arc, the harpoon retracted, sending the BST model three tumbling through the air. Automatons were scattered like bowling pins as the great weight bounced and skidded, but there were hundreds more ready to replace those who had fallen. "*Ssspider* for the win!"

Danielle and Kota rushed forward, the Artificer already making motions with his hands which caused the nearest mindless machines to either step out of the way or begin rolling the Beast to the side for easier access to his core. Within moments, they were at his side, struggling against rust and years of poor maintenance to try and force its internals open.

The Enchantress whacked the Comte on his arm to break

his attention as he fiddled with tools. "Stop being delicate and *chop* his core out if you need to! We're officially out of time."

Blinking at the barked order, the Artificer nodded once and motioned for the machines around him to get to work dismantling the Beast. It was the work of a few minutes to get through the thick armor, welded-on plating that had been added when sections rusted through, and faulty, broken internals. When he pulled his arm out of the Beast's chest, both his clothing and the core were soaked in various mechanical fluids.

"I never stopped to think how badly he must have been damaged over the years." LeKrout sighed gently as he cradled the glowing rectangle in his hand. "I can only be glad my creations don't feel pain, or he would've been suffering terribly."

With a quick swipe of his stylus, the Artificer removed the self-destruct portion of the Beast's rune design. When Danielle didn't respond to his words, he glanced over at her, only for his eyebrows to shoot up, practically vanishing under his thick hair. "By the system, what are you *doing*?"

"Grabbing... *this*!" Danielle grunted as she dug through the Beast's chest, absolutely coating herself in filth. She shoved a thick plate of metal out of her way, coming up with the Comte's preserved heart. "What's going on with this thing? Why's it floating? Is that *blood*?"

"Ah, I'd wondered what the Beast and your father had been doing." Kota's offhanded remark caused Danielle to sweep the room for her father, but one sigh of relief later, she still hadn't found him. "That's a much lower-end health potion. Essentially, all it will do is provide enough healing and nutrients to keep that organ healthy. If it breaks down too much, it's likely that some of the oaths etched onto it will degrade before we want them to."

"Enough of this! Your toys are defeated, and your monstrosities are nothing compared to me! Soon, you will have no choice but to accept that!" Gasteel's voice was filled with madness and venom, "I will... *crush* you... and take what's mine!"

"I've already *warned* you, Baron!" the Artificer shouted back with great annoyance. "All of this is working against you. The more impressive your reward would have been, the farther you'll fall now that you've proven you have no honor!"

The bubbling laugh of a madman caused Danielle to feel a sinking pit in her stomach as Gasteel answered, "You think I'll lose my rank for this? That I'll be slapped down all the way to a Greenhorn? *Good*! This! This is what I love! Living on the edge, one mistake away from absolute destruction. The *growth* zone! If I can't be the most powerful, *respected* noble, I'll be the most feared man in the entire kingdom!"

"Comte LeKrout!" Gasteel howled as he swung his sword hard enough to send metal soldiers tumbling through the air. "By the authority of the king of Verdelune, cease this resistance! You're ordered to report for wartime duty under *my* banner!"

CHAPTER
THIRTY-SEVEN

THE SWORDS in mechanical hands stopped swinging. Steam, fire, and acid was held back instead of constantly being released at the attackers in great clouds. What only moments ago was unceasing motion began to falter, coming to a halt as Comte LeKrout sent out frantic instructions for them to stop attacking. Now that the order had been given, any intentional aggressive action from the Comte or his creations against the baron would be enough for the oath to be considered as broken.

Seeing the machines going still, the human soldiers also stopped their assault, pulling back slightly as they waited for their enemies' total surrender... with one notable exception: Gasteel.

The hulking warrior swung his borrowed sword in great arcs, furiously venting his rage on the now-helpless automatons in his path. Because of the constraints the Artificer had put on them, they could only accept the blows, doing nothing to retaliate. They could still attempt to block, but these older-style automatons were ill-balanced and designed to be chopping and slashing, with very little effort put into allowing them self-defense.

Gasteel cleaved through two to three of them at a time, opening a wide space around himself, then moving forward, his eyes now locked on the silent Comte. A ragged shout broke through the spreading silence. "Is that all? You're not going to argue, or tell me that I've still somehow truly lost, even though I've won?"

"What do you want me to say, Baron Gasteel?" Kota replied evenly, reaching out and taking Danielle's hand to reassure her. "You were warned, and I'm not going to have to deal with you for much longer, anyway. I'll be under the banner of whoever *replaces* you soon enough. Most likely, I'll be sent back to the capital city to produce soldiers, while whoever is in charge of you continuously sends you on missions with the intent of you not coming back."

"Are you *threatening* me?" Gasteel scoffed at the higher-ranked noble, his sword continuously swinging back and forth as he slowly cut his way toward Kota and Danielle.

"No, Gasteel. That's what I'm trying to tell you. *I* don't need to do *anything* to you." The Artificer's casual attitude only served to infuriate the fuming man even further. "As far as I'm concerned, you've just removed yourself as a threat. The real question is, what do *you* want?"

The handsome commander finally paused for a moment, "I. Want. *Satisfaction*. I want to wake up tomorrow morning and have my *wife*-"

Here, he shoved an accusatory finger at Danielle, "-make me a plate of scrambled eggs! I want her to learn how to prepare a Frontière Flip for me to drink when I get home from a hard day! I want the respect and position I've *earned* with a lifetime of bloodshed and dedication. No one's done *more* than Gasteel. In all of Verdelune's history, no one's enjoyed *war* like Gasteel!"

The baron locked eyes with the Comte, then sneeringly looked him over. "In comparison, there's *you*. Here you stand, behind a wall of armor and weaponry, weak and unable to defend yourself because you fear mere words binding you."

"*You* are the one who couldn't make me bend the knee with the might of his arm. It was *you* who invoked the oaths, using words to win the fight instead of fighting. Of course... *I* understand. You were going to lose, so you did what *any* nobleman in your position would have," Kota replied mildly, then returned the baron's sing-song statements with his own. "As a specimen, yes, you're infuriating. Oh... no one talks a big game like Gasteel... dishonors his name like Gasteel. In our history books, no one will be *defamed like Gasteel!*"

"You *dare?*" the baron roared as every speech-capable automaton in the building echoed the Comte's words. "You want to fight me? *Fight* me!"

"I'll take that as a direct order."

Kota pulled Danielle close as the immense number of metal soldiers surrounding the baron on all sides began swinging their swords. Clearly, he was attempting to spare her the sight of the man being chopped into bite-sized chunks of meat, but she easily squirmed out of his grip and pushed him to arm's length.

"I'm no wilting flower, Comte." Danielle watched grimly as the baron fought for his life against scores of flashing blades, holding his own surprisingly well. After considering the situation and coming up with a quick strategy, she turned back to the Artificer. "In order to prevent a repeat performance where he gains control by telling you to stop the attack, maybe get your metal soldiers to start stomping, clapping, or pounding on metal to drown out anything he attempts?"

The Comte had barely heard her words before he realized the wisdom in them. Within moments, the beleaguered shouts of Gasteel were completely drowned out by an *immense* clattering racket. Danielle nodded approvingly, then returned her attention to the reignited battle. Soldiers from Gasteel Company poured into the house once more, and while she was certain they were letting loose war cries and shouting orders, this only added to the ear-numbing cacophony.

"Keep the automatons on the lookout for the Wind Mage," she shouted into the Artificer's ear just to be heard. "If he has enough power to batter hundreds of combatants at once, he might be able to throw Gasteel's voice directly to your ears if he gets the chance. Might I suggest that a well-placed harpoon might be able to prevent that?"

He nodded, then turned back to yell a reply, "We've got most of the self-aware automatons' cores out; can you take the first crate of them and get to the library? I'll finish the last few and join you there."

The Enchantress glanced at him with narrowed eyes, trying to see if he was trying to get rid of her, but he only smiled knowingly and motioned for her to follow him back into the preparation area. There, she found two small crates, just large enough to hold two dozen of the cores each. The first was full, and the second was nearly there. She looked from the box to the man, her left eyebrow arching, "You aren't going to do anything foolish, are you? As soon as you have what you need, you're coming to the escape tunnel? Yes?"

"Nothing foolish, I'm making my escape with you." The Artificer's promise was the only thing that made Danielle slowly move her feet, but as she stepped closer to grab the cores, a thought froze her in place.

"They entered the hallway from the main entrance. My room was the first door, then a few... guest rooms? Coat rooms? But the library is nearly at the halfway point between here and where Gasteel Company is entering. Your metal soldiers are coming up from the workshop, which is even closer to here and completely blocking my path. Even if they weren't, Gasteel has been fighting as hard as he can to get closer. Kota, I think you might be completely blocked in."

"A very good point, and also why you should go *this* way." Kota gestured to a blank wall with a knowing smile as he stepped past her, picked up the full crate, and handed it over. A moment later, a silhouette of a small doorway appeared in the otherwise white wall, smoothly swinging out and revealing an entrance into what appeared to be a storage room. "Can I just say, this is the first time I feel vindicated in having put secret passages between all the rooms? Before now, I merely felt paranoid for doing so."

"We'll be even more paranoid wherever we live next," Danielle promised as she put the preserved heart on top of the small crate and picked both up gingerly. "Pulley systems, at least two or three escape tunnels, secret passages, hidden rooms... I'm kind of relieved, if I'm being honest. What sort of mad Artificer would you be without a few paranoid passageways?"

He was smiling widely at her, his eyes narrow and twinkling. "You said wherever 'we' live next. I never asked... does this mean–"

"A conversation for another time." Danielle replied firmly, nodding at the last few automatons needing their cores swapped out. "Let's get out of here, Kota. Then we can figure out what we want our lives to look like."

"Yeah, we-" The Comte coughed into a closed fist, cutting off whatever he was about to say. "You're right, this isn't an appropriate setting for such an important discussion. Meet you at the library. Remember, whatever goes on, don't show your face in the great hall again—they have to believe we were in here when everything went *boom*, or it is all for naught."

Moving carefully with her delicate cargo, Danielle stepped through the secret door and into what appeared to be a dry-goods pantry. Moments later, the door behind her silently swung shut, and a set of cupboards in front of her, which held dried beans and tea leaves, split horizontally, the top half rushing up into the ceiling, the lower half into the floor.

As she carefully avoided exposed piping and jagged stone reinforcements, Danielle decided that the secret corridor she was walking through must be a part of the outer wall. Only the light filtering in through the open pantry behind her allowed her to barely pick her way across the straight, narrow space. When that cut off and she was left in near-perfect darkness, the Enchantress very carefully scooted forward until the door in front of her popped open—this time splitting vertically and opening to the left and right.

Happily, this one had deposited her directly into the library, and a glance back the way she had come allowed Danielle to watch as a bookshelf she had frequently referenced slowly slid back together. "There's one mystery solved. I had *wondered* how the Beast snuck in here time and time again without me noticing."

"Danielle?" Henri's muffled voice caught her off guard, and though Danielle looked around questioningly, she was unable to find her father. "Over here... I don't know how to open this *abyssal* door from the side. It's—oh, there it goes."

As the passageway hidden behind the bookshelf slid open, Henri stumbled into the library, appearing disheveled and exhausted but otherwise unharmed. Carefully setting her burden on the table, Danielle rushed over and swept him into a hug. "You're safe! Where were you? I was so worried! I thought you might've gotten trapped down in the workshop."

"No... no, I remained there for..." Henri studied her intently with sunken eyes before allowing a tight smile to cross his face. "Never mind *me*, I've been waiting here since the Beast sent me through the tunnel, being worried sick about *you.*"

"Is that all that's going on?" Danielle pulled back slightly, studying his face with great concern. "Did the Beast say something to you? You seem... distracted."

Her father shook his head, but it didn't escape Danielle's notice that he was avoiding her gaze. "Just trying to stay out of sight and waiting for you. That and, well, thinking. But!

Let's focus on getting you out of here; I'm sure LeKrout didn't ask you to wait around for him, right?"

"He didn't, but I'm not going anywhere until I know we're all ready to go. Kota's grabbing the last few cores, but he should be joining us any moment now." Danielle squinted at her father, who was acting odd and cagey, but decided that perhaps now was not the time to press him. "I don't know if you saw or heard, I suppose, but the Beast fell in combat against a cowardly sneak attack from Gasteel when the man had already surrendered."

"The Beast is down?" Henri visibly winced at that news, shaking his head and muttering, "Well, *that* complicates things."

"What do you-?" Danielle went silent at that moment, as the nightmarish sounds of battle were overridden by a distinctive voice.

"Fall back! *Fall back*, prepare to charge!" Gasteel could barely be heard over the symphony of clashing metal, and only because he must have been almost to the doors of the library. Strangely enough, it sounded like he was full-on *running* when he was shouting, leading the retreat back to the main entrance of the manor.

"What's going on?" Danielle's eyes were fixed on the oak doors, gouged from where Doc had flipped into them, and found herself drifting toward them almost in a trance. "Just a quick peek… I've got to know what he's doing."

There was no more clashing, only the sound of feet jostling as the metal soldiers pushed forward to retake the ground they'd lost in the hallway. More flooded up from the workshop, replacing their destroyed brethren as they hurried to remove the invaders from their lord's estate. "Stop! What're you *doing*? Don't go out there!"

Henri's voice reached Danielle just as she touched the door handle, snapping her out of the odd introspection that had been driving her to give away her position. She pulled her hand back, brow furrowing in confusion at her nearly very foolish decision. "I don't know why I was-"

"Tremblar, rexum, somberia… dazzle sharp hysteria! Calmort, aether, turm-a-lyn, first ray of dawn's light now begin…" It was a low, ominous murmur, slowly increasing in intensity as the words were chanted over and over. The sound started as a vibration in the floor, seeming to slowly crawl along the floor and coil around her legs before slithering up to her ears.

"What's happening out there? Why does it feel like I'm breathing oily smoke?" Danielle lifted her hands, running her fingers against her thumbs to try and feel if it was an actual sensation or a byproduct of whatever was happening.

As the air grew heavier, each breath carrying the tang of ozone, the tempo of the chanting increased, a vibration resonating with her bones. Henri quietly called out to Danielle, but the urgency in his voice was unmistakable. "You need to get away from that door… right now! I've heard this before, Danielle. Don't walk, *run!*"

By the time she turned and started running toward her father—veering off to grab Kota's heart and the box of cores, much to his dismay—the once quiet library had become a resonant chamber as the air itself began to hum. A spark jumped from the crate Danielle scooped up, causing her to flinch and almost drop the precious cargo as everything in the area began to crackle with latent power.

It was only as the charged atmosphere sent rippling shivers down her spine that she recognized the feeling. "Is this system energy?"

Henri's eyes were wide and darting, his mouth clenched so hard he could only nod frantically in response. As she got close, he pulled both of them around a sturdy bookshelf and yanked her to the ground, shielding her with his body as the shadows in the room twisted and elongated, created by flickering lights which danced into and out of existence with each moment.

A piercing whistle split the air, so sharp and high that Danielle reflexively clamped her hands over her ears—but that barely took the edge off the noise. The room was filled with blinding beams of light, and across the library, books burst into flame wherever the incandescent energy touched.

Danielle waited for an explosion of power, but between one blink and the next, the energy faded away. No more noise, no more light. "What was that?"

The Enchantress blinked as she realized her words were muted, as though she were holding a pillow to her mouth. Pulling her hands away from her ears, she noticed small spots of blood from where her ears had taken damage... but her father's sharply whispered response was still easily heard.

"*War wizards.*"

THIRTY-EIGHT

HENRI COUGHED from the light smoke as he tried to stand to his full height, only for his legs to buckle. A glance down revealed that his prosthetic leg was bubbling and melting, a white-hot line drawn across it as perfectly as if it'd been done with a quill and protractor. "By the system, I haven't seen magic used like that since the last battle for the independence of…! What was that *light*?"

"Radiance." Danielle looked over her father, noting that even the reflection of the light had caused blisters to spring up across his body. A deep well of anger was building in her as she looked at the man who'd taken care of her for her entire life and even now was protecting her. "Do you know how I know? Because someone attacked Gasteel's men recently, the conscripts and such. There was a Radiance Mage who killed off a huge swath of them."

"You don't mean to say—*blast* it!" Henri winced as Danielle waved her hand over his scorched skin, leaving behind an area which didn't look *nearly* as rough, though it hadn't been healed. "At least the pain is in nice, neat lines now, instead of just generally… everywhere. Ugh. Do you mean Gasteel attacked his own men? Why would he do that?"

"I think he was trying to draw me out." Danielle chose her words carefully as she watched her father's skin lay itself flat where it had been blistering in fouled disorder. "Me or the Comte. Either way, it would've been a win for him, but to so casually sacrifice his men?"

"I'd ask if you were certain, but this is a type of spellcaster you don't encounter randomly. If they want training or instruction, they will almost always need to swear an oath to their kingdom early on, when they're first discovered." Henri was still speaking quietly, his eyes now trying to pierce the acrid smoke beginning to fill the library. "It's time to go. If I wasn't certain before, I am now. The manor is burning down around us. "

Another brilliant flash seared through the hallway, the magic proving itself to be from a different source, as it was followed by a wall-shaking explosion. The force of the blast sent a wave of hot air rushing into the doors of the library, slamming them open and nearly taking them off their hinges. Books rained from shelves, and the duo were sent stumbling as rapidly moving shapes rushed past the opening.

"*Charge!*" Gasteel's voice passed by quickly. The father-daughter duo hunkered down, peeking between books on the lowest shelf to see what was happening. "Get a shield wall set up around that opening! It doesn't matter *how* many there are if they can't get up here! *Gasteel Company!*"

"*Gasteel Company!*" The return shout came from dozens of voices as men rushed to fulfill the baron's orders.

"Let's get into the passage, at the very least," Danielle whispered urgently to her father. "We can wait for the Comte there and be ready to run."

"Good plan!" Henri nodded, his face set with determination as they began scooting across the floor. Here the shifting smoke played in their favor, offering cover and disguising their movements.

Each time they came to some burning debris, Danielle

carefully swept it closer to the door, building up their smoke screen further. The fifth time she did so, she sucked in a sharp breath as her hand swiped across a shard of glass, opening a shallow but wide cut on her palm. Barely managing to stop herself from cursing out loud, she followed her father to the passage—only to go cold as a voice rang out behind her.

"Secure these rooms! Someone get those fires out; there's valuable information being lost every second we waste!" The Enchantress looked out into the hall, which had cleared enough for her to see a scene of utter devastation. Automatons lay in slag heaps, the few who remained unmelted having been shattered and scattered by the second magical strike. An armored man was in the doorway, luckily looking outward as he ordered other people to start moving through the space.

"If we can see him, he can see *us*, if he but looks. Go," Henri whispered into her ear, startling Danielle into motion once more. They scuttled around a fallen bookshelf, remaining low to the ground, both to avoid the searching soldiers, as well as to stay under the thickening smoke. "Where's the Comte? Time is not in our favor at this moment."

"I don't *know!*" Danielle quietly hissed back her reply, her eyes on the doorway as a dozen men hurried into the now-open room. For a moment, she thought about making a run for the passageway she knew would bring her back to the dining room, but she bit her lip as her eyes darted to her father's leg. Shaking her head, she murmured under her breath, "No… there's no way we can move fast enough."

Deciding to get her father to safety before trying to make any moves of her own, Danielle followed closely behind Henri as he led them to… "Father, do you know where the entrance to the escape tunnel is?"

"What?" Henri looked back at her, the pupils in his eyes practically vibrating from the intensity of his stare. "I thought *you* were showing *me* where to go!"

"Then why are *you* leading? You came out of it; I thought you'd know how to get back in!" Danielle's frantic words received no reply. Instead, her father stopped looking at her, his gaze trailing up, and his eyes going blank.

She turned her head, a pair of boots coming to a stop next to her capturing all of her attention. Ever so slowly, trying to draw in breath around the sudden vacuum in her lungs, Danielle looked up, and up...

With the most false smile on her lips that she'd ever before forced into position, Danielle spoke in a weak, conversational tone. "Le-*froupe*. *He~ey*... come here often?"

The scribe stared down at her, curiosity and apprehension battling on his face as he lifted the dagger he was gripping tightly. "Madame... why are you in here?"

"We're trying to escape, Lefroupe." Danielle kept her voice steady, though she wasn't sure how she managed. "Please don't give us away. This isn't the life I want to live, and... and... how'd you find us?"

The scribe pointed the tip of his blade at Danielle's hand. "There was a blood trail leading right to you. You're... you're injured? That's not good. You're not supposed to get hurt. Gasteel will literally tear someone apart for this."

At that moment, the baron in question rushed past the door of the library, sword held high as he bellowed furiously, "*Where are they?* Find them! Rip this place *apart* if you need to!"

"He was going to kill my father, Lefroupe." Danielle poured every iota of willpower she had into getting all of her skills working on her behalf in every possible way. "*Please.*"

Her head tilted back, her eyes littered with unshed tears, but... it was only as Lefroupe watched the slow drip of blood from her hand that his hard, indecisive eyes shifted to tender understanding.

"I was sent in here to grab valuable texts and rescue knowledge before it was lost forever." Lefroupe stepped back and glanced away, his voice dropping further as his lips trembled. "I have my orders, and I'm going to follow them. When I come around this way again… that's when I'll need to decide if I was telling myself a story about being the hero who found Gasteel's fiancée and turned her over. Maybe there were just a couple books laying here that I got a little too excited about?"

"Thank you, Lefroupe," Danielle whispered softly as he started to turn around. "I'll never forget that you were kind to me."

The scribe froze in place, and for a moment, the Enchantress worried she'd said something wrong. Then he backed up a step and another, revealing the sword pressed to his chest. A moment later, the Comte came into view, a half-dozen metal soldiers flanking him. The Artificer's scowl fell away as he took in Danielle and Henri's state, flickering to relief, then to an unreadable expression as he returned his attention to Lefroupe.

"Your life for your silence." The Comte stepped closer to the prone duo, pulling them to their feet. "Just stay quiet, and you'll make it through this."

Lefroupe swallowed hard, watching as the Artificer helped Danielle pull her father to his feet. Henri started moving once more, but Danielle—holding the crate with a heart in a jar—stayed a moment longer to look into the scribe's eyes, mouthing the words 'thank you' one last time before she started backing away, following her father around yet another shelf.

The metal soldiers broke off to follow her, and she paused to make sure nothing happened to the scribe who had just saved her life. Kota leaned in, his words just loud enough for her to make out. "Do you want a better life than this, Lefroupe? You can come with us. I know someone like you wouldn't have signed a bad contract."

"I have a future here," Lefroupe answered numbly, blinking in surprise at the sudden offer. "Gasteel's star is on the rise, no matter what you say."

"You think *Gasteel*...?" The Artificer shook his head and stepped back, slowly following after Danielle. "I guess you've made your choice, then. You could have done something better. Instead, you'll always be the lackey to a terrible man. I don't understand it, Lefroupe. From what Danielle's told me, you're *nothing* like him."

"I'm...?" Lefroupe's face twisted with anger, his pale face flushing as he rapidly blinked. "I so *am* like him! I'm talented. *Smart*. Celestial feces, I'm strong! By the system, what am I doing? No one holds a grudge like Gasteel, no one's fury is hotter than the *sun* like Gasteel!"

The more he spoke, the louder the man got, and just as Danielle stepped forward to try and calm him, his gaze snapped to her like a chameleon who had just seen a particularly delicious bug. "You ensorcelled me! No! I'm a loyal man, and I will never betray..."

"*Gaste~eel!*"

He shouted the final word at the top of his voice, turning and sprinting for the entrance to the library as if the Comte were about to silence him with a sword thrust.

Kota *was* actively attempting to skewer the man, so it was an apt decision on Lefroupe's part.

"The Artificer! The Enchantress! The Tinkerer! All of them are in the library with the metal men!" Lefroupe was sobbing as he screamed and ran. "*Gastee~eel!*"

"Well, *that's* not good," Kota murmured as he sheathed his sword and jogged around the bookshelf, meeting Danielle's angry glare with a sheepish shrug. "I have *no* idea what I said to set him off like that."

She could only shake her head and wait as he started pulling on books in sequence. In the distance, she heard the baron roar with excitement over his targets having been found. Footsteps pounded toward the library, and the Comte was sweating furiously as he quickly swiped the last book out of the way, and a thick cloud of dust burst from a nearby bookshelf.

The passageway creeped open, years of disuse and poor maintenance making it a heart-poundingly slow process. Henri all but shoved Danielle into the opening as soon as she would fit, but she twisted out of his grasp and pulled him in after her. "Kota! Get in here and close the door!"

"It's not time yet, Danielle!" Henri growled at her, trying to slip away from her in return. "It's not *believable* yet, I need to-"

"*Comte LeKrout!*" Gasteel's howl whipped through the library. "I demand that you get over here right this instant!"

The passageway was still shifting open, but now none of the trio were moving. Henri and Danielle stared at the Artificer in horror, and the man himself simply let out a sigh of frustration and nodded at them. "Go… I'll catch up."

"To the abyss with *that* idea!" Danielle snarled at the man, reaching out for his arm, only for her father to grab her wrist. "Let me *go*! I'm not going to let him sacrifice himself so we have a few more minutes to run. Don't make me hurt you."

"I'm your father, I know you've fallen in love with him. But be *reasonable*-" was all Henri got out before Danielle twisted, sweeping his false leg out from under him and sending him to the floor.

"I'm so sorry, and I love you, but you can't tell me what to do." Danielle grabbed his flailing arm as he fell to make sure he didn't hit the ground too hard, then gave her struggling father a quick kiss on the forehead before chasing after the Artificer. "I'll be right back, I *promise!*"

"Danielle!"

THIRTY-NINE

BLAM!

The Enchantress skid to a halt as the wooden endcap of the bookshelf she was passing exploded into a shower of splinters.

"Abyss!" Dropping into a crouch, she clutched at her furiously pounding heart and slowly crept forward once more. As Danielle peeked around the wooden barrier, she watched as Gasteel tossed his smoking musket to the side.

"At this range, that could've been your head, Comte," the baron growled, tilting his head side to side and cracking his neck before staring down the smaller man and slowly licking his lips—as though savoring the impending violence. "Instead of putting you down like the feral beast they all say you are, I'm just going to tame you with my fists. You should *thank* me for my benevolence. "

Even with his back to Danielle, she could hear the disbelief in LeKrout's response. "All of the authority of the kingdom at your beck and call, and the first time you get to use it on me properly… it's so you can beat me up?"

"No one splits skulls like Gasteel, demands *respect* like Gasteel." The baron was humming in an unhinged tone as he stepped across the smoky space between them. "By the end of this, you'll beg for a *deal* with Gasteel!"

"No." Comte LeKrout shook his head and let out a long-suffering sigh. "It's time for me to crush the dream of Gasteel. Attack."

The order was so nonchalant that the baron didn't react immediately, not understanding that the Artificer wasn't speaking to *him*. It was only as the first sword whistled through the air, and the hunter-turned-noble instinctively dodged, that he realized what was happening. Gasteel dodged yet another swing from the automatons that had been escorting LeKrout, his eyes going wide in concern. The huge man started backpedaling, both to avoid the attacks, as well as to try and undo what had just been done. "No. *No*! You can't attack me, you'll-"

"Yup. That's right. This is me breaking my oath. I finally get to live as I've always dreamed." The Artificer spoke almost cheerfully, though Danielle could detect a hint of trepidation in his voice. "Death before enslavement."

Danielle's breath hitched, and the world itself seemed to have frozen in shock. A tangible, physical tension filled the space, causing the hair on the back of her neck to rise and her heart to pound. Trying to inhale, the Enchantress found that the air was heavy and oppressive.

The system was turning its attention to Comte LeKrout, and it was *not* happy.

"It's not too late, yet!" Gasteel shouted into the room which should have been silent, but instead had a low, rumbling roar rising in intensity and echoing through every speck of matter in the library. "Take a knee; I'll accept your apology! You still have a chance-"

"No." LeKrout firmly replied, refusing to break his stare down with the baron. "I'm taking you with me. Or, if nothing else, I can be a lesson to you. Sometimes, you just can't make other people do what you want. Sometimes, Gasteel, they'd just rather die."

The smoke swirled through the room as the system began to pass its judgment. A deep, ominous, throbbing green light washed out the surroundings, before quickly collapsing in to surround the Comte. The man spasmed, his body held in place and trembling as it was gripped by impossible force.

Danielle watched as the light poured into the Artificer, but as she was behind him, she was able to watch as the target of the system's wrath shifted. As the last of the light streamed into his body, it burst out of his back, flashing past her in an instant, the noise reaching a crescendo, only to be replaced by an unsettling tearing sound. For just a moment, she was able to hear what could only be described as delicate cloth tearing before the sound of shattering glass reverberated through the air.

The light and noise cut off in the next moment, the heaviness in the air vanishing as if it had never been. Ever so slowly, Kota LeKrout collapsed, falling to his knees, then to his back... his eyes wide and staring up at nothing.

"*Kota!*" Danielle's shriek was drowned out by Gasteel's screech of failed ambition, and the Enchantress found her eyes pulled to where the baron was fighting for his life against six automatons.

These were clearly the newly upgraded versions, which used her captured motion, as they had been dancing around the viciously attacking nobleman, returning his fury with finesse. Yet, as the oaths on the Artificer's heart were physically destroyed, a ripple of chaos was sent through all the automatons, which hadn't had the self-destruct sequence scrubbed away before his fall.

The coordinated and precise movements of the metal soldiers immediately turned erratic, but the sudden drop in efficiency was *more* than made up for in their increased attack speed.

Their runescripted systems began to overload, and Gasteel's enormous sword cleaved through one of them which had begun to jerk and twitch, throwing off its combat capability. As the metal soldier fell, the baron's eyes landed on Danielle. His surprise shifted to avarice, but he only managed a single step in her direction before the automatons closed the gap in their ranks. Sparks were flying from their joints, the air filled with the sound of grinding gears and hissing steam—even so, it wasn't loud enough to drown out his shouts.

"Now you see how I'm the better man, Belle!" Gasteel cackled as he continuously tried to fight his way through the metal soldiers, slowly gaining ground as he came for her. "No one's *forgiving* like Gasteel, at least to the future wife of Gasteel!"

"You're insane!"

"Just crazy for you, my bride! *Haa*!" Despite his immense experience and unceasing ferocity, the nobleman was struggling to hold off the automatons—who were now fighting with an absolute disregard for their own longevity.

Their overheating was starting to reach a critical point, and their chassis were beginning to glow white from the heat radiating off their cores. As the wall of fighters stepped closer to the shelves, books all across the first five rows burst into flame, adding to the rapidly increasing temperature of the library.

"I can't give you another chance after this," the baron warned Danielle as he carried a wild, desperate arc of a sword, brutally retaliating and sending the metal soldier to the ground as scrap metal—which started melting into slag as soon as it couldn't move enough to vent its heat. "Can't do it! Belle! You once told me you couldn't be with someone who didn't understand you. Well, now you've seen the strength of my convictions. *You* understand *me*… so aren't we already halfway there?"

Not saying a word, Danielle began slowly backing away,

her view of the wild-eyed baron quickly becoming hidden by books and smoke.

He did *not* appreciate her choice.

"So be it! You can burn with the rest of this cursed place!" For just a moment, his face appeared through the smoke, twisted with rage. Then, with a mighty swing of his sword, he knocked back the nearest metal soldiers, turned on his heel, and ran for the exit to the library. "I'll make sure of it! If I find out that you managed to worm your way out of here, I swear by the *system* I'll hunt you down and finish the job! Cross my heart, and *hope to die!*"

A burst of golden light in the shape of a bright 'X' flared through the smoke, then Gasteel was gone, chased by the four remaining superheated soldiers. One of them threw itself after the fleeing baron, blocking his advance for a moment, but also pushing itself beyond its limits. It exploded at that moment, sending molten shrapnel surfing along an energy-filled shock-wave that shattered the oak door and left deep cracks along the stone floor and walls.

Danielle heard a groan, and for a moment, assumed it was Gasteel... until it came again, followed by a familiar, if weak, voice.

"Uughh... looks like it worked?"

"*Kota?*" The Enchantress paused for a moment, uncertain if she should believe her own lying ears. Then she rushed out, dropping and sliding across the polished floor to the Comte's side. "You're alive? I thought for sure the system killed you out of hand while it was trying to fulfill your part of the oath."

"Nope..." Kota started to chuckle, but it turned into a deep, wracking cough. "Looks like I found a loophole with crossing my heart. All I needed to do was have the organ itself pulled out of my chest and replaced with a different version, not forgetting to leave the main heart intact. There, it could act as a decoy and pull the system's attention to it... to take the punishment of an oathbreaker—*hack*—instead of me. I was pretty sure my hypothesis would work. But who would be foolish enough to test this in my stead?"

"Only you would try something like that. No one else is fool enough to think they can pull one over on the *system itself*." Danielle's bluntness caught the Artificer off guard, and he could only nod as he tried to catch his breath. "Then again, no one else would even be able to think of making something like that work, let alone pull it off. You're... I can't believe how amazing your mind is. How amazing *you* are. Can you stand?"

The man tried, but the invasive energy of the angry system had left him greatly weakened. "That's a no. Maybe with some help?"

Danielle pulled him to his feet, surprised at how easy and natural the motion felt as she swung his left arm over her shoulders and wrapped her right arm around his waist to support him. They began walking toward the hidden exit as quickly as they could manage. "How long do we have?"

"Minutes. At *best*," Kota intoned heavily, before turning to look at her with hooded eyes. "I'd tell you to go ahead, that I'd catch up, but if there's one truth I know about myself, it's that I learn quickly. I can only ask that you use me as a shield if things start to collapse."

"Why is *everyone-*" Danielle grunted as she stumbled over the remains of a fallen shelf, "-so abyssally *determined* to make sure I make it out of here without so much as a scratch? By the system, just close your mouth and move your feet!"

A series of explosions rang out, and a wash of superheated air flowed over them. Danielle felt her hair scorch and twist, small blisters rising on her skin where the airburst had touched. Both she and Kota cried out in pain as the unbearable heat began to increase even more.

The Artificer spoke in gasping breaths, his voice raspy from the dry, smoky air. "The building is going to come down; its self-destruct failsafe must be on the verge already."

"There you are!" Henri's relieved voice felt like a healing

balm to Danielle's ears. He continued to speak, so she used his voice as a beacon, stumbling toward him with her eyes scrunched shut so the heat couldn't burn them. "Get in, right here! There you go…"

Danielle stepped into a cool, dark space, finally managing to gulp down air that didn't burn on the way down. She tried to open her eyes but found that she could only squint, her skin inflamed and swollen. Henri gently directed her, and only moments later, she found herself pushed down onto a seat.

"Father, what is this?" Her words were ever so slightly slurred, as her lips had begun to char. "Why are we sitting? We need to *run*!"

"Don't worry… the barrel will take care of that." Henri pried her hands away from where they were grasping onto Kota and pressed a cold, glassy object into each of them. There was a *ploink*, the sound of a cork being pulled from a bottle, and Henri lifted her right hand toward her mouth. "Drink half of this, then give the other half to Comte LeKrout."

"Not a Comte," Kota slurred through his own damaged mouth, a scoff that was half disparaging, half-filled with amazement escaping his steaming lips. "Without my oath to the Kingdom of Verdelune in place, I'm just another commoner. It's… it's *wonderful*."

"I bet it is."

"Why can't *you* help him with the healing potion?" Danielle blinked rapidly as her skin filled with moisture once more, the potent healing potion already starting to have an effect. "Father, what are you doing?"

"What needs to be done, Danielle," Henri spoke with a tone of grim finality. "That man will never stop hunting you if he has even the slightest inkling that you escaped. I've met his type before. If he can't have you, he'll want to make sure no one can. I can't have that. I can't have you running for the rest of your life. There's only one way I know he'll believe you didn't leave, and that's if he sees the building fall on me."

"*Don't you dare!*"

Her father wasn't listening. "Take care of her... Kota."

"I will-"

"You get your butt in here this *instant!*" Danielle tried to stand, but found a strap holding her in place. She fumbled with its mechanism, but her hands hadn't had enough time to heal, certainly not enough for the fine motor control needed to undo the latch.

"Oh, my sweet girl." Henri gave her a kiss on the forehead. "I'm so sorry, and I love you, but you can't tell me what to do. I hope you live a *wonderful* life. There's no one in this world that deserves you, but he comes close. You two have my blessing to be married, when you're ready."

With that, he slapped the back of the barrel, and it jerked forward like a horse that had been spurred into action. Kota and Danielle were tossed back and forth as the oversized container ran forward on two legs, the harsh shifts back and forth making it impossible for the Enchantress to maintain her grip on the strap and unhook it.

As they raced down the tunnel, surrounded on all sides by absolute darkness, she could only look back and reach out as Henri watched them go.

"*Father!*"

FORTY

THE TWO-LEGGED barrel burst through a sudden opening in the darkness, leaving Danielle and Kota blinking in the sudden daylight. Both of them were silent as the contraption continued *barreling* along, jostling them back and forth.

Opening his mouth to offer condolences, the Artificer glanced at Danielle and thought better of whatever he was about to say. Instead, he looked down at his hands, where the last of the blisters along his fingers were fading back into healthy skin.

"Why would he do that?" Danielle was the one to finally break the silence between them, jostled out of her ruminations as their ride navigated around a tree. "He could have been sitting right here next to me, and instead..."

"What father doesn't want to protect their daughter?" Kota carefully and quietly replied, seemingly uncertain how his words were going to be taken at the moment. "I fully understand... if I had thought I would be able to protect you better by forcing you away from me, I wouldn't have hesitated, either. He sees how bright you are. Borrowing the words of that sycophant, he sees your star is on the rise."

"That's just it, isn't it?" Danielle's chin sank to her chest as tears streamed from her eyes. "Stars don't just shine, they *burn*. It seems like I'm burning everything around me to ashes just by being there. Even if I actively try to stop it, people keep throwing themselves in front of me as a sacrifice to 'help' me. I didn't *need* him to sacrifice himself… I needed him here. It's what I've been working on ever since Gasteel took him in the first place!"

Choosing to remain silent, Kota could only nod in response to her vehement outburst. His gaze trailed down as he lowered his head in a moment of silence, only to lock onto a large crystal still clutched in Danielle's left hand. "You have a memory crystal?"

"This?" The Enchantress looked over at the object with a dull stare, listlessly handing it over. "Here. Take it. My father forced it into my hand before he threw me out of the house and let himself be killed."

Kota pulled away from her, at least as far as the strap in the jostling Tinkerer's contraption would allow. "That is *not* what happened. You can't seriously think he had no reason for what he did. The man loved you more than-"

"I know he had his reasons. Most likely, he was ensorcelled by my system skills and made to think he needed to rescue me." Danielle's words were dark, and the Artificer's face immediately set in a resolute expression.

"Let's find out, shall we?" LeKrout took the crystal and began tapping on it, his movement slowing after a few moments. From there, he focused on empowering the crystal with his skills, and after a moment, the cloudy interior of the crystal changed—showing a scene Danielle couldn't help but recognize. "The memory *just* finished being inserted? Let's see what he did."

From the positioning of the memory, the Enchantress realized it must be from the perspective of the Beast as it walked along next to her father. Far in the distance, past thousands of metal soldiers, she saw herself and the Artificer dancing on the platform as he got used to piloting his own body once more.

Her father's voice resonated out from the crystal, and Danielle felt a renewed surge of emotions as she heard his voice once more. "They look good together, don't they? I was worried he would be... different. Worse. More like what I've been told about him."

"The Comte is nothing but honorable, dutiful, and perhaps a *touch* work-obsessed." The Beast's mechanical voice boomed out over the sound of the metal soldiers beginning to shift. "Come now, there is an invasion happening at this very moment, and I will not arrive too late to help. My master seems to think it *funny* that I am unable to access his pulley system, but I find myself greatly inconvenienced."

"You know there's no winning this fight, yes?"

Henri's nonchalant words caused Danielle to gasp in agitation as she clutched at her ruined dress. "Father... we could have won. We were so *close* to a clean escape."

"I understand the inevitable outcome, if that is what you mean." The Beast spoke in a soft growl. "At this point, tensions have escalated too far. The king and queen have been informed of our... *indiscretion* with saving you. Since they are undoubtedly involved, eventually, someone will arrive to force the issue. That is, assuming we even *do* manage to defeat Gasteel Company."

Henri stepped in front of the beast, forcing the enormous machine to come to a halt or risk crushing him. Danielle stared at her father, watching as passion burned in his eyes as he in turn stared up at the automaton. "Then you *must* know that the best option for your master, and my daughter, is to be set upon a path to a new life. Escaping is not enough. We need to fake their deaths and make sure to do it convincingly enough that no one will ever doubt it."

BST model three hesitated for a long moment, and the perspective shifted from staring down at her father to up where Danielle's past self was just starting to get off of the platform. "He will never accept this. Comte LeKrout is no coward, and this *reeks* of-"

"Are you an *automaton* or a *puppet*?" Henri's heated voice cut through whatever the machine was about to say. "I need you to help me with the machinery and set the stage for their escape. If we are able to drive the baron off, all the better, but before we commit ourselves to battle, we *must* have a contingency in play."

The image in the crystal suddenly sped up, the Beast walking across the room in the blink of an eye next to Henri. The Tinkerer drew out a schematic with lightning swiftness, his hands and mouth moving in conversation that must have taken far longer than what was being shown.

As soon as the blueprint was complete—what Danielle could easily recognize as the transport barrel they were in even now—her father and the Beast got to work building the machine from the spare parts available in the workshop. Suddenly, the memory slowed to a normal speed, "-then all they'll have to do is hit this button, and it will power down the barrel. But we need to make sure it's hard to notice until they are too far away to stop it and turn around."

"The escape tunnel will be filled with darkness. Let's cut down on the shocks on the legs to make them clutch at the support bar. That'll make it harder for them to feel around and perhaps accidentally press it. Once it powers down, it will not restart without significant effort." The Beast's view zoomed in on the button, staying there for a long moment before they were once more moving incredibly swiftly.

"What is *happening*?" Danielle looked around for the button, finding it out of her reach, but easily within Kota's. "Stop this contraption immediately! We need to go back!"

Instead of immediately following her order, the Artificer simply continued staring at the crystal, where the duo was adjusting one of the upgraded metal soldiers to have long hair, matching Danielle's appearance enough for a distant observer to be fooled. "Pull out the core, Beast! All I need it to do is walk when I'm pushing on it, and that's easy enough to work manually."

"You can't just *damage* the master's items like-" whatever argument the automaton had been making was cut off, clearly won by Henri moments later.

The Artificer spoke into the silence. "What's happening is called 'fast forwarding'. I can't stop it. This memory was placed in the crystal with the intent of skipping the tedium of what they were doing, to highlight only the important parts."

"Kota. Press that button-"

"Danielle." Her father's words, directed specifically at her with the knowledge she would hear them, caused the Enchantress's throat to close up. She turned her teary-eyed attention back to the memory crystal. "I know how hard it is going to be for you to listen to what I'm going to ask of you. But please... don't come back. It's time for you to have your own life, with someone who can appreciate you for *all* of you. Whatever you choose to do, whether it is going off on your own, acting as a researcher with Comte LeKrout, or even if you were to choose to marry him someday... know you have my blessing."

"As for *you*, Artificer Kota LeKrout." Henri's eyebrow arched. "You owe everything, including your *life*, to the woman beside you. I fully expect you will never forget this fact, until your dying breath. Whatever she chooses to do in her life, you will enable that, or by the *system*, I hope that your skills fail you. But... I don't think I need to threaten you. You were not the System-Forsaken Battle Beast you were made out to be, and I don't think you ever will be."

Once more, the image 'fast forwarded', and Danielle watched as the Beast reached to its chest and pulled out two of its six crystalline eyes, one of them perfectly matching what she held in her hand even now, with the other being the one used as a recording device. That second crystal, her father hooked to his artificial leg, dropping their perspective to that of a six-year-old as he went up the stairs, through a secret passage in the wall, and made his way through the library.

"Ah… *that's* how the memory managed to continue to be captured," LeKrout muttered softly as he tapped the crystal. "The Beast's eyes were all linked."

The Beast went with Henri, opening the final escape tunnel and gently setting the enormous, leggy barrel several meters in before sealing Henri into the space. Several long moments of darkness passed before the door opened once more, and Danielle saw her own face appear. Then there was a rapid recounting of the radiance magic being used, Lefroupe appearing, and Danielle sweeping Henri's feet out and running off.

As the library exploded into flame, only for her and Kota to stumble out of the burning area, she heard her father let out an exclamation of absolute relief she had missed. His hands reached out, clasping onto the nearly blind couple and pulling them into the passage, even as his own arms broke out in blisters.

She saw how she had looked before the healing potion— swollen, burned, sores weeping blood, and how her father had been shedding tears as he got her to drink her half of the potion. Finally, she saw the barrel racing into the darkness.

Then, Henri stood tall and turned to reopen the tunnel door, pushing out into the inferno. His position shifted slightly, and Danielle saw a flimsy imitation of herself that he wrapped one arm around. The automaton—no, the *simulacrum*, since it had no core—began moving forward.

Though the image was moving quickly, not letting any sound through, Danielle could tell her father was in a great deal of pain, no doubt because the top layer of his body had already begun to burn away. He and the machine made it into the hallway, where hundreds of overheating automatons were pushing out of the manor door, chasing after Gasteel Company—specifically Gasteel himself, as they viewed him as the person responsible for their Master's 'death'.

Bright red lights were flashing, practically *strobing* due to the increased viewing speed. In an instant, the view changed slightly, and Danielle realized her father had been knocked to the ground. Almost as quickly, he was back on his feet, walking toward the gaping hole where a section of the grand hallway had been standing.

"An explosion of some kind?" Danielle could barely get the whisper past her dry lips, but she knew she didn't truly want an answer.

Henri stepped out onto the lawn, sound once more coming through the crystal as the speed reduced to a human level. The sounds of combat filled the air, metal clashing with metal, booming retorts as cores overloaded, and the screams of people burning from the proximity of the melting mechanical soldiers. The Tinkerer looked around, and for a long moment, stared at a section of the estate where there were no troops, neither human nor machine.

Then, slowly, resolutely, he turned and started limping his way toward where the baron stood fighting off a swarm of automatons. Even with the intensity of the combat, Gasteel was able to survey the battlefield. Moments after Henri started moving toward him, the baron noticed the discrepancy between the limping walk of the Tinkerer and the full sprint of the overloading machines.

"*You*! The two of you are *alive*? After all this? No. No… you're dead. You just don't know it yet." The huge man darted through a break in the flashing sword wall, sprinting toward Henri like a starving wolf.

The old man let out a curse and turned around, doing his best to rapidly hobble back into the building. Danielle could tell he wasn't going to make it—Gasteel was too fast, too strong. As the baron's enormous, meaty *paw* of a hand reached out for the false version of herself, Gasteel suddenly lurched back, dodging to the side as a heavy spear flew through the air he had been occupying only a moment previously. No… not a spear.

A *harpoon*.

"Ssspider for the win!" The projectile slammed into 'her', and the false Danielle tumbled to the ground, only to be *yanked* through the gaping wound in the side of the building.

Henri played his part perfectly, raising a hand after her as if to pull her back, and screaming as she vanished into the flames. Then he was grabbed and yanked into the air by his ankle, held upside down as Gasteel sneered into his face.

"At the end, those war toys even turned against *her*. This will look good in my report… they were too dangerous to keep around. It's actually a *fantastic* thing I got rid of the Artificer." Gasteel's eyes were bright red, both from fury as well as the irritants in the air. "Haaa… he's gone! That means no military advancement. *She's* gone, so no social climbing, thanks to having an Enchantress at my beck and call. The only win I have remaining…"

"…is an *execution*!"

Gasteel spun around, then seemed to recede and shrink, though he remained firmly in place, watching to see where the old man would land. The bright daylight was replaced with smoke, then flame… and as Henri landed back within the manor, the building rumbled and collapsed in on itself.

The memory crystal went dark as Danielle buried her face in Kota's singed shirt, holding on for dear life.

EPILOGUE

THE BARREL CONTINUED to tirelessly run in a straight line toward the border of Verdelune. All too soon, the day gave way to night, and the landscape was shrouded in velvety darkness.

Despite the intense discomfort of the confined space—the jostling and the subdued but continuous noise of the hydraulics forcing the legs to push ever onward—to the duo who had just had their lives turned upside down, this was simply a safe mode of transportation gently rocking them into a fitful slumber.

Though they woke up several times throughout the night, they were always able to return to sleep... until finally the construct came to a halt as the first light of true dawn painted the horizon with brilliant colors. Birds began chirping, and the gentle rustling of grass in a steady breeze contrasted starkly with the chaos they had just escaped. With a loud *hiss* of steam and ruptured hydraulics, the mechanical legs attached to the barrel gently sank down, easing Danielle and Kota to the ground.

Danielle stood and stepped out with a wince, stumbling ever so slightly. As per usual, her skills took over, translating the motion into a smooth, perfect landing on the ground. She shook the stiffness from her legs, stretching side-to-side to overcome the strain of their journey. Once the Enchantress had her blood flowing once more, she moved to the side and offered a hand to Kota, helping the Artificer out and guiding him through the same motions.

As he did not have system skills helping him and had spent more than a decade walking in the bodies of his creations, Kota had a far harder time managing for himself. She gave him a reassuring squeeze on the shoulder and guided them both to the ground. There, they simply took a moment to breathe in the fresh, cool air.

Danielle took a deep inhale, slowly letting it out and saying, "Smells like freedom. Wonderful, terrible, *bittersweet* freedom. Where do you think we are?"

The sun chose that moment to fully crest the horizon, and a line of light rushed along the grassy slope they were sitting on until the world was alight around them. The terrain was utterly unfamiliar to Danielle: lush, green, a vast expanse of grassy mountain stretching out below them.

"I recognize this place from paintings; it's a fairly famous location. The locals call it 'Mountaindale'. It's the juxtaposition of a mountain and a broad, grassy valley—a dale. A place for only the highest of achievers, especially among artists. To get up here and paint? As I'm sure you can see for yourself, that takes a special kind of determination." LeKrout paused for a long moment to take in the sight. "Unless I miss my guess, we're three-quarters of the way to the estate I had purchased in your name. We're far beyond the border of Verdelune, high above the worries and dangers of that kingdom."

"Then we should be able to make it by the end of the day?" Danielle's optimism bubble was popped by Kota letting out a soft snort.

"If you can sprint uphill until sunset, then you *might* be

able to reach the outskirts of the city tonight. Otherwise, it's going to be a two, maybe three-day walk."

"Well…"

Kota let his head loll on his shoulders as he sent a meaningful stare at the Enchantress. "What am I saying? Of *course* you can endlessly run for a full day. You're humanity perfected. Well, even if *you* can, I can't. Besides that, we need to find food and water up here-"

"My father wouldn't have sent us out to die on the side of a mountain, no matter how beautiful it was." Danielle painfully got to her feet, her muscles still cramped and sore from the long ride. Going over to the barrel, she poked and prodded at the sides until she found the door to a compartment and pulled it wide. "There we go. A few sacks of dried meats, some water skins, and… the cores!"

"They *made* it?" Kota was at her side in a flash, reaching a trembling hand into the open space and gently running it along his creations. "This… I thought we lost them in the fire! With this, we have everything we need to rebuild. My life's work isn't destroyed. Perhaps… it's merely changed? For the better?"

Danielle grasped his hand before it went too far, pulling him away from shards of glass littered through the space. "Looks like your heart made it in as well. What's, um, left of it. Why would he have put this in here?"

Four perfect sections of a heart were in the storage space, all of them shining gold except for where a single 'X' had turned a malevolent green and cut through—leaving perfectly straight lines through the organ. "A heart of gold can be used to make powerful magical items. I would even go as far as to say enchanted items… but not this. Magical is the best I can hope for, as the cuts of an oath breaker are permanent and will always reduce the final product into something lesser than it could have been."

"Still…" He sent a crooked smile to Danielle. "I could

always auction it off to the highest bidder and fund the next decade of our research and projects."

"Before that..." Danielle swept the food pouches out, shaking off the broken glass and stacking them to the side. "Before all that, we need to get to our new home. We need to warn them that Verdelune is secretly building up an army and is planning to invade."

Kota froze for a moment, slowly turning to stare at the Enchantress as she organized all of the goods they would be taking with them in a pleasing manner. "But...? A quiet, hidden life? Isn't that what you wanted? If we bring this news to someone who can do something with it, there will be no escaping our part in it."

"We will give them a warning; I didn't say we had to deliver it ourselves." Danielle hefted her portion of the load and gave Kota a bright smile. "Let's get going! No time like the present, and it's the start of a beautiful new day. I could use some time to... process. To grieve, if I'm being honest."

The Artificer slowly nodded as he listened to what she was saying, lifting his own burden and taking the first step toward their new destination. "You're right. They deserve to know what's coming."

"After that's in the past, we need to find a place to rebuild, where we can continue our work and live a life worth living." She turned her eyes, meeting his and finding a shared determination. "Together?"

"I'd like that very much. Yes... together, if you'll have me." Kota agreed warmly, beginning to climb the mountain stretching out before them. "We'll warn the kingdom, carve out a new home, and rebuild our lives. Whatever you choose to do, I'll be right there with you. No matter what."

Danielle looked at the Artificer closely, sensing that he was being completely sincere. "Whatever I choose, for the both of us? You trust me enough that you would bind your fate to mine? What if I choose wrong?"

"I'd very much like to follow through on your fathers words, and marry you… if you'll have me. I've decided that it's high time I follow my heart." Kota raised an eyebrow as Danielle lifted the jar and let loose a weak chuckle. "Not like that. Danielle… you had my heart far before you held it in your hands."

"You have an uncanny ability to turn every moment into pure poetry. Kota, it's not *just* your heart I treasure." She swallowed hard, not bothering to hold back tears as she reached for his hand. "It's that wonderful, brilliant mind. So… yes. I accept. Let's go choose the life we want to live together… *together*."

Continue the Damsels of Distress series on Patreon.com/ DakotaKrout - or order on Amazon, geni.us/DamselsSeries.

Rob X Punzel
Snow X Dwight
Red X Wolf
Cinder X Bella

ABOUT DAKOTA KROUT

Good. Clean. Fun.

Dakota Krout is a celebrated author known for infusing fantasy novels with fun, punny, and clean humor. With multiple best-selling series—including "Divine Dungeon", "Completionist Chronicles", "Cooking With Disaster", and "Full Murderhobo"—he brings joy and laughter to readers. Dakota's work, renowned for its wit and creativity, earned a place as one of Audible's top 5 fantasy picks in 2017, a top 5 bestseller rank featured on the New York Times, and was chosen by Audible as among "the top 100 fantasy books of all time" in 2024.

Dakota's journey in publishing has been filled with gratefulness, and a deep desire to continue bringing smiles and laughter to the readers. "_I hope you Read Every Book With A Smile!_"

Connect with Dakota:
MountaindalePress.com
Patreon.com/DakotaKrout
Facebook.com/DakotaKrout
Instagram.com/DakotaKrout
Twitter.com/DakotaKrout
Discord.gg/mdp

ABOUT MOUNTAINDALE PRESS

Dakota and Danielle Krout, a husband and wife team, strive to create as well as publish excellent fantasy and science fiction novels. Self-publishing *The Divine Dungeon: Dungeon Born* in 2016 transformed their careers from Dakota's military and programming background and Danielle's Ph.D. in pharmacology to President and CEO, respectively, of a small press. Their goal is to share their success with other authors and provide captivating fiction to readers with the purpose of solidifying Mountaindale Press as the place 'Where Fantasy Transforms Reality.'

Connect with Mountaindale Press:
MountaindalePress.com
Facebook.com/MountaindalePress
Twitter.com/_Mountaindale
Instagram.com/MountaindalePress

MOUNTAINDALE PRESS TITLES
GAMELIT AND LITRPG

The Completionist Chronicles,
Cooking with Disaster,
The Divine Dungeon,
Full Murderhobo, and
Year of the Sword by Dakota Krout

Metier Apocalypse by Frank G. Albelo

A Touch of Power by Jay Boyce

Ether Collapse and
Ether Flows by Ryan DeBruyn

Unbound by Nicoli Gonnella

Lion's Lineage by Rohan Hublikar and Dakota Krout

Wolfman Warlock by James Hunter and Dakota Krout

Axe Druid,
Mephisto's Magic Online, and
High Table Hijinks by Christopher Johns

Tower of Jack by Sean Loomer

Dragon Core Chronicles by Lars Machmüller

Pixel Dust and
Necrotic Apocalypse by D. Petrie

Viceroy's Pride and
Tower of Somnus by Cale Plamann

Henchman by Carl Stubblefield

Artorian's Archives by Dennis Vanderkerken and Dakota
Krout

www.ingramcontent.com/pod-product-compliance
Lightning Source LLC
Chambersburg PA
CBHW020514260626
47156CB00006B/1999